EXILE

A BIRCH FALLS NOVEL
BOOK TWO

POPPY FITZGERALD

Dear Reader,

I would like to say a few words before you dive into Exile, in an effort to ensure that this is the right book for you. Exile is a dark romantic suspense that deals with heavy topics, including emotional and physical abuse (not by the MMC), abuse of power by police officers, mentions of racial profiling and injustice by the police to people of color (MMC is pulled over and profiled without cause), mentions of protesting, civil unrest and police in riot gear, SA, dub con (on page) non con (off page) (not by the MMC in either case), death of a parent, and taking care of a parent with a disability.

When I wrote Astray, the first book of the Birch Falls series, I wanted to do my best to be inclusive with my cast of characters. I wrote Serena as a Black police officer who went into that line of work because of her lived experience. This book is her story. Her experience is not unique to any race or ethnicity; it is, sadly, familiar to women of all demographics. That is to say, she just so happens to fall in love with an asshole.

I have utilized sensitivity readers every step of the way and have found their feedback invaluable. Without them this story wouldn't be what it is, and I am grateful for every single one of them (more on them in my acknowledgements at the end).

This book is about men who abuse their power and privilege to take advantage of women and control them. It is about women who find themselves in dire situations with lack of support from society, isolated and robbed of their power, unsure who they can turn to for help.

Many women suffer this kind of exile. I wish them all the true Happily Ever After they deserve.

If you have found yourself in a similar situation, visit the National Domestic Violence Hotline website for help thehotline.org or call 1.800.799.SAFE(7233)

EXILE PLAYLIST

- Exile - (feat Bon Iver) Taylor Swift
- Falling - Florence and the Machine
- Lose Control - Teddy Swims
- Daylight - David Kushner
- Can I Kick It? - A Tribe Called Quest
- Redbone - Childish Gambino
- Try Again - Aaliyah
- Running Up That Hill - Kate Bush
- Summertime Magic - Childish Gambino
- Break You Off - The Roots, Musiq Soulchild
- Umbrella - Rhiannan, Jay-Z
- I Feel It Coming - The Weeknd, Daft Punk
- Stellar - Incubus
- What Was I Made For? - Billie Eilish
- Safe and Sound - Capital Cities
- Stay With Me - Sam Smith
- ove The Way You Lie - Eminem, Rhiannan
- Love Me Like You Do - Ellie Goulding

- This Is America - Childish Gambino
- Stay - Rhiannan, Mikky Ekko
- My Silver Lining - First Aid Kit
- Real Love Baby - Father John Misty
- Girl On Fire - Alicia Keys
- Clouds - JVKE
- Dog Days Are Over - Florence and the Machine

CHAPTER ONE

SERENA

"Small Americano, banana muffin!" I call out the to-go order as I place it on the counter before turning to start the next ticket in line. It's 7:15 a.m., deep in the morning rush of commuters on their way to work. I've been here since five, working the early shift before my classes start at ten. I do this five days a week, waking up at the obscenely early time of 4 a.m., so I can get in twenty hours a week while attending school full time. On weekends, I'm a waitress at a dive bar downtown and get paid under the table. The exhaustion I feel seems beyond what a twenty-year-old body should be capable of, but if I don't work this hard then food won't be put on the table, and there is more than a slight chance of the lights being cut off. If it weren't for scholarships, there would be no way I could afford to get a degree, so I consider myself lucky I only have to come up with money for life, not school.

A flurry of dings from the bell over the front door signals a flood of customers. I close my eyes and take a deep breath as I wait for the milk to foam for a cappuccino, trying to keep my cool. André called out this morning, claiming he had the stomach flu. Eddie and Marge are in the back, baking muffins and making the breakfast orders that come in. That leaves only Marie and me to handle the front counter during the morning rush. This is the third time André's had the stomach flu this month. If it weren't for Marge having a soft spot for him—because his mom's an addict, and his dad's out of the picture—he probably would've been fired months ago. Don't get me wrong; Andre is a good guy, just…unreliable.

Brewed Awakening has been a staple in Birch Falls for nearly thirty years. Eddie and Marge opened it when they were a young married couple. There seems to be an understanding in the community that no crappy mega chain coffee shops are to encroach on their territory downtown. It probably doesn't hurt that Eddie's dad is the mayor. For that matter, so was his grandfather. There must be bylaws written about it, considering how there are no fewer than four chain coffee shops in the next town over, but here in good old BF, there are only Brewed Awakening and Rosa's, a little cafe next to campus.

A sharp elbow in the ribs forces me to open my eyes and return my attention to the pitcher of milk that has nearly foamed over. Facing me, Marie tilts her head towards the register, causing my eyes to track what is happening behind her. Three of Birch Falls' finest stand in line in their crisp, navy uniforms, waiting to place their usual orders. This trio seems to have the morning patrol shift. They come in together almost daily, smiling, turning on the charm and flirting shamelessly. I've been serving them coffee for the two years I've worked at Brewed Awakening and have built up a rapport with them. Marie is pregnant and married to her high school sweetheart, so every time they come in, she pushes me to work the register so she can live vicariously through me, since I am not above flirting to sweeten my tips.

"I'll finish the drinks. Why don't you go see what Officer Orgasm is drinking today?" She shoots me a wink before nudging me away from the espresso maker with her impressive baby bump. She's only six months along but looks like she's ready to pop. I'm very concerned about the state her vagina is going to be in once she gives birth to the baby elephant she is apparently incubating. To be fair, her husband is built like Bigfoot, over six-and-a-half feet tall, close to 300lbs and a former college linebacker. My concerns are not unfounded.

"Hello, Officers, what will it be today?" I saunter over to the register and put my hands on my hips, initiating the dance we do every morning. I ask them what they're having, Eric pretends to flirt with me—even though he's much older—doing his best to goad Dominick into making a move. Their partner, Dane, the youngest and quietest of the trio—a rookie, still—hangs back to let the two more seasoned cops do the talking. Dane is cute, but in a very boy-next-door kind of way that doesn't do much for me. Dominick is older than me, but only by six or seven years, if I had to guess, and he's handsome in a mature way that boys my age have yet to achieve.

He's big. Not Bigfoot big, like Marie's husband, but tall

enough and broad enough to make me feel petite, even at my above average height of five foot nine. His body is well-built, like he works out and takes care of himself, but there is a slight softness to him that says he enjoys pizza and beer on the weekends. He keeps his dark beard trimmed neatly and his head shaved on the sides with just enough length at the top to run his fingers through. If it wasn't for his police uniform, I would assume he was in a biker gang with his intimidating appearance.

However, it's his eyes that draw me in the most. They're such a striking silver color, you'd almost swear he was a werewolf shifter from a fantasy romance novel. They're the kind of eyes that scare young punks into confessing their crimes and stop all logical thoughts from existing in my brain if I stare into them too long. He has an aura about him that is calm and controlled, like he has an energy that is contained but so very dangerous when unleashed. Like the eye in the middle of a hurricane.

Eric leans his elbow on the counter while biting his bottom lip, giving me a once over. For a man in his forties, he's attractive, with salt and pepper hair, laugh lines in the corners of his eyes and a neatly trimmed silver beard, but I'm not into that much of an age gap. I know he used to work with my grandfather on the force before he retired, and knowing that puts him squarely in "old man" territory for me. There's no way he's checking me out because I'm hot. It's barely past 7 a.m., and I've been up for three hours already; the bags under my eyes could count as carry-on luggage. I'm wearing ripped jeans and a Brewed Awakening sweatshirt, and my curly hair frizzes into a halo, barely contained by the bandana I'm using to hold it back.

He's doing it to get a rise out of Dominick. They seem to think he has a thing for me but won't act on it. He doesn't seem like the kind of guy who gets told no often or is too afraid to ask a woman out, so I'm not convinced of that theory. But I enjoy Dominick's attention, so I play along, hoping maybe one day he will take the bait and ask me out.

"Darlin', Dane and I'll have the usual, and our boy Dom here will have a pumpkin spice latte, extra pumpkin." Eric winks at me when I quirk an eyebrow at Dominick for his uncharacteristic order.

"You lose a bet or somethin'?" I ask as I key in their order and fight to control the smirk threatening to take over my lips.

Dominick rolls his eyes at Eric and mutters, "Or somethin'," under his breath.

Eric's broad face splits into a smile when he leans in like he's going to let me in on some big secret.

"You see, Dom lost a bet last night at The Sip. There was a group of cute young girls throwing darts, and he seemed to think he could challenge them to a round and win. Easy pickin's, right?" He side-eyes Dominick pausing for dramatic effect. I can't help but notice the slight pinkening of Dominick's ears when he looks away, trying to ignore Eric by engaging Dane in conversation about last night's basketball game.

"Well, these Basic Sorority Barbies kicked his ass, and the wager was if they lost, they'd have to try a round of straight rotgut whiskey, and if he lost, he'd have to drink pumpkin spice lattes every morning for a month. I'm here to keep our boy honest, because we are officers of the law, and we uphold our end of a bargain."

I lose my battle to contain a fit of giggles over Eric's story. Doubling over in laughter, I turn to Marie and tell her, "Be sure to add extra pumpkin spice to that latte!" Spinning back to face the three men, I find Dominick looking at me with a strange intensity I've never experienced from him before. It pins me in place and makes me think he probably uses this look when intimidating a suspect into confessing. My mouth goes dry, my cheeks heating under his scrutiny. The words that come out of his mouth next steal the air from my lungs.

"If drinking a daily frou-frou coffee is the price I have to pay to hear your laugh, I'll suffer it gladly." His voice is husky, and a shiver races down my spine as my brain struggles to process the meaning behind his words. My eyes are locked with his, but at my periphery I see Eric backing away with a satisfied smirk on his lips. Pressing his advantage during my momentary stunned silence, Dominick leans in closer and asks, "Can I get your number, Serena?"

The moment turns awkward while I take too long to respond, still too stunned to answer his question. Dominick clears his throat and looks down at the counter, almost bashfully, as if he feels like he might have crossed a line. Marie fortunately comes to the rescue with a nudging me from behind with her baby bump, starling me out of my stupor. "Reenie, don't leave the poor man hanging. He's clearly already suffered a pumpkin-sized hit to his ego." Marie places Dominick's coffee on the counter, and he gives her an appreciative nod.

"Uh…um, yeah…sure." I nod and stand there, hands hanging limply by my side, my brain still not entirely rebooted from the short circuit his question caused. Marie takes matters into her own hands, sliding my phone out from my back pocket, swiping her thumb over my lock screen (*wait, how does she know my password?*) before handing it to Dominick. He shoots her a grin before taking my phone and adding in his information. I hear a ringtone sound briefly from his pocket before it shuts off, and he returns my phone to me with a wink and a nod.

Marie finishes the transaction, while I stand off to the side, my brain still struggling to catch back up. I see Eric stuff a generous tip into the jar before the three police officers retreat, making room for the next customers in line. The morning rush is still in full swing, so I force myself to put my phone away without looking at it in case seeing his number on the screen causes another full body shutdown.

TWO HOURS LATER, things have calmed down, and I'm getting ready to clock out so I can head to class. I finally chance a glance at my phone, and I see an outgoing call under "Tall, Dark and Pumpkin Spiced," along with a few unread text messages from the same contact.

> Tall, Dark and Pumpkin Spiced: Can I take you out for dinner sometime this week?

> Tall, Dark and Pumpkin Spiced: This pumpkin spice thing isn't so bad. Don't tell the guys I said that.

> Tall, Dark and Pumpkin Spiced: I've never been so happy to lose a bet.

Biting my lip, I type out a response, hoping I can recapture some cool points I might have lost when I had my little mind meltdown earlier.

> Me: Your secret is safe with me. How about Thursday night? I work evenings on the weekend.

I don't have to wait long for his response. It comes through so fast I can't help but feel like he might've been staring at his phone, waiting for me to text back.

> Tall, Dark and Pumpkin Spiced: Thursday it is. I'll pick you up at 7. Just send me your address.

> Me: Looking forward to it, Pumpkin. ;)

I grin at the nickname I dub him with, then I put my phone away and grab my backpack, ready to head to my psychology class. Marie tosses me a wave as I head towards the front door and gives me a singsong, "You're welcome!" in parting while the door closes behind me.

I head to class with a lightness in my chest I haven't felt

in years. Not since Mom's accident left her unable to work, forcing me to be the primary caretaker for the both of us. Maybe things are finally looking up for me. I allow myself to get lost in daydreams of meet cutes and first dates as I walk to class, still not entirely believing my luck that a man as drop dead gorgeous as Dominick Reeves wants to take me out.

CHAPTER TWO

SERENA

"You want to grab some lunch?" my friend Kai asks, bumping my shoulder with his as we pack away our psychology books. As if on cue, my stomach lets out a mortifyingly loud rumble in response. Kai chuckles as my cheeks flush with embarrassment.

"I'll take that as a yes."

"I'm good; I've got this." I pull out my sad PB&J I packed at 4:30 a.m. before heading into work. Kai lifts his eyebrows skeptically and shakes his head, rejecting my excuse.

"I know you've been up for six hours now and probably haven't eaten more than a muffin and chugged some coffee at work. That PB&J isn't going to be enough to stop your stomach from embarrassing you during stats class. Come on ReRe—I'm buying." Kai hooks his arm around my shoulders and leads me out of the classroom, guiding us towards the dining hall on campus. He steers us toward the tantalizing aromas of greasy cheeseburgers and French fries.

Kai knows my situation better than anyone, having been there when I got the news of my parents' car accident that fateful night two years ago. He and I had been cramming for finals at my place, just weeks away from graduation, when the police knocked on my front door and turned my world upside down.

"HELLO, ARE YOU SERENA MALCOLM?"

The voice that greets me when I open the door is gruff, but softened by something that sounds a lot like remorse. His face is half-hidden in shadows, sporadically lit up by the blue and red lights of his police cruiser parked in our driveway, but when I catch glimpses of his eyes, I can tell he hates this part of his job.

"Y-yes," I manage to stammer out. I feel the heat of Kai's body at my back as he places a protective hand on my shoulder.

"I'm Officer Jones, and I'm sorry to tell you, but there has been an accident involving your parents." I feel my legs threaten to buckle, and Kai immediately pulls me into his side. He wraps me up in a tight hug, keeping me from collapsing onto the ground.

"Are...are they...okay?" is all I manage to eke out in a whisper as my vision begins to tunnel and my chest constricts from the pressure of the impending panic attack building inside of me. I

know the answer before he says anything. Of course, they're not okay. He wouldn't be here if they were.

"Your mother has been rushed to Birch Falls Memorial in critical condition. They were hit head on by a drunk driver, driving on the wrong side of the highway, and—"

A jagged sob escapes my chest as my knees finally give way completely. Kai goes with me as we collapse in a heap on the floor, him cradling me against his chest while my tears soak his BF High Class of 2012 t-shirt.

"What about her dad?" I hear his voice, even though it's muffled by his arms wrapped so completely around my head.

The long silence before the officer's response is answer enough, but the words that follow break me completely. "Unfortunately, he didn't make it."

"Hey, ReRe, where did you go?" Kai gives my shoulders a tight squeeze, bringing me back to the present. We walk through the doors of the dining hall, the scent of greasy fried food hitting us as soon as we enter. Kai immediately guides me to Grease Pit, the term we affectionately call the fast-food section of the cafeteria. More often than not, one or both of us will wind up regretting eating there but the smash burgers are so legendary, a little upset stomach is worth it.

Kai and I have been best friends since our freshman year of high school when his family moved in next door.

His parents relocated from the other side of the country to give their kids a quieter life away from L.A. Kai's sister isn't around much—she was a high school senior when they moved and is now going to college for nursing a few hours away. Kai and I bonded immediately on the bus our first day as freshmen at Birch Falls High, and he's been my rock since my parents' accident. He can usually tell when I'm up in my feelings and missing Dad.

"Just thinking about Dad. His birthday is in three days…"

We grab our trays and load up on burgers, fries and two large Cherry Cokes, our mutual favorite. Kai pays, because he always does, even when I protest. He is very good at developing selective hearing when it comes time to pick up our tab.

"Do you wanna do something? I can pick up some pizzas, and we can have a movie night to keep your mind off of things." Kai's offer sooths some of the melancholy that had begun to creep in. It's on the tip of my tongue to accept his offer but I remember Thursday is in three days, and I have a date.

"Can I have a rain check? I, um, have plans?" My response comes out more like a question, and Kai lifts one of his dark brows as he stares, waiting for me to elaborate.

Sometimes looking at him is like looking in a mirror. His hair mirrors mine in the sense it often resembles a fluffy cloud of curls, and he conveys most of his emotions through quirked eyebrows and dubious stares. The main difference being our complexions. His is a sepia brown while mine is a lighter tawny color due to my mom being a fair Irish woman with freckles. We can have an entire conversation with just a look. It's probably why we hit it off so well in the first place. Our silent form of communication has served us well in the past, especially when trying to come up with a cover story when my parents would catch us sneaking back from late night parties in high school.

"It's a date. I have a date Thursday night." A flicker of something passes over Kai's face, an expression I don't think I've ever seen from him, but it's gone before I can place it and he begins his interrogation.

"A date? With who? When? Where? What does he do? How'd you meet him?"

I take a large bite of my burger, chewing slowly before I answer his barrage of questions. Growing impatient with my stall tactics, he nudges me with his elbow.

"Come on, give me the deets. Do I need to be standing on your porch with a shotgun when he comes to pick you up?"

A guffaw escapes my mouthful of burger as I hold up a finger, telling him to wait a moment. "Please don't do that —he's a cop. I don't think that would go over too well."

Kai's expression turns stony at my confession, and an uncomfortable silence falls over us for a minute.

"You're going out with a cop?" His voice is clipped, not his usual warm honey baritone.

"Um, yeah? He's a regular at the shop. Comes in every morning. He asked me out when he came in today," I stammer out, slightly confused as to why I am having to defend who I choose to go out on a date with.

"He's not one of the assholes who pulled me over in my own neighborhood, is he?" There is an edge of bitterness in Kai's voice that I didn't expect. I hadn't known he'd been pulled over recently.

"When were you pulled over?"

"Which time?" he responds with venom in his voice.

I raise an eyebrow at him, pulling the same move he just used on me, waiting for elaboration.

"Well last month I was pulled over on my way home from work for a supposed broken tail light even though I just had my car inspected. Before that, it was around Easter. I was pulled over for *failure to signal*. Then last year, they stopped me right after I pulled into my driveway claiming I looked like a 'person of interest' in a home invasion earlier in the evening, while I was at work. Thank God my boss answered when I called and gave me an alibi, so they fucked off pretty quick."

I suck in a sharp gasp, shocked by Kai's recent run-ins with the law. Birch Falls, the sleepy college town where we live, where I have spent my entire life, isn't exactly known for high crime rates. Aside from the disappearance of the Cassidy Grainger, a BFU student, a couple of years ago, Birch Falls is a quiet and safe community.

He lets out a dark chuckle when he continues, "You know what's most fucked-up? They got the guy who did the home invasion. It was a sixty-year-old white meth head. I know you think the cops are the good guys, ReRe, but they're not all like your Granddaddy."

I think about the framed portrait of Granddaddy, hanging in our living room. In it he wears his uniform, decorated in medals from his many years of service. He used to take me for rides in his cruiser as a small child and let me play with the lights and siren. Granddaddy was my hero in every sense of the word, and when he passed away from cancer a year before my parents' accident, it crushed me. He is where my entire sense of justice comes from. He taught me how to look for the helpers if I got separated from my parents in a public place. He was a good man, and the idea that there are men out there wearing the same uniform as him, tarnishing that reputation, turns my stomach. I'm not dumb, I know not all cops are good, but here in Birch Falls, under the influence of my Granddaddy, I assumed crooked cops would not be tolerated in his force.

Suddenly I'm not so interested in my burger, and the bite I had been chewing turns to sawdust in my mouth. The idea that Kai Roberts, the sweetest, most selfless person in my life, could be harassed by cops, my cop specifically, makes me sick.

I push away my food, and Kai notices. He shakes his head before nudging my tray back towards me. "I'm sorry. It probably wasn't your Officer Dudley Do-Right. Don't let me rain on your parade. Just be careful, yeah? It's been a while since you put yourself out there, and I wouldn't be doing my job as your best friend if I wasn't keeping an eye on you."

He bumps my knee with his and force feeds me a French fry. Relenting, I snatch at the fry with my teeth, chomping down on his fingers as he holds it, forcing a pained, "Brat!" to escape his lips.

We finish our lunch in a lighter mood with no more

mention of my upcoming date, then go our separate ways: me to stats, Kai to his photography class. Kai has already figured out his major— he plans on getting into photojournalism once he graduates.

I'm still floundering, taking mostly general education classes while I try to figure my life out. I'm doing all I can, working enough to support Mom and me and trying to keep my head above water while taking a full load of classes. I know I need to make a plan for the future, but it's hard when I know, no matter what, she will need me to take care of her. I'm mostly just here so I can get a degree that will allow me to get a decent job. If only life would slow down enough to let me figure out what it is I want to do once I get that degree.

AFTER MY LAST class of the day, I head home to check on Mom. While I'm at work and class, our neighbor, Mrs. Gregory, comes by to keep Mom company. I feel guilty relying on her so much, but she insists she doesn't mind, claiming she'd be bored out of her mind sitting at home alone all day. I don't argue with her too much since I can't afford to pay someone to come stay with Mom, but I do try to make sure I feed her dinner on the nights she can stay and eat with us.

"Honey, I'm home!" I call out in my best Ricky Ricardo impression as I walk through the front door. *I Love Lucy* is

Mrs. G's favorite show, and she gets a kick out of a young millennial like me actually understanding the dated reference. I spent entirely too much of my childhood watching TV Land reruns late at night with my dad when we both couldn't sleep. He spent a lot of time away from home on business, so when he was home, that was our special time to hang out and bond, just the two of us. I inherited his insomnia gene and his love for old and wholesome sitcoms from yesteryear. I never did understand the latest *Gossip Girl* or *Gilmore Girls* reference, but I could quote the *Golden Girls* from memory.

Walking into the living room, I find Mom and Mrs. G sitting at the table in front of the bay window, putting together a puzzle. Mom suffered a traumatic brain injury during the accident that killed my dad. It left her in a coma for almost three weeks and when she woke up, she had what the doctors described as anterograde amnesia. Like Drew Barrymore's character in *50 First Dates*.

Mom remembers basically everything up until the day of the accident, but she doesn't remember anything from that day or almost her entire hospital stay. Forming new short-term memories is extremely difficult for her, so she's unable to work anymore. She does remember Mrs. G though, so having her around to keep Mom company during the day is a godsend. They keep each other busy. On the good days, Mom can tell me what they got up to. On the bad days, she may not remember what they had for lunch.

Mom and Mrs. G always take time each day to journal and take pictures of what they do so Mom can look back and "remember" what she did. Sometimes, she's lucky enough for certain things to stick, and she retains those memories. She understands her condition fairly well thanks to the journaling and the constant repetition of Mrs. G or me explaining to her what happened.

"There's my baby girl. How was school?" Mom smiles up at me, eager to hear all about my day. I know she will make a note of it in her journal so if anything important happened she will be able to ask me about it in the future.

"It was good Momma. How was your day?" I drop my backpack next to my favorite chair—where I do most of my studying—and lean down to give Mom a kiss on her head.

"Oh, you know, same old, same old. Gloria and I made some of her famous pumpkin muffins today. They're in the kitchen if you want one." Mom waves a hand towards the kitchen before she returning her focus back to the puzzle she and Mrs. G are working on.

I smile, enjoying the aroma of pumpkin spice in the air. I can't help but think of my upcoming date with Dominick. It must have been a good day for them if she remembers the muffins. Comforted by those two thoughts, I go into the kitchen and snag a muffin off of the counter while I start pulling dinner out of the fridge. "Mrs. G, are you staying for dinner? I have plenty of lasagna I can heat up!"

"Don't worry about me, ReRe. I've got bridge club tonight." Mrs. G comes into the kitchen to put away the muffins while I heat up dinner. "Laura had a really good day today. It was her idea to bake the muffins. She remembered how much you liked them last fall." She rests a hand on my back, making me pause to absorb what she just said. She smiles up at me with a kind understanding in her soulful brown eyes. She better than anyone understands the toll Mom's condition has taken on me.

"She remembered that?" I think back to last fall when I had come home from class one day to find Mom and Mrs. G baking muffins for the senior center where Mrs. G volunteers. I stole a muffin or three and declared they were the best thing ever. Mom then insisted on baking a fresh batch every day that week in an attempt to memorize the recipe. The doctors always insist they can't tell us how permanent Mom's memory loss is or if she will ever regain the ability to create new memories, so anytime she does, it feels like I'm getting a piece of her back.

I scoop Mrs. G into a big hug, squeezing her tightly.

"Don't give up on her, Re. She does better every day."

Mrs. G goes back to packing away the muffins, and I remember I need to ask her to stay late on Thursday. "Um, I need to ask you a favor." I bite my lower lip nervously, hoping I'm not imposing too much on Mrs. G by asking her to stay for me to go out on a date.

"Anything for you, ReRe. What do you need?"

"Can you stay with Mom Thursday night? I, um, kind of have a date..." My request barely has a chance to escape my lips before Mrs. G squeals and clasps her arms around me, this time giving me a bone-crushing hug.

"It's about damn time, sugar! I was worried I was going to watch you turn into a spinster, working so hard and never going out! Who's the lucky fella? Is it that handsome boy next door, Kai?"

My face scrunches in confusion at the mention of Kai. "What? No, um, it's not Kai. His name is Dominick. I met him at work. He's a regular."

Mrs. G waves her hand dismissively, "Oh, his loss then. One day that boy will come around and realize what he's missing. Tell me about this Dominick."

"He's a cop; he comes in every morning. He asked me out… It's no big deal, really." I pop a shoulder, trying to come across as nonchalant. I don't want to get my hopes up in case my complicated life is too much for him.

"Ooh, I like a man who comes with his own set of handcuffs!" A wicked gleam shines in Mrs. G's eyes as she claps her hands together. She bursts out laughing when she takes in my shocked expression.

"Don't be so scandalized, child. Ol' Mr. G and I had some fun times when we were younger. You don't stay married to the same person for thirty years without getting a little creative from time to time."

"Um, yeah, but you're my surrogate grandmother, and I *really* don't need to hear how you and Mr. G got 'creative' with handcuffs." I make an exaggerated gagging sound, and the next thing I feel is Mrs. G's hand slapping the back of my head while she mutters explicit curses about ungrateful shithead kids.

"Keep that up, you little shit, and see if you have anyone to come sit with your mama while you go on this 'hot date.'" Mrs. G keeps muttering under her breath about one time in Cabo with Mr. G and the cabana boy, and I do my best to tune her out while I throw the lasagna in the oven to heat. I usher her out the door just as she gets to the so-called "good part", doing my best to talk over her and ignore her comparison of the cabana boy's dick size to actual vegetables.

"You know those zucchinis that get left in the garden for too long and turn into giant green baseball bats?"

"Uh huh, yeah, okay, that's nice Mrs. G... See you tomorrow! Byyyyeee!" I close the door in her face, and I can tell by the mischievous look in her eyes she loves nothing more than to embarrass me with her sexcapades. I make a mental note to not let Dominick anywhere near Mrs. G when he comes to pick me up on Thursday.

CHAPTER THREE

SERENA

It's the next morning, and we are deep in the prework rush again. I feel another jab in my side while I'm restocking the bakery case. "Psst, your boyfriend is here," Marie stage whispers to me when Dominick and crew walk in.

"Shit, how do I look?" I ask as I straighten up and try to dust the powdered sugar from my black shirt. I leaned too far over the donut tray while stocking and now have two white circles on my boobs for everyone to see.

"Like you got in a fight with a donut and lost." Marie bites her lip as she tries to hold back her laugh and fails miserably.

"Shut up, you twat." I hip check her on my way to the register.

"Hey, cops like donuts! Ask him if he wants a bite of yours!" My face heats with embarrassment as I look up and realize she said that last part loud enough for Dominick,

Eric and Dane to hear. All three are holding back smirks, and Dominick is not-so-subtly checking out my chest.

"You know, if this is your idea of foreplay, I have to admit it's working." Dominick's velvety baritone washes over me, and the heat of embarrassment ratchets up another hundred degrees.

"I was, uh, um, stocking…donuts…sugar everywhere." I flounder as my brain tries to boot back online after being short-circuited by his voice.

"I can tell there appears to have been a struggle. Do I need to take a report? Perhaps eat the perp so it can't cause you any more trouble?" Eric and Dane both chuckle at Dominick's joke, and I fight back a smile. He's never been so playful before, and I can't help but feel excited about how our date will go if this is what he's really like. Before I can say anything, Marie leans over with a box holding two powdered sugar donuts, sans some sugar on top.

"Here you go, Officer. The suspects, in case you'd like to take them in for questioning. On the house, since they've been on her tits." She jabs her thumb at me, and I hiss at her in embarrassment.

"That's enough out of you." I shove Marie back to the espresso machine before she can humiliate me further. "Now that we have that out of the way, what else can I get you fellas? Two usuals, and pumpkin spice, extra pumpkin?" I quirk a brow at Dominick, trying to regain some of the cool factor I might have lost during the donut fiasco.

"Actually, it'll be three pumpkin spice lattes, extra pumpkin. These two losers didn't think I'd have the balls to ask for your number, so now they have to suffer with me."

Dominick's full lips turn up in a smirk as he gives his coworkers a side eye.

"Boys, if you want to drink a PSL, drink a PSL. You don't have to make up excuses about losing bets if you want to get your basic bitch on. I promise I won't judge… too hard." At this point I give up on the fight to hold back my smile. Joking around with Dominick is doing a lot to settle my pre-date jitters, and his smile is so disarming. The intense, ball-busting cop who was in here yesterday is nowhere to be found today, and I find myself really wanting to get to know this side of Dominick.

"I assure you, Serena, I am secure in my manhood enough to order a pumpkin spice latte without any pretense. If it puts that smile on your face, I'll drink that shit in the middle of July, just to watch you light up." My brain goes offline again as I try to process his words. He said something about smiles and lights and pumpkins in July, but I can't make any sense of it. A long awkward moment passes before I realize he's looking at me expectantly, like he's waiting for an answer to a question.

"Um, I'm sorry, did you ask me something? I, uh, got lost…" *Nice save, dumbass*, I mentally berate myself.

Dominick lets out a sultry low chuckle that causes me to clench my thighs together. "I asked if I could call you tonight. I get off shift at six."

I smile, nod, and shake my head all at the same time. "Yes, no. I mean yes, you can call, but not at six. I have a late class tonight. I'll be home around eight." At this point Marie reappears, placing the three coffees on the counter.

"Alright boys, wrap it up. The line is getting long. You

can continue with your flirting tonight. We have other customers to serve."

With that, they pay and head out, Dom tossing me one of those sexy head nods in goodbye, and I'm fairly certain I'm making heart eyes at him while he walks out. Marie shoves me back to the kitchen so I can compose myself while she takes care of the next customer in line.

After a silent freakout session and a few box breathing exercises, I make my way to the front and see that Kai is next in line. I go to help him while Marie works on the previous order.

"Hey! What's up?" I start working on my latest creation, a maple-pecan latte with a dash of nutmeg that I'm debating naming Sweater Weather. Kai is my official guinea pig, and I make him try any new drinks before we put them on the menu. He's never afraid to tell me what he really thinks, and he's the main reason why the passion fruit latte didn't make it on the menu during the summer. He wasn't wrong about that one; it wasn't my greatest idea. I blame my binge watch of the *Great British Baking Show* and the copious amounts of passion fruit the contestants use in their recipes for that particular bout of inspiration.

"Hey, you wanna get together tonight after class to work on that assignment for psych? You're better at the outlining part of paper writing, and I'm stuck," Kai asks, throwing a five on the counter that I ignore in favor of making his drink. It's on the tip of my tongue to say yes before I remember I agreed to talk to Dominick tonight after class.

"Um, I can't tonight. Plans. How about we work on it tomorrow? We've got until next week to turn in the outline. I haven't even started mine yet." A flash of something that looks like surprise crosses Kai's face. He's not used to me not being available outside of work and school hours. He knows I usually stay home with Mom once I'm done for the day.

"Plans? What kinda plans? I know it can't be anything good because they're not with me." He leans down on the counter on his elbows, leveling his cocksure grin at me.

"None of your business, you ass. Here, try this." I plunk the coffee creation down in front of him and quirk a brow at him, waiting for his judgment. I know this one is good. It's got maple in it, and it's almost as basic as a PSL. The college girls will go nuts for it.

Kai takes a sip, closes his eyes and makes a humming noise as he savors the flavors of the drink. "It tastes like you need to spend more time with your best friend and help him get his outline done."

"Ha-fucking-ha." I roll my eyes and shove the five back across the counter at him. We do this dance every time he comes in. He slaps a five-dollar bill down, I ignore it, he ignores me ignoring it, and eventually he stuffs it into the tip jar.

"Seriously, what are you doing tonight?" He takes another long drink of the latte, sucking half of it down in one go. I made his iced because Kai doesn't believe in drinking hot coffee.

I ignore his question, still feeling weird about his reaction from the previous day about the news of my date with a cop. I'd rather not step back into that hornet's nest if I can avoid it.

"Better than the passion fruit?"

"Much. Very Basic. The white girls are gonna love it. Is it Dudley? I thought your date wasn't until Thursday?"

Rolling my eyes, I huff out a sigh. "If you must know, yes. He's going to call me tonight. I would like to get to know him better before our date. And his name is Dominick."

Kai doesn't say anything for a long moment before nodding once, backing away to make his exit. "Alright, just be careful with him, ok? It's been a while since you've put yourself out there. I don't want to see you get hurt. Or fall for a cop and get all lame."

"Fuck you. You wish you were as cool as me." I reach across the counter and punch him in the shoulder.

Kai grins wide, showing off his perfect white teeth before saying, "Every day, baby." With that, he walks out, slinging his backpack over his shoulder while putting his headphones over his ears.

LATER THAT NIGHT, I'm walking in the parking lot on campus after class when my phone rings. Glancing at the screen I see it's Dominick calling. I answer, slightly out of breath from the long trek across campus to the student parking lot.

"Hey! What's shakin' bacon?" I cringe when I hear the words come out of my mouth. What the hell did I just say?

"Bacon? Is that some sort of cop joke?" Dominick chuckles while I stop dead in my tracks, desperately hoping a hole will open up in the ground and swallow me whole.

"No. It's just me being a colossal dork. If you want to hang up and lose my number, I completely understand."

"And miss more zingers like that one? Not a chance." The amusement in Dominick's voice washes over me like a warm blanket. I continue on my trek across the dark parking lot to my car while we talk.

"How was class?" he asks as I start digging through my backpack looking for my keys.

"Long. Just got out so I'm walking to my car. Prof held us over by like twenty minutes. I'm dead on my feet right now."

"You're walking across campus right now? Do you have anything for protection?" Dominick's voice is suddenly less warm, colder and more serious. It must be hard to turn off that kind of vigilance at the end of the day, or ever, for that matter.

"I've got a rape whistle somewhere," I mutter as I drop my backpack on the ground to crouch down and dig through the pockets looking for my keys. "Damnit, why do they always go to the bottom?"

"You're walking alone in the dark, without your keys in hand? Serena, you need to be more aware of your surroundings. I want you to stay on the phone with me until you get to your car." I'm simultaneously annoyed by his lecture and thrilled he cares about my safety. It's been so long since I've felt looked after—it's nice hearing the concern in his voice.

"Yes, sir," I respond with a mocking seriousness to my voice as my hands finally snag the keys in the bottom of my bag.

"Watch your tone, Serena, or I'll give you a reason to call me sir." The gravel in Dominick's voice causes me to clinch my thighs together as it shoots straight to my pussy. Holy shit, his cop voice is hot.

"Yes, sir," I respond automatically. A car door slams behind me, and the crunch of shoes on gravel reminds me I'm still in the middle of a dark parking lot, alone. I hoist my backpack back over my shoulder and resume walking, keys threaded between my fingers like Dominick instructed.

"So, what class did you have tonight?" Dominick's soft, friendly tone, the one he used today at the coffee shop, is back.

"Creative writing. It's a class I take for fun. We were reading our latest assignments, and class time went over." I finally see my car in the back corner of the lot. Parking here in the student lot is a nightmare on most days if you don't have an 8 a.m. class. Which I don't most days since I work the early shift.

"Anyway, we were going over some short stories we wrote last week..." The sound of footsteps close by causes me to trail off as I turn and look behind me. I don't see anyone, but the feeling of being watched slowly creeps over me, causing goosebumps to raise all over my skin.

"Everything okay over there? You got quiet." Concern laces Dominick's voice, drawing me back to our conversation.

"Um, yeah, I thought I heard something. But I'm almost at my car." I start moving again, half jogging the rest of the way. I've never felt unsafe walking through the school lot before, but maybe I was just oblivious to how dangerous it is. Dominick has me looking over my shoulder, feeling paranoid now.

Once I'm safely tucked inside my car, with the doors locked, I focus back on my call with Dominick. "Okay, I'm in my car, heading home. Since it's not a fancy new one with the Bluetooth speakers, I'll have to hang up so I won't get pulled over for talking while driving." I let some humor slide into my voice as I start up the car, and I melt at the sound of Dominick's husky chuckle from the other end.

"Okay, Kitten. Drive safe, text me when you get home, and for the love of God, buy some mace and keep your keys in hand when you are walking in a parking lot."

"Yes, sir," I say with a smirk before hanging up the call. It might be the lack of a father figure in my life, but Dominick's protectiveness has me feeling all warm and fuzzy on the inside.

CHAPTER FOUR

SERENA

After getting home, I sent Dominick a text that I arrived safely, and that turned into another phone call that lasted until almost midnight. We talked a little about everything but kept the conversation light. He asked about my classes; I asked him how he decided to go into law enforcement. He told me more about his partners, Eric and Dane, and I told him about my favorite drinks at the coffee shop. We talked about movies too—his favorite (*Fight Club*) and my favorite (*Shaun of the Dead*)—and what our date would be like on Thursday. He didn't go into much detail other than he would be picking me up at my house at seven, and the rest would be a surprise. I tried to argue and say I'd meet him somewhere so he wouldn't have to go out of his way to pick me up, but he insisted.

Now I'm sitting in psych class, head bobbing from tiredness. Professor Stein's droning voice is a struggle to pay attention to on the best of days, but today, running on only four hours of sleep, it has me fighting to stay awake.

A pinch on my thigh has me jerking my head up from where I had it resting on my hand. "Ouch. What the fuck," I angry whisper at Kai.

"You were drooling," he responds, not taking his eyes from the white board up front where Professor Stein is writing up the traits of narcissistic personality disorder.

"Was not," I huff indignantly, folding my arms across my chest. His only response is to tap his pen on my notebook page where there is a noticeable wet spot smearing the ink on my notes. My cheeks flush in embarrassment, and I see his lips quirk up in a smirk out of the corner of my eye.

"Keep your mouth shut," I mutter as I go back to taking notes. He just presses his full lips into a flat line, trying his best to contain the chuckle trying to escape.

"So where is Dudley taking you on your date?" Kai asks as he shoves a huge bite of pizza into his mouth. We have a long break between classes right now, so we are eating lunch and working on our outlines for our psych papers.

"Dunno." I pop a shoulder as I take a sip of my Cherry Coke. "He won't tell me. I just know he's picking me up at seven."

"Do you need me to hang out with your mom or anything while you're out?" Kai's offer surprises me. He's stayed with Mom before when Mrs. G couldn't be there, but it's usually only when I have no other options. He's busy himself with work and class so I try not to intrude on his free time when he gets to work on his photography.

"Nah, Mrs. G is staying. She won't miss the opportunity to embarrass me in front of Dominick, I'm sure. Did I tell you about her cabana boy story?"

"No, and I really don't need to hear it either." Kai grimaces as he puts his large hand over my mouth in an attempt to hush me. He should know by now that move doesn't work on me. I stick out my tongue and lick his palm, causing him to pull away.

"Dude." He shakes his head in disgust when I giggle at him.

"But she said his tally whacker was as big as one of those giant zucchinis!" I do my best impersonation of Mrs. G while Kai tries covering his ears to block me out. "They don't make them like they used to, ReRe! That boy damn near split me in half!" I double over in a fit of laughter as Kai starts singing loudly, trying to drown me out. Kai just rolls his eyes at me, familiar with the kind of stories Mrs. G likes to tell. She has regaled him with a few when she has cornered him at my house.

We draw a few curious looks from other students nearby, so I cool it on the zucchini talk and focus back on our work. "What are you writing your paper about?" I lean over, trying to sort out the mess that is Kai's notes. Kai is brilliant but disorganized. He always struggles with getting his thoughts in order, so that's usually where I come in when we work on assignments together.

"I dunno. I think borderline personality disorder or

maybe the narcissistic one he was talking about today. Seemed interesting. You?"

I shrug, unsure of which one I want to write about. "I'm leaning towards the dependent one. It reminds me a lot of you, needing someone to take care of them all the time." My lips quirk up in a grin, and Kai gives me a playful shove.

"Yeah, fuck you too." He laughs as he goes back to sorting through his notes. We resume our work as we finish off the pizza that Kai bought us. He thinks he's subtle about how he takes care of me, but I notice. I always notice how he always buys me lunch, always tips on his free coffee in the morning and all the ways he looks out for me, like making sure he's available on my dad's birthday and anniversary of his death. Kai is my best friend, and I don't know how I would've made it through the last two years without him.

I lean against him and rest my head on his shoulder. "Thanks for lunch. You want to come over for dinner tonight? I'm making tikka masala." Kai wraps his arm around my shoulders and gives me a squeeze.

"Can't tonight. There's a protest happening in the square over a police shooting that happened a few towns over. I'm going to document it for the school paper."

"A protest? What happened?" I sit up, shooting him a concerned look. A protest sounds scary, and I'm worried about him going to one.

"Some kid got pulled over on his way home from work. When he was reaching into his glove compartment to get his papers, the cop freaked out and shot him through the door thinking he was grabbing a gun. He was only sixteen. It's fucked up. The cop hasn't even been put on suspension for the investigation." Kai's lips press into a thin line while he shakes his head. "You know, that's the third shooting this year of an unarmed teenager by the police? Shit is fucked. So now all the demonstrations are popping up across the country, trying to bring some change."

"Is it safe for you to go?" I bite my lower lip, looking up at my best friend, fear niggling at me after the stories he told me about his own encounters. He's been my rock and my biggest source of support since my dad died. The thought of anything happening to him causes a painful clenching in my stomach.

"Yeah, it's fine. It's just some local activists giving speeches. But I think we are on the cusp of something big happening, and I want to be there to document history."

I nod and return to my work, not really sure what to say, but unable to let go of the uneasy feeling sitting in my gut now. Kai is always on the lookout for history in the making, so I know there will be no talking him out of going to this demonstration.

After our break, we go our separate ways. I make Kai promise to call me when he gets home tonight just so I know he makes it back safe. The uneasy feeling in the pit of my stomach over this demonstration won't go away.

IN STATS CLASS, I get a text from Dominick that I check, unable to resist knowing what he has to say.

> Tall, Dark and Pumpkin Spiced: Hey, I won't be able to talk tonight. I have to pull a double to work crowd control for a protest happening. I'll be seeing you in the morning though. Can't wait for my pumpkin fix. ;)

I smile at his winky face, and the worry about the demonstration eases a bit in my gut. If Dominick is there then things shouldn't get out of control. He's a good cop and will keep things calm.

> Me: Be safe tonight. I'll miss talking to you. See you in the morning.

> Tall, Dark and Pumpkin Spiced: Wouldn't miss it for the world. Seeing you first thing in the morning is the best part of my day.

With hearts in my eyes, I tuck my phone away and spend the rest of stats class daydreaming about my upcoming date with Dominick. I'm pretty sure the professor announces a test for the next class, and I don't even care if I fail it—I'm on such a high from Dominick's attention.

It's 11:30 p.m. and I haven't heard from Kai yet. I decide to send him a quick text checking in, just to see if he made it home ok.

Me: Hey, how was the demonstration? You home?

I WAIT AROUND for twenty minutes for his response, but none comes, and my message never shows as read. I crawl into bed, knowing I need to get some rest if I want to stay awake long enough to go on my date with Dominick tomorrow, but sleep doesn't come easy with the worry about Kai creeping back into my head.

WHEN I WAKE up the next morning, I check my phone right away to see if Kai ever responded. My heart sinks when I see my message to him is still unread. It's ass-early in the morning so I don't dare call him in case he just got home late, but the anxious feeling crawling through my brain will not let up as I get ready for work. I send him one more text, just to let him know I'm worried.

Me: Hey, how'd it go last night? Call me when you get a chance.

With that, I shove my phone into my purse and head

into work, hoping that maybe seeing Dominick and hearing from him that everything was fine last night will alleviate my worries.

A few hours later, the bell jingles above the entrance of Brewed Awakening and I see Dominick and crew walk in. They all look tired and a little worse for wear. I can only assume they all three pulled doubles last night to help cover the demonstration.

"Good morning, boys. What will it be?" Dominick stands back and lets Eric do the ordering today. I can see the dark circles under his eyes and wonder if he might be planning on rescheduling our date tonight, based on how quiet he's being.

"Back to the usual for me and Dane, sweetheart. Your boy here is still on the pumpkin spice." Eric shoots me a flirtatious grin as I key in their order.

"You boys look tired—need any extra shots of espresso?" I ask, trying to get an idea of how last night went and how worried I should be about Kai this morning.

"Nah, we'll be alright once we get going." Eric brushes me off without offering up any additional information. I nod and turn to give the ticket to André to make the drinks. He finally decided to show up for work this morning, which is a good thing since Marie had a checkup with her OB. Working the morning shift alone is miserable and hectic. I'll take André's slow-as-molasses ass over working alone.

I look past Eric and meet Dominick's silver eyes. I bite my lower lip, debating how to break the ice with him. It feels awkward this morning. I can't tell if it really is, or if

I'm making up shit in my head, spiraling because of my anxiety over Kai. I settle on a barely audible, "Hey."

"Hey, Kitten." His voice is gravelly, like maybe he spent the night yelling or barking out orders. I can't help but take a moment to imagine what it would sound to hear him call me Kitten in bed.

Dane and Eric busy themselves with talk of an upcoming football game tonight, so I take the opportunity to ask Dominick how last night was. "Everything go okay last night? You seem…quiet."

"Yeah, mostly. Had a few rowdy shit disturbers in the crowd we had to throw into lock up for the night, but all in all it was a peaceful protest." I can feel the tension leave my shoulders when he confirms it was a peaceful night. I just have to assume Kai got home late and crashed before texting me. I make a mental note to give him shit about that later.

"Do you still want to go out tonight? If you're tired I—" Dominick raises his hand and puts a finger to my lips to hush me.

"I'm going to stop you right there, Kitten. We are going out tonight. This date is the one thing I've been looking forward to all week. Seeing your gorgeous face is the reason I get up early in the morning to buy coffee instead of making it at home. So shut your pretty little mouth unless it's to tell me how excited you are about our date."

I feel my mouth drop open in shock as I nod mutely at his words. The way he's looking at me can only be described as intense, but the slight upturn of his lips tells me he knows exactly the kind of effect he is having on me.

"Ah, um, yes...sir?" There I go glitching again. I can't seem to carry on a normal conversation with him any time he's in front of me.

"Good girl." Dominick flashes me a panty-dropping grin before swiping his coffee off the counter. He tips his head to André in thanks and throws some cash in the tip jar before following Eric and Dane out of the coffee shop.

I turn around after he leaves, eyes wide, cheeks flaming hot, to meet an also stunned André's shocked expression.

"Um, when did that happen? Since when does the hot grumpy cop talk?"

"It happened this week. You'd know that if you bothered to come to work more than once a week." I roll my eyes at André and turn back to the counter to serve the next customer, barely being able to contain the smile threatening to bloom across my face.

CHAPTER FIVE

SERENA

I'm in my bedroom, standing in my underwear, chewing on my fingernails while I debate my clothing options. It's almost 7:00 p.m. and I'm no closer to deciding on what to wear when I hear the doorbell ring.

"Shit!" I hiss out in panic as I stare down at the pile of clothes on my bed.

I hear Mom call out that she will get the door, and I grab a dress at random to throw on, frantic to not leave Dominick alone for too long with my mom and Mrs. G. Fortunately, my hair and makeup are already done, so getting dressed is the last step in the process. I just didn't expect to look at everything in my closet and hate it. Looking at my ripped jeans, college hoodies, Brewed Awakening t-shirts and the small assortment of dresses leftover from my high school days made me realize how little I've done for myself since my parents' accident. Aside from high school graduation I haven't had an occasion to dress up for in the last two years.

I take a quick look in the mirror, scanning over my appearance. I pick a black skater dress that is kind of plain but hugs my figure in just the right way, showing off my curves and my legs, which are my best assets. It laces at the front, and I loosen it a bit to show off more cleavage, hoping to distract Dominick from my teenage wardrobe with my tits. I'm mildly freaking out about how much older he is than me, and I hope he won't take one look at me and realize he's too mature for me. On my way out of my bedroom, I shove my feet into a pair of black booties and grab a jacket to fight off the autumn chill that has begun to settle in.

As I descend the stairs, I hear voices in the living room. Oh no, they've already got Dominick in the house. I send up a quick prayer, hoping that Mom hasn't already broken out my baby pictures. I round the corner and stop at the sight of my mom gazing adoringly at Dominick from her seat on the couch while he takes a bite of one of the muffins she and Mrs. G baked today. They were trying out new recipes, and apparently Dominick gets to be the guinea pig taste tester. Mrs. G is standing next to him with an expectant look on her face, holding a glass of milk for him to wash down the muffin with.

"Wow, Mrs. Malcolm, this is really good," Dominick says with a mouthful of muffin.

"Call me Laura." Shit, she likes him. She's already on a first name basis.

"These are amazing, Laura." Dominick corrects himself before polishing off the rest of the muffin and accepting the glass of milk from Mrs. G.

"Hey, sorry! I was just finishing getting ready. I'm ready to go." When I speak, Dominick turns and rakes his gaze all over my body. The heat in his stare causes goosebumps to erupt all over my flesh and the way he licks his bottom lip before making eye contact with me causes me to forget how to breathe. The way he is looking at me is entirely too carnal for my mom to be in the room, but I'm too stunned by his smolder to do anything but stand there.

"Serena, you look beautiful, and now that I've met your mom, I know exactly where you get it from." The smile Dominick unleashes is blinding, and I can see the hearts in my mom's eyes already. Mrs. G looks like she is smitten too, the way she stands behind him with her hands clasped under her chin.

A blush creeps across my cheeks as I stammer out a quiet, "Thank you." My mom and I do look a lot alike. I may have my dad's darker complexion, full lips and curly hair, but my gold eyes, button nose and the freckles that dot along my face are all from Mom. Dominick reaches out for my hand before placing a gentle kiss along the back of it while shooting me a discreet wink.

"Alright you two, go have fun! Get on, get out of here." Mrs. G begins shooing us towards the front door. You'd think she's the one that has had the dating dry spell by how excited she is for us to go out. Dominick takes my coat and helps me into it before leading me to the front door.

"It was nice meeting you Laura and Mrs. G—"

"Call me Gloria!" Mrs. G interrupts him, before he gets out the rest of his goodbye.

"Gloria, it was lovely to meet you," Dominick corrects

himself. "I'll have Serena home safe and sound. You ladies have a good night."

Dominick ushers us out the front door with Mom and Mrs. G hovering behind us, watching our departure. I should consider myself lucky they aren't trying to come along on our date. As the door closes, I hear my mom call out, "Have fun, kids. Don't do anything we wouldn't do! We won't wait up!" Just when I thought I was done being embarrassed for the night, she had to get one more comment in.

"Sorry about that. I know they're a lot." I bite my lower lip as I look up at Dominick, hoping he isn't already regretting this night. The smile he gives me is nothing short of panty-melting. Before I realize what's happening, Dominick leans in and places a gentle kiss on my cheek as he wraps his arm around my shoulders, pulling me into his side. I find myself easily nestling into his warmth, like it's the most natural thing in the world.

"Don't worry about it, Kitten, I like your mom and Gloria."

I feel my heart swelling with that declaration. "You are totally going to make it into her journal, you know," I say without thinking.

"Her journal? Does your mom keep a suspect log of every guy that takes her daughter out?" He asks with an incredulous laugh, and I realize I'll have to explain Mom's condition to him if he's going to be coming around more. I freeze on our walk to his car as I process how I am going to explain our situation. I'm so protective over Mom and it's just been us, Mrs. G, and Kai for so long. I worry about people taking advantage of her if they know about her memory loss, so I don't often mention it to outsiders.

"Hey, where did you go?" Dominick stops and turns to me, lifting my chin to look up at him so he can look me in the eye.

"It's kind of a long story. I'll explain in the car." I flash him a smile that doesn't quite reach my eyes as I take his hand and give him a tug towards his black Dodge Charger. Dominick gives me a terse nod of understanding before opening my door for me like a gentleman. I can't help but bask in the feeling of protectiveness and being cared for that washes over me from such a simple gesture. Outside of Kai, who I wouldn't exactly call gentlemanly, my dad was the only other man in my life to look after me, and I've missed that feeling of being taken care of. I've been carrying such a weight on my shoulders, taking care of Mom and myself—it feels nice to let go for once and let someone else be in control.

Once my butt hits the smooth buttery leather of the seat, Dominick leans in without hesitation and buckles my seatbelt for me. His hard body is so close to mine, I can feel the heat radiating from him, and his sandalwood cologne invades all my senses. I can't help but gasp and take in a deep breath, becoming intoxicated by his entire presence.

Before he pulls away, I feel his lips brush against the shell of my ear as he whispers, "I take care of what's mine, Serena. Get used to it." My core clenches as a rush of arousal pulses through my body at his possessive words. I find myself thinking that I will have absolutely no problem getting used to being taken care of by Dominick.

FOR OUR DATE, Dominick takes us to a nice restaurant. One of those locally sourced, seasonal menu type places with handcrafted cocktails and words used to describe foods I have never heard before. I'm pretty sure half of them are either in another language or entirely made up. This type of dining experience is not within my work-two-jobs-to-get-through-college budget. I am staring at the Mortar and Pestle menu, trying to discreetly puzzle out what Maître d'Hôtel Butter is, when a waitress in a crisp white button-down shirt accessorized with a skinny black tie approaches our table.

"Good evening, folks. My name is Kelsey, and I'll be your server tonight. Can I start either of you off with a cocktail or a glass of wine?" Kelsey's voice is friendly, but all of her attention is directed at my date.

"I'll have a glass of Blanton's Single Barrel, neat." Dominick orders without hesitation. I bite my lower lip as I look over the drink selection on the menu. I don't turn twenty-one for another three months, and I'm not sure what Dominick's stance is on underage drinking, so I decide to play it safe and order a blackberry and basil mocktail.

"Wonderful, would you like any appetizers to start while I get your drinks started?" Kelsey keeps her eyes glued to Dominick when she speaks, making me feel completely invisible.

"That'll be it for now." Dominick dismisses Kelsey without even a second glance. His eyes are fixed on me, with a mischievous glint in them. Kelsey lingers for a moment longer, seemingly hoping he will finally look up and notice her, but gives up after a long awkward moment.

"I'll have those drinks right out to you, sir." She leaves with a tight smile on her face that doesn't quite reach her eyes anymore.

"You worried I'll bust you for drinking, Serena?" Dominick says as he hides his sly smirk behind his water glass.

"I'm not twenty-one until November eighteenth. I didn't want to risk you tarnishing your stellar reputation as Birch Falls Officer of the Year, three years running, by being seen out with an underage delinquent." I shrug one shoulder as I take a sip of my own water, hoping I am coming across cool and nonplussed about Dominick mentioning my age.

The surprised guffaw that leaves him is contagious, and I find myself laughing as well. "Oh, Kitten, I can't wait to show you how tarnished my reputation actually is." Dominick winks at me, and I can feel heat rising up my cheeks as I take in the implication of his words. I hide my face behind my menu, perusing it studiously like it holds the answer to the meaning of life while I wait for the burn of embarrassment to cool from my face.

"Nuh-uh, Kitten, don't hide from me," Dominick commands as he reaches across the table and pulls down my menu. "I don't ever want you to hide that pretty face from me. Your face is my favorite view."

Kelsey returns with our drinks then, ready to take our orders. My mind is still in blue screen of death mode from Dominick's compliment, so I just order the first thing my eyes land on. Pan-seared halibut and dashi broth with a side of crispy Brussels sprouts. I have no idea what dashi broth is, and I'm not even sure if I like halibut, but the ability to parse the fancy terms on the menu has completely abandoned me for the night, so I will make do with what arrives at the table. Dominick orders the bison ribeye with the fancy butter I was puzzling over and confit Dutch potatoes.

"Can I get you anything else at all, sir?" Kelsey asks, a false sweetness to her voice as she keeps her attention fixed on the man sitting across from me. Dominick hands her his menu without sparing her a glance as he keeps his eyes trained on me.

"I have everything I need right here, Katie."

I bite my bottom lip, trying to hide my smile at his obvious dismissal of our waitress. Normally I'm not one for being rude to waitstaff, but with the way she's ignoring me and overtly flirting with my date, I don't feel even a little bad about him putting her in her place.

From that point on, our date is full of easy conversation while we eat delicious food (it turns out I do, in fact, like halibut, and Mâitre d'Hôtel Butter is just a fancy way of saying compound butter). I tell Dominick about my mom and her memory issues from the accident. I see a flicker of sympathy cross his face when I recall the night of my parents' accident, and he never lets his attention stray from me once. We are sharing a dessert of maple brûlée custard when my phone chimes out with a text notification.

"Oh shit, sorry. I thought I turned my ringer off," I apologize as I reach into my purse to turn off my phone. I glance down to see who the notification is from, and I see a new message from Kai on my home screen. I almost give into temptation to open my phone to see what he has to say after being radio silent for over twenty-four hours but Dominick clears his throat, drawing my attention back to him.

"Your mom checking in on you?" he asks, his expression serious and maybe a tad bit annoyed.

"Oh no, it's my friend Kai. I guess he's finally responding to my text message from last night."

"Who's Kai?" Dominick's tone turns from light to serious in a heartbeat.

"My other boyfriend. Why? You jealous?" I joke, trying to bring the lightness back to our evening.

Dominick's eyes darken from silver to a stormy gray when he responds, "Incredibly. I want to be the only man you refer to as your boyfriend." My mouth goes dry at the molten heat in his gaze licking over my skin. Instead of poking the bear more, I slide my phone, ringer now turned off, back into my purse.

"Come on, Kitten. Let's get out of here." He signs the receipt left by our waitress and leads me out of the restaurant by the hand.

"What are we doing now?" I ask as I let him pull me along to his car. He doesn't answer me until we reach the vehicle. His response comes as he cages me in with his large body against the hard metal of the passenger door, cool from the crisp fall air.

"Now, we are going to kiss, and I am going to show you how thoroughly you belong to me." One of his large palms grips my hair at the base of my skull as he tilts my head back, angling my face up so he can crush his lips against mine. His lips are full, soft and demanding. He tastes sweet, like maple and vanilla, with a hint of smoky caramel from the bourbon he was drinking. His other hand cups my cheek as he licks against my lips, seeking entrance into my mouth. I open for him, becoming pliant under the heat of his body. How long we stand there kissing in the moonlit parking lot, I have no idea, but it's long enough for my breathing to grow ragged and my panties to become damp from my arousal. When Dominick finally pulls his lips away from mine, he leans in, whispering into my ear, "You're mine now, Kitten. I better be the only man you refer to as your boyfriend from now on."

I respond with the only two words my brain is capable of forming, "Yes, sir."

CHAPTER SIX

SERENA

It's the end of my shift at Brewed Awakening, and I'm counting out my tips when Kai walks through the door. He looks rumpled and disheveled in a way I rarely ever see him, outside of cramming for finals. There are dark circles under his eyes, deepening the tone of his skin. Stubble coats his chin, making it seem like he hasn't bothered shaving in a couple of days, which is extremely unusual for Kai. He claims his dimples are his secret weapon to charming the ladies, and he refuses to cover them with a beard, stating it would be a crime to deprive womanhood of them.

I quickly pocket the money I've been counting and rush around the counter to pull him into a hug. "Hey, where have you been? I've been worried sick about you!" Kai doesn't say anything, but he squeezes me tightly, like he's afraid I'll disappear if he lets me go. "What's going on, Kai?" I mumble into his chest, unable to loosen myself from his hold. Kai just stands there, holding me for another minute before releasing me and taking a step back.

This close, I can see the shadows under his eyes. The whites of his eyes are red from lack of sleep. His haggard appearance has me on high alert, and I grab his hand and tug him to the love seat at the back of the shop, one of our favorite places to study together. Kai leans back on the plush sofa and covers his face with his hands while he gathers his thoughts. "I just got out of jail last night." He pulls his hands away from his face and turns to look at me. His eyes shimmer with unshed tears, and my mouth falls open in shock. Whatever I thought he was going to say, that was not it.

"Excuse me? You got out of what?"

"Jail. A couple of dudes got rowdy at the demonstration the other night. Got up in the faces of some pedestrians walking by. I was off to the side shooting with my camera, and I tried to break it up and keep things calm. But when the cops showed up, they grabbed us all and took us in."

"Jesus, Kai. Seriously? Are you okay? I'm so sorry I didn't answer last night." I scoot over and wrap my arms around his waist and lay my head on his chest, trying to give my friend any comfort I can. He wraps his arm around my shoulder and drops his head into my hair. His next words are muffled as he speaks into the mass of curls.

"I saw your messages when I got my phone back and was calling to let you know I was home and okay. I got my boy Ryan to pick me up when they finally let me out." Kai lets out a weary sigh before speaking again. "I think I'm gonna skip class today. I'm tired as fuck. I don't know if you know this, but city jail isn't exactly the Hilton. Plus, those drunk assholes kept bitching all night about their rights, like the fucking bastards that put us in there gave any shits."

"Sure, yeah, that makes sense. I'll take notes and drop them by for you after class." I pull away and give Kai another thorough once-over. He looks defeated, his natural charisma and energy nowhere to be found. "You want me to bring some lunch too? I can hang for a bit before I have to go to work tonight."

On Friday and Saturday nights, I waitress at Mavericks, a college dive bar known for their cheap beer and unlimited wing nights. The tips aren't great there, but the owner lets me keep them all and doesn't hassle me about not being twenty-one. He's not exactly known for caring about the rules on underage drinking or serving, hence Mav's popularity with the college crowd. Freshmen and sophomore students in particular.

Kai flashes me a tired smile that doesn't quite reach his eyes, his dimples nowhere to be seen. "Sure, ReRe. That'd be great." With that, Kai stands from the couch and pulls me up with him to give me one last hug before he leaves. As I watch him go, my mind starts spinning about what happened to Kai, and I wonder if Dominick was the one that put him in jail. Is the man I'm currently falling for responsible for the defeated and broken heaviness emanating from my best friend?

After class, I stop by our favorite local sandwich shop and pick up a couple of our favorite subs. It's not exactly in my budget for the week, but Kai spends so much time taking care of me, it's only fair I return the favor. Especially after he's had one of the worst experiences of his life. On my way to Kai's with our lunch and psychology notes, my phone rings. I glance down at the screen and see Tall, Dark and Pumpkin Spiced with the selfie Dom and I took on our date lighting up the display. I hit the speaker button and return my attention to the road.

"Hey there, Pumpkin. I was just thinking about you." I try to infuse lightness into my voice when I answer the call. My words aren't a lie. I have been thinking about Dom. Agonizing over the possibility that he could've been the one that locked up Kai for no reason at all and what I'll do if he is. Dominick is the best thing that has happened to me in years, and the idea of him hurting the second most important person in the world to me causes my heart to seize up.

Dominick's laughter comes through the speaker in a low rumble. "I'm never going to live that nickname down, am I?"

"Nope," I respond, popping the p. "You're stuck with it now."

"I suppose it is a cross I must bear if it means being with you, Kitten. I was calling to see if you wanted to grab some lunch. You're done with class for the day, right? There's that burger place close to campus; I can swing by and pick you up. I've got an hour before I'm back on shift."

I bite my lower lip, debating my response, wondering how to bring up the protest from the other night. "Um, actually, I already have lunch plans today." There is hesitation in my voice. I don't want to accuse Dominick of something he didn't do and ruin our fledgling romance, but I need to know if he was the one that arrested Kai.

"You do?" Dominick's tone turns from cheerful to serious in a heartbeat.

"Yeah, um, I'm taking some class notes and lunch over to my friend Kai. He's had a rough week and missed class today." I pause briefly, working up the courage to say the next part. "He was arrested at the demonstration Tuesday night…d-did you…arrest anyone that night?"

In the ensuing pause, I find myself holding my breath, waiting for Dominick's response, silently praying he won't have any idea what I'm talking about.

"No, Kitten, I didn't arrest anyone. There were a few aggressive protestors and a few fights, but I wasn't involved in any of them. Dane or Eric might have, or it might've been one of the other guys from the county office. I'm sorry about your friend, but that's a risk he takes when running with a crowd like that."

The breath I was holding whooshes out, and the relief I feel at Dominick not being involved in Kai's arrest is palpable. "Right…um…okay. That's good. I think it was just the wrong place, wrong time. Kai said he was trying to get some dudes who were fired up to calm down, and I guess he got caught up in the crossfire."

"That's probably what happened, Serena. Hopefully your friend learned his lesson. Do you want to get dinner tonight instead? I'm off shift at six." Dominick's sudden change of subject sends me into a tailspin. I'm so relieved by his answer and desperate to be near him again I almost tell him yes, momentarily forgetting I have to work tonight.

"I'd love to but I'm working tonight at Maverick's." I let out an exhausted sigh at the thought of the long night of waitressing while dodging drunk college bros and their attempts to flirt with me while leaving shitty tips.

"You're working tonight? How late?"

"Until the kitchen closes. I'll probably be there 'til midnight."

"Damn, Kitten, when do you get a day off?" Dominick's voice is laced with concern and I close my eyes, relaxing into my seat, letting the smooth baritone of his voice settle into my bones. "You work more than I do, baby. I'm worried you're going to burn yourself out."

A small smile tugs at the corner of my mouth as I revel in his concern. "Unfortunately, there's nothing to be done for it. Mom can't work, so I have to. The settlement from the accident paid off the mortgage on the house, but there's still bills to pay and food to buy. It's okay though. Once I get through school and graduate with my degree, I'll be able to get a better job with saner hours. I'm not the only girl that's had to work her way through school, and I haven't had to resort to stripping yet, so I've got that going for me." I let out a small laugh that has no actual amusement behind it.

"Kitten, I'll make sure you never have to resort to that." The tone Dominick uses is firm and commanding, brooking no argument from me.

"I'll hold you to that, Pumpkin," I say with a much

bigger smile blooming across my face. "Hey, I gotta go, but do you want to go out Sunday? It's my only actual day off."

"Absolutely. I need to see you again. I can't stop thinking about that fucking delicious mouth of yours. How about I pick you up for brunch, then we can find a more comfortable place than my car to get to know one another?"

A warmth seeps into my core as I think about our make out session in his car and how fogged up the windows had gotten. I'm pretty sure we could have fucked right there on the street, and no one walking by would've been able to see what we were up to. The idea of "getting to know" Dominick more personally lights up every nerve ending in my body, and a flush creeps across my cheeks.

"It's a date, sir."

AFTER HANGING UP WITH DOMINICK, I grab my backpack and the bag of sandwiches before making my way across my yard to Kai's house next door. Technically it's his parents' house, but they spend six months of every year traveling the country in their RV, enjoying their early retirement. Kai's dad made some smart investment decisions in his thirties, and now they get to live their best lives. Currently they're somewhere in the southwest United States exploring the national parks.

When I knock on the door, it takes a few minutes for a

bleary-eyed Kai to open it. He's shirtless, wearing just a pair of gray joggers, and stifling a yawn behind a fist. My eyes snag on the way his abs flex as he stretches, temporarily short-circuiting my brain. I shake my head and mentally chide myself for ogling my best friend.

"Shit, I'm sorry. Did I wake you up?" I take a step back, ready to retreat and let him get his rest.

"Nah, I just got up a few minutes ago… Oh shit, is that what I think it is?" Kai's eyes light up with excitement when he spies the bag of food in my hand. Kai grabs the sandwiches before I have a chance to answer and takes off to the living room, leaving me completely forgotten as the aroma of tandoori chicken and crispy homemade French fries wafts from the open bag.

"You're welcome," I mutter as I close the door and slip my shoes off by the welcome mat before following Kai into the living room.

"You'rethabest," is the muffled response I get from my friend as he shoves a handful of fries into his mouth.

We spend the next hour going over the notes I took during class while finishing our lunch. I can tell Kai is antsy and not completely focused on the work we are doing. His mind is clearly still on his night in lockup, so I grab his computer from his lap and close it before setting it off to the side. "Let's take a break. You're on edge, and I'm too tired to focus. I just want to chill before I go to work." The smile Kai gives me doesn't quite reach his eyes, but he nods in agreement all the same.

"Good call. My head isn't in the right space to retain this shit anyway." With that, he wraps his arm around me, tugging me into his side, making us comfortable on his parents' plush oversized couch while he pulls up our favorite season of *Supernatural* to watch. I grab the throw blanket from the back of the couch and drape it over us, snuggling into Kai's muscular frame. The scent of his citrus and sage body wash envelops me, and the comfort of our old familiar routine soon has my eyelids heavy with sleep. I drift off not long after the monster of the week is introduced in the episode he chose.

"Hey, ReRe, wake up." A gentle shake on my shoulder slowly rouses me from the dream I'm lost in. It's a good dream about Dominick and his hot, possessive kisses.

"Mmm…no…leavemelone…" I grumble as I tug the blanket over my head and nuzzle deeper into Kai's side.

"You gotta get up, ReRe. It's time for you to go to work." Kai stands up suddenly, jerking the blanket off me, letting me collapse into the couch cushions completely. "And you've drooled all over me. You're worse than Archer." At the mention of his name, the giant Great Dane bounds into the room, jumps on top of me and starts licking my face.

"Gah! Noooooooo! Archie! Bad dog!" I let out a shrill scream as I throw up my arms trying to fend off the slobbering animal. "Get ooooff meee!" I wail as Kai laughs at my predicament. Archer is undeterred by my flailing and continues to slobber on my face.

"MALAKAI DEMETRIOUS ROBERTS! GET YOUR BEAST OFF OF ME!" Archer's tongue licks up my face and sneaks into my mouth as I yell at Kai. "ACK! NO! GROSS!"

"Aw, ReRe, Archie is just trying to looooove you." Kai is still laughing as he finally, mercifully, pulls the giant dog off me. I sit up in a huff and shoot him a glare that I only hope conveys exactly how much trouble he is in.

"Archer, spot!" With one firm command Archer immediately bounds over to the dog bed by the fireplace and plops down with a thud that shakes the floor.

"What time is it?" I ask, wiping the dog drool from my face with one of Kai's hoodies that is draped on the back of the couch.

"Hey! I just washed that!" He jerks the shirt from my grasp with a frown and points to the clock. "It's four-thirty, and as much as I enjoyed listening to your symphony of snores, I'm pretty sure you're supposed to be at work in half an hour."

"Shit, why'd you let me sleep so long? I'm gonna be late." I hurriedly pack up my notes and computer, shoving everything into my backpack haphazardly.

"Seemed like you needed the rest. You were out like a light. You didn't move through three whole episodes of *Supernatural*. My left arm was starting to raisin from all the drool." Kai shoots me a playful wink as he walks with me to the front door.

"Ha-fucking-ha." I mutter, rolling my eyes at him. He reaches out, grabbing my arm, stopping me before I open the door.

"Seriously, ReRe. You look wrecked. Have you thought about cutting back your hours at work?"

I look up to see my best friend looking down at me with so much concern in his eyes. The bridge of my nose begins to sting, and I look down, blinking back the tears threatening to form. He's not wrong. I am exhausted. I'm worn down. I'm so tired of working constantly and not having any time for fun. I'm so damn tired of taking care of everything and worrying about Mom and bills and my grades and if I'm taking advantage of Mrs. G's kindness too much. I'm just...so. Damn. Exhausted. Instead of confessing this to him, I deflect.

"Yeah, I'm fine. I just had a late night, that's all. Maybe after the holidays I'll cut back on my hours some. I gotta go. See you later."

I jerk open the door and head out before Kai gets the chance to probe some more. After a quick pit stop at my house to change and say hi to Mom and Mrs. G, I head to my second job, ready for a long night of waitressing and come-ons from douchey frat bros.

CHAPTER SEVEN

SERENA

"App sampler for table twenty!" Marcus, the line cook, calls as he places the tray of food in the passthrough window.

"Serena, can you run that to twenty? I've got to change a keg; the natty just kicked." Adam, the head bartender, nods over to the table hosting what looks like half a frat house. This is their fourth order of appetizers, and they are on their sixth pitcher of shitty light beer. I've successfully managed to avoid their table for most of the night, but it looks like my luck has run out. Stacey is busy mixing drinks, and Veronica seems to be devoting all of her attention to the table of professors in the back, probably very aware that is where the best tips for the night are waiting.

I let out a weary sigh as I grab the food from the window. "Thanks, doll." Adam flashes me a smile before disappearing into the back. I plaster a strained smile on my face, mentally counting down until the kitchen closes. I'm desperate to get home and fall face first into my bed.

"Here you go, guys. Just a heads up, the kitchen closes in a half hour so if you need anything else, speak now or forever hold your peace." I lean over to set the plate of food in the center of the table. As I'm bent over, a large hand slides over my ass and gives it a firm squeeze.

"Oh, I'm definitely in need of something else. I'm in need of your phone number, gorgeous."

I straighten up, spine stiffening at the intrusion on my personal space. Glancing to my left, I see a disarmingly attractive guy wearing a pink polo shirt paired with a backwards baseball cap, flashing me what I'm sure he considers a charming smile. I try to take a step back, out of his reach, but he tightens his grip, pulling me until I stumble and land on his lap.

"I'm Brad. What's your name, sweetheart? Why haven't you come over to see us all night? We've been hoping you'd come…serve us." His blue eyes shine with the confidence only granted to rich white boys of privilege, used to always getting what they want.

"This isn't my section, now if you'll excuse me…" I move to climb off his lap, but before I can extricate myself from his grasp, his friend to my right turns towards us, caging me in further. He is built like a linebacker. Big, beefy, square head, featuring a crooked nose that's been broken more than once.

"Come on, sweetheart. My boy Brad just got dumped, and he's feeling lonely. Hang out with us for a few minutes. Have some fun. We won't bite."

The smile Brick-head flashes at me is anything but reassuring. I glance over to the bar to see if Adam has returned, but he's nowhere to be seen. Veronica is still flirting with the professors, and Stacey has her back turned to us while she shakes up a cocktail. The rattling of ice in her shaker is barely audible over the bass of the latest Nikki Minaj hit. My stomach flips when I realize I'm not going to get out of this situation without causing a scene.

"Sorry about your luck, Brad, but I really have to get back to work." I lean forward, making a move to stand up, but Brad bands his arm around my waist, pulling me back against his firm chest.

"Don't be like that, gorgeous. I think we could have a lot of fun together. I promise we'll make you feel so good."

His hot breath washes over my neck as he whispers in my ear. I can smell the stale beer wafting from him. I swallow back the nausea roiling in my stomach. Brick-head leers at me as he scoots closer, invading my space until all I see and smell is them. The rest of the guys at their table seem completely oblivious to my discomfort and ignore us. They continue eating and chugging beer while laughing about whatever the fuck it is that frat bros find amusing. My heart hammers in my chest as Brad's hand starts sliding up my waist and grazes the side of my breast. His friend's big meaty hand slides up my thigh, and my breathing starts to become panicked and shallow.

"Please, just, don't…." I close my eyes, squeezing them shut, trying to will myself out of this situation. Pray for Adam to return and notice what is going on. As I feel the urge to scream begin to build in my chest, a familiar, smoky voice sounds from behind Brick-head.

"Why in the fuck do you have your hands on my girl?"

My eyes pop open, and I see Dominick looming over Brick-head, his hand grasping the back of his neck causing Brick-head to grimace in pain. Dominick doesn't wait for an answer before he gives Brick-head a forceful shove, face planting him into the table, causing a loud crack when his nose makes contact with the surface.

Brad immediately senses the danger he is in and lets go of me. I don't hesitate and jump off his lap, letting Dominick pull me into his side. "Woah, dude. We were just having some fun, weren't we, sweetheart?" Brad looks to me with pleading in his eyes and some misinformed notion that I will help him out of this situation.

"Kitten, is that true? Were you having fun? Because to me, it didn't look like you were having fun." Dominick's voice is cold and lethal. He doesn't take his gaze off Brad as he gently guides me behind him, shielding me from what he's about to do.

"No. I was trying to get back to work." My voice sounds much stronger than I feel right now. My body is still trembling from the panic attack I was on the verge of having.

"Yeah, I didn't think so. If you two douche bags don't want to get arrested for sexual assault, I suggest you and your friends pay your tab and get the fuck out of here. Right fucking now. Don't make me tell you twice." The entire table is silent as Brad and Brick-head exchange a silent conversation.

"Yeah, man, whatever you say. Come on, guys. Let's get out of here." Brad pulls out his wallet and throws some money on the table. He moves to leave, but Dominick places a hand on his chest, holding him in place.

"I want you to apologize to my girl for making her feel uncomfortable." Dominick's tone is so cold, it sends a shiver down my spine. Brad jerks a nod and leans over to look at me around Dominick's broad frame.

"I'm sorry that I made you uncomfortable. I apologize for my behavior."

"Yeb, we're sorby," Brick-head follows up, words muffled by his hand pinching his busted nose, trying to stem the flow of blood.

"Don't ever let me catch you back in here. Find a new bar." With that, the group vacates the bar, and I let out the breath I didn't even realize I was holding. Dominick turns to me, wrapping me up in a tight embrace as I relax into his hold. "Are you okay, Kitten? Do you want me to arrest them? Break some kneecaps? Your wish is my command."

I huff out a chuckle as I shake my head back and forth against his solid chest, melting into the safety of his embrace. "That's not necessary. As long as they don't show their faces here again, I'll be happy. Thank you for that. I was two seconds away from screaming and really causing a scene."

"More of a scene than me breaking that asshole's nose?" Dominick laughs and plants a kiss on the top of my head.

"You don't know how loud I can scream." I smirk up at him, feeling the tension melt away from my muscles, relaxing now that the danger has passed.

A wicked gleam shines in his eyes as he leans down and whispers into my ear, "Oh, I can't wait to find out how loud I can make you scream." Heat creeps up my cheeks at the salacious wink he shoots my way.

"Go finish your shift, Kitten. I'll have a beer while you work, then I'll follow you home." Dominick gives me a light tap on the ass as he turns me back towards the bar. Adam is back pouring beers, Stacey is busy with a new group of customers, and Veronica has finally decided to pay attention to the other tables in her section. It's back to business as usual at Maverick's, no one seeming to notice what went down just a few minutes ago.

"Did you come here just to see me tonight?" I can't hide the smile that threatens to bloom across my face. The idea that Dominick couldn't wait until Sunday to see me makes my heart race.

"I did, and it's a good thing too. Sounds like I've got myself a gig as a bodyguard now until I convince you to quit this job and let me take care of you." I let out a nervous laugh at his comment, but Dominick's eyes darken on the last part of his sentence like he isn't joking at all.

I decide to sidestep that comment for now and make my way back to the bar to close out the rest of my tables for the night. The kitchen is closed now, so I am almost done.

"I just have to close out my tickets and do some side work. I should be done in the next half hour."

"Take your time, Kitten. I'll wait for you as long as I need to."

AFTER I FINISH COUNTING out my tips and clock out, Dominick escorts me out to my car. "I'll follow you back to your place to make sure you get home safe." Dominick reaches past me, opening my doorlike a true gentleman.

"You know you don't have to do that. It's a ten minute drive, I think I can handle it." I try to give Dominick an out, so he doesn't feel obligated to follow me but he shakes his head in dismissal. He places his hands on the roof of my car, caging my body against the cool metal in the same move he used on our date. Heat radiates from him like an inferno, and I feel my pulse quickening in excitement at his proximity.

"What did I tell you, Serena?" Dominick leans in, letting his lips ghost against mine in a feather light touch. "I take care of what's mine." His hand cups the back of my head as he crushes his lips to mine. It feels like he is trying to devour my soul with his kiss, and I wrap my arms around his neck, pulling him closer, desperate to let him. Dominick's kiss is needy, possessive and everything I'm missing in my life. His tongue sweeps into my mouth, and I taste the malt and hops from the beer he drank. His body is so firm and solid against mine. I want to mold myself against him and feel every inch of his skin against mine. I hook a leg against his hip, as he grinds his growing erection against my core. We kiss for so long I think I forget how to breathe, I become so light-headed. When we break apart, we are both panting for air, hearts pounding, breath mingling.

"Kitten, I'm gonna need you to get in your car before a patrol comes by and winds up arresting us for indecent exposure. Because if we don't stop now, I can guarantee you that's what is going to happen."

I laugh into his chest, not quite believing my luck at finding such an amazing man. "Oh, surely they wouldn't arrest one of Birch Falls' finest officers." Dominick lifts my face up with a finger under my chin so he can hold my gaze.

"Oh, Kitten, with all the filthy, depraved things I want to do to you, I can guarantee they would most definitely lock me up. Those acts are NOT meant for public consumption." The grin he flashes at me is positively feral, and my core heats with arousal. He plants one more searing kiss on my lips before directing me into the car and buckling my seatbelt. "Lead the way, sugar. I'll be right behind you."

I start my car and drive home with a smile plastered across my face the entire time.

CHAPTER EIGHT

SERENA

It's Sunday morning, and I'm once again digging through my closet, clad only in my underwear, hunting for something to wear on my date with Dominick. What does one wear on a brunch date? He told me to dress comfortably before he said goodnight after following me home Friday, but he refused to divulge more information than that. Does comfortably mean my favorite ripped jeans and oversized hoodie? Would leggings be appropriate? Most of my comfortable clothes are barely fit for public consumption, but considering all I ever do is work, go to school or hang out with Kai, I haven't really given my wardrobe much thought in the last few years.

I'm busy pulling out some of my more casual dresses from the closet when I hear the doorbell ring downstairs.

"I've got it, Sweet Pea!" Mom calls up the stairs as I start panic dressing with the first thing I grab out of the pile I made on my bed. I skip the dresses in case Dominick has planned something active and pull on a pair of skintight black leggings and an oversized boatneck sweater. It's a burnished gold color and falls off my shoulder for a slightly sexy touch. I'm hoping he will take the bare skin as an invitation to kiss it, like he did Friday night when we came so close to doing indecent acts in public. After our intense make out session, the memory of Dominick's body pressed against mine has been occupying my mind relentlessly. I was so turned on after I got home, I had to get my favorite purple vibrator out to take the edge off.

After slipping on my favorite pair of black boots I go downstairs expecting to see Dom, but instead find Kai in the living room with Mom. "Hey, what are you doing here?" I stumble to a stop at the bottom of the stairs, confused, trying to recall if I have forgotten a study date with Kai.

"Mrs. G came over this morning all worked up. Her sister fell and broke her hip, so she needs to go to the hospital to be with her, but she said you had 'very important plans,' and she was supposed to sit with your mom today. She asked if I could come over instead."

Heat climbs up my cheeks, embarrassment flushing them with color at the thought of Mrs. G calling my date with Dominick "very important." I know she wants me to get out there, but recruiting Kai to watch my mom so I can go on a date is not at all what I had in mind.

"No, it's okay… Don't worry about it. I can cancel." As the words leave my mouth, the doorbell rings. My stomach drops in disappointment, knowing it is Dominick this time, and I will have to cancel our plans. I close my eyes and take a deep breath, readying myself and hoping he won't mind taking a rain check. Before I can move to the door, Kai's hand lands on my shoulder.

"Hey, ReRe, it's okay. I don't mind hanging out with your mom. Go. I've got this." I open my eyes and look up at my friend, expecting to see resignation, but his expression is a warm smile in support.

"You sure? I really can cancel. It's not that important." Instead of responding, Kai walks past me to open the front door, revealing Dominick looking devastating in dark wash denim and a black henley top that looks almost molded to his body. I hold my breath, waiting for the moment when Kai realizes my "very important plans" are a date and decides he has better things to do than babysit my mom.

Instead, he just opens the door and steps to the side so Dominick can fully see me, standing in the foyer, biting my lower lip, feeling guilty for using my friend like this. Dominick only spares him a quick glance before zeroing his focus on me.

"Good morning, Kitten. You look gorgeous." He swoops in and places a kiss on the corner of my mouth before turning to greet my mom. "Good morning Mrs. Malcolm. I hope you don't mind me borrowing Serena for the day. She works so much; it's hard to get this girl pegged down for a date."

"Hello, nice to meet you..." Mom trails off for a moment, trying to recall if Dominick is someone she should remember.

"Dominick Reeves. We've met briefly before." Dominick leans in to give Mom a quick kiss on the cheek in greeting.

"And with any luck, you'll see enough of me that I'll be impossible to forget." Mom glances over at me, pink tingeing her cheeks from Dominick's charm and mouths "he's going into the journal." I laugh, rolling my eyes, knowing he's already in her journal.

"You ready, Kitten?" Dom turns to me, extending his hand in invitation for us to leave. I glance up at Kai one more time to make sure he really is okay with this, and he nods once, but his expression is closed off and unreadable.

"How long do I get to keep you today, Kitten? What time does your mom's nurse go off duty?" Dominick asks as he helps me into my coat. I hesitate, not sure how to answer. Kai and I hadn't had a chance to discuss how long he would be willing to stay before Dominick showed up. Guilt claws at my gut over using my friend so I can go out and have fun.

"I'll stay as long as ReRe needs me." Kai's response to Dominick has a coldness to it that is out of the norm for my warm, goofball friend.

"Kai—" I start to interject, saying we won't be out long, but Dominick cuts me off.

"Excellent. I've got big plans for spoiling my girl today. We'll see you all later." Dominick gives Kai a hard clap on the shoulder as he tugs me out the front door. I glance back one last time to see Kai's expression. His eyes are narrowed, lips flattened in a thin line like Dominick is a problem he needs to solve.

I manage to squeak out a quick, "Thank you," to Kai before he moves to close the door, and his expression softens when his eyes meet mine.

"Have fun, ReRe. You deserve it," is his only response before closing the door.

DOMINICK WASN'T LYING about the spoiling. Our date starts with a brunch picnic in the park by the duck pond. Dominick packed a variety of pastries, fruit, yogurt, cut cheeses, and ingredients to make mimosas. He even has a selection of fancy macarons for dessert. We sit and talk for hours. I tell him about my dad and his love for old TV classics and impress Dominick with my pop culture knowledge from shows well before my years, even busting out my best Lucy Ricardo impression.

"Wait, so you're telling me you can quote *I Love Lucy*, but you've never watched *Breaking Bad*? *The Wire*? *Big Bang Theory*? *Friends*?" Dominick looks at me in disbelief, like I'm some sort of rare zoo animal.

I shrug my shoulders and pop another strawberry in my mouth. I lie back on the gingham blanket and stare up at the cloudless sky above us, savoring the warmth of the sun on my skin.

"Dad was an old soul and loved black and white shows. After the accident I've been too busy with school, work and taking care of Mom that I haven't really kept up with the latest shows. My life is a constant cycle of work, study, sleep, repeat. My entire social life is conversations with customers at the coffee shop, hanging out with Kai and begging Mrs. G to not tell me about her sexcapades with her husband."

"Hanging out with Kai? The nurse that was staying with your mom?"

"Oh, he's not a nurse. He's my best friend. He lives next door, and sometimes when Mrs. G can't stay, he will come over and sit with Mom while I work. I can't afford to hire nurses with what I make, so I rely on him and Mrs. G to keep Mom company when I can't be there. She does okay for the most part, but I worry about her deciding to cook or go out of the house and then forgetting what she was in the middle of and something terrible happening. The memory lapses are kind of unpredictable."

Dominick's brow furrows for a moment in a look I'm not sure how to interpret before smoothing back out. "Good thing you have me now, Kitten. Now you have someone to take care of you and your mom." Without warning Dominick leans over me, capturing my lips in a kiss. He teases my mouth open with his tongue, and I open, letting him in. He tastes of champagne and chocolate-covered strawberries, and I lose myself in the intoxicating feel of his body pressed against mine, the silkiness of his tongue mingling with my own.

Soon our breaths are coming in short, excited pants, and I can feel my arousal dampening my panties. Dominick's rough, calloused hand slips under the waist-band of my leggings, and I part my legs in invitation for him to explore further. "I want to make you come on my fingers, Kitten. I want to taste you."

"Oh god..." I let out a breathy whimper as I feel him

trail his finger up the center of my slick heat, my panties the only barrier between us. "But…we're in public…" My protest is weak. I don't actually give a shit if anyone sees us. I'm so turned on, I would gladly fuck him with an audience just to relieve this ache between my thighs.

"There's no one around, Kitten. I'm going to fuck you with my fingers now." Dominick's voice is a low rumble in my ear while he slides his hand under my panties and swirls a finger in my wetness before plunging all the way in. My hips buck up, involuntarily, seeking more friction. Dominick's mouth finds mine again, this time his kisses turning greedy and hungry. He devours my moans as he slides another finger into my pussy while his thumb circles my clit, sending sparks of electricity through my body. I can feel my orgasm building, and I know it won't be long until I make a mess of both of us.

"Oh god…Dom…I'm gonna…" My breath goes ragged when he curls his fingers in a come-hither motion, hitting that magic spot deep inside. My back bows, my orgasm taking over. Dom slides the top of my sweater down along with my bra cup, exposing my breast. He captures my nipple between his teeth and bites down gently, eliciting another cry of pleasure from me.

"That's it, baby. Come for me." My body shudders, hips arching off the ground, vision darkening, as I ride out my orgasm. It feels like eternity before my muscles relax enough to let me collapse limply on the ground, feeling boneless and completely spent. When my vision comes back into focus, I see Dominick licking his fingers with a self-satisfied smirk dancing across his lips.

He looks down at me, his silver eyes darkening with arousal to the color of a storm cloud. "Kitten, I think the taste of your pussy is my new obsession. We need to get out of here before I lay you bare and feast on you for God and everyone to see." Too weak and befuddled by my toe-curling orgasm, I just nod and let him pull me up so he can pack up and take us home.

On the car ride home, I'm so drowsy and relaxed from the amazing orgasm Dominick gave me, I can barely keep my eyes open. He keeps one firm hand on my thigh in a possessive grip, just shy of cupping my wet pussy. I'm so aroused, I'm half-tempted to spread my legs open and let him finger me while he drives, but the guilt churning away in my gut for using my friend's kindness to get laid keeps my lust at bay.

"You sure I can't talk you into coming over to my place to watch a movie?" Dom's thumb makes a soothing pattern rubbing circles on my thigh, and I fight to stay conscious and not fall asleep in his car.

"Rain check? I feel bad making Kai blow his Sunday watching my mom while I'm on a date." I put my hand on Dominick's and give it a reassuring squeeze. "I had an amazing time today. Thank you for the picnic...and... everything else. I haven't been this relaxed in months."

Dom lifts my hand to his mouth and kisses the back. "Stick with me, Kitten, and you'll always be taken care of."

CHAPTER NINE

SERENA

"Soooooo…how did your date with Dominick go?" Marie nudges me with her shoulder as we stock the pastry case before the Tuesday morning rush. This is the first shift I've worked with Marie in almost a week.

"Which date? Thursday night? Friday night when he came and kept me company at work? Or Sunday afternoon when he took me on a picnic?" I can't stop the smile that splits my face when I remember the way he worked my body expertly with his fingers while stealing my soul with his kisses.

Marie's eyebrows shoot up in surprise. "Damn, that boy isn't wasting any time, is he? Kai spent too much time fucking around, and now he's going to find out what happens when you don't shit on the pot."

My brows furrow at Marie's weird mash up of idioms. "Um…what?"

Marie shakes her head and turns to the fridge to check

the stock of dairy and nondairy products. "Like you don't know? Everyone has been shipping you two for years. We thought for sure he would've asked you out by now."

"No, it's not like that between us. Kai's my friend. My best friend. He doesn't think of me that way." I shake my head and laugh off her comment. "That would be like dating my brother."

"Uh-huh. Sure." Her flat tone says everything in those two words. She doesn't believe me. It's okay though, she doesn't have to. Kai and I know where we stand.

The bell above the door dings, and I head to the register, ready to let this line of conversation drop. It's no surprise when I see Dominick strolling in, Eric and Dane trailing behind him with shit-eating grins on their faces. They haven't stopped ribbing him since he asked me out, and I don't think they have plans to stop any time soon. I run around the counter, and Dom immediately wraps me up in a hug that squeezes the air out of my lungs and lifts me off the ground. He takes my lips in an absolutely not-safe-for-work kiss, and it's not until Eric and Dane both start hooting and Marie starts coughing in a comically exaggerated way that he breaks away from me.

"Good morning, gorgeous. I missed you." His velvety baritone sends shivers down my spine.

"You just saw me yesterday morning." I give his shoulder a gentle slap and move to get back behind the counter. Dominick stops me with a possessive hold on my wrist, tugging me back into his body.

"Every hour I go without seeing you is too long." His possessive, claiming words make me weak in the knees.

The bell over the door dings again, signaling the arrival of another customer. I push away from Dom, trying to get back to work, and he lets go of me grudgingly.

"Hey ReRe, got anything special for me this morning?" Kai's voice calls out, letting me know he's my new customer. I look around Dominick and see my Kai strolling in with a smile on his face that melts away when he sees Dominick crowding into my space.

"You're early. You're not usually here until you're almost late for class." I tease my friend and move behind the counter. There's a stiffness in the way Dom holds himself that wasn't there a minute ago, and I chalk it up to male posturing. He moves to the side to let Kai order first.

"I have a tutoring session this morning. Need some help with the psych paper, and since my usual tutor has been busy having a life…" He shoots me a wink as he gets out his wallet. Guilt slithers through my stomach when I realize I had promised to help him over the weekend and never got the chance to.

"Shit, I'm sorry. I can come over and help tonight?" I begin making his drink, a new concoction I came up with that includes butter toffee and salted caramel, making it reminiscent of kettle corn.

"Don't worry about it, ReRe. We're good." Kai's words are reassuring, but his voice seems sad and resigned. Out of the corner of my eye I see Dominick's posture shift, his expression flat and unreadable.

"Actually, Kitten. I was hoping I could bring dinner over for you and your mom tonight. Give you a night off and hopefully have a chance to let your mom get to know me better. You know, since I plan on coming around a lot." I glance over at Dom, surprised by his suggestion. He hadn't mentioned anything about dinner in any of our conversations since Sunday, so his offer takes me off guard.

"Yeah, it sounds like you have plans tonight. I'll catch up with you later." Kai takes the drink I offer him and stuffs a five-dollar bill into the tip jar before leaving. I stare at my friend, confused by his sudden departure, Marie's words from earlier echoing in my mind. Does Kai have feelings for me? Is he jealous of Dom?

Dom takes Kai's place at the register with Eric and Dane flanking him. I begin making their usual order while Dominick waits patiently for my answer.

"You really want to come over and hang out with my mom?" I raise a skeptical eyebrow at him, and he stares back with a no-nonsense expression on his face.

"Why wouldn't I want to spend time with my girl? You're busy, so I'll take any spare moment I can with you."

"Damn dude, calm down with the charm. You're making the rest of us look bad. If my wife hears about this, she's going to start dragging me to her mom's house for Sunday dinner." A laugh escapes me at Eric's chiding.

"Yeah, Dom. You need to be careful. If you raise the bar too high, no man that comes after you will have any hope of impressing me."

His silver eyes darken to the color of a storm cloud, the intensity shining from them nearly taking my breath away. "Who said any man would come after me?"

After Dom and the boys leave, I get swept up in the rest of the busy morning crowd until it's time to rush off to class. I don't see Kai for the rest of the day either. We don't have any classes together today, and he is scarce during lunch, so I eat my sad peanut butter and jelly sandwich while revising my paper for psych class. It's due before Thanksgiving break and counts for thirty percent of our grade. I pick up my phone, debating on texting Kai to see if he wants to get together one night this week to read over each other's papers, when a text notification comes through from Dom.

> Tall, Dark and Pumpkin Spiced: Dinner at 6 okay? I'll pick up something from Roma's.

> Me: You know you don't have to do that, right?

> Tall, Dark and Pumpkin Spiced: Kitten, don't argue with me. I'm bringing dinner and making your mom fall in love with me, so she won't get mad when I monopolize all of your free time.

I bite my lower lip, grinning like a loon at Dom's response. How did I get so lucky to find a man this attentive? I shoot off a quick *Yes, sir.* in response and put my phone away to finish working on my paper.

DOM'S PLAN TO win Mom over works like a treat. I warn her about him coming over so she can refresh her memory by reading her journal entries. This at least ensures she doesn't reintroduce herself to him for the third time. All through dinner, he is careful to ask her questions about her life before the accident so she doesn't stumble over her missing memories, and I can see the joy shining in her eyes at being able to tell someone new about my awkward teenage pop princess phase and the time I flashed my underwear to the mall Santa when I was only three years old, showing off my new Christmas dress.

Dom sits next to me, his left hand never leaving my right thigh, his touch possessive and grounding at the same time. He laughs at her stories, gives all the right responses to her questions about his life, and even cleans up after dinner. Mom might as well have cartoon hearts for eyes as she watches me walk Dominick to the door when it's time for him to leave.

Once we are outside and the front door closes, Dom turns me around so my back is against the column holding up the roof of our covered porch. He leans in, lifting my chin so he can gaze into my eyes. There is a banked heat shining in his silver eyes, burning like the embers of a blazing bonfire. He licks his lips in a move that is reminiscent of a predator sizing up their prey. I can't help the hitch in my breath when my eyes focus on the movement of his tongue over his lush, full lips. Every cell in me is screaming for him to lean in and claim me with his mouth. My body hums with anticipation. My core is wet and needy for him, and I am desperate to feel the press of his hard body against mine. I want to pick up where we left off on Sunday and take things further. I want to fully belong to Dominick.

"Kitten, if you keep looking at me like that, I'm going to do obscene things to you right on your front porch and undo all of that goodwill I just earned from your mom." Dominick whispers into my ear and a shiver runs down my spine. I lick my lips, taunting him in response.

"Don't threaten me with a good time."

"Fuck, Kitten. You are asking for it." The groan that leaves him is purely animal. "Come home with me tomorrow. Stay with me. I promise you; we will have a real good time." Dom kisses his way up my neck, along my jaw and ghosts his lips over mine in the briefest phantom of a kiss.

"God, I wish I could. I can't leave Mom alone overnight." The reality of my situation crashes over me like a bucket of cold water dousing the flames building between us. Something that looks like disappointment flashes across Dominick's face briefly, but it's gone as quickly as it comes.

"I'm sorry, Dom. Dating me isn't easy. My life is complicated, and it's just Mom and I. My whole life revolves around work, taking care of her, and school. If it's too much to deal with, I understand."

My head drops and I close my eyes, trying to ready myself for the moment he realizes dating me isn't worth the hassle. The silence between us stretches for what seems like an eternity. Eventually I gather the courage to look up, to let him dump me face to face. All I see are his lips pressed in a thin line, a look of determination on his face.

"Kitten, if you think I'm going to let little things like

work or taking care of your mom prevent me from claiming the most beautiful woman I've ever seen and calling her mine, you are seriously delusional. I am going to make this work. Don't worry your pretty little head about it." He presses another kiss to my mouth, sealing his promise to me and causing all of my fears to melt away.

CHAPTER TEN

SERENA

The next few weeks pass with Dom and I forming a cozy routine. We see each other most mornings at the coffee shop when he stops in. At least once or twice a week he comes over to have dinner with me and Mom. When I work at Mav's Fridays and Saturdays, Dom will come after his shift to lurk on a bar stool and keep the frat boys at bay. Brad and his merry band of douche bros haven't been seen since Dom took them down a few pegs, and I can't help but be grateful for his insistence in hanging around. Our dates out of the house are nonexistent thanks to my crazy work schedule and studying for finals. Plus Mrs. G has been helping her sister during her recovery, so she hasn't been able to stay with Mom again. My guilt won't allow me to ask Kai to stay with Mom.

Speaking of Kai, outside of class and his occasional stops by Brewed Awakening (never when Dom is there), I have barely seen him, thanks to Dom taking up whatever free time I have available. A pang of longing hits me when I think about my friend, and I decide to text him to see if he wants to come over tonight for a movie night. It's Sunday afternoon, and Dom is off golfing with Eric and Dane, so my evening is wide open.

> Me: You, me and a movie marathon tonight? And by marathon, we will watch half a movie, and I'll pass out from exhaustion?

I don't have to wait long for Kai's response, which loosens a knot of uneasiness that had been building in my chest.

> Kai: Depends. Which movie am I listening to you snore through, and will there be popcorn?

I bark out a laugh at his response, his humor enveloping me like a warm blanket. Hanging out with my best friend is exactly what I need tonight.

> Me: Zombieland and Shaun of the Dead. Duh. And I'll even throw in some M&Ms to go with the popcorn since I'm feeling generous.

> Kai: See you at 7.

At 7:00 p.m., Kai waltzes in through the front door, a six pack of fruity ciders for us to share. He knows I'm not big on most alcohol, so he always brings something I'll like even if the fruity stuff isn't his favorite. He claims he only drinks the stuff because I do, but I've seen half-drunk six packs of ciders in his fridge that I know I had nothing to do with.

I've got a frozen pizza fresh from the oven, a big bowl of popcorn, two sharing size bags of M&Ms spread out on the coffee table with *Zombieland* queued up and ready to go. Mom has gone up to her room claiming a headache, but I think she just wanted to give Kai and I time to hang out on our own.

Kai stops after he enters the living room, eyeing me suspiciously. "Where did you get that?" I look behind me, trying to figure out what he could be talking about.

"Get what?" I ask, spinning around trying to see what he sees.

"That," he says again, pointing directly at me, his lips pressed in a flat, unamused line. It's then I realize I'm wearing my favorite oversized hoodie. A.K.A. Kai's favorite *A Tribe Called Quest* hoodie that he got when he saw them on tour for his eighteenth birthday. He let me borrow it when the weather was unexpectedly chilly one day in our senior year of high school, and I might have—maybe— forgotten to give it back on purpose.

"Oh, uh, this old thing? I…uh…think you left it here. I thought you gave it to me." I smile sheepishly at him, stuffing my hands into the front pocket, hoping he won't make me take it off right this minute. I'm dressed for lounging and stuffing my face with junk food. That means baggy sweatpants, no bra and my most comfy hoodie is all I'm wearing.

"Uh-huh. Yeah, I don't think so, ReRe. You stole that hoodie. That is mine. Give it back." He lunges at me suddenly, and I shriek in alarm when he grabs me around the waist and tugs me into him so he can pull off the shirt.

"No! Kai! No! Stoooooop." I'm laughing like a loon, because he's tickling me with one hand as the other starts yanking up the bottom hem of the sweatshirt.

"This is rightfully mine, ReRe. Give it to me now, or I'll be forced to tickle you into submission." Kai's fingers dig into my ribs, and I squirm futilely trying to get out of his grasp and preserve my modesty. He knows I'm ticklish beyond reason, and I'm powerless to stop him.

"Hahastahppleasehaaa," I wheeze out, tears starting to stream down my face. Kai's arm that isn't busy tickling me has worked its way under the hoodie, and he's pulling it up, exposing my bare torso. I feel his knuckles brush against my bare skin, and even despite the uncontrollable giggles, it sends a shiver through me to feel him touch me like that.

"Give it up, ReRe, and all of this will be over." His husky voice teases my ear as his hand inches further up, until suddenly he's got a handful of the hoodie and my bare breast at the same time. We both freeze. My back pressed into his chest, his left arm banded around my waist, hand still digging into my ribs while his other hand cups my left breast. It's like time stops, and we both forget how to breathe and how to move. Not once in our entire relation-ship, in all of our many wrestling matches, or tickle fights, or goofing around, have we ever been this close to inti-macy. We are friends. Best friends. This is not a line that we have ever crossed.

I find myself acutely aware of the way I can feel his heart beating rapidly in his chest, in time with the hummingbird flutter of my own. I also find myself very much aware of the press of his now hard length pressed against my backside. Time finally seems to resume, and Kai lets go of me in an instant, backing away, hands up in the air.

"Uh…you can keep it for now. But Ima get it back before I leave." He won't look me in the eye, and I can see a red hue lighting up the tips of his ears even with his sepia skin tone. I quickly nod my head and yank the shirt back down into place.

"Yeah, I was trying to tell you before you tried to take what I rightfully stole—I'm not wearing a bra." Somehow his cheeks manage to redden even more at my confession.

"I noticed," Kai bites out as he plops down on the couch, pulling a pillow onto his lap. I can't help but smirk at his discomfort as I plop down on the other end of the couch, giving him some space to cool down. I decide to plate up some pizza as a peace offering to break the tension. There's no reason to let an accidental boob grab make things weird between us and ruin our night. It's been weeks since we've hung out, and I'm determined to still enjoy our evening. I'm so determined to not let things be awkward that I pack away the thrill of enjoyment I got from Kai's warm palm cupping my breast into a tiny little mental box made of steel and lock it away deep in the recesses of my mind. I have Dom for that kind of stuff now, and I have no business thinking of Kai in that way at all. Especially when he's clearly so uncomfortable with what happened.

"Ready to watch zombies get splattered?"

We are so engrossed in our movies that I don't notice

any notifications on my phone until after Kai helps me clean up and says goodnight. I check my phone after I climb into bed and see the missed texts and calls from Dom.

> Tall, Dark and Pumpkin Spiced: Hey, Kitten. Just got done golfing. Want me to come over?

> Tall, Dark and Pumpkin Spiced: I can bring dinner? I was thinking maybe we could do a sleepover.

> Tall, Dark and Pumpkin Spiced: Hello? Serena? Everything ok?

TEN MINUTES after that last message Dom called me and left me a voicemail.

"Hey, Kitten. I'm just checking up on you. I was hoping to come over tonight and spend some time with you. Call me back."

Guilt slithers in my stomach as I listen to the flat tone of his voice and remember what happened tonight with Kai. Logically I know it was an accident, and I have nothing to feel bad about, but I still can't completely silence the little voice in my head saying I did something wrong. I debate calling him back, but it's almost midnight, and I'm exhausted. I send him a quick text instead in apology.

> Me: Sorry, was hanging out with Kai
> tonight and didn't see your messages until
> now. I'll see you in the morning?
> Goodnight, Pumpkin. *kissy face emoji*

I wait a few minutes for a response, and when one doesn't come, I assume Dom has gone to bed and decide to do the same. I'll see him in the morning anyway, so we can make plans then. With that, I fall into a restless sleep with dreams of the strong, safe and very familiar arms of my best friend wrapped around me.

CHAPTER ELEVEN

SERENA

It's Monday morning, and the rush is almost over at Brewed Awakening. I haven't seen nor heard from Dominick. An uneasy feeling squirms in my stomach as I wonder if he's mad at me for not answering him last night. The rational part of my brain tries to tell me it's not *that* unusual for him to miss a morning coffee run, but the insecure, needy, new-to-dating part of my brain won't shut the fuck up.

"Where's Officer Orgasm today?" Marie sidles up next to me, giving me a nudge with her shoulder.

"I don't know. We didn't get a chance to talk last night. I was busy hanging out with Kai. He probably had to get to work early or something." I pop my shoulders in a casual shrug and hope my tone comes across indifferent and not as anxious as I feel on the inside.

Marie does that thing where she quirks her brow and tilts her head to the side. The look on her face tells me she absolutely does not buy what I'm selling.

"For real. Kai and I hung out and watched some movies. By the time I saw the missed texts from Dom, it was late. I'm sure I'll talk to him later. He's not obligated to come see me every morning at work." Thankfully, my voice doesn't sound nearly as uncertain as I feel on the inside.

"Uh-huh…well…just be mindful of how you spend your time with Kai. You have a boyfriend now, and when you're in a relationship, sometimes you have to choose how you spend your time more…wisely." Her voice hesitates on the last word, like she's trying not to hurt my feelings.

"What are you talking about? Kai and I are friends. We hang out. Dom knows this." I immediately get defensive.

"Riiight…but you and Kai are close. Like…really, really close. So close, someone who doesn't know your relationship might assume you were dating. I'm just saying, you might want to be mindful of that now that Dom is in the picture, so he doesn't get the wrong idea about you two."

Immediately, my mind goes to the moment last night when Kai's body was pressed up against mine, his warm palm cupping my breast, his erection solid and firm against my ass. My cheeks immediately heat at the memory, and Marie doesn't miss it. She purses her lips and nods her head like I just confirmed everything she said. She returns to restocking the pastry case, leaving me alone to stew in my guilt.

AFTER WORK I decide to call Dom and leave him a message to smooth things over. *"Hey, it's me. I missed you this morning. Sorry I didn't see your texts until late last night. If you want to come over tonight and spend the night, I'd really like that. Um...call me back,"* I finish lamely and hang up. I hope I haven't already messed things up with Dom. He's the best thing that's happened to me since the accident and I'm determined to make it work.

I'm walking to class, near the building that houses my psychology class, when my phone vibrates in my pocket. Glancing down, I see it's Dom, and I take a small detour to an empty bench at the entrance to the arboretum next door.

"Hey! I'm heading to class so I can't chat for long, but I'm glad you called!" My voice is breathless and excited when I answer, giddiness filling me up at finally being able to speak to Dom to make sure we are okay. His response comes after a few beats, causing my giddiness to turn into nervousness.

"Oh, I'm sorry Kitten. Am I interrupting again?" His voice is stern, his tone flat and dry.

"Um, no...I can talk. I have a few minutes before I need to be in class. I missed you this morning," I stammer, suddenly feeling like a child being scolded.

"I missed you last night," is his terse response. I wait for him to elaborate, but he doesn't.

"I know. I'm sorry. I invited Kai over to hang out and watch some movies since it had been a while since we got to chill. I thought you'd be busy with your friends...so I didn't think you'd be planning on coming over." I sit on the bench, the cool metal—chilled from the brisk fall air— sending a shiver through me as it seeps through my thin leggings.

"You didn't think to call and ask me if I was planning on coming over? Or mind if another man spent time with *my* girlfriend?" My stomach bottoms out at his harsh words.

"I-I'm sorry. I didn't think—"

"You didn't think. That's obvious." Dom cuts me off before I can finish my thought. "Look, Serena, I know you're new to this whole relationship thing, but it's not a good look to spend time alone with another guy when you have a boyfriend. I've seen the way he looks at you, and I don't want you to keep giving him false hope when there is none." My mouth falls open at his accusation.

"No, Dom, you have it all wrong. Kai and I are friends. He doesn't think of me that way." My protest feels false as I say it, thinking about Kai's reaction to touching me last night.

"Doesn't he?" Dom clips.

"No, he doesn't. If he did, I'm sure he would have said something by now. He's...like my brother." I make a face as the denial falls from my lips, hoping he believes me and doesn't hear how much I don't believe my own words. I bite my lower lip so hard it hurts.

"*Brother* or not, I don't think you should be spending time alone with him. I'm not the type of boyfriend that lets another man cuckold me. If you want this relationship to work, Serena, you need to respect my boundaries." My heart stutters over his use of the word boyfriend. That's the second time he said it. He also called me his girlfriend. Is that how he sees us? We hadn't had any talks about official labels but apparently this is how he sees us. How did I not realize that? We do spend almost all of our free time together. That should've been obvious to me.

"Dom, I…I'm sorry. I guess I didn't realize how serious you were about me. About us. You're right. I haven't done the relationship thing in a long time."

The campus clock tower starts to chime, signaling I'm late for class.

"Shit, Dom, I gotta get to class. Will you come over tonight? Please?" I lace my words with as much pleading as I can.

He lets out a sigh, sounding weary and resigned. "Sure, Kitten, I'll come over tonight." I let out a relieved sigh.

"Good. Um, I'll see you later, then?"

"Yeah, you'll see me later. This conversation isn't over. Now get that fine ass to class before you're late."

WHEN I FINALLY MAKE IT TO class the seats next to Kai are taken, leaving only a few seats in the front row open. He gives me an apologetic shrug, but I'm honestly relieved to have an excuse to put some space between us. After my conversation with Dom and Marie's words of warning, I'm full of doubts about how much time I should be spending with my best friend.

CHAPTER TWELVE

SERENA

That evening I'm pacing in the living room, nervously gnawing on my thumbnail while I wait for Dominick to come over. It's almost 8:00 p.m. We never agreed on a time, but he's usually around for dinner when he does come over during the week. Mom and I already ate the stir-fry I threw together, and I have some set aside for Dom in case he hasn't had dinner, but I'm starting to feel more and more sure he isn't coming over.

"Sweetie, you're going to wear a hole in the floor if you keep that up," Mom says from her seat on the couch, her favorite romance novel perched on her lap face down, holding her place. "Talk to me, Sweet Pea. What's going on?"

I let out a sigh and flop down on the couch next to Mom. She pulls me into her side, wrapping me up in a motherly hug, and I rest my head on her shoulder. "Dom and I had a fight. I think I messed up, and I don't know how to fix it."

"Dom…is your new friend?" Mom asks, hesitation in her question as she tries to remember what she knows about him. He's come around enough now that he's become familiar to her, but she still doesn't truly remember him.

"Yeah. He's my boyfriend…I guess… We haven't really talked about it, but I think that's how he sees it. I didn't realize that, and I think when I hung out with Kai last night and missed Dom's texts, he got mad."

"Oh, sweetie, relationships are hard. Disagreements are inevitable, but it's how you work through them that's important. Kai is a big important part of your life, and now Dom is too. It's going to be hard trying to navigate those new boundaries, but if Dom is right for you, he will give you grace and patience."

Just then, the doorbell chimes, causing relief to flood my system and the taut bowstring in my muscles to loosen. He came. We can fix this.

"I think that's my cue to head to my room. I'll see you in the morning sweetie." Mom plants a kiss on the top of my head and retreats to her room with her tea and book.

WHEN I OPEN THE DOOR, Dom is standing there looking devastating in a tight black Henley that looks like a second skin. His eyes are the color of silver moonlight shimmering in a starless night, and his lips are curled up in a contrite, sheepish smile. He's holding a bouquet of flowers and a box from Baked!, the local cupcake shop.

"You came—"

He cuts my words off with his lips, crushing them into mine in a claiming, possessive kiss. He swallows the lusty exhale that escapes my mouth and plunges his tongue deep inside, taking everything I have with everything he is. A soft thump of the cupcake box landing on the entryway table registers in the back of my mind, but I'm too consumed by his hot drugging kisses to do anything but follow his lead. Dom pushes us into the house, kicking the door shut behind him. His hands cup my face possessively, not giving me a centimeter of space as he devours me with his sinful mouth. My back hits the wall, and his body presses against mine, his hard muscles pinning me in place, dominating me until I'm pliant, soft, and melting into him.

He pulls away, just a fraction, his lips still ghosting against mine as he commands, "Kitten, take me to your room. I'm done waiting to show you how thoroughly you belong to me."

"Yes, sir." My response is barely more than a breath as I take his hand and lead him up the stairs to my bedroom. As soon as we cross the threshold to my room, Dom pulls his shirt off with that one-handed move that can only be described as panty-meltingly hot. My eyes greedily drink in his body. This is the first time I've seen him shirtless, and my mouth begins watering at the sight. He's power-fully built, with broad shoulders, a fine dusting of dark hair across his chest that leads down to his abs that are just defined enough to know he spends time in the gym.

Dom stalks toward me, a predatory gleam in his eye

that triggers my flight instinct. I back away until the backs of my legs hit my bed causing me to fall on it. Dom is on me in an instant, his huge body between my thighs, his chest pressed against mine, his lips sucking and nipping at my neck.

"Are you ready for this, Kitten? Because I'm getting ready to teach you a lesson about who owns you." His voice is a gruff reverberation in my ear. My only response is a low, keening moan as I try to grind my center against his straining erection, desperate for more.

Just as suddenly as he was on top of me, he's gone. My eyes fly open at the chill I feel from the loss of his body heat. "Dom, what—"

"Up, Kitten. Take your dress off, and get on the bed on your hands and knees." His voice is dark and rolls through me like thunder. I can't fight the compulsion to obey his every command. I sit up and pull my dress off, leaving me in my matching red lace bra and panties. They were an impulse purchase I made after class today, in hopes Dom would be able to enjoy them tonight. His gaze is like molten steel as his gaze slides over my body. It feels like flames licking my skin leaving me flushed and uncomfortably hot.

"Are you wearing that for me, Serena?" Dom licks his lips, and my eyes trace the movement eagerly, desperately, wanting to feel his tongue on me again. I nod mutely, my brain unable to form words at this moment.

"Am I the only one you wear those pretty, lacy underthings for?" His voice darkens, a threat sliding through it that sends a shiver down my spine.

"Yes."

"Yes, what?" he clips out.

"Yes, sir," I correct myself.

"Good girl. Now get on your hands and knees. Let me see that pretty round ass of yours."

I do as he says, crawling back onto my bed on my hands and knees. In this position, I can see him in the mirror of my dresser, and I watch, transfixed, as he removes his belt with one hand and then opens the fly of his jeans, revealing the delicious V of his lower abs that leads to his cock. He pushes his jeans down, and his cock springs free. My mouth goes dry at the sight of him, nude, angry, and hard behind me. His cock is thick, long, and intimidating. I suck in a sharp breath, suddenly realizing it's been *years* since the last time I had sex and none of my vibrators rival Dom in the size department. How in the fuck am I going to be able to handle him?

"Dom wait— Ahh!" The sharp crack of his hand lands on my ass, and I cry out in surprise, cutting off what I was going to say.

"Did I say you can talk, Kitten? I told you, I'm going to teach you a lesson. Now close that pretty mouth, and take your punishment." He doesn't give me a moment of reprieve before another two sharp, stinging smacks follow the first. I bite my lower lip to keep from crying out again, but tears still spring to my eyes, blurring my vision. I clench my eyes shut, waiting for the next blow, but I'm surprised when the next touch is a gentle soothing caress over the glowing heat left behind from the previous strikes.

"God, Serena. You are so beautiful like this. So obedient. So good for me." I open my eyes, his praise lessening the sting left behind by his hands. I see his reflection in the mirror, and he's looking at my ass almost reverently, admiring his handiwork.

"Who do you belong to, Serena?" He looks up, his eyes meeting mine in the mirror.

There is no hesitation in my response. "You."

The grin that spreads across his face is dangerous and feral. I see a glimpse of something dark and sinister lurking in the shadows of his eyes, but in the next instant, he is ripping the thin lace of my panties and shoving the engorged head of his cock into my wet, slick pussy. I bury my face into the blanket, muffling the cry of surprise and pain as I am obliterated by the sudden, swift intrusion of him. My hands fist, clenching the blanket as I try to muffle my moans. Dom sets a relentless pace, pounding into me so hard it feels like he is trying to burrow into my body. At this angle he is hitting the perfect spot deep inside of me that causes a tingle to build in my core. It hurts, but it feels so good. My mind liquefies at the overwhelming sensations until I'm no longer sure where up is or what my name is.

"This. Pussy. Is. Mine." Dom punctuates each word with a thrust, his fingertips digging into my hips in a bruising grip. "This." Thrust. "Ass." Thrust. "Is." Thrust. "Mine." Thrust. I nod mindlessly. It's all I am capable of at this moment.

"You. Are. Mine. Serena." This time he reaches one hand up to collar my neck, cutting off my breath while the other reaches around and pinches my clit, setting off a detonation in my body. The cry that tries to escape is cut off by his vise-like grip on my throat, my body seizing and convulsing from the most mind-blowing orgasm I've ever experienced. I feel Dom stiffen and his dick thicken, pulsing inside of me as he comes. Dimly in the haze of oxygen deprivation, I realize he didn't use a condom. Fuck.

CHAPTER THIRTEEN

SERENA

Lying in bed after the most intense sexual experience of my life, my body and mind feel disconnected. My limbs are leaden, and I feel like I'm sinking into the mattress while my brain drifts off into space. I feel used, wrung out, sore, but in the best possible way. It feels like Dominick owns a piece of my soul now.

Dom arranges us into the spooning position with my back pressed into his front, my head resting on his bicep, and his huge body curled around me, enveloping me in his heat. My thighs are wet and sticky from his release, and I can feel his cock, still semi-hard, pressed into my backside. I want to go to the bathroom so I can clean myself up, but I don't have the strength to move, and being surrounded by Dom's warm embrace feels like a drug.

"You did so good for me, Kitten. You take my cock so well. This pussy was made for me." Dom kisses the back of my neck gently. I let out a low happy hum at his praise and let myself sink into his embrace.

"Mmm…I should get cleaned up. You…you didn't use a condom. I'm a mess." My words are sleepy and lacking conviction. My body and mind are exhausted, more than ready to fall into the deepest sleep. "I feel like this is an important conversation we should have." I try to pry myself out of Dominick's hold, but he tightens his grip, one arm banding around my shoulders, the other moving lower until his free hand is cupping my pussy, wet and dripping with his cum. A startled gasp escapes my lips as I feel him gather up his release and push it back inside me.

"Nu-uh, Kitten. Not yet. I like knowing part of me is still inside of you. It's so fucking hot." Dom nips at my ear playfully as he lazily finger fucks me, causing my core to clench in arousal.

"Dom…" His name is a plea, but I don't know what I'm asking for. My hips buck mindlessly into his hand as he grinds his erection against my backside. The arm banded around my shoulders shifts so he's cupping my breast, pinching and rolling my nipple between his fingers. He nips and sucks at my neck as I writhe against him, consumed by arousal.

"That's it, Kitten. Take it." Dom removes his hand from my center, and uses it to lift up my top leg, spreading me open for him. In the next instant he is thrusting his once again rock-hard cock into my aching core from behind.

"Oh God, Dom…" This time Dom thrusts into me, lazily, like he has all the time in the world to make me come. What was previously a frantic claiming has turned into a languid, sensual coming together of two souls. Soon, the ache between my legs dissipates as another orgasm builds, becoming the only sensation I can focus on. This orgasm isn't the explosive release from before. It comes over me like a wave breaking against the shore, drowning every thought in my head in pleasure. Seconds later, I feel Dom stiffen, coming undone again, filling me with himself. Any urge or need to move has left me completely, and I let my eyes fall closed as I drift into an exhausted, satisfied sleep.

A SCREAM and the sound of breaking glass startles me out of my dreamless sleep. I sit up in bed, frantic, looking around for the disturbance. My room is dark, and the left side of my bed is empty.

"Dom?" I call, climbing out from under the covers. I slip on his shirt and crack open my bedroom door to figure out what is going on.

"Who are you?! Why are you in my home?!" I hear my mom's distressed yell and immediately jump into action. Shit, she must've woken up and seen Dom, not remembering he was coming over tonight.

"Laura, calm down…I'm here with Serena."

I hear another crash, and the sound of shattering glass echoes through the house.

"Mom! Stop! It's fine!" I yell down the stairs. My heart is pounding in my chest as I race downstairs. It's been a long time since Mom has had a freak out over her memory.

Routine and consistency are key to dealing with her condition and keeping her from realizing just how much she's lost. An unknown man surprising her in her own home in the middle of the night must have scared her to death.

When I reach the kitchen, I see Mom standing by the sink, eyes wild with fright, another glass in hand, ready to throw it at Dominick. Dom is standing on the other side of the island, hands up in a placating manner, shirtless and only wearing his boxer briefs, his jaw clenched in frustration. I move to push past him, but he grabs me, stopping my progress before I step on the glass-covered floor.

"Mom, please. Stop. This is Dom, my boyfriend. You know him. You've met him plenty of times. He spent the night with me." My mom jerks her gaze over to me, taking us in, standing side by side.

"I...I know him?" Her voice is soft, uncertain. She looks back at Dom with a dubiousness clouding her eyes.

"Yes, Mom, you know him. He's been here having dinner with us every week. He brings us food from your favorite Chinese restaurant. We've been dating for almost two months."

"Oh...God. I'm so sorry." Mom's face crumples in despair, and I push past Dom, mindful to step around the glittering shards of glass that litter the floor. When I get to her, I wrap her up in a hug, applying pressure, hoping to stave off the panic attack I know is coming.

"It's okay, Mom. I should've left you a note letting you know he stayed over." Mom's shoulders shake as she cries into my, well, Dom's shirt. I make soothing noises as I hold her, letting her cry out her fear and shock. In my periphery, I see Dom grab the broom and start sweeping up the broken glass. His face is dark and unreadable.

"I'm going to take Mom to her room. I'll be back."

Dom doesn't say anything, just gives me a terse nod in acknowledgement as he crouches down to brush the mess into the dustpan.

"Honey, I'm so sorry. I didn't mean to attack your boyfriend. I got up to get a glass of water and saw a naked stranger in my kitchen. I-I thought he had done something to you." My cheeks heat as I remember exactly what Dom did to me tonight. I help Mom into bed and kiss her forehead.

"It's okay. I'm sorry, I should've planned better. It's okay; Dom understands your condition. He's not mad." At least, I hope he's not mad. The thunderous expression on his face wasn't exactly reassuring.

"You deserve so much better than this, Sweet Pea. You shouldn't have to be the one supporting me. You are young. You should be enjoying your life and having sleepovers without worrying about your mom freaking out on your boyfriend." A tear slips down her cheek, and I wipe it away gently.

"Mom, hush. I'm lucky to even still have you in my life after the accident. Go back to sleep, okay? I'll see you in the morning." I kiss her forehead and finish tucking her in.

Back in the kitchen Dom has finished cleaning up. He's leaning against the counter, shoulders bunched and tense, jaw clenched. My heart stutters at the sight, worried this might be the last straw, and he will realize I'm not worth the hassle.

"I'm so sorry about that. Mom didn't know you were staying…you caught her by surprise. She doesn't do well with surprises. It will get better the more you come around. I promise. She does build new memories sometimes. It just takes a long time. But…I understand if this is too much for you…" My panicked ramble trails off as I watch his expressionless face give nothing away. "I know it's a lot to deal with." My head drops, and I break eye contact. My cheeks flushed with embarrassment, eyes stinging with the tears threatening to fall.

Dominick strides across the kitchen, and in the next breath I am wrapped up in his arms. "It's fine, Serena. We are fine. I will help you deal with this. It's going to take something much bigger than this for me to be done with you. You're mine now, remember?" I melt into his embrace, his words of reassurance exactly what I need to soothe the splintered pieces of my soul.

CHAPTER FOURTEEN

SERENA

The soothing dulcet tones of the NPR announcer slowly pull me from sleep. My alarm must be going off. My body feels heavy, sluggish, and my eyes do not want to open. "Fuck…too early…" I attempt to reach out to hit the snooze button on my alarm, but my arm is pinned to my body by a lead weight. A hot, muscular lead weight. I open my eyes and see a large arm draped over my body. Dom is pressed into my back, cuddling me like an over-sized koala.

"Turn it off," Dom mumbles, his voice rough with sleep.

"I'm trying to, but you are heavy, and you're holding my arm hostage." Dom lets out an aggravated grunt before reaching over himself and hitting the snooze button, then snuggling back into the pillow we are sharing.

I almost let myself drift back off before I remember I have to work this morning. I don't build any snooze time into my morning routine.

"Babe, I've gotta get up. I need to get ready for work. I

need to take a shower and wash last night off. You made me all…crusty." Dom's only response is to tighten his hold on me and snuggle into me harder. I bite back a smile as I try to harden my tone.

"Dom, baby, please. I don't want to be late." I wiggle, trying to loosen his hold on me, but the man's arms are a steel band wrapped around me. He doesn't allow me an inch of movement.

"It's too early. Go back to sleep, Kitten." Dom's voice is muffled in my hair as his warm breath tickles my neck.

"I know, but I get up too early every morning. I have to be at work by five. Let me up." Dom heaves out a defeated sigh before finally rolling onto his back, releasing me from his hold. He cracks one eye open, pouting when I climb out of bed.

"You didn't tell me sleeping with you would require waking up before the sun is even up."

"It's the price you pay for loving a barista. Sorry babe," I joke before I realize I just casually dropped the "L word" in front of him. I freeze, waiting for his reaction.

He flashes a playful grin at me as he props his hands behind his head, shooting me a wink.

"Worth it." A warm flush creeps over my body while I take in the sight of him, naked, beautiful, and sex-rumpled in my bed. He is staring at me with a feral gleam in his eye, like he's more than ready to go for round three. The sight nearly takes my breath away. I tear my gaze away from the sex god in my bed and hook a thumb toward my bathroom.

"I'm just gonna go hop in the shower… You can snooze

while I'm getting ready." I turn to make my way into the en suite, but seconds later he is out of bed, wrapped around me from behind once again, pressing hot kisses into my neck.

"What, you're not going to invite me into the shower with you?" Dom nips at my ear with his teeth as he grinds his rigid cock into my ass. "I could be so helpful in getting you clean, Kitten." A low moan escapes my parted lips as my body ignites from his searing kisses. "You know what they say…many hands make quick work. I promise, I'll be quick…this time." One hand cups my breast, pinching my nipple between his thumb and forefinger while the other skates down my stomach, sliding under his shirt that I slept in, to cup my sex.

"Dom…" His name is barely a sigh, a prayer meant only for him. My head falls back against his shoulder and my eyes close as I drown in the sensations he floods me with. My hips start rocking into his hand, the wetness of my pussy slowly easing the soreness left from last night's harsh pounding. Slowly, he guides us into the bathroom, taking his time to turn on the hot water in the shower as he continues to tease me.

As steam starts to fill the room, he peels his shirt from my body, continuing to trail hot, open-mouthed kisses across my shoulders as he guides me into the shower. "Don't get my hair wet. It's not wash day." I mumble lost in the sensation of his drugging kisses.

"Whatever you say, Kitten." Dom mutters as he trails his lips across shoulder and up my neck. Once we are in the shower, he turns me so my back is against the wall, his body pressed flush with mine, his thick, hard cock pushing between my thighs, so close to entering me again. I'm not entirely sure I can handle going again after last night's activities, but as I open my mouth to tell him, he lifts my left leg, opening me up, and thrusts in one powerful movement. I let out a groan of pain wrapped in pleasure that he immediately swallows with his mouth. He kisses me like he's trying to devour me; he ruts into me like a man possessed. I just let myself fall into overwhelming sensations, and slowly the pain fades away until only pleasure is left.

After our shower, which wasn't quick at all, Dom and I are getting dressed in my room when I realize once again, we had sex without a condom. I'm on birth control, but it's not one hundred percent effective.

"Dom...we should talk." I'm staring into the mirror, watching him behind me as he tucks his shirt into his jeans. He stops what he's doing and looks at me intently.

"Don't tell me you're breaking up with me now you've gotten what you wanted from me. Did you really just use me for my amazing dick?" I roll my eyes at him, but I don't turn around. I'm not sure if I feel brave enough to face him for this conversation.

"You...you didn't use a condom, and you didn't ask me if I'm on birth control. Don't you think that's something we should have talked about first?" I bite my bottom lip and lower my eyes, hoping he doesn't think I'm trying to pick a fight.

"Are you?" His voice is dark and serious, like I confessed to being pregnant already.

"I am...I'm on the pill. But nothing is foolproof and... well, have you been tested? I haven't been with anyone since my first boyfriend..." Dom cuts me off when he comes up behind me, spinning me around to face him.

"Then there's nothing to worry about. I'm clean. You're on the pill. And there is nothing hotter to me than the idea of your insides painted with my come." I start to protest, but he crushes his mouth against mine in a claiming, possessive kiss. "I told you, Kitten, you're mine now. Whatever happens, happens. Don't worry your pretty little head about it." Dominick presses one more lingering kiss against my lips before pulling away and giving me a gentle tug towards the door.

"Time to go, baby, before I decide to fuck you again and cause us both to be late for work."

CHAPTER FIFTEEN

KAI

"God, ReRe, you feel so good." I cup her full, soft breast in my hand, pinching her nipple between my fingers. Serena throws her head back, resting it against my shoulder as she writhes in my grasp. Her back arches, grinding her ass into my length. Her shirt is half-off, and the only thought running through my head is how badly I want to rip it off her body and taste her.

"Kai..." My name on her lips sounds like a prayer. Her lips ghost my neck in the softest of kisses, and the last remaining shred of control I have snaps. I turn her so she's facing me, capturing her lips with my own and swallowing her moans. We break apart only long enough for me to finish pulling the hoodie over her head before we crash back together, frantic, desperate, and on fire. Her skin is so soft in my hands. How have I never noticed how soft she is?

I push her down on the couch, hovering over her, peppering kisses along her jawline, down her neck, between her breasts, as I explore every inch of her beautiful tawny skin. I capture one of *her dark mauve nipples in my mouth and suck, pulling another keening, needy moan from her lips.*

"Oh...God...Kai. Yes..." Her pleas are lyrical and the sexiest fucking thing I've ever heard. I switch my focus to her other nipple, and her hips buck up, seeking more friction. I give her what she wants, moving back up her body until my aching dick is lined up with her needy pussy, and I grind into her, her thin leggings and my gray sweatpants the only barrier between us. We are making out and dry humping like a couple of teenagers, and I am the most turned on I have ever been in my life. Fuck, she feels perfect under me. She feels like...mine.

I feel precum dripping from my tip, and I know I'm only minutes away from coming in my pants like a virgin, but she feels so good under me I can't stop. I won't stop. She's everything I didn't know I needed. Serena's body tenses under mine, her nails digging into my arms as her orgasm barrels through her. It's enough to push me over the edge, and I come in my sweats, not even a little embarrassed.

MY EYES FLY open as my orgasm rocks through me. My hand is gripping my dick as I fuck into it, coming in my pants, just as I did in my dream. "Fuck." I haven't had a wet dream since I was a horny sixteen-year-old and had my first crush on Beyoncé. I have definitely never had a wet dream over my best friend before.

At least not until this week. Now I've had two—ever

since Sunday night I haven't been able to get Serena off my mind. When my hand brushed against her bare breast, it was like a key opening a lock that unleashed a Pandora's Box of new, unrequited feelings for the woman who was... is...my best friend. Grumbling, I throw off the covers and head to the bathroom to shower and clean up the evidence of my embarrassing new habit.

I DECIDE to skip my morning coffee from Brewed Awakening, shame still spiraling through me over my dream about Serena. I can't face her until I get these feelings under control. We haven't spent much time together since Sunday night. She's been showing up to class late, sitting in the front of the room and skipping our usual lunch dates, claiming to be busy. I haven't pushed, giving myself some space from her while I work through my shit. I know she feels guilty about what happened, even though it's not her fault. I'm the one who crossed the line.

On the drive to campus, I'm lost in thought over my new feelings for my best friend when the flashing of blue and red lights in my rearview mirror brings me back to reality.

"Fuck me. Not again." Glancing down, I confirm I'm not speeding. I know all of my lights are functioning, and the license plate is up to date. I stay on top of my car maintenance in an effort to stay off the cops' radar in town. I refuse to give them any reasons to pull me over. Grudgingly, I pull over into an empty church parking lot, turn off the car engine and place my hands on the steering wheel in an automatic reflex. I know the drill by now. Keep my mouth shut, do not argue, and keep my hands where they can see them.

I watch the officer approach in the side view mirror and dread starts pooling in my gut when I recognize Serena's new boyfriend, Dominick, approaching my car with a smug as fuck grin on his face. I wait for him to tap on my window before lowering it.

"Can I help you, Officer?" I keep my tone neutral, voice calm. I will not give this power-hungry jackass a reason to give me shit.

"Do you know why I pulled you over?" Dominick Reeves's eyes are cold and unfriendly as he gives me a once-over, casually inspecting my car in one quick glance.

"No, sir, I do not." I keep my eyes trained forward, hands still on the wheel, jaw clenching in effort to remain calm and collected. Dominick must sense my seething frustration; it is strong enough to be palpable.

"You were going a little fast back there through the school zone." *Bullshit* is my immediate thought, but I bite my tongue and keep my mouth shut.

"I'm sorry, sir; I didn't realize I was speeding. My speedometer showed twenty-five for me." My grip on the wheel tightens as I take in a deep breath, fighting the urge to call him on his bullshit.

"I clocked you at twenty-eight on my radar. Look, Kai, I know you're *friends* with my girl, so I'll let you off with a warning in exchange for a little favor," Dominick says, as he leans down, resting his elbows on the car door, invading my space. The way he emphasizes the word *friends* is patronizing as fuck. "Do me a favor, and stay away from Serena. I don't want to hear about any more movie-watching parties with just the two of you. She's mine now, and I don't want people getting the wrong idea about the two of you. Or about her. She has me to take care of her now. You can take your little unrequited crush and move along."

I turn to look at him, eyes narrowing at his audacity. "Excuse me? Don't you think that should be Serena's decision to make?" So much for remaining calm and not arguing with the officer. I'm more than ready to get out of my car and get arrested for assaulting a police officer.

"Kai, we both know Serena is too fucking sweet to hurt your feelings by telling you to move on. But that's what you need to do. You drug your feet and missed your chance with her. Now let her live her life and be happy with a man who is willing to take care of her the way she deserves. Do what I say, or next time I won't let you off with a warning." Officer Assgoblin raps his knuckles against the door and backs away. "Oh, and be more careful in the future. I'd hate for someone to get hurt because of your actions."

A shudder runs through me at his parting words. They don't feel like a warning at all. They feel like a threat.

CHAPTER SIXTEEN

KAI

I'm sitting in my usual seat in class when Serena rushes in, her cheeks flushed with exertion, her curls floating around her face like a halo. She's not late today. In fact, we have another ten minutes before class starts, so I'm not sure what her rush is. She makes her way to the back row where I'm sitting, an excited sparkle in her jade-colored eyes. I shift uncomfortably in my seat, realizing that she's planning on sitting next to me today. Between the sexy as fuck dream I had about her and my run-in with Dominick, I'm not ready to be this close to her again.

Serena collapses into her seat, her body pressing against mine in the small auditorium seating. I catch a whiff of her jasmine and hibiscus shampoo, and it goes straight to my dick. Shit, since when do I notice what she smells like? Has she always smelled this good? I shift in my seat, trying to put some space between us, but she just turns, flashing me the most jubilant smile, and I am momentarily struck dumb by how gorgeous she is. Her smile could rival the brightest star, and the excitement radiating from her is infectious.

"Damn, ReRe, did you win the lottery or something? Did Jensen Ackles finally accept your marriage proposal?"

Serena bites her lower lip and shoots me a coy smile, sending a jolt of lust shooting through me. What. The. Fuck. She's been next to me for all of sixty seconds and I'm already painfully turned on. I shift again, lowering the book I was reading onto my lap, hiding the evidence of my arousal.

"Something like that… Dominick is taking me away for the weekend to a cabin in the mountains. He arranged it with Mrs. G, and she's going to come stay with Mom while I'm gone. Isn't that so sweet? I haven't had a weekend off in so long!" Serena leans her head against my shoulder and wraps her arm around my own, giving it a tight squeeze.

"He said he's tired of watching me work myself to death and that I deserve a break, so he contacted Mav at the bar and got me off the schedule for the weekend." She lets out a dreamy sigh, and I bite back the urge to point out to her that I've told her the same exact thing.

"That's…nice. Are you sure your mom is going to be okay with you being gone the whole weekend?" Fuck knows I'm not okay with it. Not even a little bit.

"Yeah, Dom talked to her and Mrs. G together while I was at work, and Mom got so excited, she immediately wrote it down in her journal and told Mrs. G to make sure I went. She said, and I quote, 'If that girl doesn't go on this trip, then I'll go in her place and steal her boyfriend.'" Serena cracks up at her own impression of her mom, and I force a brittle smile while a sour jealous feeling claws at my chest.

The idea of her spending the weekend away with the douchewaffle that threatened me sends a sense of dread slithering through my body.

"So anyway, we are leaving after I'm done with class tomorrow and won't be back until late Sunday." Serena continues on, completely oblivious to my discomfort. "Do you mind checking in on Mom and Mrs. G while I'm gone to make sure they're okay? I know they won't call me short of a meteor hitting the house, and I need to know someone will let me know if something happens with Mom." When I don't answer right away, still lost in my own thoughts, Serena pulls away and looks up at me, a concerned expression furrowing her brows.

"Kai? Is something wrong?" I shake off her touch and put some space between us as Dominick's threat from this morning plays through my mind.

"Yeah...no. Everything is fine. I'll try to check on your mom while you're gone." She seems put out by my noncommittal answer but before she can press me about it, Professor Jacobs clears his throat, directing our attention to the front of the room. Serena shoots me one last narrow-eyed curious look before turning her attention to the lecture.

When class ends, I pack up my computer and move to leave when Serena stands in front of me, looking up at me expectantly with her gem-colored eyes. "Wanna grab lunch?"

It's on the tip of my tongue to accept her invitation, but

Dominick's warning plays in the back of my mind. I should tell her about his behavior, but will she believe me? Or will she think I'm jealous, and I'm just trying to break them up? As I'm about to accept her invitation, her phone buzzes in her back pocket, diverting her attention away from me.

"Oh, hang on; it's Dom. Let me get this." Serena holds a finger up for me to wait. "Hey, Pumpkin, what's up?" Her face lights up when she answers her phone with a giddiness I haven't seen from her since before her parents' accident. The sick realization that Dominick might be right about him being the man for her crawls through my brain like a spider, and I decide to take the opportunity to escape to sift through my own feelings.

"Actually, ReRe, I have lunch plans. I gotta go. I'll call you later." She looks at me, a disappointed frown tugging at her full, voluptuous lips at my dismissal. I flash her what I hope is a reassuring smile before squeezing around her to make my escape, leaving her staring after me with hurt and rejection dancing across her face.

CHAPTER SEVENTEEN

SERENA

"**A**re you absolutely sure you're okay with staying?"

I'm standing in the kitchen watching Mrs. G make some tea for her and Mom instead of finishing packing my things for my weekend away with Dom. He'll be here any minute, but I'm starting to feel guilty about saddling Mrs. G with Mom-sitting duty for an entire weekend. Especially since she's spent so much time taking care of her sister lately.

"Child, if you don't finish packing your bag, I will send you out that door with only the clothes on your back. Laura and I will be just fine. I rented that Magic Mike movie from the Redbox to keep us entertained. Go on now; get out of here." Mrs. G shoos me out of the kitchen, and I retreat upstairs to my bedroom desperately wishing I could erase the mental image of her and my mom watching the movie about male strippers from my mind.

I'm busy frantically tossing clothes into my weekend bag when Dom strolls through my bedroom door, looking delicious in a black t-shirt under a red and black flannel shirt with the sleeves rolled up, exposing his muscular forearms. His dark hair is glistening from the rain, and I find myself distracted by the one lone drop of water rolling down the side of his face. I was so distracted by panicking over what to pack I didn't hear him arrive. Or realize it was raining out.

"Kitten, you're not packed. I told you to be ready to go at 3:00 p.m. sharp. Am I going to have to smack that plump ass of yours to get you to listen?" Dom's stern tone sends shivers through me as he tugs me into his body, crushing his mouth against mine in one of his demanding, panty-destroying kisses. As he pulls back, he nips at my lower lip playfully.

"I'm sorry, sir. I promise I'll be a good girl and listen better next time." I flash him a coy smile as I return to packing my bag. Dominick surprises me by reaching into my bag and pulling out my clothes, discarding them on the floor one by one.

"You won't need this…or this…or these…" He drops my pajamas, favorite leggings, extra sweatshirt, and most of my panties on the floor. (Okay, maybe I didn't need *five* pairs of panties for one weekend trip, but you never know when you will have a panty emergency.)

"Excuse me? What do you expect me to wear, then?" I narrow my eyes at him in mock annoyance.

"You can still take this." He holds up the black lace lingerie I had tossed into the bottom of the bag, an impulse purchase I made this afternoon. I had wanted to surprise him with it as a thank you for arranging this trip.

Dominick leans in, letting his lips ghost over the shell of my ear, "There won't be much need for clothes with the plans I have made." He nips at my earlobe, and I let out a low aroused moan in response.

"Well, since you put it that way, I just need to grab my toiletries and birth control from the bathroom." Before I can move in that direction, Dominick puts up his hand, stopping me.

"I'll go get it. Go get your shoes and jacket and I'll meet you downstairs." With a firm swat on my ass, Dom sends me downstairs while he rounds up the rest of my things. As I race down the stairs, eager to get our weekend started, I can't help the love-struck smile frozen on my face. Because that is exactly what I am. Love-struck. I think this will be the weekend I tell him, officially. We've danced around the topic, and it's been implied, but neither of us have officially said those three little words to each other.

Mom and Mrs. G are both standing near the bottom of the stairs, trying and failing miserably at trying to come across as nonchalant about my weekend plans. Their excitement for me is palpable, and I can't help but be reminded of my senior prom when my parents stood waiting for me at the bottom of the stairs, ready to gush over me in my prom dress. I just have to hope Mom and Mrs. G don't insist on taking dozens of pictures of me and Dom before letting us leave.

"Can you two please try not to embarrass me in front of my boyfriend?" I hiss while I slip on my favorite fleece-lined boots. Mrs. G eyes grow wide in exaggerated innocence as Mom suppresses a snicker.

"Why, I would never." Mrs. G holds her hand up to her chest, clutching at her nonexistent pearls. I respond with an eyeroll that earns me a smack upside my head. Dom's heavy footsteps pounding down the stairs save me from a scolding from Mrs. G.

"Ready, Kitten? We need to head out if we want to beat the weather. I heard this rain is supposed to turn into snow tonight." That gives me pause, worry about being snowed in at the cabin away from Mom creeping into my mind.

"How much snow are we supposed to get?" I pull out my phone to check the weather, but Dom stops me by stealing my phone.

"It's only supposed to be an inch or two. We will be fine. I just want to make it up the mountain before the roads get slick." He turns his attention to Mom and Mrs. G. "Gloria, Laura, have a lovely weekend. We will see you Sunday!" Grabbing my hand in his, Dom tugs me out the front door, not giving me a chance to protest. I look back at Mom and flash an apologetic smile while blowing her a kiss.

"Love you, Mom! I'll call you later!"

"Bye! Have fun, kids!" Mom makes a catching motion with her hand, happy tears shining in her eyes while Mrs. G stands next to her flapping her hands in a shooing motion, encouraging us to leave.

Once I'm buckled in Dominick's car, I close my eyes against the sting of tears threatening to fall. It's been two long years since I've been away from Mom and not responsible for taking care of her. I'm overwhelmed with emotion, torn between relief and guilt. Dom must sense the turmoil swirling in my head, because he grabs my chin, turning my head, forcing me to look at him.

"Eyes on me, Kitten. You are not allowed to feel guilty about this. I'm going to take care of you the way you deserve to be taken care of. The only thing I want you to feel for the next two days is spoiled and blissed the fuck out from my cock."

I blink back the tears and nod.

"What do you say, Kitten?"

"Yes, sir." With one last salacious smirk, Dominick puts the car into drive, and we head to the mountains for a weekend of bliss.

CHAPTER EIGHTEEN

SERENA

Just as we turn off the main road to follow the winding gravel lane up the mountain, the rain that had been pounding the windshield for the last hour transforms into fluffy white snowflakes. There is already a light dusting on the ground and trees, giving the dusky evening a magical feel.

"Are you sure it's only going to be an inch or two?" As pretty as the early November snow is, I can't help the worry creeping in, about not being able to get off the mountain in case of an emergency.

"Oh, Kitten, you're definitely going to be getting more than an inch or two. More like nine." Dom lets out a bawdy laugh as I smack his arm.

"You're such a child."

"You left yourself wide open for that, Kitten…speaking of wide open…" Dom wiggles his brows at me, and I clamp my hand over his mouth before he has the chance to make another double entendre. His joke does succeed in taking my mind off the weather though, so I sit back and admire the beauty of the snow-covered forest as we make our way up the mountain to the cabin.

When we arrive at the cabin, I'm taken aback by how charming it is. It's a modest two-story, rustic A-frame made out of Eastern Pine wood, overlooking the valley below. The balcony seems to almost hang right off the edge of the mountain.

"Wow, this is cozy. How'd you find this place?" I ask as I walk up the stairs to the homey front porch that houses a couple of rocking chairs and a swing off to the side.

"It belongs to a buddy of mine. He lets me use it occasionally when I need a weekend away." Dom pulls out a key and unlocks the front door, revealing what is clearly a family getaway and not the usual vacation rental place. It has an open floor plan with floor-to-ceiling windows along the back wall that overlook the valley below. There is a stone fireplace with a comfortable looking overstuffed couch in front of it and bookshelves lining the opposite wall. The kitchen has an island separating it from the living space, but the first floor is one big open space so the view of the windows can be seen no matter where you stand. A staircase off to the side leads up to the loft-style bedroom above us.

"Wow, Dom, this is gorgeous." I wander off from him to take in my surroundings, admiring the craftsmanship of the expansive woodwork throughout the room.

"Yeah, it's nice here. I try to get up here a couple of times a year to reset myself."

I'm standing at the windows, watching the snowfall blanketing the valley below us, when Dom comes up behind me, engulfing me with his warm body. He peppers my neck in open-mouthed kisses, and my body instantly melts at his touch.

"I'm going to defile you on every surface of this cabin this weekend, Kitten. I hope you're ready for what I have planned for you." Dom's voice is a low, sensual growl in my ear, and my knees go weak at his words. A low sound I can only describe as a purr escapes from me, and Dominick takes that as his cue to flip me around, pressing my back against the cold glass of the window while he cages me in with his body. His kiss is all consuming. Possessive. It's almost like an assault on all of my senses. I don't think I'll ever get used to how he seems to claim ownership of me with every kiss.

Slowly, his hands work my sweater up and over my arms, breaking our kiss only long enough to pull it off my body. In return, I claw at the flannel shirt he's wearing, stripping it from his body, desperate to feel his skin against mine. Our movements become frenzied and rushed, a frantic race to strip ourselves of every barrier separating us so we can come together as one.

Dominick lifts my legs up, wrapping them around his waist, and in one hard thrust, he's inside of me. I bite his shoulder, riding out the pain of the sudden intrusion, as he begins pounding into me. The glass against my back is cool, but sweat still beads across my forehead as he fucks me relentlessly. I'm not sure if my body will ever fully adjust to his size, but slowly the walls of my pussy relax, easing his way into me, making his thrusts pleasurable instead of painful.

"Fuck, Kitten. Your pussy is perfect. You were made for me. I can't wait to call you mine forever." Dom bites and sucks and nips, leaving marks across my collarbone and on my breasts. A wave of pleasure builds in my core. I dig my nails into his back and throw my head back against the glass as my orgasm crashes into me like a wave.

"Oh God, Dom!" I shout as my walls tighten around his cock, and my body shudders, over-stimulated and euphoric.

Moments later, Dominick is grunting while he finds his own pleasure. I can feel the warmth of his release filling me. We stay there, pressed against the glass, locked together, breathing each other in as we come down from this high.

Gingerly, I reach a finger up under Dom's jaw, lifting it so he is looking me in the eye. "I love you, Dominick Reeves. You're the best thing that's happened to me."

A dark look of satisfaction crosses his face. "I love you too, Serena Malcolm, and I never plan on letting you go."

I'M IN THE BATHROOM, waiting for the shower to heat up, when Dom strolls in, naked, cock hard again and swinging. "Jesus, Dom…again?" I laugh and back away from his predatory gaze. My pussy needs a break, and I am desperate for a shower after all our...activities. Dom just smirks at my apprehension, a hungry gleam in his eyes.

"I will never get enough of you, Kitten. You might as well get used to it." Dom leans in, capturing my lips with his, stealing the protest that was forming on my lips. He backs us into the shower together, pinning me against the tile as he ravishes my mouth with his. When he inserts one of his thick fingers into my sore and battered vagina, I wince and pull back.

"Dom, I can't. Not again. Not yet. I need a break." I try to pull away, but his hard body has me caged in, and there is nowhere for me to go.

"Come on, Kitten... I know you've got one more round for me. You can take it. Be my good girl." Dom bites my neck as he inserts a second finger. My pussy is so sore from our last round, when he fucked me so hard from behind, I'm sure he left bruises.

"Dom, no...please. We can go again tomorrow." I push at the hand cupping my sex, desperate to get him to let me go. Dom lets out an aggrieved sigh and motions to his hard-on, looking red and angry and ready to go.

"What am I going to do about this, Kitten?" I lick my lips, unsure of what to say. Dom's eyes light up as he watches the movement. "Good idea, Kitten. Get on your knees and let me fuck that beautiful mouth of yours. I want to see those pretty lips wrapped around me." When I hesitate, Dom reaches around and cups my ass, teasing my tight hole with his finger.

"It's your mouth or your ass. I'll let you choose." His lips ghost against mine and I shudder against the teasing brush of his finger against my ass. I'm definitely not ready for that.

When I drop to my knees, ready to get this over with so we can go to bed, Dom gives me a satisfied smirk. "That's my good girl. Now open up, and let me feed you my cock."

CHAPTER NINETEEN

SERENA

The next morning, I wake up to the sound of an alarm chirping from my phone. I'm so tired from the previous night's activities that I can't bring myself to move, or even bother to open my eyes. Dom's warm, hard body is pressed against my back, one of his big arms draped over my waist like the world's firmest weighted blanket. Why is there even an alarm going off? It's Saturday. Neither of us has to work. Blessedly, after a minute, the alarm stops, and my mind drifts back to sleep.

A few minutes later, the chirping resumes, and Dom lets out a sleepy, disgruntled sound. "Shutitoff." His face is buried into the pillow behind me, so his words are muffled and barely audible. Blindly, I reach one hand out, hunting for the offending piece of technology. I crack one eye open to see that the 7:00 a.m. reminder for me to take my birth control is the reason for our disrupted sleep.

I start to wiggle out of Dom's hold so I can go take my

pill, but he clutches me to him, throwing one of his legs overtop of mine, pinning me in place. "Where do you think you're going, Kitten?"

"I need to take my birth control. That was my reminder. I have to take it at the same time every day for it to be effective. I'll come right back." I try futilely to dislodge Dominick's arm, wrapped around my waist. Is this man Wolverine? Are his bones made out of adamantium? Jesus, he's heavy.

"Stay. It can wait." Dominick snuggles into me and begins pressing kisses along my neck and bare shoulder. His rather large, persistent morning wood presses into the curve of my ass, making itself known.

"It'll just take a minute. I'll be right back." I giggle as he nips playfully at the ticklish spot right behind my ear.

"Fine. Be quick. I'm in the mood for some lazy, spooning morning sex." Dominick releases his hold on me before giving me a quick swat on the ass. I jump out of the bed and run to the bathroom before he changes his mind and decides to hold me hostage again.

While in the bathroom, I take the opportunity to relieve my poor, overfull bladder and brush my teeth (because, ew, morning breath and sex do not mix), before digging through my toiletry bag in search of my birth control pack. I always throw it in the same bag with my toothbrush, toothpaste and shower supplies so it doesn't get lost in my clothes or forgotten about. But as I dig through the items in the toiletry bag and come up with everything from face wash to moisturizer but not the little pale green foil pack of pills, I begin to panic.

"Shit, shit, shit, shit..." Losing patience, I dump the contents of the bag out, desperately hoping to find the pills were just stuck in the bottom. When they don't materialize, I let out a low, frustrated groan. "Fuuuuck..."

I take the mini pill because it has lesser side effects than the combination pill, but it comes with one major downside. I have to take it in the same three-hour window every day for it to be effective. Panic begins to set in when I think about how many times Dom and I made love last night and how many times he came inside of me.

"Everything okay in there, Kitten?" Dom calls from the bedroom.

I make my way out of the bathroom, and the panic I am feeling must be evident on my face because Dominick immediately sits up, concern etched into his handsome features.

"I think I forgot my birth control. I swear I packed it. I remember getting it out of the cabinet and setting it on top of everything in my toiletry bag...but it's not there. It's not there, Dom..." My heart feels like it is trying to beat its way out of my chest, and my breathing turns shallow and frantic, signaling an impending panic attack. I used to get them often after my parents' accident, but I haven't had one in nearly a year. Now the thought of accidentally getting pregnant while I'm already carrying so much responsibility is sending me spiraling.

Within seconds I'm wrapped up in Dom's warm embrace, and he is rubbing soothing circles on my back, trying to calm me down. "Shh, shh, it's okay, Kitten. It'll be okay. I've got you. I'm sure one missed pill won't be a big deal. I've dated women who used to forget all the time. It's fine."

Shaking my head, I push away from Dom to look him in the eye. "No, Dom, it's not fine. I can't get pregnant. Not right now. I work two jobs while going to school full time and taking care of my mom. I barely remember to feed myself some days. I am not in the place to take care of a baby." My eyes sting with unshed tears, and I look down, not wanting him to see how close I am to losing it.

Dom cups my face in his palms and forces me to look at him. "Serena, look at me. I said it will be fine. What part of 'you're mine' are you not understanding? I will take care of you no matter what. If I'm lucky enough to put a baby in your belly, then I will take care of it too. You're not in this alone anymore. I've got you." Dom pulls me back into his embrace, fully engulfing me in his hold. I don't know how long we stay like that, but eventually he tugs me back into the bed, burying us both under the covers, me nestled into his side, using his shoulder as a pillow.

"Are you okay now, Kitten?"

I nod, letting out a little sniffle. "Yeah, I'm sorry for freaking out. You're probably right. It's just…been a lot the past two years, since Dad died and having to take care of Mom. Getting pregnant is absolutely not in my life plan right now."

"I get that, Kitten. I do. But remember you have me now, and you will never have to do anything on your own again." With those reassuring words, the panic I was feeling leaves my body, leaving me feeling more than a little exhausted. I let the soothing rhythmic beat of his heart lull me back to sleep.

Hours later, I am woken by Dom's hot mouth licking and sucking at my breasts. He's biting down on one peaked nipple as he pushes his rigid length into me, bringing me fully into awareness. "Dom…" His name is little more than a gasp as I become overwhelmed by the sensation of him moving inside of me.

"God, Kitten. You feel amazing when you're so sleepy and relaxed under me. Just let me make you feel good, baby." Dom captures my lips with his as he begins thrusting in earnest, his pelvis grinding against my clit, working in tandem with his thick cock hitting my g-spot to bring me to orgasm faster than ever I thought possible. As my walls clench around him, Dom stiffens, his release barreling through him.

"Wait, Dom, not in me!" Realization hits me almost too late when I remember we shouldn't be having unprotected sex right now. With herculean effort, Dom pulls out in the middle of his release, spilling himself on the lips of my pussy and thighs.

"Shit, baby, I'm sorry. I was planning on pulling out, but you felt so good coming on my cock. God, you're so perfect for me." Leaning down, he plants a gentle kiss on my lips, coaxing me to open to him so he can lick into my mouth. Once again, I find myself overwhelmed and consumed by everything Dom and can't remember why I should be worried about anything at all.

CHAPTER TWENTY

SERENA

When we finally manage to untangle ourselves from one another and go downstairs for breakfast, I am momentarily struck dumb by the view of the valley beyond the floor-to-ceiling windows. The valley below is covered in a thick blanket of snow. At least six inches of it is piled up on the deck railing, and the tree limbs are heavy and droopy from the weight of it.

"Um…Dom…" I trail off as my brain tries to process what I'm seeing. That's a lot of snow. Way more snow than "one or two" inches. Like, enough to keep us snowed in on this mountain for a day or two, until it melts off. We drove up in Dom's Dodge Challenger. There is no way we are getting off of this mountain in this weather.

"Isn't it pretty? That view is almost as gorgeous as you." Dom comes up behind me, wrapping his arms around me in a hug, and rests his chin on my shoulder.

"Um…yeah, but we are supposed to go home tomorrow. Will this road get plowed? I can't expect Mrs. G to just keep staying with Mom, and I have to work Monday—" Dom spins me around and cups my face in his hands, cutting off my panicked tirade.

"Kitten, calm down. It'll be alright. I'm sure Gloria won't mind staying an extra day, and if there is this much snow in town, I bet the coffee shop won't even open. I'm sure classes will be canceled too. Just relax and let's enjoy the next couple of days without any responsibilities." He silences my next protest with a kiss that leaves me breathless and weak in the knees. When he pulls away, he flashes me his most devastating smile and winks. "I'll make us some breakfast; you go cozy up by the fire."

While Dom busies himself making breakfast, I grab my phone off the kitchen island so I can check in with Mom. There are a few unread messages sent by Mrs. G last night. One wishing us a good weekend followed by a picture of them on the couch with the TV screen showing a half-naked Channing Tatum dancing. Then another one with a string of fire, hot face, eggplant and thumbs up emojis. I giggle at her absurd message before hitting her contact icon to call her. She doesn't answer, so I leave her a voice-mail letting her know we are snowed in up here and ask her to call me back.

When I hang up my call with her, I decide to text Kai and see if he minds checking in on Mom and Mrs. G and let him know I'll be gone longer than expected.

Me: Hey, we got more snow than expected up here. I don't think we will make it back tomorrow. Do you mind making sure Mom and Mrs. G are ok?

It only takes a minute for Kai to respond to my text.

> Kai: No prob. I'll check on them. Do you need help getting home? I can use Dad's truck to come pick you up. Just say the word, ReRe.

I grin down at my phone, heart swelling at how ready Kai is to jump to the rescue.

> Me: We're ok. Should melt by Monday. I appreciate your willingness to brave the elements to rescue us. *smile emoji*

> Kai: I never said I was rescuing you both. Officer Dudley got himself into that mess. He can find his own way down the mountain.

I SNORT out a laugh at Kai's last message as Dom comes up behind me and hands me a coffee cup. He wraps his arm around my waist and pulls me back into his firm body, and I can't help but melt into him.

"What are you laughing at, Kitten?" Dom kisses my neck, distracting me from my conversation with Kai.

"Just something Kai said." I shut off my phone and drop it back on the counter. Turning, I wrap my arms around Dominick's neck as I reach up to kiss him, but when my lips meet his, I find them firm and unyielding. He doesn't kiss me back, so I pull away, looking up at him in confusion.

"Why are you texting Kai when you are here with me?" His tone is serious, and his eyes are the color of a storm over the ocean.

"I was just letting him know I won't be home tomorrow and asked him to check in on Mom."

"I don't think you should be friends with him anymore. You've got me now, and I don't appreciate having another man panting after my girl like a dog in heat." It takes a moment for me to process Dom's words. Surely, he didn't just say what I think he said. I pull back from him, confusion drawing my brows together.

"Excuse me?"

"You heard me. It's not appropriate for you to be friends with him. You are in a relationship now, and he's going to do his best to sabotage it because he has feelings for you. I don't want you talking to him anymore." Dom snaps the word anymore with the bark of someone used to being in a position of authority.

"Dom, it's not like that at all…" I stammer out, unsure where this sudden change in attitude came from. "Kai is my best friend. He's been my best friend for years. He doesn't have feelings for me. You don't have to feel threatened by him." I rest my palm on Dominick's chest in a reassuring manner, hoping he's just having a flare-up of alpha male jealousy.

"Come on, Serena. I know you're smarter than this. I've seen the way he looks at you. He wants you." Dom's jaw clenches, and I swear he looks two seconds away from turning green and hulking out. Irritation ripples through me at his insinuation that Kai is only my friend because he has feelings for me.

"I'm not having this discussion, Dominick," I spit out his full name in irritation. "Kai is my best friend. Nothing more."

"If you're so sure about that, then ask him. Ask him if he has feelings for you. I promise you; he won't be able to give you a straight answer. He's just been waiting around for you like a sad little puppy hoping you will take pity on him and fuck him. I will *not* have some punk ass kid hanging around *my* woman waiting to take advantage of her."

I rear back from Dom, his words hitting me with the force of a slap. "Kai would never!" I jerk away from Dominick to walk away from him, disgusted by his attitude. Dom must realize he's gone too far, because he grabs my arm, pulling me back into him, caging me against his body.

"Serena, baby, I'm sorry. I know that's harsh. I shouldn't have lost my temper. But I love you and can't stand the thought of another man coming between us. You are everything to me." Dominick kisses the top of my head, and when I look up at him, I see the tell-tale sign of tears shimmering in his eyes. My anger at his attitude immediately melts away when I see them. He's just as scared as I am by this new relationship.

"I love you too, Dom. You've got nothing to worry about, I promise." Dominick nods stiffly and goes back to making breakfast, and I can't help but wonder if maybe he's right.

The awkwardness from our first argument seems to melt away over breakfast. Dom dotes on me, almost to the point of it being comical. Sitting me in his lap while he feeds me fruit and croissant and eggs from his plate while never letting my mimosa run out. After breakfast, he runs me a bath and insists I take a luxurious soak while he preps dinner for tonight. He even dumps in some Epsom salts to help with my muscle soreness from all of our...physical activity.

I'm relaxing in the tub, muscles loose from the long soak and eyes growing heavy from the lavender-scented water, when I hear my phone ring from the living room. Immediately, I am on alert. I recognize the ringtone I have saved for Kai, and I can't help but worry something has happened with Mom. I move to climb out of the tub but stop when I hear Dominick's gruff voice answer the call.

"What do you need, Malakai?" His voice is less than friendly towards my best friend, and I can't help but bristle at the tone. There is silence while I assume he listens to Kai's end of the conversation.

"No, Serena cannot come to the phone. She's taking a bath and relaxing. If this isn't an emergency, then it can wait until we get back on Monday." More silence from Dom but I can hear him walking further away from the bathroom. His next response is muffled as I hear him step out the sliding glass door out onto the balcony. By the time I climb out of the tub, halfway dry myself off and make my way back into the living room, Dom is coming back inside, his call with Kai already over.

"Hey, what did Kai need? Is everything okay?" I reach

for my phone, but Dom slides it into his back pocket, out of my reach.

"Everything is fine, Kitten. Your *friend* just wanted to make sure you were okay and didn't need a ride down the mountain." I don't miss the bitterness in his voice lacing the word *friend*. I can see Dominick's jaw pulsing from where he's clinching it.

"Nothing is wrong with Mom?" I ask again, trying to reassure myself all is well back home.

"Nothing is wrong, other than your friend being too codependent to let you be away for one weekend."

Before I can come up with an apology for Kai, Dom crushes his mouth to mine, swallowing the words forming on my lips. My body is already pliant and relaxed from my hour-long soak, and I melt into him as he kisses away my worries.

"Now that you're clean, let's go get you dirty again." Dom shoots me a wink as he scoops me up and carries me upstairs to the bedroom loft. Once we make it upstairs, Dominick drops me on the bed and climbs on top of me, kissing every inch of my exposed, damp skin. He peppers hot, open-mouthed kisses down my neck, along my collar bone, down to my breasts, taking each nipple into his mouth, lavishing them with his tongue. Somehow, he manages to undress himself while turning me into a panting, needy mess.

Just as I feel the head of his thick cock notch at my entrance, I pull away from his kiss and push back on his chest. "Wait, do you have a condom? I think we should use them until I get back home and start taking my birth control again." A pained look crosses Dominick's face as he holds himself back from sinking balls deep into my slick heat.

"Kitten, you're killing me." He pleads, nudging the tip of his cock against my clit, making me moan.

"Dom, I'm serious. Please." I give him my best puppy eyes as I push at him again, trying to resist the temptation to give in to the moment. "Do you keep one in your wallet?" I glance over at his wallet on the nightstand, hoping like hell he has one stashed in there. I want to fuck as badly as he does; I just want to be careful knowing I'm not able to take my pill for two days. Dom lets out an aggrieved huff but reaches over to snag his wallet off the nightstand. I watch his face as he flips it open to look inside. When he pulls out the small foil packet, I sigh in relief.

"Oh, thank God. Get that on, right now." Dom lets out a dark chuckle at my command.

"Oh, I'll put it on, Kitten. But it's the only one I have, so I'm going to make it count. I hope you're ready for this." With a look that can only be described as wicked, Dom slowly rolls the condom down his length without breaking eye contact. I resist the urge to watch him sheath his impressive cock in the rubber, our eyes locked together in the world's sexiest stare off. I don't break until Dom thrusts into me with one powerful snap of his hips, forcing my eyes to close and my mouth to cry out in pleasure.

Dom wasn't lying about making it count. We have sex for what feels like hours, in every position he can rearrange me into. When he finally comes, it is with a roar, fucking me from behind, my hair wrapped up in his fist, my entire body trembling and weak from exertion. When he releases his grip on me, I collapse onto the bed, limp, satisfied and more than a little sore. I feel bruises forming on my hips from where he had been gripping me earlier, and my vagina feels battered from his rough pounding.

After a few minutes, I finally work up the strength to stand so I can make my way to the bathroom, but as soon as I am vertical, I feel a warm dampness leaking out of me, coating my thighs. Dom is already in the bathroom cleaning up, so I call out to him, "Uh, Dom...did the condom break?" Dread pools in my gut as I wait for his answer. When Dom pokes his head out of the bathroom, a sheepish look on his face, I know the answer. My knees give out from under me, and I land sitting on the bed, mind already whirring with consequences.

"Hey, hey, hey. Kitten, look at me." I keep my head down, arms wrapped around myself, rocking as I spiral into panic. "Serena! Look at me!" Dominick's sharp bark snaps me out of my thoughts, bringing my attention back to him. He cups my face in his big hands, keeping my attention on him.

"Listen. To. Me. It will be alright. I'm sure the odds of you getting pregnant from missing a couple of pills are super low. It will be alright. You will be alright. Even if you do get pregnant...You. Will. Be. Alright. You have me, and I will take care of you and any baby we make. Do you understand?" I give a small nod, head still held in place by Dom. His face lights up with the most brilliant smile, and I can't help but melt from its beauty. "Good girl. Now go clean up, and no more worrying."

Dom pulls me up to my feet and sends me on my way with a swat to my ass, my worry about pregnancy tamped down for now. It's difficult to remember why it would be the worst thing in the world to become pregnant when Dom is right there in my face being so rock solid, so reassuring. So, fucking, perfect.

CHAPTER TWENTY-ONE

SERENA

Monday afternoon brings a warm front to the area that melts the snow that had been preventing us from leaving the cabin. While I'm happy to finally go home, a big piece of me is sad about leaving. This cabin has felt like a sanctuary for the last three days, sheltering me from all of the stress and responsibilities of life. Dom has doted on me, made love to me, used me, and pleasured me to the point that I'm not even sure I remember how to walk. After his only condom broke, I made him pull out every other time we made love. I'm still not feeling great about that particular backup method, so I plan on asking him to stop by the pharmacy on the way home so I can pick up some Plan B.

My good intentions to pick up emergency contraceptives go up in flames when my phone rings as we get into town. I see Kai's name on my screen, and I hesitate to answer his call, not wanting to irritate Dom by talking to Kai. The call rings out and goes to my voicemail. Instead of leaving a message like I assume he would, Kai must decide to call right back, because my phone immediately starts ringing again. This time I do answer it, a sick feeling of dread settling in my stomach. He wouldn't call like this if it wasn't an emergency.

"Hey, what's going on? Is Mom okay? What's wrong?" My words come out in a breathless rush, panic already making my throat tight.

"Your mom's fine, ReRe. Don't freak out. Mrs. G slipped on some ice. We think she might've broken her arm. The ambulance just took her to BF General, but I wanted to let you know I'm here with your mom." My heart sinks at hearing the news about Mrs. G.

"Shit, is she okay?"

"She was flirting with the paramedics who came to help her, if that tells you anything. Cussin' up a storm too, saying it hurt like 'a sonofabitch' and complaining about having to miss bridge club tonight." I can hear the smile in Kai's voice, and I can't stop one from forming on my lips to mirror his.

"Sounds like she's just fine then. Good. Look, we just got into town; we will be home soon. Do you mind staying with Mom until I get home?"

"Re, you don't even have to ask. I'll be right here until you get back. Your mom is already insisting on making muffins for Mrs. G as a get well soon present."

"You're going to bake muffins?" I raise an eyebrow and let the incredulity seep into my voice.

"Oh, hell no. Your mom is going to bake, and I'm going to lick the batter bowl and keep her company." I laugh, knowing Kai is one hundred percent telling the truth.

"Alright, keep her company. We will be there soon."

When I hang up, I look over at Dominick and see his eyes locked on the road, expression stormy. He doesn't look my way when he bites out, "Why was Kai calling you?"

A little hurt and a lot bewildered by his tone, I immediately find myself on the defensive. "He was calling to let me know Mrs. G slipped on some ice. She's been taken to the hospital, and he is staying with Mom until I get home." Dom doesn't respond, just jerks a nod, keeping his eyes focused on the road.

Instead of starting another argument, I turn my focus to my phone and start composing a text to Marie to let her know I won't be at work tomorrow. I've got to make a plan for what to do about Mom while I work and go to class. It's not like she can't be alone, but her memory lapses can be unpredictable, and the idea of her forgetting and going out into the world without someone there with her sends my mind into a panic spiral.

It happened a few times when she first got home after the accident, when it was just the two of us trying to learn how to live with our new normal. One day she went to the mall while I was at school and forgot where she parked the car and couldn't get back home.

Another time she forgot Dad had died in the accident and went to his office to surprise him with lunch. When his coworkers called me to come get her, she was inconsolable with grief in the middle of his office. That was probably the second worst day of my life. Watching my mom relive the agony of losing Dad all over again gutted me. There have been other times when the grief came back, fresh and raw, but that day in the office was just like being in the hospital when she finally woke up and I had to tell her the news. I find myself lost in the haze of memories from those early days when I had to break the news to my own mother that her husband, her life partner of twenty years and the father of her only child, had died.

THE STEADY BEEP of the heart monitor is like a metronome, but instead of keeping time for a beautiful piece of music, I only hear the symphony of hospital noises. The soft whoosh of air from the oxygen cannula, the low murmur of chatter from nurses at their stations, occasional overhead pages for stroke alerts or incoming traumas, the mechanical hum of the portable x-ray machine roaming the hallways.

I've been sitting by this hospital bed for three weeks now, for as long as they allow me to stay, sometimes well past visiting hours. I've hardly been to class, but thanks to my stellar grades, my teachers are giving me a pass on the last few weeks of school. Mrs. G, Kai and his parents have all stopped by regularly, checking on me and Mom, bringing me food and books to read, but I have never felt more alone in my life. All I want is for my mom to wake up and a hug from my dad. One of those things I know I will never get to have, and the other seems less likely with each passing day.

Visiting hours are almost over, and I am resigning myself to leaving this godforsaken hospital again with no progress from Mom, when I feel a light squeeze on the hand I am using to hold Mom's with. My heart immediately begins to race when I see her fingers twitch, and I feel another light squeeze.

"Mom? Can you hear me?" My voice is an excited whisper, hope bubbling in my chest at the possibility that she is here with me. She doesn't say anything, but she gives my hand another squeeze. My vision goes blurry as tears silently pool in my eyes.

"Mom, it's Serena. I'm right here. I'm here, Mom. Please, please, wake up. I need you." My words are a plea. A prayer. I keep repeating myself, willing her to open her eyes and fully wake up. I've never needed anything more than for my mom to open her eyes and look at me so that I know she is okay.

When she does, and her eyes meet mine for the first time since the day of the accident, I break down. The floodgates open, and the tears come pouring out in a tsunami of loss, grief, sadness and anger. But also, there are tears of relief and hope and happiness that I still have her. That I didn't lose her too.

A FIRM HAND on my leg brings me back to the present, and I realize with a start that we are now parked in my driveway, and I'm crying.

"Hey, Kitten, what's wrong? Talk to me." Dom turns my

face so I'm looking at him, and he wipes away the tears sliding down my cheek with the pad of his thumb. "Why are you crying, baby?"

"I-I was…just thinking about how it was in the beginning. After the accident and how hard it was. I'm okay… I'm just…worried about how I'm going to take care of Mom without Mrs. G's help. I can't leave her alone, Dom. I can't…" Dom surprises me by unbuckling my seatbelt and pulling me into an embrace. He kisses the top of my head while rubbing soothing circles on my back.

"Don't worry, Kitten. You're not doing this alone anymore. I'll take care of it. You've got nothing to worry about. We will figure it out together, and I will make sure you, and your mom, are taken care of. You're mine now. My responsibility." I nod, my head resting against his chest, his strong heartbeat calming the wave of panic that had been threatening to take over. Knowing Dominick is here, ready to help in whatever way possible, gives me the strength I need to get out of the car and face this new obstacle in my life.

As we walk up the steps to the front porch, my phone starts buzzing in my hand with an incoming call from Marge. Marie must have let her know what's going on. "Hey, I need to take this. I'll be right in." I tilt my head towards the door, inviting Dom in while I hang back to talk to Marge.

"Hey, Marge, I guess Marie told you what happened?"

"Yeah, sweetie, she did. Take all the time you need; your job will be here waiting. Do you need anything from us?" Marge's raspy voice comes through the line, offering reassurances that help ease some of the tension building in my shoulders.

"I just need some time to figure out how long Mrs. G is going to be in the hospital and line up someone else to stay with Mom. I don't exactly have a long list of volunteers for free babysitting, so I might have to call around or hire someone." Mentally I start tallying up how much hiring someone to stay with Mom will run me, and I wince. I make enough between my two jobs to cover the basic living expenses for us, but there usually isn't a lot leftover.

"Okay, you just let me know when you're ready to come back. We will be fine at the shop. And if you need anything at all, don't hesitate to ask. You're like a granddaughter to Eddie and me, and we are happy to help any way we can."

"Thanks, Marge. I'll call you once I have things sorted."

WHEN I ENTER THE HOUSE, Dom and Kai are standing in the foyer locked in silent standoff. Kai's face is closed off and angry, his chin tipped up in defiance. He is bristling like an angry porcupine. Dom's stance is wide, arms crossed, and he's looking down his nose at Kai with his *cop* look. It's the same expression I saw when he dealt with the frat douches at Maverick's weeks ago.

"Hey, Kitten, I was just telling your *little friend*, Malakai, he can go. We've got it under control now." Dom doesn't turn to look at me when he speaks—his eyes are locked on Kai. His words are neutral, but the tone behind them is anything but. Kai doesn't break eye contact with Dom when he speaks, either.

"And I was just telling your *boyfriend* that I'm happy to stay with Laura as long as you need me to." Shit, I need to diffuse this before two of the most important people in my life come to blows.

"Kai, thank you so much for staying with Mom and checking in while I was gone." I turn to Dom and give him a gentle nudge toward the kitchen. "Will you give us a minute, babe? Please?"

Dom doesn't budge at first. He just continues to stare Kai down. Kai breaks the tension first by looking at me. Whatever he sees on my face melts away the anger from him. He moves away from his standoff with Dom and wraps me up in a hug.

Speaking low in my ear he says, "ReRe, I'll be around to help any way I can. My parents will be back in town this week, and I'm sure they will be more than willing to give you backup so you can get to work and class."

With one last squeeze, he lets me go and heads to the front door. When my eyes travel back to Dominick, there is a storm of emotion swirling in his steel gray eyes as he watches Kai leave. A pit opens up in my stomach as I realize there is no way I am going to be able to keep both of these men in my life. At some point I am going to have to choose, and I don't know how I will.

CHAPTER TWENTY-TWO

KAI

Serena hasn't been able to make it to class or to the coffee shop this week. I've been stopping by every day to drop off notes for our shared classes, despite Dominick's warning to stay away from her. Fuck if I am going to abandon my best friend when she needs me most. My parents will be getting back in town today from their epic cross-country trip to the Southwest. I already filled them in on the situation, and they're both more than willing to hang out with Ms. Laura so Serena can get back to her life. Serena hates asking for help and relying on others—the guilt eats at her, I know—but I am not about to let her shoulder this on her own.

Bounding up the front steps of the Malcolm home, I give a light knock on the door before letting myself in. Serena is used to my afternoon visits, so she should be expecting me. When I enter the house, I hear the low murmur of voices in the living room. One is deep and male. Shit, Dominick isn't usually here when I come by. He better not start up with his posturing bullshit again. As I approach the living room, I realize Dominick is talking to Laura, and Serena isn't around

"I know it feels like a big change, Laura, but I think this would be best for Serena, don't you? I know you hate the fact that she has to work so much to support you both, and I want to help. Serena deserves to be able to live her life and know you are safe and taken care of."

"I don't know, Dom…it's too much." I pause in the hallway, just outside the door, listening, unease building in my gut. Why is Dom here talking to Ms. Laura without Serena? What is he trying to talk her into?

"Nothing is too much when it comes to Serena. I promised her I was going to take care of her and you, and I intend on keeping that promise. I am going to propose to her, so we will be family soon. Let me do this, Laura. It's a really nice independent living facility. You'll have your own apartment, around-the-clock care available, and they have a neurologist on staff that is an expert in memory loss."

My heart drops when I hear the word propose come out of his mouth at the same time Laura lets out a surprised gasp.

"You're going to propose?" Laura's voice is excited. I hold my breath waiting for Dominick's response.

"I have the ring already. Look, Laura, Serena won't decide to do this on her own. I know how hard she's fighting to keep you at home. You're the one who is going to have to suggest this to her. If she believes this is what you want, she will go with it. Once she accepts my proposal, she will move in with me. We can sell this house to help cover the costs, and she won't have to spend every free moment working. Don't you want what's best for your daughter?"

Dominick's words slide over me like an oil slick, leaving a disgusting residue behind. I can tell Serena's mom is buying into his bullshit. I'm about to speak up and interrupt when the front door opens behind me, and Serena walks in, carrying groceries.

"Oh hey, Kai!" Her face breaks out into the briefest of smiles before falling away when she sees my expression. "What's wrong? Is everything okay?"

I must be doing a shit job of hiding my feelings about the conversation I overheard, but before I can say anything, Dominick appears in the hallway, eying me with suspicion.

"What are you doing here, Malakai? I didn't hear you knock." His tone is accusatory, and I bristle at the under-lying accusation.

"I was stopping by with notes for Serena from class today." I look at Serena when I answer, ignoring him. That doesn't change the fact that I can feel him staring a hole into the back of my head. Fucking prick. I can't let Serena marry this asshole. She deserves better. *I would be better.* A little voice in my head speaks, and I shake it off, knowing now is not the right time to let my mind venture down that road.

Serena eyes Dominick and me warily, sensing the tension between us. Instead of feeding into Dominick's attitude, I move to grab some of the grocery bags hanging off Serena's arm. She follows me into the kitchen with Dom right on her heels, like he's afraid to leave me alone with her for even a second.

"I've got this, Malakai. You can go now." Dominick pushes in front of me, separating me from the bags I just dropped on the counter. The move also places him between me and Serena, with her behind him, unable to see the daggers he is glaring at me. He looks pointedly behind me, towards the front door.

"Right. Well, here are the notes from today, ReRe. If you need any help with the assignment, just call." I pull the notebook from my backpack, dropping it on the counter. "Mom and Dad will be in town tonight. Mom already said she's happy to stay and hang out with your mom tomorrow so you can get to work and class."

Dominick crosses his arms over his chest, trying to intimidate me when he speaks again. Joke is on him though, this chucklefuck doesn't intimidate me. Not where Serena is concerned.

"I'm sure Serena appreciates your offer, but that won't be necessary. We've got it covered." Serena steps out from behind Dominick, her brows furrowed in confusion. She doesn't know about his plan to send her mom away, and I don't think she's going to like it. It's on the tip of my tongue to speak up and say something. To warn her, but before I can, Serena shoots me a small smile, soothing some of the anger that is threatening to boil over.

"Thanks for stopping by, Kai. I'll call you if I have any questions. Tell Grace and Luther I said hi. They're more than welcome to stop by when they get settled in."

I look at my best friend. Really look at her. I see the quiet pleading in her eyes and the stiffness in her posture. She's uncomfortable, and she doesn't know how to handle it. I can see her pulse fluttering in her neck and the way she's nervously biting her lower lip. The tension between me and Dominick is causing her distress, and I refuse to be the reason for her discomfort, so I nod and back towards the door.

"Sure thing, ReRe. I'll see you in class." I leave without another word but with the undeniable feeling that I am losing my best friend.

LATER THAT NIGHT after helping Mom and Dad unload their RV and get unpacked, I'm sitting in the living room staring into space when my mom plops down on the couch next to me, pulling me to her, forcing me to lay my head on her shoulder like I used to as a kid.

"What's going on Kai, baby?" I don't know how she knows, but somehow, like always, she does. I've never been able to hide from my mom, and any time something is weighing on me, she is there—with a hug and comforting words—ready to ease my burden.

"Nothin', Ma. Nothing at all."

Mom tuts her disapproval at my response. "It doesn't sound like nothing to me, baby. Come on, talk to me. Is it about that handsome new boyfriend Serena has?" I let out an involuntary groan at the mention of Dominick, and Ma's face lights up like she hit the jackpot. "I knew you'd figure it out eventually. I had a feeling it would take having some other man show some interest to finally light a fire under your ass."

"Ma, what? No. It's not like that." My protest is half-hearted at best, and my mom quirks an eyebrow at me, giving me her "don't bullshit me" look.

"Okay, maybe it's like that. But it can't be. Serena is really into this dude, even if he's a complete douche-nugget."

"Douche-nugget?" Mom lets out a chuckle as she echoes me.

"Such a douche-nugget. He won't leave Serena alone with me—he told me to stay away from her! Can you fucking believe that shit? She's my best fucking friend. Who is he? Some asshole getting his dick wet."

"Malakai Demetrious Roberts! Watch your mouth." Mom smacks the back of my head, and I give her a contrite look.

"Sorry, Ma."

"You're right though, he does sound like a douche-nugget. Have you talked to Serena about your feelings?"

"No. How can I when I'm not even sure what my feelings are? I just...I just want the best for her, and I don't think he's it. She deserves the world..."

"And you want to be the one to give it to her." Mom chimes in, and I can't bring myself to deny it.

I do want to be the one to give it to her. It's been her

and I for so long, and I just assumed it always would be, even if I didn't recognize the feelings I had buried for her.

"Yeah, Ma, I want to be the one to give it to her. But now she's with—"

"The douche-nugget," Mom interjects.

"Yeah, the douche-nugget, and I'm too late. I overheard him talking to Ms. Laura today, and he's planning on proposing to her. They've only been dating for a couple of months. Who does he think he is?"

"It sounds like he's a man who knows what he has and doesn't want to let it go. Now the question is, what are you going to do about it?" Mom never minces her words, and I wince at her no-nonsense question.

"What can I do about it? She doesn't feel that way about me." Dejected, I lean back, dropping my head on the couch, closing my eyes. All I can see is Serena. Serena's bright smile. Serena's golden honey-colored eyes. Serena's halo of curls. All I can see is her.

"Are you sure about that?" With that final question she gives me a hug before leaving me to wallow in my self-pity.

CHAPTER TWENTY-THREE

SERENA

It's nearing the end of my Friday night shift at Maverick's. Thanks to Kai's parents' generosity, I've been able to get to both my jobs and class today. Mrs. G is still in the hospital waiting for surgery on her shoulder and clavicle, and after she's healed from that, she will need physical therapy. I've been calling around looking to hire someone to stay with Mom, but it's been impossible to find someone to fit within my budget.

Being out of work for the better part of the week has me stressing about money. So much so, I can't even bring myself to be pissed that Brad and his frat bros are back in Maverick's. I had hoped after their run-in with Dominick they'd steer clear of the place, but clearly, they do more of their thinking with their dicks than their brains. Fortunately, they're sitting in Stacey's section, and I've been able to avoid their table.

Dominick hasn't stopped by yet. He's been a constant presence during my evening shifts at Mav's since I refused to quit, but they were going out for dinner tonight for Eric's birthday, and he wasn't sure what time he would be here.

"Hey, Serena, can you take out the ladies' room trash? It's overflowing, and a couple of Karens complained about the mess." I look up at Adam and see him jerk his head to a couple of older women sitting at one of the high-top tables, both dressed like cougars on the prowl for some young stud to take for a ride.

"Yeah, sure. Wouldn't want to upset the Karens and lose their business. That would be tragic." My tone is thick with sarcasm as I leave my post behind the bar to take out the trash. The route to the bathrooms takes me by the table near the back, occupied by Brad and his crew. I do my best to ignore them, but I catch a snide "slut" comment as I walk past. Clenching my teeth I press on, determined to stay as far away from them as possible.

After gathering up the trash from the ladies' room, I head out the back door that leads to the parking lot. The dumpsters are at the back of the lot, which is mostly empty this time of night. My breath forms a cloud in front of me when I step out into the cold night air. "Fuck me—it's cold."

"Gladly." A deep voice comes from behind me, and a second later my head slams against something hard as I find myself pressed up against the rough brick wall next to the door, garbage bags abandoned on the ground. Brick-head has me pinned against the wall with his beefy hand wrapped around my throat, cutting off my oxygen. Brad looms next to him, a hateful sneer marring his generically handsome face.

"Where's your boyfriend, slut? Did he break up with you already? Is this gorgeous ass back on the market?" I close my eyes against the spit that flies from Brad's mouth, the reek of shitty beer wafting over me like a noxious cloud.

"Yeah, I think you owe me a turn with that tight little cunt of yours for what your pig of a boyfriend did to my nose. Then my boy here is gonna take your ass." Brick-head uses his free hand to cup my breast and gives it a painful squeeze that brings tears to my eyes. I reach up, clawing at Brick-head's arm, desperate to make him let go. Desperate for air. He hisses in pain when my nails dig into his flesh, but he doesn't let go. His grip on my neck gets tighter, and my vision begins to go fuzzy around the edges.

Brad grabs my arms and pins them against the wall above my head. Terror floods through me; my heart pounds erratically in my chest so hard I'm afraid it's going to burst. I feel the hot, wet slide of his tongue up my cheek the same time Brick-head yanks at the fragile buttons of my shirt, ripping it open. Bile rises up my throat and the bitter taste coats my tongue and the urge to vomit becomes overwhelming. They're going to rape me. I know it in my bones, and there is nothing I can do to stop them. As his rough hands fumble clumsily with the button on my jeans, I hear an angry shout in the distance.

Suddenly the crushing pressure on my throat is gone, and clean, cold air rushes into my lungs.

"Hey man, it's not—" Brick-head doesn't finish his

sentence. The deafening crack of a gunshot silences him. I watch in horror as his eyes go wide in shock before looking down with a dumbfounded expression at the red circle blooming across his chest. It feels like it takes an eternity for him to fall. It's almost like his mind doesn't recognize what has happened to his body, so he stands there, in shock, the color rapidly draining from his face. Brad releases his grip on my arms and starts backing away, freaking the fuck out.

"Fuck. Fuck. You fucking psycho! You fucking shot Todd. What the fuck? What did you do? Fuckfuckfuck." We both watch, transfixed, as Brick-head, A.K.A. Todd, collapses face first onto the pavement. I let out a scream the same time Brad turns to run, and an angry voice shouts, "Freeze! Police!"

AN HOUR LATER, I'm sitting in the back of an ambulance, blanket wrapped around my shoulders while an EMT assesses my injuries. The parking lot is illuminated by flashing red and blue lights as police officers secure the perimeter of the crime scene and redirect the crowd forming at the edge of the parking lot. Todd's body lies under a sheet, still on the ground. Brad has been taken to the police station already. I scan the crowd of officers milling about, trying to find my rescuer. My eyes finally lock on Dominick standing off to the side, a dark rage clouding his expression. He's speaking to the detective who seems to be in charge, and I can feel the tension radiating from him all the way from my perch in the ambulance.

Everything after Todd being shot is a blur for me. Brad freaking out. Dominick yelling. My screams. Vomit. Shouts for help. Sirens.

"Hey, Kitten, baby, are you okay? Serena, talk to me." Suddenly Dominick is in front of me, cupping my face, peppering it with kisses.

"Oh God...Dom...You...I—" I break. Sobs burst forth from my chest with abandon and I find myself engulfed by Dominick.

"Ssh, ssh. It's okay, Kitten. I'm here. I saved you. You're safe now."

I sob into Dominick's shirt, all the emotions that had been held in check by shock now crashing out of me with the fury of a dam burst.

I don't know how long he holds me like this. It could be seconds or minutes or hours. My mind is still trapped in those moments when I watched the light go out of Todd's eyes.

"You killed him. You killed him. Youkilledhim." I can't stop repeating the mantra. My mind is locked in an endless loop, short-circuited by trauma.

"Damn right, I did, Kitten. I'd do it again. He was assaulting you. He was going to rape you. I protect what's mine. I won't let anyone touch you."

"I'm sorry to interrupt, but we need to get her to the hospital to be checked out and make sure she doesn't have a concussion." The female EMT who had been doing my exam interrupts us. "You can ride with her if you want."

"Oh, I will be. I won't be leaving her side."

AFTER A CT SCAN of my head and neck and a rape kit that I refused—much to Dominick's chagrin—I am forced to recount my story to the officers who came to take my statement. Dominick only leaves my side for the duration of the CT scan and only at the insistence of the radiology tech. He is back holding my hand as soon as it is over.

Dominick holds me as I tell the officers how Brad and Todd had pinned me against the wall and groped me. Threatened me. Violated me. I can feel Dominick tense when I speak of how they said they were going to fuck my ass and pussy. When I get to the part where Dominick shot Todd, I freeze. My mind won't process what I saw. It won't accept that I watched someone die. Die because of me. Dominick takes over telling the officers our story, and they seem to be familiar with him. I can sense their admiration for him, and I can tell they don't believe Dominick will be in any trouble for killing Todd.

"Sounds like you did this town a favor, D," one of the officers mutters as he closes his notebook.

"Let's just say I won't be losing any sleep over that piece of shit." Dominick gives me a reassuring squeeze and I nestle closer into his body, eyes heavy from exhaustion.

The adrenaline that had been keeping me going through this whole ordeal has finally been depleted, and staying awake becomes impossible. I hear Dominick say something to the officers taking our statement, and they mutter their goodbyes.

"Lie down, Kitten. Rest. I've got you." Dom's soft, reassuring words are the last thing I hear before sleep finally claims me.

"LET ME SEE HER."

"Fuck off, Malakai, she's sleeping."

"I swear to God, Dominick, if you don't let me check on Serena, she won't be the only one admitted to this emergency room tonight. Let. Me. See. Her."

The hushed, angry argument filters into my sleep-fogged brain, rousing me. I crack one eye open to see Dominick blocking the door to my room, barring Kai from entering.

"Kai?" My voice comes out in a rasp, and I realize it hurts to talk. Apparently, Todd did some damage to my throat when he had me pinned against the wall.

"ReRe, I'm here." Kai shoves past Dominick and wraps me up in a suffocating hug. The warmth and comfort of Kai's embrace settles over me like a weighted blanket, and I melt into him. The spicy, citrusy scent of his cologne fills my senses until all I can feel, smell and hear is Kai. We stay like that until something wet drips down onto my nose. When I pull back and look up, I see Kai's eyes, red-rimmed and shimmering with tears. I reach up and cup his cheek, hoping to reassure him with my touch.

"I'm...I'm okay, Kai." My voice cracks, betraying my words. I clear my throat and try again. "Dom saved me before they...before they did anything. He got there just in time." I watch Kai as he studies me intently, like he's trying to tease out the truth from the dark circles shadowing my face. I've never felt his gaze on me like this before. It feels... intimate. Like in this moment we are two souls tethered together in this dark abyss of trauma. I see so many emotions whirling in his eyes. Terror. Anguish. Relief. But the one that stands out the most is love. It's at this moment that I know Dominick is right about Kai's feelings towards me.

Dominick clears his throat, breaking the spell, severing the tether holding us together. I drop the hand that was caressing Kai's face and look over his shoulder at Dom. His face is a blank mask, but I can see the way his jaw is clenched and the hardness in his eyes as his stare bores a hole into the back of Kai's head. Kai doesn't move, doesn't acknowledge Dominick's presence. His focus is still solely on me, like he's afraid I will disappear if he looks away.

Carefully, I scoot back, putting some distance between us, while my mind grapples with the revelation it just made. "How did you hear about the shooting? How'd you know I was here?"

"It's all over social media. People were live streaming the crime scene investigation, and it came up on my feed. I heard someone say your name on the stream and came straight here." My stomach plummets when I realize what I just went through is already all over the internet.

"Oh God, does Mom know? I need to call her." Frantic, my eyes bounce around the room, trying to locate my cell phone.

"It's fine. I told Mom to stay with your mom while I checked on you. Pretty sure she had already gone to bed before shit went down, so she's just hanging out until you get home." A relieved breath whooshes out of my lungs. I did not want her to get the news of my attack online without hearing from me first. I glance over at Dominick who still looms in the doorway, arms crossed like a sentry.

"Any idea when I can get out of here? Did the doctor say anything while I was asleep?"

"They were waiting for the report from the CT scan to make sure you didn't have a concussion." Dom's tone is clipped, his stare never wavering from the back of Kai's head. I wonder if he can feel the daggers Dominick is staring into him.

I shoot Dom a pleading look. "Can you go check? I need to get out of here. I want to go home." The only part of Dominick that moves is the muscle in his jaw as he clenches and unclenches it. "Please?" I beg, desperate for him to leave the room so I can have a moment with Kai. With a huff, Dominick jerks a nod and leaves the room, but not before shooting one last glare in Kai's direction.

When he's gone, Kai pulls me into another bone-crushing hug and kisses my forehead. "Fuck, ReRe. I've never been more terrified in my life. If anything had happened…I don't know what I would do without you."

His words get choked off as he buries his face in my hair. There is a sense of peace and rightness I feel in Kai's arms. I let myself revel in it for a moment. Absorbing it, letting it wash over me. Because this is the last time I can let him be this close to me if I want my relationship with Dominick to work.

"Kai, hey, it's okay. I'm okay." Gently I push back, putting space between us again. "Thank you for coming, but…I think you should go." Kai's eyes go wide in surprise, and I lower my gaze, staring at my hands, trying to avoid the hurt I know I will see if I look back at him.

"It's…it's just that Dominick is uncomfortable with our friendship. He thinks you have feelings for me. I know that's crazy"—I huff out what I hope sounds like a dismissive laugh—"but I need to respect his boundaries. He just… he just killed a man to protect me. I owe him that much."

"It's not that crazy." Kai's voice is barely a whisper, but it rings through my ears like a gunshot. I jerk my head up and look at him. *Really* look at him. I am transfixed by his expression. I see it. I see the kiss coming before it happens, but I can't bring myself to stop it. The first brush of his lips against mine is soft, tentative. A test. He presses his lips against mine more firmly, and mine part without a thought from me, letting him in. His kiss is tender, warm, and sends electricity surging through my body. "It's not crazy at all," he whispers against my mouth before pressing in again.

Emotions war inside of me. The rightness of Kai's lips

against mine. The wrongness of the timing. The guilt of letting him do this with Dom just steps away. The devastation of knowing this is the end of our friendship. The beep of the overhead page jerks me back into reality, and I push back against Kai, separating us.

"Kai…no…we can't. I can't. I need you to go. Please. I love him…I can't do this." My eyes sting from the tears threatening to fall.

"Serena, please, give me a chance." Kai's hands cup my face, and I shake myself free from his hold.

"Just go, please. I can't deal with this right now. It's too much." Kai doesn't move, doesn't say anything for a long moment, and I keep my eyes fixed on the starched white of the hospital linens covering my bed. I can't look at him. I can't see how my words are hurting my best friend. There has been too much hurt tonight, and my heart can't handle any more. Finally, he leans in and presses another kiss to my forehead.

"Fine, I'll go, but this isn't the end of this conversation." With that, Kai moves to leave, and I immediately feel bereft from his absence. When I hear the quiet snick of the door shutting behind him, I curl up on my side and let the tears fall.

CHAPTER TWENTY-FOUR

SERENA

It's a little after 3:00 a.m. when I am finally discharged, with a clear report from the CT scan and strict instructions for vocal rest to let the swelling go down in my throat. The silence in Dominick's car is charged while he drives me home. He's been in a cold fury since Kai stopped by the hospital, and I don't know how to break this awful tension thrumming between us. My emotions are in such turmoil, I don't know if I'm capable of saying anything that won't make the situation worse.

"I hope you know that was your last shift at Maverick's." Dominick's voice is a low rumble that pulls me from the guilt I'm busy drowning in.

"Um, what?" My own voice is still little more than a hoarse whisper that barely manages to squeak out.

"That was your last shift at Maverick's," Dom repeats in a low growl. "I've been trying to get you to quit for weeks now to avoid something like this happening, and now that it has, I'll be damned if I let you go back to that shithole and work. If they let scumbags like Brad and Todd in through their doors, there is no fucking way I am letting you continue to work there."

"But—" I begin to protest, but Dom cuts me off.

"No fucking buts, Serena. You are not to go back there. I can't always be there to keep you safe, and it's lucky I got there when I did tonight. What would have happened if I had been even five minutes later? Huh? Did you think about that? He probably would've had his pencil dick inside of you. Are some shitty waitressing tips worth more than your safety?"

The bridge of my nose begins to sting from unshed tears as I drop my gaze to my lap. Dominick's harsh words cut, but he's not wrong. Those shitty waitressing tips aren't worth what I just went through, but losing part of my income isn't an option. I don't argue though. It hurts too much to talk right now, and all I want to do is go home, crawl into bed and forget this awful night ever happened.

We finish the drive in silence, and when Dominick moves to get out of the car, I put a hand on his arm, stopping him. "You don't have to come in. I'm beat, and I just want to go to sleep."

"Kitten…" His tone is gentler now. The look in his eyes softens, and it stirs the guilt churning in my stomach still. I shake my head, cutting off his protest.

"Please, Dom. I need sleep and some time to process all of this. You can come by tomorrow if you want." My voice cracks from use, and I give him a pleading look, begging him not to fight me on this. Fortunately, he doesn't. He just leans in and presses a soft, chaste kiss to my lips. I cringe internally, paranoid that he will be able to sense the ghostly remnants of the kiss Kai burned into my soul earlier tonight.

"Alright, Kitten. Get some sleep. I'll be back in the morning, okay? I can help you explain what happened to your mom if you want."

Relief floods through my system at his words. Relief from what, I'm not entirely sure. Relief of getting distance so I can process the guilt from Kai's stolen kiss? Knowing I won't be alone when I have to relive this horrible nightmare to tell Mom? Or the fact that the icy fury that had been making him edgy and prickly for the last few hours has finally melted away, revealing the warm, kindhearted man I fell in love with in its place.

Dragging my tired body through the front door, I am nearly tackled by Grace as she launches herself at me, wrapping me in another bone-crushing hug, like the kind Kai gave me in the hospital.

"Sweet, ReRe, are you okay? Let me look at you." Grace cups my face as she looks me over, checking for injuries. Her eyes narrow, then begin to shimmer with tears when she takes in the bruising on my neck. "Oh, baby girl, what did that monster do to you?" She pulls me back in for another hug, and I melt into her, savoring the comfort she is offering.

"It's okay, Grace. It could've been a lot worse." I try to pull away to give Grace a reassuring smile, but her hold on me doesn't relent.

"Kai called me and told me what happened, and I've been a mess worrying about you. I wasn't sure if I should wake your momma up and tell her what happened. I can go get her now if you want." Grace finally releases her hold on me and turns like she is going to go wake Mom up. I place a hand on her arm, halting her in mid-step.

"No, let her sleep. It hurts to talk too much now. It'll keep until the morning. I don't want to have to explain this to her more than once." Grace gives me an "are you sure?" kind of look, so I give her my most reassuring smile.

"I really just need to get some rest. Dominick is coming back in the morning so we can tell her what happened. You can go home and get some sleep, Grace. Thank you so much for staying so late."

After a few more minutes of fussing, Grace finally leaves, promising to return in the afternoon to check on me. I climb the stairs to my room on the second floor with herculean effort, the last several hours weighing on me mentally and physically, but I refuse to get into bed with the ghost of Todd's touch still lingering on my skin. After showering, putting on PJs, and brushing my teeth, I finally feel clean enough to climb into bed.

My last thoughts as my eyes drift closed and sleep overtakes me aren't of the monsters who assaulted me or of the man who saved me. They are of the soft, plush lips of my best friend and the way they fit so perfectly against mine.

CHAPTER TWENTY-FIVE

SERENA

Late the next morning, I wake, head pounding, feeling like I've been run over by a truck. Bleary-eyed and groggy from lack of sleep, I shuffle into the bathroom to relieve my bladder. Standing at the sink, I take in my appearance. My eyes are still swollen and red from crying, dark shadows under them highlighting exactly how tired I am. Bruises circle my neck like a choker, my complexion sallow like I haven't seen the sun in weeks. In a word, I look like shit. After brushing my teeth and splashing cold water on my face in a futile attempt to freshen up, I head downstairs, not feeling at all ready to tell Mom what happened and relive that nightmare.

When I reach the bottom of the staircase, the low murmur of voices in the kitchen catches me off guard. I pause for a moment, trying to discern who is here in my house, but my mother's choked sob spurs me back into action. In the kitchen, I find Dominick hugging my mother, consoling her as she breaks in his arms. Something twists in my gut when I realize what's happening. Dominick told her about my assault last night while I was upstairs asleep. Dominick notices me standing in the doorway to the kitchen, but he continues to hold my mom, rubbing soothing circles on her back.

A storm of emotions rages through me over his audacity to do this without me here to console her myself, but before I can open my mouth to say anything, my mom's muffled words, sobbed into Dom's chest, cause my righteous indignation to catch in my throat. "Thank you, thank you, thank you. You saved her."

Dom looks me in the eye when he says to my mom, "I would do anything for your daughter, Laura. You'll never have to worry about Serena as long as I'm around." The irritation that flared up at the thought of him breaking this news without me dies a sudden death.

"Mom." My voice comes out in a choked whisper when I speak. She immediately tears herself out of Dominick's arms and flings herself at me, engulfing me in her arms. I bury my face in her shoulder and let myself become a little girl who needs her mom's comfort. It's been so long since I let myself fall apart in front of her, needing to be strong for both our sakes after Dad's death.

"I'm so sorry baby. I'm so sorry you had to be in that situation. I'm so sorry." I feel wetness on my skin as my mother's tears mix with my own. We cling to one another like a life-raft adrift in an ocean of tears and sorrow.

I don't know how long we stay like that, but eventually the sound of cabinets opening and closing and mugs being set on the counter brings us out of our emotional trance. I pull away from Mom just enough so I can look her in the eye when I say, "I'm okay, Mom. They didn't hurt me. Dominick got there in time." Mom nods once and pulls me in for a forehead kiss. When we break apart Dominick has set three full mugs of coffee on the table.

We follow Dom's lead and take a seat at the table. Mom won't let go of my hand though. She continues to cling to me as if she's afraid if she fully lets go, the horrors of last night will come back and steal me away.

"Laura, I already told Serena she is done working at Maverick's. It's not safe for her there, and I will not allow her to continue to put herself in danger. She is mine to care for and I want to take the next step with her." My eyes snap to Dominick's at his words. My heart begins to race at their implication and what might be coming next.

"Laura, I know you don't remember me, but hopefully the longer I'm around, the more you will grow to trust me, because I'm not going anywhere. I want to marry your daughter. I want to give her the life she deserves to have and not this hamster wheel of work and survival that she's stuck on. Serena shouldn't have to shoulder this burden alone, and I won't let her. Not anymore. Will you let me take care of you and your daughter?"

My heart ceases to beat, and my breath catches in my throat as I process Dominick's question. Is he asking what I think he's asking? Our eyes are locked together, Dominick's searing intensity boring into my soul as my mind comes to grips with what he is saying.

"Serena, will you marry me?" The words, while technically a question, sound more like a command. Dom places a small black box on the table and flips it open. Inside sits an ostentatious princess cut solitaire diamond engagement ring. I feel locked in stasis as I struggle to form a coherent answer to Dominick's question. Mom's hand squeezes my own, directing my attention to her. When my eyes find her, I see her red-rimmed eyes shining with more tears, her lips turned up in a small, reassuring smile. She gives me an encouraging nod, as if to say, *"It's okay. Say yes."*

When I turn back to Dominick and meet his gaze, I know there is only one answer.

"Yes."

CHAPTER TWENTY-SIX

KAI

I knock on Serena's front door, fidgeting from foot to foot, desperate to see her again. Touch her again. Talk to her about what happened last night. I haven't been able to take my mind off how her lips felt pressed against mine, and the feeling of completion that settled over me when I held her in my arms. We've hugged before. Cuddled even, but there was a charged energy last night between us. I let every tumultuous feeling that has been whirling through me out in that kiss, and nothing has felt more right in my life. I know without a doubt that a gravitational shift happened in our relationship, and there is no going back to the way things were. I need to make Serena understand the depth of my feelings for her. I can't waste my chance, before it's too late and Dominick makes her his forever.

Serena's mom opens the door looking flushed and excited, which is wholly unexpected after the events of last night. "Oh, Kai! I'm so happy you're here! Come in, you can celebrate the big news with us!" Laura grabs my hand and tugs me through the door, down the hall to the kitchen. The unmistakable rumble of Dominick's voice reaches me before I see him and dread pools in my stomach at what this "big news" could be.

"Look who just showed up!" Laura announces when we enter the kitchen. I see Dominick sitting with Serena perched on his lap, one of his arms wrapped around her waist locking her in place, a smug smile plastered across his face. A giant, sparkly diamond ring sits on Serena's left ring finger, catching the light, mocking me. Serena looks like she's been crying, but her expression is unreadable. She doesn't look sad, but she doesn't exactly look happy either. She sucks in a sharp breath when she sees me, her eyes flaring in guilt, like I'm here to spill our secret to Dominick.

"Serena, tell Kai the good news!" Laura squeezes my hand in excitement as it lies limply in her grasp while I take in the scene before me in stunned paralysis. It takes a long moment before I find the ability to speak.

"W-what's going on?" The voice that leaves me barely sounds like my own. It's cold and suspicious. My gut is roiling with nausea as my mind screams, "No!" at the realization that I'm already too late.

It's Dominick who answers me, Serena averting her gaze to the floor, unable to look me in the eye when he shatters my world. "Kai, my man, you're just in time to say congratulations. Serena and I are getting married." Dominick couldn't sound more like a smug asshole if he tried. I can see the victory in his eyes. The bitter taste of defeat coats my tongue. I know I should say congratulations for Serena's sake, but I can't force the word past my lips. This is wrong. She isn't supposed to be his. She can't marry him. If she does, I'll lose her forever.

"ReRe…" Her name is a plea on my lips. I need her to look at me, to see how wrong this is. It shouldn't be him. He's manipulated her into this after one of the most traumatic experiences of her life. There's no way she actually wants this. Dominick barrels on, needling his victory into the very marrow of my bones.

"After last night, I knew I couldn't take the chance of something like that happening to *my girl* again. I take care of what's mine, and I'm going to give Serena and her mother the life they deserve. Isn't that right, Kitten?" Dom tugs her against his chest and kisses her neck, while never breaking his eye contact with me. I don't miss the emphasis he puts on "my girl" and my hands clench into fists as I fight the urge to punch the smug look off the fucker's face. He doesn't miss the tension thrumming through my body, and a slow wolfish grin spreads across his face. He's won, and he knows it.

Serena finally looks up, meeting my eyes. She looks haunted and not at all like a woman excited to be getting married. I'm momentarily buoyed by the thought that maybe she doesn't actually want this, but then she speaks, destroying the fragile bubble of hope forming in my chest. "Kai, Dom asked me to marry him, and I said yes. He's what we need. What *I* need. And I love him. I hope you're happy for me." Her smile is a soft, broken thing, and it cuts me deeper than any knife could.

I force a smile that feels brittle and fake before saying

the words that burn my tongue like acid as I speak them. "Congratulations, ReRe. I'm happy if you're happy." It's the best I can offer under the circumstances. Her eyes shine bright with unshed tears as she nods, accepting my half-hearted blessing. She looks like she wants to say more, but I need to get out of here before I lose my shit completely. "I just wanted to come by and make sure you're okay. Looks like you're more than okay and have some celebrating to do, so I'll leave you guys to it." I lean down and give Laura a quick hug before making my exit. "Take care Ms. Laura, I'll see you around."

With that, I walk out of my best friend's house, and possibly out of her life, for good.

CHAPTER TWENTY-SEVEN

SERENA

"I don't know, Dom. This is too much…we can't afford this." Dom, my mom and I sit around the kitchen table staring at a brochure for an independent living facility called Whispering Grove. It features individual apartments, a community center, tennis courts, walking trails, a dining hall, indoor pool, and a state-of-the-art memory care center.

I glance over at Mom who is staring at the brochure, a pensive look on her face while she bites her bottom lip nervously. I'm worried she thinks we are trying to get rid of her so we can get married and live happily ever after. My stomach pitches at the thought. "Mom, we don't need to do this. I'm sure you can stay with us. We'll figure it out." I look to Dom, seeking reassurance, but his eyes are locked on my mother while she studies the information in front of her.

"Dom, we can't afford this. We are barely getting by with free help from Mrs. G," I say again, reaching to pull the brochure away from Mom, not interested in entertaining this dream that will never become a reality. I'm not even sure if it's a dream I want. The idea of being separated from my mom after it's been just the two of us for so long makes me queasy.

"We can if we sell the house." Mom's voice is barely a whisper, but it makes my blood run cold. My hand stops its movement, my body frozen as my mind tries to process what she just said. Mom lays her hand on top of mine and squeezes, drawing my attention to her face.

"We sell the house; you can move in with Dom, and I can live at Whispering Grove. You won't have to worry about supporting us both or working two jobs, you can focus on school. You can have the life you're supposed to be living." The air in my lung catches, and I can't believe she could seriously be suggesting this.

"No. No! That is not an option. You and Dad bought this house when you got married! I was born here. Raised here. Dad lived here! I can't believe you would even suggest that. What if moving makes your memory loss worse? What if you forget more? What if you forget Dad?" I choke on the last words when a sob catches in my throat.

My mother pulls me into a hug and cradles my head against her chest. "Sweet Pea, nothing could ever make me forget your father. A once in a lifetime love like that never goes away. I don't want to see you struggle anymore, Rennie. You've carried this weight for far too long, and what did it get you? Attacked? Almost raped? I won't have my daughter, my life blood, putting herself in that position again. Not for me. Let me take care of you for a change.

And who knows, maybe the memory care rehab will help me? We can give it a try."

The woman who gave me life pulls back and cups my face, forcing me to look her in the eye. She's a blurry silhouette, the tears pooling in my eyes obscuring her face. "You've been strong for so long, precious darling. It's okay to let someone else take the reins now. I believe Dom will take care of you the way you deserve, and I want you to be happy."

"She's right, Kitten. I will take care of you. You can't count on the help of your elderly neighbor forever, and I want you with me in my house, where you won't have to worry about anything ever again. Let's go tour the facility and see what it's like. We don't have to decide right now, but I think once you see it in person, you'll realize it's exactly what your mom needs."

I look over at Dom, and his eyes are the color of steel—cold and unyielding. Even though his words are reassuring, my heart still feels like it is being squeezed in a vise. This doesn't feel right. Selling the house doesn't feel right. Losing the last tie to my father does not feel right. When I look back at Mom, she is staring at Dom like he hung the moon. I know there is no winning this argument now while I'm emotional, so I accept his suggestion to hopefully buy more time to talk Mom out of this crazy idea.

"Fine, we can go look. But if it isn't perfect then we aren't selling the house."

Mom gives me a sad smile as she nods her understanding. "Of course, Sweet Pea."

With the moving discussion tabled for now, Mom

excuses herself and goes to her room to write in her journal about our overwhelming morning. Alone with Dom, the full weight of everything that has happened in the last twenty-four hours hits me. The assault. Seeing Todd die. Kai's confession. Dominick's proposal. His suggestion to move Mom into a care facility. Mom's suggestion to sell the house. My breathing becomes rapid and shallow, and a buzzing starts in my ears as the beginning of a panic attack claws its way into my chest.

"Serena! Look at me!" A rough shake of my shoulders snaps my head back, pulling me out of my panic. Dom is kneeling in front of me, his hands gripping my shoulders tight enough to bruise, a somber look on his face.

"You're hurting me." My voice comes out small and weak. Dom winces at my words and releases his hold on me.

"Sorry, Kitten. You weren't responding to me. You were having a panic attack." Dom offers up a bashful smile as he brushes a tear from my cheek. "Aren't you happy? I know it's a lot, but these are good changes." His voice is tentative, like he's unsure of where we stand now.

"No—yes. Yes, I'm happy. It's just…a lot. I think everything from last night has caught up to me." I stammer out, hoping it will ease the hurt I see in his eyes. "I am excited, Dom. I love you. The idea of selling the house—where I still feel most connected with my dad—just broke me. It was too much." Dom jerks a tight nod before he pulls me into him in a tight embrace.

"It's okay, Kitten. I forgive your reaction. I know you

love me, and I won't let you regret this decision. I will make you so happy."

I close my eyes and let myself melt into his hold. I know Dom loves me. I know he will take care of me. Intellectually, I know he will be good to us. So why does it feel like I'm having my whole world ripped away from me?

CHAPTER TWENTY-EIGHT

As we approach Whispering Grove, slowly driving up the winding gravel lane—its stately grounds forested with mature oak, maple, and yellow-poplar trees —I feel my throat constrict, and I lose the ability to breathe. It is beautiful. There is a serenity about the repurposed manor that seeps from every detail my eyes take in. From the soft babbling brook lined with willow trees that parallels the driveway, to the flower garden carefully maintained with seasonal blooms, to the carefully curated walking paths that crisscross the verdant lawn leading to little gazebos and benches settled in the cozy shade of the towering trees. From the quiet gasp Mom lets out from the back seat, I know she is equally taken by Whispering Grove's calm beauty.

We park in front of the main building, which in its former life was an impressive mansion belonging to an early 1900s railroad baron. When the baron's wife suffered from early onset dementia, he brought in the best doctors he could find and slowly his home transformed from just their home to a care facility for those unable to care for themselves.

Now the estate consists of the manor house, plus four other buildings with apartments that allow for independent living, an assisted living building for tenants who need more help, a community center, a greenhouse, walking trails, and of course the new state of the art memory care unit.

As we exit the car, the front door of the manor opens. A woman, in what appears to be an oversized hand knit sweater made of yarn scraps, steps out and waves at us in greeting. Her hair is a wild mass of curls floating around her head, and glasses dangle from a chain around her neck. Her smile is warm and inviting and seeing her genuine enthusiasm to meet us causes me to release the breath I had been holding.

"You must be Dominick, Serena and Laura. So lovely to meet you! I am Bethany, the director of Whispering Grove." We each take turns shaking hands with Bethany, and I take a moment to take in her appearance. Her earrings are chunky, multicolored hoops that match her sweater. Her glasses are rainbow-colored, and her shoes are those god-awful holey foam shoes favored by chefs and nurses. Her style is eclectic, and I find it reassuring, knowing she isn't some serious CEO in a pantsuit only driven by the bottom line. I open my mouth to greet her in return, but Dominick beats me to it.

"Nice to meet you, Bethany. I'm Dominick; I'm the one who called to set up the tour. We are here to see if this is a good fit for my mother-in-law, Laura." Dominick waves a hand over at Mom. My mouth snaps shut as Dominick takes the lead and guides us to follow Bethany through the front door. Mom reaches out, taking my hand in hers, giving it a reassuring squeeze. I can tell by the look on her face that she is already fully on board with this place, and it feels like a vise is squeezing around my heart.

I find myself only half-listening to Bethany as she gives us the grand tour, guiding us across the impressive grounds and through the modern apartment buildings, while pointing out all the lovely homey touches like the greenhouse and gardens. Words like holistic combined with modern, cutting-edge memory research filter through the haze of thoughts I find myself lost in. Mom seems to be hanging on every word she says while Dominick asks pertinent questions, but I can't seem to break free of the mental loop I'm in as I consider the future that lies before me now.

I'm picturing selling the house I grew up in. Imagining losing my last connection to my dad. No longer being neighbors with Kai or Mrs. G. Uprooting my whole life to move in with Dom. No longer needing to work two jobs to support Mom and myself. No longer coming home and seeing my mother every day and asking how her day was. It's almost too much to bear, and I feel the tell-tale sting in the bridge of my nose from tears threatening to fall.

"What do you think, Kitten? It's perfect, isn't it?" Dominick's low voice in my ear draws me out of my panicked thoughts, and I realize we are back in the front lobby, standing in front of Bethany's office door. I don't even remember half of what she told us or what we saw. I blink owlishly at Dominick, trying to come up with a response, but the best I can muster is a nod and a quiet, "It's nice."

"Shall we get the paperwork started? We tend to stay full, but you guys are in luck. We have a vacancy available right now, so we could have Laura move in as soon as you're ready." Bethany's words finally snap me out of the trance I've been in during the entire tour.

"I don't know…I think we should talk about it," I hedge, glancing at Dominick for back-up. "It's a big step, and we still have so much to do to get the house ready to sell. I'm not even sure if I am ready to sell it, and we need that money to afford this place."

"If we don't start the process now, it may be months or another year before another apartment opens. We have another tour booked this afternoon, and I can't guarantee we can hold a spot for Laura. I can give you all a little time to talk it over, but I would recommend starting the paper-work before you leave. I'll go wait in my office; you all come in when you're ready." Bethany gives me a reassuring smile before slipping through her office door, leaving us in the large echoey foyer.

I turn to Mom and take in her hopeful expression, and I know I'm the only holdout in the group. "It really is perfect, Serena. Did you see how cute those apartments are? And the neurologist they have on staff is one of the best in the country for his research in memory loss. I could take up gardening, make some friends, and you could finally be free to live your life, Sweet Pea." Mom reaches up, cupping my cheek. She gently swipes away the tears that have started falling without my knowledge.

"But…I am free, Mom. My life isn't a prison."

"I know, sweetie, but you deserve more. You deserve to be a twenty-one-year-old who doesn't have to arrange babysitters for her mom so she can go out on a date. You deserve to find a job you want to do, not just one you must do to make ends meet. You deserve to be young and have fun. To experience love and get married and have babies and make your own life, not just live to take care of me." Now my mother's eyes are shining with tears as well.

"But…Dad…" My lower lip trembles as my words get choked off by a sob.

"We will never forget your dad, Sweet Pea. He lives here"—Mom presses her hand against my heart—"and here." She taps my temple gently. "He's always with us, and nothing will ever take him away from us. I know it's a big change, a scary change, but sometimes change is good." We stare at one another for a long moment before I nod in resignation.

I hear Dom clear his throat, and I look over to see him gesturing to the partially open door leading into Bethany's office. "Come on, Kitten. Let's begin the next stage of our life together." With one hand still clasped with Mom's, I let Dom take my free hand, and we walk into the office together. The crushing weight of the wrongness of this decision is no less oppressive, but I soldier on, determined to do the right thing by Mom and let her make this choice for herself, no matter how much it hurts me.

CHAPTER TWENTY-NINE

KAI

It's been a week since I last spoke to Serena. I've avoided going to Brewed Awakening, and she has reverted to showing up to class late, sitting in the front, putting what feels like an ocean of distance between us. I know she's doing her best to avoid me after I confessed my feelings in the hospital. I can't blame her, not really. I chose the exact fucking worst time to finally admit my feelings for her and destroyed our friendship in the process. Every day I hate myself a little more for being so selfish and taking advantage of her vulnerability in that moment. I'm no better than Dom in that respect, and now he has her, and she can't bring herself to look me in the eye. There's no way I can win her back from him without seeming petty or jealous.

As I head out the front door to go to class, I stop dead in my tracks at the sight of a rectangular metal sign posted in the yard next door. It is red and white and reads: "For Sale" in bold lettering with "Campbell Realty Group" under that. At the bottom, a smaller sign is attached with a phone number.

Without thinking, I march over to Serena's front door and knock. I don't have a plan or even a sense of what I'm even doing other than following this uncontrollable urge to get answers. I honestly don't even expect her to answer, so I'm surprised when she does. Her eyes widen in surprise when she opens the door and finds me standing there; clearly she was expecting someone else.

"Kai, hi. Um, what are you doing here?" Serena takes a step back, and I look past her, revealing stacks of moving boxes littering the hallway behind her.

"I saw the sign, Serena. You're moving?" I don't recognize my voice. It's harsh and bitter sounding. It doesn't match the hurt feeling slithering through my chest right now.

"Oh, um, yeah. We are selling the house so Mom can go to Whispering Grove. I'm going to move in with Dominick. It…it just makes sense." I can sense her hesitation, and I hear the uncertainty in her voice. She doesn't look me in the eye, instead opting to look anywhere else, but I can see the tell-tale shimmer of unshed tears in her eyes.

"Why? I thought the house was paid off? Do you need help? You know my parents and I are here for anything you need." I step over the threshold, reaching for my friend, but Serena backs up, keeping the space between us.

"I know. But Dom suggested it, and Mom is all for it. We toured the facility the other day, and she loved it. She… she doesn't want me to feel like I have to take care of her anymore. She doesn't want to be a burden to me." An edge of bitterness creeps into Serena's voice at the end of her statement.

"Who said Laura was a burden? I know you didn't."

"No, I didn't. She said it. I think she wants me to be free to live a normal life. Especially now that Dominick is in the picture. She wants me to be happy." Serena finally looks at me, and I track the lone tear sliding down her cheek.

"You don't sound happy," I say in a low, careful tone. I see it in her eyes. She hates this as much as I do. She's loved this house and fought so hard to keep it for the last two years. I know the idea of selling it is killing her as much as the idea of her marrying Dom is killing me.

"It's a lot. Too many big changes at once. I'll be fine... I...I just need some time to get used to it." Her words are wholly unconvincing.

"ReRe, this is a big decision. You can't take it back... Once the house is sold, it's done. Are you sure you want to do this?" I step closer to her, and she backs up again, pressing her back against the wall. Gently, like I'm coaxing a feral kitten out of a tree, I lift Serena's face so she's looking me in the eye, when I say my next words.

"You don't have to do this, ReRe. This is your home. This is your life. Don't let him push you into anything you're not ready for. This isn't Dom's call to make." We stare at one another for a long moment. My eyes track every micro expression that flits across her face. We are close enough that we are sharing the same air, and I feel the rapid flutter of her pulse against my palm where it gently cups her jaw. "Serena, listen to me. This is the rest of your life you're talking about. You have to be one hundred percent sure about this decision." Silently, I'm begging her to reconsider. It's one thing for her to be engaged to the domineering asshole, but to know he's taking over her whole life and forcing her to give up everything she knows is too much to bear.

"It's for the best, Kai." Her words are like a knife to the heart, and I know I'm losing her. "He's going to take care of me, of us. He's going to front the costs of Whispering Grove until we sell the house and make sure Mom gets the best care she can have. Dominick doesn't want me to work at Maverick's anymore, and I can't support us on what I make at the coffee shop. We won't have to rely on Mrs. G or your parents when I need to work, so you'll be free too. I'll be okay, Kai, I will…" Serena trails off when she looks at my face and sees the devastation written across my features.

"I'm sorry, Kai. I think we need some space from each other. I need to focus on my relationship with Dominick and we…we need some time apart. I don't think it's good for us to be around one another right now." Now the tears are falling more freely, and I wipe them away on impulse.

"ReRe…no. You don't mean that. You're my best friend." My own words are a choked whisper as I lean down and press my forehead against hers, silently pleading with her not to cut me out.

"But that's just it, Kai. I'm not *just* your best friend, and I can't be more. Not now. Dominick loves me and I need to respect that. We need a break until…until you move on…"

"Serena—" I try to speak, but she pushes against my chest, forcing space between us.

"Kai, no. Please, go. Don't make this harder than it already is. Just go. Okay? I have packing to do. We are having an open house tomorrow I need to get ready for. I can't deal with this right now." Serena looks at me with a coolness in her eyes that chills me to my core. I have never seen her look like this. So disconnected. So cold. Slowly, I nod and back away, back towards the open front door.

"Alright, ReRe. If space is what you need, I will give it to you. But know you can always count on me. Always. Call me when you need me, and I will be there. Promise me you will call me if you need my help."

It feels like an eternity stretches between us before Serena gives the most subtle nod at my request. She doesn't say the words though. All she does is choke out a tearful goodbye before turning and walking deeper into her house, leaving me alone and adrift in a tumultuous sea of heartbreak.

Back outside, I breathe in the crisp fall air, trying to cool the roaring inferno of emotion building inside of me. As my eyes land on the street in front of the Malcolm house, I see Officer Asshole himself climbing out of his penis extension on wheels.

I stop at the bottom of the stairs leading up to the porch, crossing my arms, readying myself for a confrontation. Dominick is still in his uniform, apparently having just gotten off shift. As he approaches me, his hand rests lightly on the holster on his hip, and a tingle of fear creeps up my spine. After our last confrontation and the high he probably got for getting away with murder, I'm not entirely sure he wouldn't shoot me and make up some bullshit self-defense story to cover his tracks.

"Malakai, did I or did I not tell you to stay the fuck away from my fiancée?" Dominick's expression is as icy as his tone.

"You don't fucking own Serena. If I want to check on my friend when I see a 'for sale' sign in front of her house that she's lived in her entire life, I damn well fucking will." I lift my chin in defiance, daring him to make the next move, right here on Serena's front lawn. I'd love to see him explain that shit to her.

Dominick's jaw clenches, and his thumb strokes the leather snap holding his gun in its holster like he's considering using it. Instead, he leans in close enough to speak menacingly into my ear. "I'd hate for your *friend* to pay the consequences of your choices. Serena knows she needs to keep her distance from you, but if you can't abide by the same rules, then maybe I'll need to punish her to make you stay in line. Now be a good boy, and fuck right off." The blood in my veins runs cold at his threat. With a patronizing slap of my cheek, Dominick pushes past me and jogs up the stairs while I am rooted in place by fear that my stubbornness will wind up causing harm to the woman I love.

CHAPTER THIRTY

SERENA

Christmas break has finally arrived. The last few weeks have been a whirlwind of packing, house staging and open houses, all while trying to take my final exams and hold down my job at the coffee house. Dom, Mom and I agreed moving during break would be best, so today she finally moves into her apartment at Whispering Grove, and I will move in with Dominick. There are already several offers over asking price for the house, so now it's up to the realtor to sift through them and make sure we accept the best one.

Every day has been an exhausting drain of my mental fortitude, reminding Mom each morning why the house was packed up and about the changes coming. She's handled it surprisingly well, but my stomach is still twisted in a knot of anxiety. I'm constantly nauseous and have barely slept since our visit to Whispering Grove. It's a small miracle I got through my finals without failing in my zombie-like state.

I'm standing in our empty kitchen, staring blankly at the bare walls, my vision clouded over with tears. The wall that used to host all the artwork I brought home from school throughout my childhood is now a stark white empty space. The sweet, spicy scent of gingerbread cookies is noticeably absent. We've been too busy getting ready for the move, so Mom and Mrs. G haven't had their annual Christmas cookie bake-a-thon. There are no festive Christmas decorations bringing cheer to our home. No tree that we picked out together and decorated while drinking eggnog. My home is as empty and sterile as an operating room, and my heart is breaking over it. The worst part is, I don't even have my best friend to lean on right now to get me through this.

I haven't spoken to Kai since the day he saw the for sale sign out front. Grace and Luther have stopped by to help with packing while I went to work or class, but Kai has been notably absent. *You told him to stay away*, I remind myself, shoving down the feeling of longing that slithers through my veins when I think of him. Mrs. G has done her best to keep Mom excited about the move, which is precisely what I need, since I am dreading every moment of it myself.

Mom enters the kitchen, disrupting the pity party for one I'm busy throwing. "Hey, Sweet Pea. You okay?" She comes up to me, cupping my face in her warm, gentle hands, and peers into my soul the way only a mother can.

"No, Mom. I'm not." That's all I get out before the dam bursts, and the tears begin falling in earnest.

"Oh baby. I'm here. Tell me what's wrong." Mom pulls me into a hug, and I bury my face in her neck, inhaling her familiar scent of warm vanilla and sweet berries. She's smelled like strawberry shortcake for as long as I can remember. I let her hold me through my sobs until I'm able to talk.

"It feels wrong. Leaving here, I mean. This is our home. This is where we lived with Dad. I feel like I'm losing him all over again, and now I'm losing you too." I hiccup on my last word, and Mom squeezes me tightly as she soothes me.

"Serena, listen to me. You aren't losing me. I'm still here —I'll just be getting the professional help I've needed for the last two years—and you're going to finally be able to focus on your dreams and goals without having to worry about me. I want that so badly for you, Sweet Pea. Your dad will always be here with you." Mom presses her hand to my heart. "He would be so proud of the young woman you've become, and I know he would want you to be able to chase your dreams uninhibited."

I nod, wiping my tears away as I do my best to accept Mom's words.

"I know, Mom. I know. It's just so many big changes at once."

Just then the sound of the front door opening disrupts our heart to heart. A moment later, Dominick strides into the room, a wide smile on his face as his eyes alight on us. "How are my two favorite girls today? You ladies ready for moving day?" Dom pulls my mom into a firm hug before wrapping me up in his embrace and dropping a kiss on top of my head. He pulls back, his brows furrowing in concern when he takes in my tear-streaked cheeks and red eyes.

"Is everything okay, Kitten?" Dom cups my face in his hands while he studies my face, trying to discern what has me so upset.

"I'm fine, I was having a moment about leaving home. I got overwhelmed by it all." I force a smile as I reach up on my tiptoes to plant a reassuring kiss on Dominick's lips. Before I get the chance to pull back, Dominick tightens his hold and deepens our kiss until I am breathless and dizzy. He doesn't pull back until Mom clears her throat with an amused grin playing across her lips.

Dominick shoots Mom a bashful look. "Sorry, Laura. I just don't like seeing my girl looking so sad."

"Right, well how about we get this show on the road, and after you kids drop me off, you can...carry on without an audience." Mom waggles her brows at me, and my cheeks burn with embarrassment.

"Mom!" The woman in question cackles at my mortification as she turns and walks out of the kitchen.

"I'm going to say goodbye to Gloria. I'll meet you two lovebirds at the car."

Hours later, after getting Mom settled into her new apartment, we arrive at Dominick's house. It's a modest two-story farmhouse built in the early 1900s, just outside of town. According to Dominick the house has been in his family for over a hundred years. It is nestled on a private lot, surrounded by trees, without any immediate neighbors. We've been bringing stuff over for the last few weeks, but tonight will be the first night I will sleep here in his home. *Our* home, I mentally correct myself.

I take in my new home, from the cozy front porch with a swing to the bay window in the dining room that lets in the morning light from the east. Fruit trees dot the large yard. Dominick told me his family used to have an apple orchard, hence the large plot of land the house sits on now. They got out of the business when his grandfather passed away years ago, but a few of the trees remain. It really is charming in a rustic sort of way, but I am slightly unsettled by the absence of neighbors and the calm quiet of the secluded area. Gone are the noises of suburbia, cars driving past, neighborhood dogs barking, the low persistent hum of power tools being used by Mr. White who lives two houses down on the other side of Mrs. G. The only sounds are of wildlife and the creaking of limbs as the wind rushes through the bare branches of the trees.

"Welcome home, Kitten." I let Dominick help me out of the car and lead me up the steps to the front door. I find myself taking small, hesitant steps, still partially resisting the idea of this being my new home. Dominick must not pick up on my hesitancy, because he picks me up without warning and carries me across the threshold bridal-style.

"Dom!" I let out a surprised laugh as I clutch his neck. "What are you doing?"

"I'm taking you to my bed, Kitten and giving you a

proper welcome. I've been waiting entirely too long to have your scent on my sheets, and I'm not wasting another moment."

CHAPTER THIRTY-ONE

SERENA

"Girl, don't take this the wrong way, but you look like run over dogshit."

I cast a baleful look at Marie as I finish stocking the pastry case before we open for the morning.

"Thanks, Marie. You really know how to make a girl feel good about herself." My sarcasm is as dry and brittle as my current emotional state. Despite moving in with Dominick over the weekend and having him dote on me for the last forty-eight hours, I still feel raw and unsettled about moving and selling my home. Marie must sense how unamused I am by her observation, because she comes up to me and takes the tray of baked goods out of my hands.

"Hey, what's wrong? I thought you'd still be delirious from all the cohabitation dicking down happening?"

"Maybe that's the problem." I blow out a sigh as I rub my tired eyes. "Dom and I spent all weekend 'celebrating', and I haven't slept well in weeks. Between packing, moving Mom into Whispering Grove, selling the house, working here and barely passing my finals, I'm dead on my feet. I haven't been able to keep any food down either, thanks to the stress." I don't even mention the nightmares that have been plaguing me since the shooting. If it's not that night coming back to haunt me, it's dreams of Dom catching Kai and I in compromising positions and him leaving me high and dry, homeless while footing the bill for Mom's care on my own.

Even though I did the right thing and told Kai we needed time apart, guilt still eats at me for not confessing to Dominick about the kiss between us.

An indecipherable look passes over Marie's face, like a cloud blocking out the sun. "What's that look for?" I ask, narrowing my eyes in suspicion.

"You say you're not sleeping and have been nauseous? How long has that been going on?"

"I dunno, three or four weeks? However long I've been dealing with this bullshit?" I pop a shoulder, too tired to do the mental gymnastics required to remember beyond what I had for dinner the previous night.

"Maybe you're PMSing—is it time for a visit from your favorite aunt? Tell Dom to pick you up some chocolate and a bottle of wine and to give your kitty the night off." Her voice has that light, forced airiness to it that someone uses when they're trying to make a joke that falls flat.

I open my mouth to laugh off her suggestion and snap it shut when the cold realization hits me that she's not entirely wrong. I should be PMSing. In fact, I should be three days into shark week at this point, based on how many of the inert sugar pills I've taken in my birth control pack. I always start on day two of the off week. *Always.* Marie immediately picks up on the panic that must be showing on my face.

"Shit, Rennie. When are you due to start?" Her voice takes on a hushed, serious tone when she asks the question that might upend my entire world.

"Three days ago…"

I'M SITTING in the bathroom, staring blankly at the line of pregnancy tests on the counter as the timer on my phone counts down three minutes. After my shift ended, I made a stop at the pharmacy and picked up three different pregnancy tests to bring home. Marie offered to come with me for moral support, but the idea of her watching me have a mental breakdown over being pregnant while knocked up herself was more than I could bear.

Being faced with the very real possibility of carrying a child at this stage of my life has my stomach in knots, and it feels like I can't breathe. As the timer on my phone goes off, the sound of the front door opening and closing carries up the stairs to where I am. Shit, Dom is home. Hurriedly I attempt to decipher the lines and symbols on the little sticks in front of me, desperate for answers.

"Hey, Kitten, you home? What's for dinner?" Dominick's voice calls out as he makes his way up to our bedroom.

I ignore Dominick's call as my eyes scan over the tests. One horizontal line. One vertical line. One digital readout that says not pregnant. Not pregnant. *Not pregnant.* My eyes blur with tears as I crumple to the floor in relief.

"Hey, baby, what's going on?" Dominick finds me in a heap, sobbing. I must look like a disaster, surrounded by empty pregnancy test boxes, still in my coffee-stained Brewed Awakening hoodie, makeup already half-ruined by tears.

"Are you hurt? What happened? What—" Dominick's line of questioning cuts off as he takes in the mess surrounding me. I wipe the tears from my face in a bid to compose myself enough to tell him that I'm okay. Before I can say anything, I see his face light up as he realizes I've taken a pregnancy test. *Multiple* pregnancy tests.

"Serena…are…are we—" There is a manic glee in his words, so I cut him off before the excitement takes hold.

"No, Dom. No. I'm not. I, uh, thought I might be. I'm late, but the tests are all negative."

"Negative?" Dom's voice almost sounds…disappointed.

"Yeah, it's okay. It must be the stress of the move making me late." Something dark passes over Dominick's face that forces the relieved smile on my face to falter.

"You're right. It's okay, Kitten. We can keep trying." Dominick pulls me into a hug while patting my back reassuringly. It takes a moment for my brain to catch up to his words.

"Keep trying?" I push away from Dom, unsure if I heard him right.

"Yeah, we can try again. You're right, you have been

under a lot of stress. It's not your fault; we can keep trying." Dom pulls me to my feet and leads me to the bedroom while I try to process his words. When he leans in to place a kiss on my neck I pull away from him, my spine stiff with fear.

"We weren't trying Dom. I am not in a stage of my life right now where I need to be pregnant. I'm not ready." I back away from Dominick, needing space. The dark shadow that had passed over his face moments ago was back. "You can't be disappointed. We're nowhere close to being ready to have kids. I have another year of college to finish. We just started dating months ago... I'm only twenty-one."

"I can't be disappointed? You're telling me what I'm allowed to be feeling? I'm not allowed to be disappointed the woman of my dreams isn't pregnant with my child? Do you know how much hope you gave me when I walked into that bathroom and I saw those pregnancy tests? The idea of your body growing my child is the fucking hottest thing I can think of. We live together. We are getting married. Is having a child really so unthinkable?" My back hits the wall, and I realize Dominick has advanced on me during his tirade and has me caged in by his hard body. My pulse kicks up as fear floods my system at the harshness in his voice.

"Are you saying you don't want to have my children?" Dominick's eyes are the color of a storm over the sea, and my mouth goes dry at the coldness of his stare. Swallowing, I do my best to diffuse the situation.

"I-I just mean I'm not ready yet. I'm still enjoying our

relationship being just us and getting to know you. We've had a lot of big changes recently and maybe we should settle in to our new life first before bringing a new one in. Of course I want to have babies. Just not right now." I cup his cheek and lean up, placing a soft pleading kiss on his lips. After a long tense moment Dom pushes away from the wall and walks across the room.

When he turns back to me, he looks stricken with remorse. "I'm sorry, Kitten. I just got so excited when I saw those tests. The idea of your carrying my child, it's…it's everything." My heart crumples at his confession, and I stride across the room, wrapping my arms around him in a hug. Selfishly, I was so consumed in my relief of not being pregnant I didn't think about how Dominick would handle the news. I didn't realize he was so eager to be a father. Silently I chide myself for being so self-absorbed.

"You're right, baby. We've got time. We've got all the time in the world." Dom's words sound reassuring, but they don't feel reassuring at all.

CHAPTER THIRTY-TWO

SERENA

Because Mother Nature has a sick sense of humor, I wake up the next morning with unbearable cramps and my boy shorts covered in blood. Grumbling, I shut off my alarm, roll out of bed, and carefully make my way to the bathroom to clean myself up. Hellacious periods and I aren't strangers, so I pop a couple of painkillers and hop in the shower to get ready for work.

In a perfect world, I'd call out and stay home curled up in bed with a heating pad, chocolate and my favorite 2000s rom-coms on the TV, but the guilt from already missing so much work the last few weeks spurs me on. Not to mention, based on the size of Marie's baby bump, I'm convinced she is just days away from recreating the chest-burster scene from *Alien*, so I need to be at work in case she goes into labor.

By the time I'm done getting ready for work, I've decided that this-regular-periods-with unbearable-cramps-and-free-bleeding-from-my-vagina-plus-the-pregnancy-scares, is for the birds, so I make plans to call my local health clinic to have an IUD inserted.

Dominick is still sleeping soundly when I leave the bathroom, so after a quick check of the sheets to make sure my mess was contained to my underwear, I drop a kiss on his head and leave for work.

"GIRL, don't take this the wrong way, but you *still* look like run over dogshit." Rolling my eyes, I ignore Marie's comment and throw my hair up in a bun before tying on my apron.

"For the record, I feel like run over dogshit. I woke up this morning with my period, and I'm cramping like a mofo." My tone is snippier than I intend for it to be, but I can't be blamed for my level of bitchiness this early in the morning on the first day of shark week.

"Ah, so no tiny little Dominicks in our immediate future? Damn, I was hoping our babies could be cousins." Marie mock pouts at me while I scowl at her.

"Don't you dare go wishing that shit on me, M. I am in no condition to be caring for another helpless human being. My mom is finally getting professional help; let me just breathe for a minute."

Marie must sense I'm not in a joking mood because she pulls me in for an apology hug. "I'm kidding Reenie.

Misery loves company and all that. How are you feeling? Are you...you know...sad? Relieved?"

My grumpiness fades at my friend's concern. "Honestly? I'm relieved as fuck. I really don't want to be pregnant right now. Not with all these big changes going on. But Dom definitely seemed...disappointed. I swear, if I didn't know better, I'd think he is trying to get me pregnant." At that admission Marie quirks a brow at me.

"What do you mean? He knows you're not ready, right? You guys just started dating a few months ago. Surely he doesn't have baby rabies already?"

"It's nothing. I think he's just one of those dudes who likes feeling virile and loading me up like he's my own personal jizz dispenser. I'm gonna make an appointment to get an IUD though, so I can avoid future pregnancy scares."

Marie nods at my statement. "I can give you the number to my OB's office. She's super nice and not that booked out. I'll even go with you if you want. You might feel pretty crampy afterward for a few hours. I've heard they're more painful when you haven't had kids previously."

I give her a grateful smile. "I'd appreciate that."

AFTER A QUICK VISIT from Dom and company during the middle of the rush, the rest of the morning passes by uneventfully. I catch a short break, just long enough to call

Marie's OBGYN to schedule an appointment in two weeks for an IUD insertion and save it on my calendar. When I clock out for the day, I am mentally patting myself on the back for making the appointment and not chickening out, but the cramps from the procedure can't possibly be any worse than what I'm dealing with now.

"Alright Marie, I'm off. I'll see you tomorrow!" On my way out the door, I run into Kai on the sidewalk, doing his best impression of a brick wall while standing right in front of the entrance to the shop.

"Shit, ReRe!" He catches me by the arms, pulling me back to him before I stumble backward and land on my ass. His hold lingers a touch too long, like he's afraid I'll disappear if he lets go. I bask in the warmth of his touch, his familiar citrus and sage scent, for entirely too long before shaking myself out of my daze and pulling away from him.

"Kai, what are you doing here?" He looks around, avoiding making eye contact with me, like he's trying to come up with an excuse. Eventually, he must realize he can't come up with something that doesn't sound like bull-shit, so he blows out a breath and lowers his head.

"I wanted to check on you. We haven't talked since… well, since you moved. I just need to know you're okay. I know you said you needed some space, and I'm respecting that, but I miss my best friend." When he finally looks at me and I see the hurt and sadness in his rich brown eyes, my heart crumples in on itself. I miss my best friend too. Being away from Kai for this long has felt like I've been missing a piece of myself.

Before I can stop myself, the words tumble out of my mouth and tears spring to my eyes. "I miss you too Kai. I miss you so much." Kai doesn't miss a beat, wrapping me up in one of his all-encompassing bear hugs that shut out the rest of the outside world. I blame my hormones for turning me into such a weepy mess. That has to be the reason I find myself sobbing into his chest and making a mess of his white t-shirt with my makeup and tears. I don't let myself entertain the possibility that I'm crying because I really do miss him that much, and I made the wrong choice in upending my entire life to be with Dom.

Kai holds me together with his quiet strength while I fall apart and let all the stress from the last few weeks weighing me down finally burst free. It takes an embarrassingly long time before I'm ready to pull back from his comforting embrace.

"Sorry, I...it's...been a lot. I guess I didn't realize how much stress I've been under." Kai nods, understanding dancing in his eyes as he wipes the tears from my cheeks. As he opens his mouth to speak, a rough voice clears their throat to our left, and I look over to see Eric, Dominick's partner, staring at us with suspicion in his eyes.

I hastily push out of Kai's hold, hoping I don't look guilty of something, and plaster on a smile I direct at Eric. "Hey, you back for a refill already?"

"Had to run an errand in the neighborhood. Everything okay here? You need me to call Dom, Serena?" Eric casts a wary glance at Kai, and I step further away from him, hoping to avoid casting further suspicion on him.

"No, no. I'm fine. I ran into Kai, and I'm a hormonal

mess thanks to Aunt Flo visiting, and he was just giving me a hug. I'm heading to class now. Speaking of…I, uh, gotta go. Good seeing you!" I cast a glance at Kai, giving him an apologetic smile while simultaneously avoiding the hurt rejection in his eyes, before turning and heading to the lot where my car is parked. Once inside the safe confines of my car, I mentally berate myself for falling apart all over Kai for no damn reason.

"Damnit, Serena, get your shit together."

CHAPTER THIRTY-THREE

SERENA

When I get back to Dom's house later that evening, after my last class of the day, I find him sitting at the kitchen table, drink in hand, with a thunderous expression on his face.

"Hey, babe…how was your day?" I approach Dom with caution as I drop my purse on the counter, wondering if something bad happened at work today. Dom looks up at me with an anger in his gaze that I swear I can feel, like heat radiating from the sun.

He doesn't say anything, just flips his phone around and slides it towards me. On his screen is a picture of Kai and I, mid-embrace, from this morning. Eric must have taken it before he made his presence known. My face is nestled into Kai's chest, his arms completely engulfing me, and his head is tipped down like he's pressing a kiss to the top of my head. Did he do that? I don't remember—I was so consumed by my own mental breakdown. My mouth opens, then closes as I work through the slimy feeling of having my privacy invaded during such a vulnerable moment.

"What the fuck is this, Serena?" His acerbic tone cuts through the shock that has me currently locked into place.

"I don't know, Dom. What the fuck is it? Why do you have a picture of Kai giving me a hug?" I surprise myself with the amount of righteous indignation I am able to muster. Good, I'm out of the weepy stage of my hormone fluctuation and now into the bitchy stage.

"Why is Kai giving you a hug after I explicitly told you to stay away from him?" Dominick stands, looming over me like an angry, dark god, and I take a step back instinctively.

"I ran into him as I was leaving work. I was a hormonal mess because I started my period, and it was the first time I'd seen my best friend in weeks! I was crying, and he comforted me." I bite out my response in the most even tone I can muster, but I can feel heat rising in my cheeks, and my heart begins to race. I hate confrontation, and I hate fighting with Dom.

"That's not what a hug between friends looks like, Serena. I know Kai wants to fuck you. He's been sniffing around you nonstop since we got together. I saw him make a move on you at the hospital, and now he's fucking lurking around your work after being told to stay away. Don't you get it? He's obsessed with you, and I will not have him putting his hands on you again."

I rear back like I've been slapped at Dom's admission. He saw Kai kiss me at the hospital? "Why didn't you say something?"

"Because you did the right thing by telling him to leave. I thought he'd get the goddamn point after you told him no and then accepted my proposal. Clearly, he didn't. Apparently, I'm going to have to give him a reminder of who you belong to." Dom steps forward, and I take another step back, finding myself pressed against the wall. The heat radiating from his body is almost searing with its intensity, and my heart rate ratchets up another notch.

"Dom, calm down. Seriously, I ran into him, we talked for like two minutes, he gave me a hug and then I left. That's it! You don't need to be giving reminders to anyone about who I *b-belong* to." That word feels vile on my tongue, but I say it anyway, trying to appease the man-shaped tempest in front of me.

Dom looks at me for a long moment, like a lion studying its prey. The heat in his eyes seems to change from raging inferno to something darker, more slow-burning. "Maybe you're the one who needs the reminder."

Before I can react, his body is pressed against mine, his hand around my throat, his mouth covering my own, devouring my cry of surprise. He kisses me like he's trying to burrow his way into my soul, and it takes a long moment before I realize I can't breathe due to his grip on my neck. I push against his chest, but he ignores my silent plea, instead using his other hand to squeeze my breast in a punishing grip that forces a squeak of pain past my lips.

Just when dark spots begin to dance across my vision, Dom pulls his mouth away so he can growl into my ear, "You're mine, Serena, and I am not going to give you up."

He jerks away from me as suddenly as he launched his

attack and goes back to the table to collect his phone and his jacket. While I'm leaning against the wall, barely able to keep myself upright while I desperately try to calm my racing heart, Dom is the picture of cool, calm and collected as he shrugs on his jacket. "I'm going out with the boys. Don't wait up, Kitten." I stare at him in total disbelief as he walks out the door, so completely unbothered, like we didn't just have the biggest argument of our relationship. I can't help but wonder if it was me, making a bigger deal out of the situation because of the guilt I feel about my feelings for Kai.

Instead of trying to examine that train of thought too closely, I make my way to the en suite in Dom's bedroom to take a hot bath before crawling into bed with a heating pad and psychology notes.

I'M ROUSED from sleep by a hard body pressed against my back, rough hands tugging down my pajamas and Dominick's hot mouth on my neck. I can smell whiskey on his breath as his hot open-mouthed kisses trail along my jaw. "Dom, no…" His mouth captures mine, swallowing my protest as he rolls me onto my back and wedges his solid length between my legs while my pajama bottoms pool around my ankles. I push against his chest and turn my head to the side in an attempt to escape the boozy haze rolling off of him.

"Comeonkitten...let me makeyoufeelgood." Dominick nips at my ear, and I feel the press of his cock at my entrance.

"DOM! NO! I'm on my period. I'm not in the mood. Stop! Please." My plea finally cuts through his drunkenness, and he peers down at me like he's trying to decipher my words. With Dominick looming over me like this, I feel like I can't catch my breath while my heart tries to beat its way out of my chest.

"Dom, I can't. Not tonight."

"Is it because I'm not him?" Dominick's voice takes on that tone from earlier tonight that's sharp edges, and it cuts me.

"Not who?" My brows furrow in confusion.

"Kai. Is it because I'm not Kai? Is he the one you want?" Dominick's hips shift and remind me how close he is to entering me.

"Jesus, Dom, no. I'm here with you. I'm just bleeding like a fucking stuck pig and have cramps from hell. Let me get dressed before I make a mess of the bed."

Instead of responding to my shove to get him to move, Dom leans in closer, whiskey wafting off of him while he whispers into my ear, "I don't mind making a mess, Kitten."

Just as he shifts again, I find my strength and shove him back with everything I have.

"I said, NO!" Clumsy from intoxication, Dom rocks to the side and falls onto the floor in a heap. I grab my pants and pull them up as I run into the en suite, locking myself in. I collapse against the door, tears falling freely, wondering if I really even know the man I've just tied my life to. This is not the charmer from the coffee shop, or the man who takes me on picnics or listens to my mom's stories about my embarrassing grade school exploits. This man is a stranger.

A loud pounding on the door makes me squeak in surprise. "Serena, open the door." When I don't respond, Dominick lets out a frustrated growl, "Let me in, goddamnit. I'm sorry, okay?"

"Dom, leave me alone!" A sob rips out of me as I bury my face in my hands. One more angry, frustrated thump rocks the door before I hear Dom stomp out of the bedroom and slam the door behind him. I sit there so long, I fall asleep in a heap on the bathroom floor, cheeks damp and salty from tears, feeling more alone than ever.

CHAPTER THIRTY-FOUR

KAI

After my run-in with Serena, instead of heading to class like I had planned, I drive home instead, the need to do *something* to help my friend burning a hole in my chest.

When I get home, I notice a well-dressed Caucasian woman standing on the front porch of the Malcolms' house, greeting couples, as balloons advertising an Open House dance in the wind on the mailbox. They had a big house showing the previous week, so I can only assume whatever offers came from it didn't pan out. Which means Serena's house is still on the market. As I turn to head inside my own home, an idea hits me like a lightning bolt. It's crazy, impulsive, and probably financially irresponsible, but the pull of it is irresistible. I veer to the left, cut across both front yards, and bound up the stairs to the house next door.

I don't miss the assessing look the woman, whose name

tag reads Chelsea, gives me as I approach her. "Can I help you?" Her question comes out guarded and skeptical.

"Yeah, I live next door, but my parents are thinking of buying this house for my Grams, I was wondering if you had a flyer with the price and details on the house?" Chelsea the Realtor visibly relaxes when I mention my parents are interested in buying the house.

"Oh, yes, I do! Here, let me give you the flyer and my business card. Would they like to take a tour too? We have an open house going on right now. A house like this won't stay on the market long. It had an offer last week that unfortunately fell through, but I have no doubt we will have more after this showing."

I take the flyer from her and immediately start backing down the stairs. "Oh, yeah, that's a great idea. Let me just see if they're home. Thanks for the flyer, ma'am."

"Like I said, tell them this house won't sit long! If they really are interested, make sure they know they need to get their offer in a.s.a.p.!" I toss Chelsea the Realtor a wave while I jog across the lawn back to my house, a manic excitement flowing through my system as a plan starts to come together in my mind.

"LET ME GET THIS STRAIGHT. You want to use your inheritance from Grams—that's supposed to be for your education—to buy Serena's house?" I sit across the dining room table from my parents, the flyer with the house listing laying flat between us, my pops staring at the asking price with a pained look on his face.

"Yes. I have the money for the down payment, but obviously getting the loan will be an issue. I'll make the payments to you guys, like I'm renting it. I can still keep an eye on your house when you're traveling, but I'll have my own space." I try to keep my voice cool and even. I am doing my best to make a level-headed case for buying the house, but the longer we talk about this, the more my panic about letting this slip through my fingers grows.

"Kai, baby, I know you're ready to get your own place, but you can rent an apartment. Grams wanted you to pay for college with that money." Mom makes a move to grab the flyer, and I flatten my hand on it, preventing her from tossing it.

"I've got a full ride scholarship, Ma. I haven't touched that money, and I won't need to."

"Kai, you can't know that. Sometimes things happen –"

Frustration rising, I stand up, throwing my arms up in the air. "I need to do it for Serena!" The words explode out of me before I can stop them.

"MALAKAI!" My pops jumps up from his seat, ready to tear me a new asshole for losing my cool on my mom. "Watch your tone, young man! I raised you better than that." Pops is a master at using the *I'm not mad, I'm just disappointed* tone, and the anger building in my chest deflates under his withering gaze. I toss a sheepish look at my ma as I sit back down.

"Sorry, Ma. I just…it's just…something I need to do."

"Kai, baby, tell us what's really going on. Why do you need to do this for Serena? I know you have feelings for her, but buying her house isn't how you win her back." My mom reaches across the table to hold my hand, like she used to do when I was younger and had trouble with bullies in school. Just the feeling of her soft, warm hands holding my own brings a sense of calm over me that settles into my bones and eases my racing mind. Closing my eyes, I take a deep breath, inhaling the sweet scent of her cocoa butter lotion, before voicing my biggest fear.

"I don't think Serena is safe with her boyfriend." The sharp inhale of my mom's shocked gasp is the only sound she makes. Shifting forward to lean his elbows on the table, my dad is the first one to speak.

"What do you mean you don't think she's safe with her boyfriend, son?"

"He's threatened me, telling me I need to stay away from her. When he saw me with her again, he escalated their relationship by proposing to her after she was attacked. He's convinced her to move her mom into an assisted living facility and sell her house. Last time he saw me leaving her house, after I saw the for-sale sign, he threatened to hurt her if I don't stay away. He's a textbook narcissist, and I think he's dangerous." When I open my eyes again, my parents are a blur, and I realize there are unshed tears clouding my vision. Instead of burying my face in my hands, hiding my weakness, I let them see the fear shining in my eyes.

"Kai, you need to go to the police if you think she's in danger. You need to tell them about how he's threatened you." My mom's voice rises an octave as her righteous fury builds. She stands, ready to hunt down her phone to call in the cavalry.

"Ma, he is the police." I don't need to say any more. Mom sits back down in her seat, as if the admission is physically weighing her down.

"I saw Serena today and she looked...broken. I think he pushed things too fast trying to lock her down, and she's realized it but doesn't know how to slow it down. I want to buy her house so when she needs a safe place to land, she will have one. I know how much she loves that house and the memories of her dad she has there. I don't think selling it is what she truly wants. If we buy it, we can make sure she can get it back once she leaves him."

"Kai, what makes you think she's going to leave him?" My dad's question sends a bolt of fear through my heart. I don't even think before I respond.

"Because I will die before I let that asshole lock her into an abusive relationship. I will not let him rip away everything she knows and loves. She is my everything, and I will do whatever it takes to get her back."

My parents exchange a long look, a silent debate raging between them. Mom thinks of Serena as a daughter, and I know—like me—there isn't anything she won't do to make sure she's safe. Dad turns to me, resignation written on his face.

"And in the event this doesn't work out like you hope, you're gonna be living in the house that reminds you every day of the girl who got away. Think about that for a moment and let it sink in."

Taking in a deep breath, I close my eyes and picture the worst-case scenario. Serena doesn't leave Dom. They get married and have babies, and I wind up living in a house that will always remind me of her. No, that's not the worst-case scenario. The worst-case scenario is Dom seriously hurts Serena or she winds up dead because she has nowhere safe to go because I didn't try hard enough for her.

"I know, Pops. But it's a chance I'm willing to take."

"Alright, son. Let's go buy a house."

Mom calls Auntie Shay, who is a realtor, letting her know they're planning on putting an offer in on a house and need her to help negotiate. Then—as a unit—we march next door to "take a tour" and put an offer in, well above asking. Refusing to leave anything to chance, we make an offer that will be impossible to refuse.

CHAPTER THIRTY-FIVE

SERENA

A light knocking on the door rouses me from my disturbed, fitful sleep. It takes a few moments for my brain to process where I am and why my body aches so much. As I slowly begin to unfurl from the ball I had curled myself into on the bathroom floor, the knocking resumes.

"Serena, baby. Will you let me in? Please, Kitten?" The sound of Dom's voice freezes me, and adrenaline causes my heart to begin racing. He sounds apologetic. Contrite even, but the memory of the previous night flashes through my mind like a sick highlight reel. Dom's hand closing around my throat, cutting off my air. The anger and accusation in his eyes during our argument. Waking up to find him on top of me, trying to enter me before I was even fully awake. The way the whiskey on his breath had made my eyes water. How I had to scream and shove at him to get him to stop.

"Go away, Dom." My voice is raspy from sleep, my

words lacking the snap I want them to have, mostly due to the exhaustion weighing me down.

"Please, Kitten. I'm so sorry. I know I was out of line. Will you come out so we can talk? I…I'm so embarrassed." His voice catches on the last word, like he might be holding back a sob.

The remorse in his voice thaws the icy chill surrounding my heart, but I still take my time freshening up by splashing cool water on my face at the sink. My eyes are red and puffy from crying, dark circles under them highlighting how little sleep I had curled up on the bathroom floor. I lean in closer, trying to find evidence of our fight—from when he put his hand around my neck—but there is nothing. I can still feel the ghost of his touch closing off my airway, but there is no visible evidence of what he did. Maybe it really wasn't as bad as I remember. Maybe it was my panic that caused my inability to breathe. He was drunk when he got home, and he did say he wanted to make me feel good. God…maybe I was the bitch in this situation?

When I open the bathroom door, Dom is sitting on the end of the bed with his face buried in his hands. When he looks up at me, I take in a sharp inhale of breath. He looks as rough as I feel. His eyes are red-rimmed and shadowed by dark circles, much like my own. Dark stubble dusts his normally smooth jawline, and his hair is sticking out in every direction, like he's been running his hands through it. Before I can say a word, he's up and on me, wrapping me in a hug so tight I can barely breathe, his face buried against my neck.

"I'm so sorry, baby. I was an ass. Can you forgive me?" I feel something wet and warm against my skin, and I realize it is his tears. The last of my resistance melts, washed away by the remorseful tears he spills as he begs for my forgiveness. "You're the best thing in my life, and I got scared when I thought Kai was going to try to take you from me. I promise I won't ever do anything like that again. It was completely out of character for me. I just had too much to drink last night and lost control of myself. You know who I am. You know I love you." Dom leans back so he can look me in the eye as he cups my face. "Can you forgive me, Kitten? Please?" It's the please that does it. The please and the tear slowly trailing down his cheek until it meets the corner of his mouth, stopping there, glimmering in the morning light streaming in from the windows.

I nod, my cheeks damp from my own tears. "I forgive you, Pumpkin."

The relief that floods out of Dominick's body is palpable as he tugs me back into his embrace, peppering my forehead and hair with kisses.

"Hey, I hope you don't mind, but I called the coffee shop and said you wouldn't be at work today. I took the day off too. I thought we could spend the day together."

"Dom, you shouldn't do that. I don't want to leave Marie to work alone when she's so far along..." I try to push out of his hold, but Dom holds me close, rubbing soothing circles on my back.

"It's okay. She said some dude named André was working today. Don't worry; just let me make up for being an asshole, please."

"Okay, you win." I lean back so I can look up at him and give him a small smile. Dom's face lights up like the sun before he leans in and kisses me so deeply it makes me breathless. This is the man I fell in love with. The man I trust with my heart. The man who makes me feel cherished.

THE REST of the day passes in a blur of romantic gestures and sweet moments. After we make up, Dom tucks me into bed so I can nap while he makes us breakfast. Then we spend the day wrapped up in each other in bed, watching movies, eating junk food, and cuddling. Dom doesn't try to push for more than the occasional kiss, content to hold me like I'm his most precious treasure. For dinner he runs out to pick up food from my favorite Thai restaurant, and he even makes a detour to return with the most decadent-looking cheesecake I've ever seen.

By the time we fall asleep, me tucked into Dom's body as the little spoon, surrounded by his spicy masculine scent, the events of the previous night feel like nothing more than a bad dream.

BY THE TIME the weekend rolls around, my fight with Dom is a distant memory. There are no more appearances by the possessive controlling side of him, and my realtor let me know someone made an offer on our house that was unbelievably generous. When I walk up to Mom's apartment door at Whispering Grove, it's with a lightness to my step I haven't felt in weeks.

"Hey, Sweet Pea! I'm so glad you're here; come in!"

When Mom opens the door, I'm taken aback by how happy she looks. There is an excited light shining in her eyes that I haven't seen since the accident.

"Hey, Mom..." I trail off as she pulls me into her apartment, like a kid eager to show a new friend their bedroom. There is greenery everywhere. Potted plants sit on every flat surface. Small succulents crowd her dining table, while leafy ferns hang from the ceiling. A large monstera sits by the sliding glass door leading out to the balcony.

"I'm so glad you came by. Come, come, tell me how it's been living with Dom."

I follow Mom to the kitchenette and sit at the island while she sets to work making us some tea.

"Um, it's good. I'm mostly unpacked. When did you become a plant lady?" I inspect a plant with little pearl-like buds dripping over the edge like a necklace.

"Oh, it's one of my assignments from Dr. Chapman. I'm supposed to build a daily routine with activities that have a lot of repetition to them. It's supposed to help improve my memory. I decided to take up plant care. It's repetitive, soothing, and each one has their own different needs, so I get to work on remembering the details of caring for the different plants. I've also taken up knitting. By the time you and Dom have a baby, I'll already be a proper Grandma!"

I wince at her mention of having a baby, but she misses

it while she pours the hot water into mugs. I won't burst her bubble by mentioning I have zero desire to get pregnant any time soon.

"So…I take it you like it here?" There is uncertainty and hope in my question. I want her to be happy, I do, but a small part of me is hurt by the thought that she may be happier now than before, when it was just the two of us.

Mom turns around to look at me when she answers, a knowing look in her eyes. She takes my hands in hers before responding. "I do like it here, Serena. My therapy sessions have been helping, and I'm making some new friends already. I'm building a life that feels like my own again. A life that doesn't make me feel like a burden." Guilt stabs in my chest at her words.

"Mom, you were never a burden. If I ever made you feel that way—"

She cuts me off by putting a finger to my lips. "No, baby, you never did. I did. I made myself feel like a burden. Daughters shouldn't have to take care of their mothers. Not at this age. I shouldn't have let you work yourself into the ground like that when you still have so much life to experience. This place is good for me. It's giving me the chance to find out who I am now, after the accident. Let it be good for you too. It's time for you to find out who you are, now that you can focus on yourself."

The relief I feel at her words causes an uncomfortable feeling to swirl in my gut, so I decide to make a joke in hopes she won't pick up on my conflicted emotions. "Well, it's a good thing you like it here, because we accepted an offer on the house. You're stuck here now." It works and

Mom laughs at my joke. Once we have our tea, Mom gives me a tour, introducing me to all of her plant babies.

"This is Monty. He's a monstera and loves living indoors. Supposedly he's a hardy plant and isn't too delicate, so they thought he would be a good one for me to start with."

"Hold up. You named your plants?" I try my best to hold back my laughter, but Mom doesn't miss a beat.

"Yes, and I talk to them too. I recount my day to them, tell them stories about your dad, do some of my memory exercises with them. The doctor says saying things out loud is just as important as writing down things in my journal."

"Alright, so you're now a crazy plant lady who talks to herself…coolcoolcool…you sure you're doing okay here?" This time the laugh I was trying to contain escapes when Mom smacks me on the arm.

"Hush, you brat. You'll be singing a different tune when I start remembering things again and can move out on my own." I can't help it when her words cause a small seed of hope to sprout in my chest. All I've ever wanted was our lives to go back to how they were before the accident, and if selling the house so Mom can get the professional help she needs here is the price I have to pay, I will gladly do it.

CHAPTER THIRTY-SIX

SERENA

"Are you sure you don't want me to go with you?" Marie asks as I ditch my Brewed Awakening apron and grab my purse out of the small cabinet we have in the back to store our personal belongings. It's the day of my IUD insertion, and Marie is hovering around me like a mother hen.

"I'm a big girl, M. I can take myself to the doctor."

"You should at least have Dom go with you so he can drive you home in case you're in pain after."

I actually haven't mentioned my IUD appointment to Dominick, but I don't tell her that, afraid of the can of worms it might open. He and I haven't spoken any more about the night of the pregnancy scare, but with the fervent way he's been making love to me every chance he gets, I've been hesitant to bring up using a more effective form of birth control, worried about the fight it might trigger between us. I know he's eager to start a family, but I'm hoping he will be fine just practicing while I finish getting my degree. What he doesn't know won't hurt him.

"Oh, he couldn't get off today. I promise, it's no big deal. I took some Tylenol, and I'm heading home after, so I'll be fine."

"Alright, if you say so. I'll see you next week. Text me if you need anything!"

SITTING in the doctor's office waiting room, my phone buzzes in my pocket with a text notification.

> Tall, Dark and Pumpkin Spiced: Hey, Kitten, I stopped by the coffee shop to see if you wanted to grab lunch, but you weren't there. Where are you?

> Me: Sorry, I have an appointment. Must've forgot to tell you. Raincheck?

> Tall, Dark and Pumpkin Spiced: What kind of appointment?

I bite my lower lip, debating on what to tell Dom. This isn't something I planned on getting into with him over text.

> Me: You know, girl stuff. I'll be home in a couple of hours. Love you.

I add on a few hearts and a kissing emoji to make my

text seem less evasive. Just then a heavy-set woman with fiery red hair, in a set of navy scrubs, pokes her head into the waiting room to call my name.

"Malcolm?"

"That's me." I close out of the texting app and tuck my phone back into my pocket so I can follow the nurse back to the exam room before I can let my nerves get the best of me. She leads me through a set of maze-like corridors with doors that all look the same before stopping in front of an open one with a yellow flag flipped out next to it. There's a scale she has me step on before handing me a little plastic specimen cup.

"Hi, sweetie, I'm Angela. I'll be the nurse during your exam. First, I'll need you to pee in the cup so we can do a quick pregnancy test. There are wipes to use in the bathroom; leave the cup in there once you're done. When you're finished, you'll come in here, strip down and put on the gown. It will open to the back. I'll be back with Dr. Torres, and she will do a quick pelvic exam before inserting the IUD. Do you have any questions?" I shake my head, and Angela leaves me to my business.

Sitting on the exam table, wearing the stiff patient gown, I can hear my phone buzzing in the pocket of my jeans like there is an incoming call. After two seconds of quiet, the buzzing starts up again. "What the hell?" I slide off the table and fish my phone out of my jeans pocket to see an incoming call from Dom, and a notification for a missed call from him. Before I get the chance to answer it, a soft knock at the door lets me know the doctor is here.

This time I shut my phone off completely before putting it away and climb back onto the exam table.

"Hi there, I'm Dr. Torres. You must be Serena?" I reach out to shake the young doctor's hand. She looks like she could be in her late twenties, tops, with her gorgeous tawny skin, warm honey-colored eyes and a kind smile that must put so many patients at ease, but she carries herself with the confidence of a woman who's been in her line of work a long time.

"Nice to meet you, Doctor. You came highly recommended by my friend, Marie."

"Ah, yes, Marie, pregnant with the baby yeti. She told me she was sending a friend of hers my way." I laugh at Dr. Torres' completely accurate description of my friend and find myself immediately at ease in her presence. "Alright, so I'm going to do a quick pelvic exam before we get started. This will likely be pretty uncomfortable for you since you haven't gone through childbirth yet, so feel free to take some ibuprofen after to help with the pain. You'll feel a slight pinch and maybe some cramping afterward. You may also experience some spotting or light bleeding for a few weeks after the IUD has been inserted, but that is completely normal."

Once Angela the nurse joins us, we get started. The whole procedure takes ten minutes tops and winds up being exactly how Dr. Torres described it. A slight pinch with some cramping afterward.

"Alright, so this will be good for the next five years. If you experience any sharp pelvic pain or uncontrolled bleeding, contact my office, okay? You don't have to stop and check out—you're free to go." I nod my agreement, and she leaves me to get dressed.

On my way out of the clinic, I'm busy looking over the discharge instructions given to me, so I don't see who is standing by my car in the parking lot. It's not until I'm in his shadow that I look up and see Dom leaning against my driver's side door, his face wearing a thunderous expression.

"Is there something you need to tell me, Serena?" His voice is cold and sends a chill of fear down my spine. Shock doesn't even begin to describe how I feel, finding him standing by my car waiting for me outside of the clinic.

"What are you doing here, Dom?"

"I asked you first, Kitten. Is there something you need to tell me?" He steps forward, looming over me, forcing my back against the car, caging me in with his body. He's so close to me, his belt with his holster presses into the soft, tender flesh of my now cramping belly. I can feel the heat of his anger radiating from him.

"I told you—I had an appointment. I just got done. Why are you here?" Dom ignores my question, zeroing in on the paper in my hand with my appointment summary. He snatches it from my grasp and begins to read it.

"Hey! That's mine!" I try to grab it, but he captures my hands in one of his while he holds onto the paper and continues reading.

"What. The. Fuck." The fury that flashes in his eyes when he looks at me sends me cowering, pressing my back further into the cool metal of my car. "Why did you have an appointment for an IUD insertion without telling me about it? Don't you think this is something we should have discussed together first?" His grip on my wrists tightens to the point of being painful, and I let out a whimper in response.

"Dom, you're hurting me." My eyes burn with unshed tears. I try to pull out of his hold but his grip is vise-like. The more I try to squirm free, the tighter it becomes.

"I asked you a question. Don't you think this is a decision we needed to make together?" This time Dom asks his question against my ear, speaking in a tone that can only be described as a growl. Before I can respond, he pulls me away from the car, only to open the door to the back seat and toss me in unceremoniously. By the time I get myself upright, he's in the driver's seat, pulling out of the parking lot, steering my car back towards home.

"What the fuck, Dom? What are you doing?" My fear gives way to righteous indignation, but Dom ignores my question. He doesn't say another word to me on the drive back to his house, and by the time we pull into the driveway, it feels like my heart is going to explode out of my chest. I move to get out of the car before Dom can reach me, but I find myself trapped by the childproof lock. Dominick yanks the door open, grabs me by my arm and jerks me out of the car. I flop out of the vehicle like a rag doll and do my best to stay on my feet as he marches me up the stairs of the front porch.

"Dom, you're hurting me! Let go!" I try my best to wrench out of his hold, but it is useless.

"I'm hurting you? I'm hurting YOU? *I'M* HURTING

YOU?" Dom's voice gets louder and scarier as he drags me by the arm, nearly jerking my shoulder out of its socket. "I'm not the one who started this battle, Serena. Maybe you should've had an adult conversation with me before you unilaterally made a decision that affects both of us!" In a fluid movement, Dominick yanks open the front door and throws me through it. I land on the floor in a heap, my knees slamming into the hardwood. I barely catch myself before my face meets the same fate.

I scramble back, trying to escape his wrath. He looks like a dark god in his all-black police uniform as he stalks toward me. I don't make it far before he pulls me up by my hair, tearing a pained yelp from my throat. "Dom, stop! Please! I'm sorry! I didn't think you'd mind!" My vision is blurred with tears, my words gasping sobs as I scratch at his hands, trying to make him let go.

"You didn't think I'd care?! After everything I've done for you? After everything I've done for your mom?! This is how you repay me? Go behind my back and take away my choice to have a child with you? I thought we were starting our lives together, Serena?! How could you do this to me?" With my hair wrapped around his fist like a leash, Dominick leads me up the stairs, leaving me no choice but to follow along unless I want him to rip it out by the root.

"Dom, it's an IUD! It's not permanent!" I scream at the top of my voice, trying to talk reason into him. When we make it to the bedroom, he tosses me onto the bed, and I scramble back, pressing my back against the headboard, trying to put distance between us.

"You saw how devastated I was when you found out

you weren't pregnant. Then you decided to turn around and make extra sure it can't happen? Are you just using me to escape your mom but have no real intention to make a life with me? Are you fucking playing me, Serena? I KILLED A MAN FOR YOU. I *SAVED* YOU. Is having my child really that fucking awful of a fate to you?" He is in my face now, his large hand wrapped around my throat, cutting off my air while holding me in place, forcing me to look him in the eye. "I love you. How can you betray me like this?"

I can't respond while he chokes me, so I do the only thing I can think of to try to calm him down. I cup his face in both of my hands and pull him to me, pressing a wet, salty kiss against his lips. I pray he feels the apology in my kiss and accepts it. The punishing grip he has on my airway lessens. I open my mouth to gasp in some air, and he takes the opportunity to dive in, shoving his tongue into my mouth, taking control of the kiss, devouring me with his intensity. Just when I think his anger has begun to ebb away, his hold on my throat tightens again, cutting off my air. My eyes fly open in surprise when he pulls away, and the look he gives me is both wicked and terrifying.

"Oh, Kitten. If you think you're going to avoid a punishment by distracting me with your mouth, you don't know me very well at all. You lied to me. You betrayed me. You're going to have to do better than a kiss if you want to earn my forgiveness."

Black spots dance in my vision, and my lungs begin to burn from lack of oxygen. Weakly, I slap at his arm—trying to get him to let go—but he doesn't even react. With his free hand, Dominick undoes the button on my jeans and starts yanking them off. I dig my nails into his arm holding me in place, tears and snot making my face a mess. My head begins to pound from lack of oxygen, and I'm terrified he won't let up before he chokes me out completely. I don't want to know what he will do to me if I'm not awake to stop him.

Just as he gets my jeans down to my ankles, his work phone comes to life, its obnoxiously loud ring bringing him out of his rage-induced fog. I lie there, held in place, trembling like a lamb cornered by a wolf, waiting to see what he will do. Just when I think I'm going to lose the battle to stay conscious, Dominick lets go of my throat, allowing cool air to rush into my lungs. I begin gasping and choking, afraid I'm going to vomit. I do my best to swallow back the bile, afraid to anger him even more by losing my lunch all over his bed.

While Dominick answers his phone, I lie there, shivering from the adrenaline crash, trying my best to calm my racing heart. I listen in on Dominick's call, wondering what would be so important that he would interrupt his assault for a phone call.

"Hey, man, sorry I ditched you." He goes quiet, listening to whomever is on the other end of the call. "Yeah, I found her. I had to give her a ride back home after a doctor's appointment. Can you come pick me up?" More silence while he listens to the caller. "Nah, she'll be fine. She isn't going anywhere else today." Dominick levels a look at me when he says the words, the dead look in his eyes sending another wave of terror crashing over me. "Yeah, I'll see you in ten."

Dominick hangs up the phone and begins tucking in his uniform shirt back into his pants. It must've come undone during our fight. I remain still, afraid if I move, I will reawaken the monster that resides under his skin.

"I am needed back at the station. Eric is coming to pick me up. You're going to stay here until I get back. This conversation is not over."

I'm too stunned by the sudden change in his demeanor to speak, so I nod dumbly. I don't move from my spot on the bed until I hear the front door open and close with Dom's departure. Then I rush to the bathroom to vomit up all of the terror I experienced in the last half hour.

CHAPTER THIRTY-SEVEN

SERENA

I don't know how long I lie on the bathroom floor, numb from the shock of Dominick's anger. Eventually, I manage to drag myself upright and check my reflection in the mirror. Once again, there is no visible evidence of Dominick's assault, but the ghost of his punishing hold still lingers on my skin. Deciding I have no desire to risk facing his wrath when he returns home, I head downstairs to leave. I don't know where I will go, only that I can't remain here.

I scan the first floor, looking for my car keys, but they are nowhere to be found. Dread pools in my gut as I desperately hunt for the keys to my escape. When I determine they are not in the house, I head out to the car hoping against hope that Dominick was so focused on punishing me that he left the keys in the ignition. The small flicker of hope is quickly snuffed out when I get to the car and find it locked, keys missing, along with my purse that had been left in the backseat.

"Fuck!" I smack my palm against the window, frustration and terror bubbling up inside of me. Dominick's house is secluded, with no close neighbors, and it is far enough from town that walking will take hours. Without my purse, I have no phone to call for a ride and no money. Panic begins to take root when I realize how few options I have. Do I hide? Do I walk and hope someone picks me up? Do I stay and pray Dominick comes home in a better temper, ready to apologize for his outburst?

The thought of staying and facing him causes bile to rise up in my throat. I can't do it. I can't stay. Without thinking about it, I start walking down Dominick's long gravel drive, heading to the main road. I'll hitchhike if I have to, but there is no way in hell I am staying here a minute longer.

Ten minutes into my walk, I'm cussing myself for not thinking to grab a jacket. The air is brisk, and the sun is beginning to set, signaling a drop in temperature will be coming soon. I am so consumed by my thoughts, I don't immediately notice the car driving past me, slowing down to pull over on the shoulder. It isn't until the flashing blue and red lights come on that I realize they've stopped a few yards in front of me. My feet freeze to the ground, fear keeping me rooted in one spot. If it's Dominick, I don't know what I'm going to do. I squint against the strobing lights, trying to make out who is getting out of the police cruiser.

"Serena? Is that you?" My knees go weak with relief when the familiar voice calling out to me doesn't belong to my fiancé. Dane stops directly in front of me, blocking the glare from the lights, looking at me with concern dancing in his eyes. "Why are you out here walking when it's almost dark? This road isn't safe to walk on without any sidewalks. You don't even have a coat. Come on—get in my car. I'll give you a ride."

Dane grabs my elbow to steer me to his cruiser, but I hesitate, my feet refusing to move while my brain tries to process my options. He turns, giving me a confused look. "Let's get you in the car where it's warm. Where are you heading?" He gives my arm another tug, and I follow him, my legs working mechanically while my brain tries to come up with an answer to his question.

Where am I going? Can I tell him what Dom did? Can his partner be trusted? After Eric sent Dom that picture of Kai and I hugging, setting off Dom's first violent outburst, I don't feel like I can trust that either man would believe me. Lost in my own thoughts, I don't realize what's happening until I'm tucked into the back of Dane's cruiser with the door shut, trapping me in. My heart begins to pound in my chest, panic rising when I realize I can't get out. Where there should be a handle to open the door, there is only flat plastic, and a steel grid separates the back seat from the front. Dane stands outside of the car making a call on his cellphone, and my heart sinks. I watch helplessly as he turns his back to me, walking a few feet away so I can't overhear his conversation.

Minutes later, he hangs up and stalks back to the vehicle, keeping his gaze trained on the ground, avoiding my pleading stare in the window. I hold my breath when he takes his seat behind the steering wheel, unsure whose side he is on. Dane glances up in the rearview mirror, conflict clearly written across his features. "I'm gonna give you a ride to the station. Dominick will be waiting for you there." My stomach plummets at his declaration, and my eyes burn from fresh tears forming. "He mentioned you guys had an argument. Even if you're mad at him, you shouldn't put yourself in danger by walking in the cold and dark alone. That isn't how you prove a point."

An argument? He told Dane we had an argument? Is that what choking your fiancée to the point of almost blacking out is to Dominick? A fucking argument? "He said we had an argument?" My voice is shrill, incredulous even. My blinding fear is momentarily replaced by anger at how flippantly Dominick dismissed what he did to me.

Dane responds by flicking off the strobe lights and steering the car back onto the road. He's on a mission to deliver me back into the arms of the monster who was once my savior.

The closer we get to the police station, the more paralyzed by fear I become. Dominick is going to be livid about my escape attempt. Will he keep his anger in check while we have an audience? Can I attempt to get help at the police station? Would anyone believe me over him? I've seen his many awards and commendations decorating the walls of his home. His reputation is spotless. Dane hasn't said anything else to me since we started driving, but the tension radiating from him is palpable. He doesn't seem completely comfortable with the situation, but he is also clearly not going to get in the middle of it.

When we pull into the lot, I suck in a breath when my

eyes land on Dominick leaning against his car, arms crossed, a cold mask of indifference on his face. A cold sweat breaks out along my hairline as I frantically try to come up with a plan to get away. Maybe if I make a big enough scene, he will be forced to play nice and let me go? He can't choke me or scream at me in public without giving up his dark secrets. I settle on that plan of action, prepared to become a screaming banshee as soon as he opens the door to retrieve me.

My plan dies a swift death when Dominick throws a wrench into it by slipping into the role of the concerned fiancé. Tears shimmer in his eyes, and his voice sounds relieved as he declares, "There you are! God, I was so worried about you." My stunned confusion allows Dominick to pull me into a hug so tight it makes it almost impossible to breathe. My body is stiff and unyielding in his hold; my skin crawls under his touch. Into my ear he whispers, "Be a good kitten. Your *friend* is currently at a protest, and I've got eyes on him. We wouldn't want anything to happen to him if it were to become a not-so-peaceful protest." His threat makes my blood run cold in terror. "Nod if you understand." Weakly, I bob my head in confirmation, and Dominick pulls back, a vicious smile playing across his lips.

"Come on, Kitten. I'm done for the day; let's go get some dinner." Dominick glances over at Dane who is looking at us, brows pulled together in what almost looks like concern. "Thanks, man, for picking my girl up. She can get kind of emotional at times, and I didn't want her wandering off, getting herself hurt to prove a point to me.

I've got it from here." Realizing he has been dismissed, Dane jerks a nod at Dominick before turning and heading into the police station, leaving me alone with my own personal monster.

Dominick doesn't say another word as he uses a bruising grip to drag me to his car. I don't fight back or complain, fear for Kai's safety ensuring my compliance. When we are both settled in the car, he speaks, his tone back to being cold and unamused. "Did you really think you were going to get away, Serena? I thought you were a smart girl."

His comment cuts, causing fresh tears to spring to my eyes. I keep my head down, blurry vision focused on my trembling hands sitting in my lap. Frustrated by my lack of response, Dominick grasps my hair in a punishing grip, turning my head, forcing me to look at him. "I asked you a question, Kitten."

"I...I...was scared. You scared me. I-I was afraid of what you'd do when you came back." My words are punctuated with sobs, my terror flowing freely now that we are alone.

"And you thought running away would save you?" Dom shakes his head and tsks like I'm a child who just told him a fantastical story. "You never have to be afraid of me, Kitten. Not as long as you do what I say. I told you before: you're mine. I take care of what's mine. I also don't ever lose what belongs to me." He leans in, capturing my lips forcefully. When I refuse to reciprocate, he pulls my hair so hard it feels like he's going to rip it out at the root, forcing my mouth to open to let out a cry of pain. He deepens the kiss, invading my mouth with his tongue. Pulling away, he licks the salty tears from my lips, the devilish smile that used to make me weak in the knees tugging his lips up at the corner. "God, I love the way your tears taste."

On the drive back home, I finally work up the courage to ask him, "How did you know I left?" My voice and body are still trembling. I don't know if I'll ever not be afraid again.

Dom lets out an amused snort like I made a funny joke. "I have motion-activated security cameras all over my property. Do you really think I'd leave something as precious as you unsupervised and unguarded? Not on your life."

CHAPTER THIRTY-EIGHT

KAI

I'm sitting in the library going through pictures I took at the protest over the weekend, trying to decide which ones to submit to the local paper. I got some excellent crowd shots and more than a few of a woman giving an impassioned speech seeking police reform. Her son was shot during a routine traffic stop. My heart clenches as I find one focused on her face, her expression equal parts fury at the injustice of it all and grief over the loss of her son. In the background, I can make out the blurry outlines of the police—all kitted out in riot gear on the perimeter— lending an ominous juxtaposition to the emotion pouring out of her. I decide this photo is front page material and send it to my contact in the newsroom at the Birch Falls Times.

The buzzing of an incoming call on my phone draws my attention away from my work. It's a local number I don't recognize, and it has me wondering if Marcus already got my email and saw the pic. I answer it while continuing to scroll through the rest of the images from the protest. "Yeah, Kai here."

"Kai, honey, it's Laura."

I sit up, my attention fully on the woman on the other end of the call. I haven't spoken to Laura since her move to Whispering Grove, and the nervousness in her voice has me on full alert.

"What's up, Ms. Laura? Everything okay?"

"Have you talked to Reenie lately? She was supposed to come visit this weekend, but she didn't. She hasn't called either. I just was wondering if she had something else going on and forgot?"

I can hear the worry and hurt in her voice that Laura is trying to mask. Her question causes a pit to open up in my stomach. Serena wasn't in class today either.

"You're...sure she didn't come?" I ask hesitantly, trying not to offend Laura by calling her memory into question. She lets out a frustrated sigh.

"Yes, I'm sure. I always write down when we speak or see each other so I can keep up with what's going on in her life. It's not like her to not at least call to tell me she can't make it. I tried calling her, but her phone went straight to voicemail."

"Right, um, she wasn't in class today either. Maybe she's sick?" I don't believe the words coming out of my mouth, but I don't want to give Laura more reason to worry until I know what's going on.

"Yeah...maybe you're right. Do you mind checking on her? I'd call Dom, but I don't have his number."

I can tell Laura doesn't want to bother me, so I do my best to put her at ease.

"Yeah, yeah, no problem. I need to hook up with her for a project in class anyway so I'll reach out to her. I'll make sure she calls you when I talk to her."

"Thanks, honey. Tell your mom and dad I said hello."

I'm already packing up my laptop before we hang up, the burning need to find my friend spurring on my movements, despite Dom's previous threats to stay away from her playing in the back of my mind.

MY FIRST STOP is Brewed Awakening to see if Serena went to work today. Marie is behind the counter looking frazzled and way more pregnant than any person should. Serena might have been on to something when she joked that Marie was pregnant with a baby yeti. When Marie sees me, she manages to flash me a tired but friendly smile.

"Hey Kai. What can I get you?"

"Actually, I was looking for Serena. Did she come to work today? She missed class, and we were supposed to meet up to study." I make up a lie, trying to get a feel for how much Marie knows without raising too much suspicion. I don't want it to get back to Dominick that I'm looking for Serena without a plausible reason.

Marie lets out a frustrated sigh before answering. "She sent a text this morning saying she was sick and probably wouldn't be in all week. I hope she's okay, but man, her timing sucks. I was seriously considering starting my maternity leave this week, but I can't leave Eddie and Marge in the lurch like that. Lord knows if they have to rely on André, nobody in Birch Falls will get the right coffee order."

"I heard that!" André hollers from the kitchen on the other side of the passthrough window.

"Good! I meant for you to hear it!" Marie rolls her eyes at me, ignoring André's indignant huff behind her. Deciding I'm not in the mood to get burned by a pregnant woman's wrath, I redirect the conversation.

"Do you have her new address? I'll drop by the notes from class so she doesn't fall behind. I'd ask her, but her phone is off and going to voicemail."

"Yeah, I think she changed it for payroll. Let me go check." When Marie returns with Serena's new address on a slip of paper, I am out the door on a mission to rescue my friend no matter what it takes.

DOMINICK'S HOUSE is located outside of town, secluded on a large lot surrounded by trees. After parking in the drive-way, I send a quick text to my parents with a pin for my location, just in case. Seeing only Serena's car present, gives me hope that she's here alone. I don't trust the asshole cop not to start some shit if he's here, but I refuse to leave without speaking to Serena myself. He can fucking arrest me for all I care—I just need to make sure she's okay.

"ReRe! You here?" I bang on the door loudly, hoping she realizes it's me at the door. The memory of how broken she looked last time we saw each other haunts me, lending a frantic energy to my knocking. "ReRe! It's Kai. Can you open up? Your mom asked me to check on you!" I press my ear to the door, listening for any signs of life coming from inside the house. I hear the faint shuffle of footsteps. The sound is light, almost timid. Definitely not Dominick. "Serena, I can hear you. Can you please come talk to me?"

The sound of the lock disengaging sends relief flooding through my system, but that feeling is quickly squashed by the scared, haunted face appearing in the small gap she allows when she opens the door. Her eyes are bloodshot, streaks of tears staining her cheeks. The look of absolute terror in her eyes is what makes my blood run cold.

"Kai! What are you doing? You shouldn't be here!" Her warning is delivered in a panicked whisper like she's afraid of waking a sleeping dragon.

"Your mom called me. She was worried about you and wanted me to check on you. Can you let me in so we can talk?" The only way to describe the look on Serena's face at my suggestion is pure unbridled terror.

"I'm fine, Kai. Please, you need to go now. Dom will be home any minute. I'll call my mom later, okay?" She moves to shut the door, but I shove my foot into the opening before she can shut me out of her life again. I am not backing down this time. Not without a fight. Serena is clearly scared and in danger and I refuse to let her deal with this alone. The move to prevent her from shutting the door surprises Serena enough that she takes a step back. I take the opportunity to push my way in, hoping if I can get her to talk to me, I can convince her to leave. What I see when I finally get a good look breaks my heart into a thousand pieces.

Serena stands before me in a tank top and shorts pajama set that more closely resembles lingerie than the normal pajamas she prefers. It is also wildly seasonably inappropriate and goosebumps erupt all across her bare skin. She crosses her arms over her chest and ducks her head like she's trying to hide herself from me, but it isn't enough. I see the angry purple-red bruises dotting her biceps and her thighs, the size and shape of fingertips. The more I look, the more of the disgusting, punishing marks I find, dotting her chest and neck. My vision goes red from anger. I reach out for her, ready to drag her to safety if I have to, but Serena pulls away before I can reach her, eyes wide with terror.

"No, Kai! Please, you need to leave. You can't be here; Dom will kill you if he catches you." Tears shimmer in her eyes as her gaze darts around the room like she's waiting for him to jump out of the shadows.

"The fuck I will, ReRe. I am *not* leaving you here with him! Are you kidding me? What did he do to you? You're covered in bruises." This time Serena doesn't pull away when I gently grab her hands, pulling her arms away from her body so I can take in the full scope of her injuries. I feel like I'm going to throw up at the sight of her trembling, battered and bruised body. The guilt I feel for letting this happen to her causes bile to rise up in my throat. Serena's face crumples as a sob escapes her. I pull her into my arms, holding her as tight as I dare while my own hot tears slide down my cheeks and land in her hair.

"I'm so scared, Kai… He's not who I thought he was. I fucked up. God, I fucked up so bad."

I squeeze her in my arms, trying to comfort her without hurting her more. "Shh, no you didn't. He's the one who fucked up by hurting you. I'm going to fucking kill him." I don't recognize the cold fury lacing the tone of my words, but I know without a doubt I mean every word I say. I hold Serena for as long as I dare, but I know every minute we waste gets us closer to being caught by Dominick.

"Come on, ReRe. Let me get you out of here and some-where safe." Serena looks up at me, fear shining bright in her eyes. Her mouth opens to tell me no, but I put my finger on her full lips, shushing her before the word makes it past them. "I am not leaving without you, so get that out of your thick skull right now. Get your shit so we can go. I am not going to let him put his fucking hands on you ever again. We good?" I feel Serena's head nod more than see it, but it's enough affirmation for me to remove my finger so she can talk.

"He took my purse, keys and phone to work. I've been trapped here since Friday. He wouldn't let me go to work or class today. I don't know if he will ever let me go back."

The broken, defeated inflection to her voice stokes the fire of rage burning inside of me, strengthening my resolve to see her to safety.

"Aight then, let's get the fuck out of here."

Serena doesn't protest when I take her by the hand and lead her out the door, away from this nightmare.

CHAPTER THIRTY-NINE

KAI

I turn left out of Dominick's drive and head away from town. If he finds out Serena left, there will be no safe place for her in Birch Falls. Not when he can send his cop buddies an APB to look for her. No, we need to be far away from Birch Falls while we come up with a game plan. I glance over at Serena and see her staring vacantly out the passenger window, tears silently trailing down her cheeks. I reach over and take her hand in mine, giving it a reassuring squeeze. "I've got you, ReRe. He's not going to hurt you ever again. I swear my life on it." Serena doesn't respond right away, just continues to stare out the window, so I leave her be while I try to figure out where to go.

I dismiss the possibility of staying with friends or relatives. It would be too easy for Dom to trace us that way, and I don't want to land anyone else on the wrong side of the police. I don't even feel comfortable driving my car right now, the memory of the last time he pulled me over fresh in my mind. We need to get off the main roads and somewhere secluded quick, before he realizes she's gone.

"He's not going to let me go, Kai." Serena's soft voice, barely audible over the hum of the tires on the road, pulls me from my thoughts. She sounds so broken and scared, it breaks my heart all over again.

"I've already got you away from him. There's no way he's getting you back now." There is steel in my voice, and I mean every word of what I say.

"Do you really think he will just throw up his hands and let me run off? He's the police, Kai! He's already threatened to have you arrested if he catches you near me. What do you think he's going to do when he sees his security footage and finds out I left with you? You should take me back before he has all of Birch Falls PD looking for you." The resignation in Serena's words is like a knife to my gut.

"ReRe, let's get one thing straight. I don't give a fuck what he threatened to do to me. I only care about what he did to *you*. I will not hand you back to that piece of shit abuser. We are going to find a place to lay low and make a plan, okay? Just trust me to take care of you. Please, ReRe." Serena lets out a small sniffle as she wipes away more tears and nods her head. "Alright, good. Get my phone and see what you can find for hotels that are at least an hour away. Preferably away from the main roads."

An hour outside of town—up in the mountains off the Parkway—we find a small motel with scenic views that seems to do most of its business during the summer and fall. Now that the trees are bare and Christmas is close, most of the parking lot is empty. I pull around to the far side of the building, parking as far away from the road as possible.

Turning towards Serena, I lift her chin up gently, directing her gaze from her lap to my face. "I'm gonna go get us a room. I'll be right back. Wait right here, okay?" She presses her lips into a thin line but gives me a subtle nod of assurance that she isn't going to wander off on some self-sacrificing mission. I debate moving the car nearer the motel office so I can see her when I go in, but I don't want to risk anyone driving by seeing it.

The entire time I'm checking in, I'm paranoid that when I return Serena will be gone. I know her, and I know how selfless she is. She doesn't want me to get in the middle between her and Dom, because she's afraid of what he will do to me. What she doesn't realize is nothing he does to me will ever hurt me as much as what he's already done to her.

When I get back to the car, relief floods my system when I find Serena still sitting right where I left her. She's staring out the window into the woods, lost in her own thoughts, so when I open the door, she startles. "Jesus, Kai, you scared me." I give her an apologetic smile in return.

"Sorry, come on. I've got us a room. Let's get inside before you freeze in those tiny pjs. Shit, we should've gotten you some clothes before we left." I kick myself for not thinking of that before dragging her out of the house, but the sight of her covered in bruises had my fight or flight instincts in overdrive. While she gets out of the car and comes around to meet me, I reach in the back, grab-bing one of my hoodies and a backpack with my gym clothes. They're still clean, since I never made it to my workout today, so I can let Serena wear them to stay warm.

When Serena reaches my side, I tug the hoodie over her head before we head to our room. It's too big by two sizes. Serena is dwarfed by the sweatshirt, but she smiles when she tucks her hands into the front pocket. "Ooh, thanks Kai for my new favorite sweatshirt."

"Don't you dare get any ideas, ReRe. That one is mine." I level a stern look at the gorgeous girl in front of me, knowing full well I'm full of shit and more than willing to give her the shirt off my back if she asks for it. She just rolls her eyes at me.

"Sure, whatever you say, Kai."

"Come on, brat. Let's get inside before you freeze." Wrapping my arm around Serena's shoulders, I lead her to our safe haven for the night, feeling slightly better after seeing a glimpse of the girl I know still hiding under the shadows Dom cast over her.

CHAPTER FORTY

SERENA

Entering the motel room and taking in its retro, sixties mod décor causes my body to release some of the tension I've been holding for the past three days. It feels safe here. After Dom lost his shit on me when we got home on Friday night, I've been living in terror of setting off his temper again. I never got my purse or phone or car keys back, so running was out of the question.

I've been biding my time, hoping to earn back his trust enough to gain a chance at freedom. I even let him fuck me when he "apologized" for losing his temper, hoping maybe it would be enough to placate him. Joke's on me. The way things went after that, I realized what an idiot I had been to imagine I was letting him do anything. He considered he had a green light to use me any way he wanted with impunity. Honestly, if Kai hadn't come looking for me, I wasn't sure if Dom would let me return to my life at all.

"I'm sorry we left before we could grab your stuff, but

I've got my gym bag with me, an extra pair of sweats if you want them."

I turn to look at Kai and the way he is holding up his gym bag in offering is almost bashful. Like he feels bad for rescuing me from my abuser with nothing more than the clothes on my back.

"Gosh, Kai. Next time you come to rescue a damsel in distress, be a little more prepared." Kai looks crestfallen and I regret the sarcastic quip as soon as it leaves my lips. He doesn't deserve my anger. He's not the reason I found myself in the clutches of a monster. That was all my dumbass decision-making.

"I'm sorry, Kai. I didn't mean that—"

Kai cuts me off before I can finish. "I don't want to hear that word out of your mouth again, Serena." Kai's stern use of my government name takes me aback. "You have nothing to be sorry about. If you need a punching bag to work your anger out on, then use me. If you need someone to scream at, scream at me. If you need someone to hold you while you break, then let me hold you. But don't you dare apologize for what you are feeling. I've got you ReRe."

Unsure of how to respond, I grab Kai's gym bag instead. "I'm gonna go take a shower. I need to wash Dom's touch off me."

Kai nods and lets me retreat into the bathroom, despite how much he looks like he wants to protest. I'm grateful he allows me some space to get my bearings.

Sequestered in the bathroom, I lock the door behind me. Leaning against the plywood door, I close my eyes, inhaling a deep breath, trying to calm my jittery nerves.

Even though we are well outside of Birch Falls' city limits, I can't help but feel like we are still at risk of being found. When I open my eyes, I see my reflection in the mirror, and it turns my stomach. Dark bruises dot along my arms in some sort of sick dot-to-dot pattern. My throat is ringed in bruises too. My eyes are bloodshot from all the crying I've been doing, and my skin is pale and ashy like I have the flu. In short, I look like shit.

Unable to bear my reflection another moment, I turn to the shower and turn the on water as hot as it will go. I grab Kai's body wash and tie my hair up on my head before stepping under the scalding stream. I don't know how long I stand under the water—trying to scrub the ghost of his touch from my skin—but by the time I'm done, my skin is red and raw.

Leaving the bathroom in a cloud of steam, bundled in Kai's oversize sweats and hoodie, I find him sitting on the bed staring pensively at his phone. He looks up when he hears me enter the room, his face tight with concern.

"What's going on? Did something happen with Dom?" My stomach pitches in worry, scared we have been found already.

"He stopped by my folks' house, looking for me. Didn't tell them why he was looking for me and he didn't mention you, so I think he's keeping it on the DL for now. Ma called me to ask why 'Serena's cop' was looking for me."

My knees go weak at Kai's words, with concern for his parents getting sucked into my relationship drama. "Oh God, Kai. I'm so sorry. I didn't want to get Grace and Luther involved."

Kai raises a displeased eyebrow at me. "What did I say about that word, Serena? Don't worry about them. They're fine. They have plausible deniability. I told them we were safe together and that we aren't in town, but I didn't tell them where we are. I want to keep our whereabouts under wraps until we come up with a game plan."

Taking a seat next to him on the bed, I bury my face in my hands. "What is our plan, Kai? You know he's going to be looking for me. He probably has his cop buddies looking for your car. We can't go back into Birch Falls without him finding out. We don't have any food or clothes. I don't have any ID or money. We are fucked." Kai nudges my leg with his knee in the way he does when he wants my attention.

"I took care of the food while you used up all of the motel's hot water." I follow his line of sight and see a pile of vending machine snacks and several bottles of water on the desk. "It's not much, but we can make do for tonight. Tomorrow I was thinking we could go to Poplar Springs and pick up some supplies…" Kai trails off like he's afraid to finish his thought.

"Pick up some supplies or…" I prod, waiting for him to finish.

"Or go to the hospital and get your injuries documented and file a report."

My blood runs cold at Kai's suggestion. The thought of going to a hospital and talking to someone about what Dom did to me causes my chest to tighten in panic.

"I can't do that, Kai. They won't believe me. Dom is too well known and too well liked. They'll say I'm making it up. Dom will find me and hurt me worse. No…no, that's not an option."

"Hey, ReRe. Calm down. Deep breaths. We don't have to if you're not ready. Okay?" Kai leans down, making sure he can look me in the eye, pulling me out of my panic spiral. "We will do this however you want, ReRe. I won't push you to do something you're not ready for."

I nod at his words as hot tears stream down my cheeks. When did I start crying again?

"C'mere, kid. Let's watch some TV." Kai tugs me against him and positions us so we are facing the TV. I settle into his side as he flips through the channels before settling on a rerun of *Supernatural*. Watching the episode, I can't help notice how much our motel room looks like the ones Sam and Dean stay in on their travels.

"What room do you think Sam and Dean are staying in? Do you think if we told them Dominick was a ghoul, they'd go take care of him for us?"

Kai laughs at my lame attempt at humor, giving my shoulder a squeeze.

"I thought the tall motherfucker standing in front of me at the check-in desk looked familiar." I laugh at his joke and settle in to watch the Winchesters hunt demons. It's like this, wrapped up in Kai's embrace feeling safer than I ever have, that I fall into a dreamless sleep.

CHAPTER FORTY-ONE

SERENA

I wake to the sound of a buzzing phone. The room I'm in is unfamiliar in the dim light of the television. The sunlight streaming in from the window earlier has dimmed to an early evening glow. I'm pressed up against a warm, firm body, and my own stiffens in fear as I try to get my bearings. The arm around my shoulders gives me a brief squeeze before I hear Kai's familiar voice. "Hey there sleepy head. Have a good nap?"

I relax into his hold as the memories from the last few hours come back into focus. Dom leaving me trapped, alone at his house. Kai showing up and stealing me away. Checking into the motel. Falling asleep while watching *Supernatural*. "You were sleeping pretty hard there ReRe. You drooled more than Archie."

"I don't drool!" I push away from Kai's chest and level an offended glare at him.

Kai smirks and gestures to the wet spot on his shirt, right where my face had been resting, causing my cheeks to burn in embarrassment. Kai chuckles as he reaches for his phone. When he sees the number on the caller ID he sits upright, expression turning somber.

"Who is it?" My stomach pitches in worry at his sudden change in demeanor.

"Your mom. Do you want me to answer it?"

I bite my lower lip, debating how to handle this conversation with Mom. Then I remember her worry over me was the reason Kai came to check on me in the first place and nod, giving him the okay to answer. Kai answers the call on speaker and holds the phone between us.

"Hey, Ms. Laura."

"Oh, thank goodness! I was worried you weren't going to answer. Have you talked to Serena? Dom is here saying she isn't at the house, and he can't get in touch with her. He's very worried."

My mouth runs dry at Mom's words, and Kai and I exchange a wide-eyed stare. Dom is with my mom. Panic surges through me at the thought of him being so close to my mother. What will he do? What can he do? He knows I'm with Kai—there's no way he hasn't checked the cameras at his house. How much can we say to her without triggering a reaction from Dom? Is she safe inside the walls of Whispering Grove?

"Kai, are you there?" Mom's voice comes through the speaker, pulling us both from our shocked silence.

"Yeah, Ms. Laura, I'm here. Uh, yeah, I talked to Serena. She's okay, and she's safe. There is no reason to worry." Kai glances at me, his look clearly asking how much he should tell Mom. "Laura? Be careful with Dom. He can't be trusted."

Mom is silent for a beat while she absorbs Kai's words before responding, "Oh, okay. That's wonderful. Tell her I said to give Arianna a hug from me and to enjoy her visit. Have her call me when she gets the chance, okay?"

Kai furrows his brows in confusion, giving me a look that says "do you know what she's on about?", clearly worried about Mom's mental state. I, however, know exactly who she is referring to.

Arianna is her best friend from high school and my surrogate aunt. She was a huge part of our lives, up until she took a travel nursing job to work in a rural hospital desperate for nurses, right before the accident.

She was the person I would go to growing up when I had questions too embarrassing for a teenage girl to talk to her parents about. She helped me navigate getting on birth control before losing my virginity to my first boyfriend. She also would come visit as often as possible and helped as much as she could in the beginning when Mom was adjusting to life post-accident. Now her visits are down to a few times a year thanks to her travelling, but there is no doubt that she will help me if I need it.

Mom is telling me I need to see Arianna if I'm in trouble. She is currently working at a hospital not too far from here. I give Kai an encouraging nod to go along with Mom's lie.

"Will do. Write this in your journal, okay? We'll talk later." Kai hangs up the call, turning his attention to me. "What was that about?"

I tell Kai what I think mom was trying to suggest we do, and he nods his head thoughtfully. "Do you feel safe going to her to report your abuse? I'll take you right now. What hospital is she at?"

I think for a moment, trying to figure out if I do feel safe enough to go to Arianna. I know she will believe me. She will advocate for me. But will her help be enough? The idea of going to a hospital, the bruises littering my skin tangible proof of my stupidity, and being examined under the harsh fluorescent lighting by a stranger sends my stomach rolling.

Kai must sense where my mind is going. Gently he cups my face, making it so that I have to look at him when he says, "None of this is your fault, Serena. *None* of it. Dom tricked you. Manipulated you. Used his charm and pretty-sounding empty promises of a happily ever after to isolate you. Abused his position of power to control you. This is *not* your fault. You did *nothing* wrong."

Kai's face becomes a shapeless blur as tears pool, obscuring my vision. I know he's right. I do. But there is a small, but very loud, part of me that won't stop yelling that I was so stupid for falling for Dom's pretty words when my gut kept screaming "No!" at so many points along the way.

Kai pulls me into him and lets me break, his warm embrace the only thing keeping me together at this point. I don't know how I still have tears left to cry at this point. They don't stop coming but Kai only continues to hold me as I let my grief of the life I lost wash over me.

Eventually, the seemingly never-ending tears do come to an end. When I pull away, Kai's shirt is soaked. "Shit, I'm sor—" I don't even get the word out of my mouth before he's pressing a finger to my lips, hushing me. With a shake of his head, I let my apology die on my lips.

"Let's eat something and come up with a plan, yeah?" Kai motions to the pile of snacks on the desk, and my stomach lets out a loud rumble in agreement.

"Yeah, that sounds good. Let me splash some water on my face." By the time I exit the bathroom, looking mildly less like a puffy-faced chipmunk with allergies, Kai has popped some microwave popcorn and spread a cornucopia of junk food across the desk. I take in the spread of candy bars, fruit candies, trail mix, toaster pastries and popcorn and can't help but laugh. Kai turns when he hears my muffled snort and grasps the back of his neck sheepishly.

"Sorry, options are limited. I tried to get a variety of snacks, but it's not exactly a four-course restaurant meal." My mind flashes back to my first date at that fancy restaurant with the words on the menu I couldn't pronounce and how uncomfortable I was in that element. Seeing Kai doing his best to take care of me, even with such limited options, causes an epiphany to come crashing through me. This is what he does. This is what he has always done. He may not have ever taken me out for a fancy meal or weekend retreat, but he has *always* taken care of me in his own way. I must get too caught up in my head because Kai's brows furrow in concern.

"If this isn't enough, I'll go out to find us some food… I think there's a gas station a few miles down the road. They might have some hot opt—"

I cross the room and steal Kai's move of hushing him with a finger on the lips.

"It's perfect. Thank you." Our eyes connect and the energy between us becomes taut with the electric need that was present the night at the hospital. The reminder of the feeling of his lips on mine causes a flush to creep up my face, but before my mind can get carried away with that memory, Kai's lips turn up in a slight smirk. Without warning he sticks his tongue out and licks my finger like a dog, causing me to squeal in surprise.

"Come on, you need to eat." Kai offers up the bag of popcorn, and I snatch it out of his hands greedily.

We don't talk while we eat. We just stuff ourselves with junk food while only half-watching the *Supernatural* reruns on the TV. I know Kai wants to figure out our next move. I *know* he wants me to report Dom's abuse and get checked out at a hospital, but my mind won't stop spiraling over the what ifs if Dom gets away with it. What if he continues to escalate? What if he hurts my mom? What if he goes after Kai? I have no home to go back to any longer. Where will I live?

"Hey, ReRe, where'd you go?" Kai's hushed question startles me from my thoughts.

"Nowhere...everywhere? I dunno, Kai. I don't know what to do. I'm so scared. He took everything from me and I'm afraid he is going to go after you next..." When my confession leaves my lips, I realize it is my biggest fear. Knowing what Dominick is capable of, him hurting Kai in any way is what scares me most. I guess we have that in common. Our only concern is the other's safety.

"That's why we are going to do this right, ReRe. I'm not going to let him get away with this. We will take it one step at a time, okay?" The certainty in Kai's tone settles my worry some. The conviction in his eyes tells me there is only one option here and he will not stop until Dominick is punished.

I take a deep breath, trying to infuse myself with some of his confidence, and nod my head in agreement. "Okay, so what's the first step?" I look into his eyes, ready to take this leap, putting all of my faith into him.

"Let me document your injuries."

CHAPTER FORTY-TWO

SERENA

"Let me document your injuries."

I stand there for a moment, absorbing Kai's words as shame paralyzes me. I can't stand the thought of him seeing evidence of what Dom did to me. The extent of it. Dom was *so* angry after my attempt at running that he completely lost all pretense of caring about appearances and left marks all over my body. It's why I haven't been able to leave the house for days. He was keeping me in seclusion until the proof of his abuse had faded away.

Sensing my hesitation, Kai steps closer, gently cupping my face in his hands and guiding my eyes to meet his. "Serena, it's important that we can prove what he did to you. The longer we wait, the more the bruising will fade. You're safe here with me. I swear."

Staring into Kai's warm, rich brown gaze, I get lost in a sea of memories. Hot chocolate after snowball fights during the blizzard of 2012. Late night movie marathons. Our between-class lunch dates that he always, always paid for. Study sessions. Kai holding me when I got the worst news of my life the night of my parents' accident. Him being there every single day after to check on me and make sure I was still putting one foot in front of the other. I am safe with Kai. There is no one else on earth who makes me feel safer. Slowly, I nod in agreement.

A look of relief flashes across Kai's face. "Alright, I'm gonna run out to the car and grab my gear. I'll be right back."

When Kai walks out the door, I decide to strip down to my underwear while he is out of the room. I'm afraid I won't have the courage to bare myself to him while he's watching. When Kai comes back, he's looking down at his camera, checking the settings. He doesn't see me standing in the middle of the room mostly naked, save for my bra and panties.

"I know this will be difficult, but we will go as slow…" Kai's words trail off when he looks up and sees me, arms crossed in front of my chest, trembling, trying to hide how exposed I feel. His eyes don't leave my face, and for that, I'm grateful. He is refusing to look until I tell him to.

"Are you sure you're ready, ReRe?" His voice is soft, laced with concern. Kai wants to nail Dominick's ass to the wall, but he doesn't want to hurt me more in the process.

I close my eyes and jerk a nod. Tears sting the backs of my eyelids, but I refuse to let them fall. Dominick has gotten enough of my tears. It's time for me to start taking my power back.

When I open my eyes again, Kai is still staring at my face, waiting for me to give him consent. "Let's do this," I say as I drop my arms, letting them hang by my side. Kai's eyes slowly trail down my body, his face growing darker and angrier as he follows the pattern of red-purple bruises down my biceps, across my chest, around my hips to the insides of my thighs. Dom was so rough the last time he took me, it seemed like he didn't leave any part of my body unmarked. Kai's jaw pops when he clenches it. I watch him, waiting to see how he will react. He closes his eyes and inhales a slow deep breath, holding it for several long seconds before exhaling. He does that twice more before opening his eyes again. I've seen him do the same ritual before when trying to keep his temper in check, but that was years ago in high school when he was dealing with a bully.

When Kai opens his eyes again, there is a look of steely determination in them. He lifts the camera to his face, and I hold my arms out, palms up, offering up my darkest secrets in the name of justice. I close my eyes while he takes his photos, willing myself to feel even a fraction of the strength I saw in his eyes moments ago. He's careful not to touch me, but I feel the heat from his body as he walks around me, crouches near me, getting images of my injuries from every angle. I'm so absorbed in the quiet click of the shutter as he works, I'm startled when he speaks again.

"Are you hurt anywhere I can't see?"

Nodding, I reach behind me and unhook my bra, letting it fall to the floor. On my right breast, there is an angry red bite mark surrounding my areola. Kai sucks in a harsh gasp when he sees it. "Fuck, ReRe. I'm going to fucking kill him."

There is one more click of the camera shutter before he places it on the desk.

When our eyes meet again, there are so many unspoken words. *I'm sorry. It's not your fault. I know. I love you.* My mind flashes back to the moment in the hospital when Kai confessed his feelings to me, and I want nothing more than to go back in time and make a different choice. The right choice.

My body moves before my mind realizes what's happening. I close the gap between us, pressing my body against his. He opens his mouth to say something, but I quiet him with a kiss. Kai stills, his hands hovering inches away from my skin, his lips unmoving, unsure of what to do. My hands travel up his chest, grasping his shirt tightly in my fists, and I pull him to me, pressing my lips more firmly against his, begging for more. Desperate for him to erase the ghostly memory of Dom's touch and replace it with his own. After a long, tense moment, the rigidity of Kai's body melts away, and he pulls me into him, enveloping me in his embrace. His lips part, his tongue licking the seam of my own, seeking entry. I part mine, granting him entrance, and our kiss goes from timid, nervous and hesitant to all-consuming in the span of a heartbeat.

A soft moan escapes me as Kai deepens our kiss. I become dizzy and forget how to breathe. Everything about this feels so right, I can't believe I didn't accept it before. My skin burns under his touch. I want more. I want it all. Suddenly we are moving, the backs of Kai's legs hitting the bed, forcing him to sit.

I push forward, climbing on his lap, never breaking our kiss, refusing to go another moment ignoring how I feel about him. Settling onto his lap, I feel the hardness of his erection pressing through his joggers. Grinding my core down on him, my panties grow damp from arousal from the effect his kiss is having on me. I lose myself as I rock my core along his shaft, shudders running down my spine as I build a rhythm that gets me close to release. Our breathing becomes erratic as our kissing becomes a frenzied tangle of tongues. And then I'm there, with one perfect thrust up from Kai, giving my clit the friction I need to go over the edge.

"Kai…" His name is a prayer on my lips. One I hope I will get to repeat over and over and over.

CHAPTER FORTY-THREE

KAI

Serena is on my lap, her chest pressed so tightly against mine I can feel her thundering heartbeat, our foreheads pressed together as we breathe each other in, lost in this moment I never want to end. She's whispering my name like a prayer, and it is the sexiest thing I have ever heard. My dick aches with how hard it is, and all I can think about is how only two thin layers of damp fabric separate us. I can feel the wet heat from her release soaking into my joggers, and it takes every ounce of self-control I have to not take this further. Not to flip our positions and drag those soaking wet panties down and sink inside of her. To really make her mine.

Serena must have other ideas, because the feeling of her hands trailing down my chest to the waistband of my sweats pulls me from my filthy as fuck fantasy. "Baby, no." Gently, I take her hands in mine, holding them against my chest, stopping her progress. Serena leans back, hurt flashing in her beautiful hazel eyes.

"You don't want me?"

My heart cracks at the rejection lacing her words. "No —yes, God, baby, it's not that. I promise you it's not that. I've never wanted anything more." My own words come out in a confused jumble as I desperately try to will the blood in my body to return to my brain before I fuck things up between us.

"Serena, don't *ever* doubt how much I want you. That isn't in question. I want to do right by you. That's all I've ever done and all I ever will do. And as much as I want to take things further, I can't. Not right now. Not yet. I don't want our first time to be when you're vulnerable and hurting. I want you to be whole and happy and ready. I want you to want it because you want me, not...not just to erase the memory of him."

Something flashes in Serena's eyes at my denial. Hurt? Apology? Rejection? She opens her mouth to speak, but I quiet her with a gentle kiss to her lips.

"Do not apologize for what happened, ReRe. It was probably the best moment of my life. I just want to wait for the right moment to take this further. We've been dancing around these feelings for a lot longer than I think either of us realize, and I'm okay with waiting a little longer. Let's get you checked out and safe from that motherfucking pig first, yeah?" A small smile plays at the corners of her mouth as she nods in agreement.

"You're right, Kai. Thank you..." She trails off like she's thinking of what to thank me for, her eyes glazing over like she's lost in thought. When she comes back and refocuses on me, there is nothing but love shining in the kaleido-scope of colors in her irises. "For everything."

Serena climbs off my lap and puts her clothes—my clothes—back on. I try to subtly adjust my raging hard-on, but the sight of her wearing my clothes, lips swollen and red from my kisses, makes getting rid of it a Herculean effort. In an attempt to cool the raging inferno burning inside of me, I change the subject.

"Do you have a way to get in touch with your mom's friend? Do you know where she is?"

"I have her number memorized. She's been an emergency contact for me since I was in kindergarten. Give me your phone, and I'll call her."

"Here, I'll, uh, be right back." Handing over my cell phone, I excuse myself to the bathroom to splash some water on my face and deal with the goddamn tent pole in my pants.

In the safe confines of the bathroom, I find myself staring into the mirror, trying to figure out how my life took such a weird fucking turn. Making out with my best friend so hard in a shady motel room, after rescuing her from her abusive boyfriend, I nearly came in my pants. Somehow one look from Serena has me reverting back to my early puberty years ready to blow a load over the swimsuit issue of *Sports Illustrated*.

I can hear her talking in hushed whispers in the other room. I should go out there and support her through this but...glancing down I see my dick hasn't gotten any less hard. "Fuck it." Knowing the quickest way to deal with my not-so-little problem will be just *dealing* with it, I pull my dick out and swipe my thumb over the tip where precum is already beading up. Closing my eyes, I conjure up the memory of Serena grinding down on me while her sweet, perfect pink tongue danced with mine. The way her dusky mauve nipples pebbled and rubbed against my chest as her breathing became more erratic and turned into whiny, needy little moans. I squeeze my shaft tighter as I increase the pace of my strokes, the tightening of my balls and pressure building signaling that I'm close to release. I think of the way my name sounded on her lips as she came all over my crotch just from grinding on me, and that does it. My release barrels through me, and I lean over the counter, spilling into my hand, making a fucking mess. It's only slightly less embarrassing than jizzing in my sleep because of a wet dream, but it's better than losing my fucking mind and taking advantage of Serena in a vulnerable moment.

Leaving the bathroom, I find Serena sitting cross legged in the middle of the bed, her phone call finished. She glances at my crotch before making eye contact with me and flashing me a knowing grin. "All better?" Her tone is teasing, and the tension I had been holding in my shoulders from the restraint of holding back from her loosens.

She's fine with what happened. She's not upset with me. Flashing her my best panty-dropping grin, I respond, "As good as it's going to get for now, but Rosie and her five sisters have nothing on you, baby."

She rolls her eyes at me, and whatever insecurity she was feeling before I disappeared into the bathroom to jerk off is gone.

"So, did you talk to your mom's friend? What's the

plan?" I climb on the bed next to her. I pull her into me and lie back so she's on her side—halfway on top of me—with her head resting on my chest. This isn't the first time we've ever cuddled, but it's the first time it's felt like more than just cuddling. It feels like two pieces of a puzzle finally coming together.

"Yeah, I talked to Ari. She's working nights and won't be off until tomorrow at seven. I don't know if I'm ready to go to a hospital, but she said we could come over in the morning and talk. She says she knows some people we can trust if I do decide to report my abuse, but she understands why I'm hesitant."

I give Serena a reassuring squeeze and kiss the top of her head.

"That sounds like a plan to me, baby."

"Baby?" Serena lifts her head so she can look at me, a smile playing on her lips. "That's the third time you called me that. Is that my new nickname?" Her tone is teasing, but I pick up a hint of hopefulness in it.

"It is if you want it to be, ReRe. Are you mine now?" I gently graze my thumb over her cheek, heart pounding like it's trying to beat its way out of my chest, as I wait for her answer.

"Yeah, Kai, I am. I'm yours."

CHAPTER FORTY-FOUR

SERENA

The chipper ringing of Kai's phone alarm drags me out of the deepest sleep I've had in weeks. My body feels relaxed and heavy, like it's being weighed down by a pile of blankets. It takes a minute before my brain wakes up enough to realize the weight is actually Kai, wrapped around me like an octopus. Arms banded across my chest, leg thrown over my own, his face buried in my neck, and his warm breath tickling my skin. His erection is pressed against my ass, hard and insistent. Before falling asleep, I stripped down to my cami and thin cotton pajama shorts. Kai must have done the same because all I feel is the burning heat of his skin against mine.

I hold my breath, waiting for the panic from being confined and held down to hit, but it never comes. Because it's Kai, and I know I'm safe with him. I decide to have a little fun with him and wiggle my ass against his erection. There's no response from Kai at first, so I press against him harder and let out a low lusty moan like I'm having a sexy dream. Kai's arms tighten around me in response, and his voice, husky with sleep, causes goosebumps to erupt along my skin when he says, "Don't start something you're not willing to finish." He nips at my neck as he rocks his hips into me, sending a new rush of arousal surging through my body.

"Who says I'm not willing to finish?" A smile plays across my lips as his arm moves down my body, stopping at the waistband of my shorts. When his hand doesn't move further south, I pout, "Now who's teasing?" I can't see Kai's smile, but I feel it against my skin when he traces gentle kisses along my shoulder and up my neck.

"Tell me what you need, baby."

"You, Kai, I need you."

"You've got me, baby." Kai slips his hand under the waistband of my shorts, finding my center slick with arousal already.

"Is this for me, ReRe? Were you thinking about me in your sleep?" He teases my clit, slowly tracing circles around it. Enough to make me desperate for more, but not enough to give me the pleasure I'm seeking.

"Kaaaiii…" His name is a needy moan slipping from my lips as I grind against him, seeking more friction. His response is to tighten his hold on me, pinning my hips in place.

"Be good and let me give you what you need, baby. Let me take care of you." When I'm too lost in the fog of lust to respond, Kai rubs his thumb firmly against my clit, sending a jolt of pleasure straight to my core. "Are you gonna let me take care of you, ReRe?" This time his tone isn't a polite request. It's a command.

"Yes. Please, take care of me." Kai resumes his slow, torturous teasing, circling my clit before dipping his fingers between my folds, coating them in my wetness.

"God, baby, you feel so good. You're so wet for me. You're desperate to come all over my fingers, aren't you?" Kai increases the pressure of his strokes, finding a pattern of dipping into my core while circling my clit with his thumb that causes my vision to go hazy and my breathing to become erratic.

"That's it Serena; let go. Let me feel you lose control." Kai's soft lips latch on to my neck, and he sucks, the final sensation I need to shove me over the edge. My thighs clench, trapping his hand between them while my body spasms through my orgasm. Vaguely, I'm aware of his hips rocking against my ass, but I'm so lost in my own bliss, I don't realize what he's doing until I hear a muffled grunt and feel a hot, slick wetness spreading along the back of my shorts. I can't help the smile that spreads across my lips as I realized he just dry humped my ass to the point of coming in his boxer briefs.

"I would've been happy to help you with that, Kai."

Kai just laughs at my teasing before pulling his hand free. "Nah, baby, this was all about you." My eyes go wide as I watch him lick his fingers clean of my release, and a new wave of arousal courses through my system. I've never seen a sexier sight in my life. How had I never realized how fucking sexy Kai is? Kai must know he's stupefied me with that move, because he shoots me a wink before rolling away to clean himself up.

"Come on, ReRe. We've got places to be, and I want to feed you a real breakfast before you wither away to nothing and lose that delicious ass of yours."

AFTER CHECKING out of the motel, we find ourselves eating breakfast at a small roadside diner not too far from Arianna's house. True to his word, Kai made sure to get a real meal into me before our next move, and after spending a whole day eating nothing but junk food, I've never been more grateful for a bowl of fresh fruit and some scrambled eggs.

I'm nervous about being out in public, unsure of how far Dominick's reach is through the brotherhood of the police force. My body tenses every time the bell above the door jingles signaling the entrance of a new customer. Kai must feel the same way because neither of us take too long to eat our meals, ready to get out of the public eye as quickly as possible.

"You ready to bounce?" Kai asks once he pays our bill. I nod and follow him out of the restaurant. On our way to the address Arianna gave us for her rental, Kai stops at a local superstore. I look over at him in confusion, trying to gauge his plan.

"Why are we stopping here?"

"I thought you might want some clothes that fit and don't smell like man-sweat. Also, I wanted to pick up a prepaid phone for you since Dom has yours. I don't want you to not have a way to get in touch with your mom if I'm not around."

I worry my bottom lip between my teeth, feeling guilty over Kai having to spend so much money on me.

"Hey, none of that." He reaches over, gently freeing my lip from my teeth. "The only one of us that will be biting those luscious lips of yours will be me."

"But—"

Kai stops me with a finger to the lips. "No buts, ReRe. I told you I'm going to take care of you. I should have gotten my head out of my ass and done this a long time ago, then we wouldn't be in this situation now. But I can't change the past. All I can do is do better for you in the future. Let me do this, okay?"

My eyes sting from tears suddenly threatening to fall. I can't believe I never saw how good Kai was to me before. How could I be so desperate and stupid to fall for someone like Dominick when Kai was there all along? Blinking back the tears I give him a small smile.

"Fine, if you insist, spend your money on me, boo. I won't argue." The smile that lights up Kai's face is almost blinding, and my heart swells seeing how happy taking care of me makes him.

After a quick trip through the store, Kai waits for me in the car while I change into clothes that fit in the bathroom —black leggings and a long sleeve t-shirt to cover the marks left by Dom. I decide to keep wearing Kai's hoodie though, because even if it smells like man-sweat, it smells like him, and it makes me feel safe. When I get to the car, he has the prepaid phone out of the packaging, activating it for me.

"Here you go. I've got my number, Mrs. G, your mom and my parents already added to your contact list." Kai hands me the phone, and I shoot him a grateful smile. Having a phone again feels like having a lifeline, and a little more tension eases from my shoulders as I slip it into the pocket of my leggings.

"You ready to do this?" Kai gives me a hesitant look as he starts the car. He knows how nervous I am to bring someone else into the shitshow that has become my life, but if anyone can help, I believe Arianna can.

"Reenie!" Arianna's excited gasp greets me as she opens the front door. She immediately pulls me into a tight squeeze, and I wince when she presses against the bruises on my arms. "Oh, shit, I'm sorry." She pulls away, guilt flashing across her face at hurting me. Her eyes dance over to Kai, and she flashes him a warm smile. "Hey, Kai. Good to see you."

"It's alright. God, it's so good to see you, Ari." I go back in for a gentler hug, resting my head on her shoulder, breathing in the clean, soft smell of citrus from her freshly washed hair. Arianna is dressed in an oversized t-shirt and leggings, clearly ready to go to bed after her long overnight shift at the hospital. "I'm sorry we're keeping you up, Ari...

You sure you don't want us to come back after you get some sleep?"

Arianna only responds with an eyeroll before pulling me through the front door into her living room. Kai follows behind, his hand on my lower back, reassuring me that he's still there.

"Do y'all need something to drink? Coffee? Water? I've got some sweet tea too."

I shake my head, my nerves jangling around my insides, causing me to vibrate with tension again. Now that I'm here, in front of someone else, covered in the evidence of Dom's abuse, I feel a new surge of terror building in my chest. What will he do if he finds out? What if nothing happens to him? How will he retaliate? My breaths start coming in short gasps, and Kai and Arianna immediately close ranks on me, pulling me onto the couch, Kai's arms wrapped around my shoulders, Arianna holding my hand.

"It's okay, baby. Breathe. You're safe here." Kai's honeyed voice is in my ear, pouring over my jagged nerves, soothing them, like a balm to my soul. I relax into his hold and take in a deep breath, steadying myself for what's to come.

"Alright, Reenie. Tell me the whole story. Take your time; don't leave anything out. I want to know the full scope of what we are dealing with here."

My mouth goes dry at the prospect of reliving the entire nightmare of my relationship with Dom. Talking about the moments I haven't told Kai about. The red flags I had ignored before now stand out in my mind like a bullfighter's red cape. The "forgotten" birth control at the cabin paired with his relentless disregard for my pregnancy concerns. The way I just let him take and take and take from my body because I thought I owed it to him. His need for control over my whereabouts and my body and how he made me so dependent on him, so quickly. Then, once he had me cornered and alone, he finally let loose with the physical abuse.

Taking a deep breath, I close my eyes, readying myself to tell my story, but Kai puts a hand on my thigh, pulling my attention to him.

"ReRe, I think we should record this. It might help if you have to recount your story again to the police. Do you mind if I turn on the voice recorder on my phone?"

I glance at the phone Kai is now holding, his thumb hovering over the red record button in the app in question. I don't relish the idea of having my pitiful life experience recorded, but I know he has a point, and I know if I do plan on doing something about Dom, this won't be the only time I have to relive this nightmare. I jerk my head in a quick nod, and Kai taps the button, beginning the recording.

As I describe every awful, manipulative, gaslighting, controlling, abusive thing Dom did, watching Ari's eyes grow wide in shock and feeling Kai grow tenser and tenser at my back, I realize how shockingly naïve I must be to have fallen for his bullshit. Silent tears stream down Ari's face as I finish my story. The room is so quiet, you can hear a pin drop.

It's a long, strained moment before Kai says, "I'm going to fucking kill him."

CHAPTER FORTY-FIVE

KAI

When Serena finishes her story, I jump up from my seat on the couch and begin pacing. My blood is boiling, anger like I've never known before coursing through me. I knew he was bad. I *knew* it, and I didn't say anything. I assumed Serena would come to me if she ever felt unsafe in a relationship. An assumption I now want to kick my own ass for. Guilt swirls in my gut when I think of how many times I should have spoken up and told her about Dom but kept my mouth shut out of fear she wouldn't believe me and it would ruin our friendship. It's a risk I should have taken if it would've saved her from this hell.

"Kai, you look like a tiger pacing its cage. Sit down." Serena looks up at me pleadingly, worry etched in her features like she's afraid I'm going to pop off and go attack Dom right this second. Her fears aren't unfounded. I want to kill the abusive, manipulative piece of shit.

"ReRe, how can you expect me to sit calmly after

hearing how he raped you and tried to fucking baby trap you?"

Serena's eyes go wide in shock, her mouth falling open like I slapped her.

"He...I—no..."

I can see the denial in her eyes. Before she can build a defense for the motherfucker I kneel down in front of her, hushing her with a finger to her lips. "Did you or did you not tell him no, and he pressured you into having sex anyway?" My voice is steadier than I feel—my body practically vibrating in anger—but I have to make her see this with reason.

She closes her eyes, takes in a deep breath, then nods.

"And did he or did he not ignore your concerns about having unprotected sex multiple times and keep pressuring you into having sex with him even if you were uncomfortable?"

Tears dance along Serena's lashes, threatening to fall. Her lower lip trembles, and I move my hand to cup her cheek, holding her, letting her know I've got her now. "Yes." Her response is a barely audible whisper. She collapses into my arms, the strength that was holding her together while she unloaded her burden finally leaving her.

"Shh, it's okay, ReRe. I've got you." I'm not sure how many times I have to remind her she's not in this alone. Not anymore. But I won't quit until it gets through to her.

After a long moment, Arianna clears her throat. I glance over at her and see her quietly wiping away her own silent tears. Her pain for Serena is palpable. She is almost as heartbroken for her as I am.

"So, how do we want to do this? I can take you to my hospital so we can do an official exam and report, but I'm not going to lie, it will be invasive and like reliving the trauma all over again, and I can't promise anything will happen to Dom. It's difficult enough to bring a regular abuser to justice, but one on the police force? The odds are against us, Reenie. He will know how to manipulate the system, and odds are charges won't even be brought against him." Arianna grasps Serena's hand, looking her in the eye when she says her next words. "I'm only telling you this because I want you to be prepared to fight this battle. I will be there every step of the way, holding your hand."

Arianna's words are a gut punch. Logically I know she's right. I've experienced how flawed the justice system is. I've seen how many police officers walk away from murder charges with nothing more than a slap on the wrist. I have thousands of photographs on my computer from protests highlighting this very real issue. But knowing Serena will probably be another statistic in a broken system makes me want to vomit.

"I...I don't know what to do. He took everything from me. He's paying for Mom's care while the house sale is in escrow. I have no money, nowhere to go, he has my ID and my bank card and my car. He's not going to let me go. Not without a fight."

"That's not entirely true." I speak up, and Serena looks at me like I have two heads.

"What do you mean? You can't seriously think Dom is just going to say 'Oh, you're right; we're better off as friends, have a nice life'!"

Arianna nods, interjecting, "She's right. A man doesn't go through that level of manipulation just to gracefully step to the side. He's very likely to escalate, and Serena is in danger."

"No, what I mean is you have somewhere to go."

"Kai, I can't stay with you and your parents. I don't want Dom setting his sights on your family." Serena shakes her head in objection, but I cup her face in my hands, halting her protest.

"You can go back to your house."

"Kai—"

"I bought it." Serena's eyes widen in surprise. I push on, seeing how she's struggling to process the bomb I dropped on her. "I used my inheritance from Grams for the down payment, and my parents helped me buy it. You didn't lose your house, Serena."

Her mouth opens and closes a few times before she squeaks, "But why?"

"Because I know how important that house is to you, and I just...didn't want you to lose it." Serena's brows furrow like she's trying to work through a logic puzzle, so I confess what I've been holding back, hoping she will forgive me for not speaking up sooner.

"I knew Dom was bad news. He threatened me to stay away from you, but I thought he was just jealous of our relationship. Then I heard him talking to your mom one day about moving into a retirement home. I thought there would be time before he put his plans into motion, but after the shooting everything moved so fast. And after you turned me away at the hospital, I was worried you wouldn't believe me about Dom, thinking I was being a bitch about losing to him. I'm sorry, Serena. I should've said something. I should've warned you.

"I just thought, maybe, if I bought the house and you realized Dom wasn't the man for you, it would be one less loss you would have to experience."

CHAPTER FORTY-SIX

SERENA

"I bought it."

Kai's words are ringing in my ears as my vision goes gray around the edges. Between acknowledging Dominick had been raping me—a brutal truth I had been denying fiercely in my own mind—and Kai confessing that he bought my house, I feel like my entire universe is collapsing and expanding all at once. I can't process. I can't breathe. I can't…

My vision goes black, and suddenly Kai's strong hands are cupping my face, his forehead pressed to mine. He's saying something, but his words are muffled by the panic that is trying to pull me under.

I'm vaguely aware of the sensation of something cold and wet on the back of my neck, dripping down my back. It's just shocking enough to force a gasp of air into my lungs. Slowly, the world comes back into focus. I see Kai's body kneeling between my legs. His warm breath tickles my lips, and I part them, breathing him in, trying to inhale his strength. His deep, honeyed voice filters through the fog, anchoring me back in reality.

"Breathe, baby. Deep breath. I'm sorry. I'm sorry. I'm sorry. Come back to me, ReRe."

I quiet Kai by pressing my lips to his, swallowing his apologies. Apologies he shouldn't be making. None of this is his fault.

When we part, a new resolve pours into the cracks of my fractured self-worth. The cracks Dom put there. Hardening, strengthening, reinforcing it into something more resilient. Better. Unbreakable. I take a long moment, sitting with this new version of myself, letting it settle into my bones, before saying, "I want to take my life back."

Arianna, Kai and I are sitting around her kitchen table, coming up with a plan for taking back control of my life—while making sure we can get Dominick locked up without fear of retaliation—when Kai's phone starts buzzing from its spot on the table.

Kai peeks at the caller ID and a frown tugs down at his full, pouty lips. "It's Mrs. G." He flicks a concerned glance at me before hitting the speaker button to answer the call.

"Hey, Mrs. G, what's up?"

"Oh, Kai! Good, you answered! Honey, have you seen

Serena? Her man, Dominick, came by looking for her, and he was all in a tizzy! He was saying crazy nonsense like you kidnapped her, and he kept asking to come into my house to make sure she wasn't here. I told him I haven't seen either one of you, but he kept threatening to come back with a warrant, so I just let him in to take a look so he'd go away. There's a police cruiser parked down the street in front of your parents' house like they're waiting to bust up a meth lab. What in the hell is going on?"

My mouth falls open at Mrs. G's words. Fuck. This is bad. I can't let Dominick drag Kai's parents or Mrs. G into this mess. He's going to harass everyone I love until I go back to him.

Kai looks at me wide-eyed, unsure of what to tell Mrs. G. We don't want her to know too much; the less she knows, the better. But we can't let Dom poison her against Kai. Quickly, I write down a response for Kai, careful not to give away that I'm with him.

"She's fine, Mrs. G. She and Dom had a fight, and she wanted to go visit her mom's friend so I gave her a ride. There's nothing to worry about. Serena is safe. I swear it." There is a long moment of silence before Mrs. G responds.

"You keep her safe, Kai. I don't like the way that man was acting. It was…irrational."

"Yes, ma'am." Kai responds, his eyes trained on me with a look of reverence, like he is swearing an oath.

When the call disconnects, I know we need to come up with a new plan. Dominick is planting seeds painting Kai as the bad guy. He's going to say Kai hurt me. I refuse to let Kai take the fall for Dominick's abuse.

"We need to get my mom somewhere safe. I can't report anything until I know she is somewhere he can't get to in case he retaliates. Then we need to get irrefutable evidence that Dom is an abuser."

I watch Kai's brows furrow in confusion at my last statement. He doesn't like where my train of thought is leading but I'm not letting that deter me.

"ReRe—"

"Don't ReRe me, Kai. I mean it. I am done letting this man ruin my life, and I will do what it takes to punish him for the hell he has put me through. I will not let this happen to another woman."

Kai doesn't say anything for a long moment before nodding his understanding.

"Alright ReRe, we will do this your way."

WHEN WE LEAVE Arianna's to go pick up my mom, she is making some phone calls to friends she has on the local police force, trying to figure out who will be most receptive to hearing my story. She is fully aware of our need for discretion until we have Mom in a safe location, out of Dominick's reach, but she wants to have the right person lined up for when I'm ready to make a report. Once we pick up Mom, we will meet up with Arianna and let Mom stay with her while we deal with Dominick.

On the drive to Whispering Grove, my body turns into

a knot of tension and fraught emotions. I'm excited to see my mom and tell her about Kai buying the house but ashamed and terrified to tell her everything that went down with Dominick. In my heart, I know she won't judge me, but the gremlin in the back of my mind won't stop whispering how I should've known better. I shake my head, trying to shake loose that line of thinking. Mentally I begin chanting, *"It's not my fault. It's not my fault. It's not my fault,"* trying not to spiral into a pit of shame and self-recrimination.

A text comes through on Kai's phone from his mom, pulling me from my doubt spiral. "Do you want me to check that for you?" Kai nods and swipes his thumb over the unlock screen before handing me the phone, not taking his eyes off the road. He's being overly cautious, driving just under the speed limit, refusing to give any cops a reason to pull him over. We can't afford to let Dom find us before we get Mom somewhere safe. My stomach drops when I read the message from Kai's mom.

> Mom: Don't come home. Officers here with warrant searching the house. Stay wherever you are.

"Shit…Kai. They're searching your house." Nausea rolls through me as I consider the consequences of this.

"It's okay, ReRe. They won't find anything." Kai tries to reassure me, but we both know it's an empty promise. It doesn't matter if there is anything to find at his house. If Dominick wants to get Kai in trouble, he's not above planting evidence.

"You know that means nothing, Kai. Dominick isn't going to leave you alone while I'm with you. He's going to set you up." My voice comes out in a high-pitched whine, panic seeping into my bones again.

"He can try, ReRe. But he's not going to win."

When we reach Whispering Grove, my body is vibrating with tension. I feel eyes on me as soon as I exit the car, and I can't get to my mom fast enough. When I rush through the lobby, it sounds like someone calls my name, but I ignore them in my rush to get to my mom. Bursting through her door, I am greeted by an empty space. No sign of my mother anywhere.

"Mom? Hey, you here? I came to see you." I walk through her small apartment, hoping maybe she's in her room laying down or in the bathroom. She is nowhere to be found and her phone is sitting on her nightstand.

"Shit, where is she?"

"Maybe she's walking on the grounds or visiting with one of her friends? Come on, let's go ask." Kai's voice is calm, a balm to the rapid beating of my heart.

Yeah, she's visiting with friends. She has friends here now. That has to be it. I let him tug me back through the door, and we run into the woman who works the front desk.

"There you are! I tried to get your attention when you came through. Your fiancé came by a little while ago and picked up your mom. He said he was going to surprise you by taking you both out to dinner. He wasn't sure what time you were coming by to visit Laura, so he told me to tell you to meet him at the house."

The blood drains from my face as I realize we are too late. Dominick has my mom.

Missing the despair that must be written all over my face, the woman smiles before saying, "He's such a sweet man. You sure did get lucky with that one." With that, she turns and walks away, taking my last bit of hope with her.

CHAPTER FORTY-SEVEN

SERENA

"Fuck, fuck, fuck, fuck."

Outside in the parking lot, I'm pacing next to Kai's car, hands snarled in my hair as I fight not to let panic take control. Dom has my mom. I don't know if he will hurt her, but I can't take that chance. She's all I have left, and I will do anything to protect her. I'm so lost in my thoughts, I don't hear Kai calling my name until his hands grasp me by the biceps, halting me in my tracks.

"Serena, we will go get her. It will be okay. He's not going to hurt her. He's using her as bait to make you go back to him." Kai's reassurances fall flat when his thumb brushes over a bruise on my arm, reminding me exactly what Dominick is capable of.

"You can't know that, Kai. If he was willing to do this to me"—I motion to my body, reminding him of the beating Dominick gave me—"there is every possibility he will do it to my mom to punish me. She might not even remember he's the one that did it! I can't take that risk. I have to go back and make sure she's okay."

"ReRe, I can't let you do that. I made a promise to keep you safe, and I am gonna keep it."

Frustration bubbles out of me and I yank myself out of Kai's hold. "This isn't up to you, Kai! This is my mother. *My family.* She's the most important person in my life, and I am not going to hide away and let Dominick unleash his monster on her."

"What do you think he's going to do once he has you back, Serena?! Do you honestly think it will end well with an 'Oops, my bad, I'm sorry I hit you'?" Kai's voice rises in volume, matching the frustration I'm feeling right now. My eyes burn from the tears threatening to fall, my chest so tight from fear it hurts to breathe.

"I fucking know that, Kai! But what else am I supposed to do? He's trying to get you arrested for kidnapping; he has my mom; he's harassed your parents and Mrs. G. I can't let him keep ripping my life apart while I'm hiding away, trying to chase away my problems by using your dick. I am going back and making sure my mother is safe."

Hurt flashes briefly across Kai's face at my dismissal of what we shared at the motel, but I can't spare any extra emotion for him right now.

"Fine, but you're not going alone. I'm going with you." Kai's jaw pulses from how tightly he is clenching his teeth, his eyes burning with an intensity I have never seen from him.

"No, you're not."

"The fuck I'm not, ReRe. I. Am. Going. With. You." Kai

grasps my face in his hands, forcing me to look him in the eye. "Serena, listen to me. You cannot go back to him."

Tears welling in my eyes finally spill over as I come to grips with what Kai is saying. I know he's right but what else can I do? "But—"

"SERENA! No buts! We will figure something out that doesn't involve you going back to him alone. Got it?" I see the anguish in Kai's eyes. It hurts him to tell me no. He knows how important my mom is. But he also has to protect me. I see that need burning inside him.

Slowly, I close my eyes and nod my agreement. Kai lets out a relieved sigh, pressing his forehead against mine.

"We will figure this out. We will get your mom back, I promise." He peppers sweet, tender kisses along my hairline and then down my nose, stopping at my lips. He gently presses his lips to mine, as if he's reassuring himself that I'm still here with him. Still his.

He tugs me towards his car, buckling me in before going around the front and getting behind the wheel. We are quiet as we leave the care facility, both sifting through the best of bad options.

As Kai pulls onto the main road, his face brightens with an idea. "Let's get someone to go with us. Maybe he won't cause a scene if we have a witness? What about Marie's husband…what's his name?" Kai snaps his finger, trying to come up with the right name.

"Ben?" I answer hesitantly, unsure if getting more people involved is the best idea.

"Yeah, Ben. He's a big motherfucker, isn't he? Wasn't he a football player or some shit?"

"Yeah, bu—" My objection is cut off with the blare of siren sounds behind us and the flare of blue and red lights. We aren't more than five minutes down the road before we are found.

"FUCK!" Kai's fingers tighten their grip on the steering wheel as his eyes flick to me, panic racing through them. He looks back at the road, then glances down at the speedometer, indecision weighing on his face. He's thinking about running.

"Kai, pull over. We can't outrun them. It'll only make it worse." I reach across the console and give his forearm a squeeze, the muscle taut and firm under my touch. He glances back at me, and I see the resolved defeat in his expression. He turns on the emergency flashers and pulls to the side of the road. He leaves his hands at ten and two on the wheel after shutting off the ignition. I place my hands on the dash as well, as a matter of precaution. If Dominick has his buddies out searching for me—with Kai as a suspect for kidnapping—we can't take any chances of provoking a response.

There's a long tense moment while we wait for the officer to approach. I don't know if I hope it is Eric or Dane or someone I don't know. Would they believe me if I told them the truth? Or do they know what he's truly like and don't care? My thought spiral is interrupted by a barked command from outside of the car.

He is standing right outside of Kai's window, gun drawn, pointed towards us. My heart feels like it is going to explode out of my chest. Bile rises up my throat as fear paralyzes me. Oh God, this is bad. This is so fucking bad.

"Get out of the car, slowly. Hands behind your head."

I watch Kai close his eyes, and his Adam's apple bobs as he swallows down his own fear. He looks at me, and all of the hurt and regret that he wasn't able to keep me safe is shining in his eyes. He blinks back the thin veil of tears as his beautiful full lips tip up into the slightest ghost of a smile.

"It's going to be okay, ReRe. I love you." My own tears spill down my cheeks as I fight the desperate need to pull him to me and hold him in my arms.

"I love you too."

With slow, deliberate movements, Kai opens his car door before placing his hands on his head and climbs out of the car.

"On the ground, now!" I don't recognize the harsh voice barking out the command. I watch as Kai drops to his knees, his head held up high with a defiant expression on his face. Fear surges through me at the thought he might try to resist. *Don't do it. Don't do it. Don't do it*, I silently pray, urging Kai to keep his cool.

A loud knock on my window pulls a scream from my throat. Kai's body jerks towards me when he hears my shout. My car door is jerked open, a strong grip pulling me from my seat while I watch on in horror as the officer in front of Kai tackles him to the ground, yelling incomprehensible orders.

"No! Kai! Leave him alone!" I squirm and jerk against the strong arms wrapped around my waist, pulling me away from Kai. "Stop! This is a mistake! Let us go!" My voice cracks as a sob escapes. I can't see Kai. I can only see the top half of the cop kneeling on his back, struggling to secure his wrists behind him. I hear Kai's pained grunts and his panicked shouts of my name as he tries to check on me.

"Serena! You okay?"

I try harder to wrench myself free from the officer manhandling me, but a large hand comes down over my mouth and nose, cutting off my oxygen.

"Nu-uh, Kitten. I'd think real carefully about your next move right now. You don't want your *friend* getting hurt over a misunderstanding, do you?"

Ice runs through my veins at the familiar rumble of Dominick's voice dancing through my ears. *No. No. No. No.* Terror wracks my body, causing me to give up my fight. Dom presses his advantage and pulls me back to a second cop car I hadn't noticed before. He unceremoniously dumps me in the backseat, locking me in. Pounding on the window, I scream in desperation as I watch him stalk back to where the other officer is dragging Kai into a standing position.

I watch helplessly as Dom pulls Kai to him by his shirt and speaks in his ear. Kai's eyes go wide as he looks towards the car I'm trapped in, terror flashing across his face before it turns into anger. Without warning he rears back and smashes his head into Dominick's nose, causing Dominick to stumble backwards, hands on his face, catching the gush of blood pouring from his broken face. Thankfully, before Dominick can retaliate, the other officer present has Kai shoved into the back of the other car.

Dominick tries to muscle his way past the other cop to get to Kai, but his buddy pushes him back, gesturing to the front of the cruiser I'm in. I look and see the flashing light of the dash cam indicating that it is recording. Shit. They've got Kai recorded assaulting an officer. My brief moment of satisfaction at seeing Dominick get what he deserves turns to dread, knowing he is going to use this against Kai. After a brief argument, Dominick turns and stalks back to the car, fury written across his bloodied face.

Dom slides behind the wheel, and the air in the car immediately becomes suffocating. His malevolent presence sucks all of the air from my lungs, replacing it with unadulterated terror. His hands are covered in sticky, dark red blood. It covers the lower half of his face, and when my eyes meet his in the rearview, mirror he flashes me a wicked, bloody grin that I know I will be seeing in my nightmares.

"I hope you enjoyed that little show, Kitten. Because that's the last time you'll be seeing your friend for a very long time. Kidnapping *and* assaulting a police officer? He's in some deep shit, Kitten."

"He didn't fucking kidnap me, you prick! I LEFT YOU! Now let me fucking go!" Anger overrides everything else as I lash out and kick the grate separating us.

Dominick lets out a low, amused chuckle, like I told him the world's funniest joke. "Oh, Kitten. Don't you get it yet? You're mine. Now and forever. You're not going anywhere, and if you don't want your buddy Kai to spend the rest of his life in prison, then you better start remembering that."

"FUCK YOU." I spit through the metal bars between us, the wet glob landing on his cheek. Dominick shakes his head and wipes the spit away, fury darkening his eyes.

"I was going to take you to go see your mother, Serena, but it seems like I need to teach you a lesson in manners first." His words are like ice water, effectively dousing my righteous indignation. I was so caught up in Kai's arrest, I forgot what set this series of events off to begin with. Dom has my mother. He has my whole world in his hands. Slumping against the seat back, the tears begin to fall as I accept defeat.

CHAPTER FORTY-EIGHT

SERENA

I sit, staring unseeing out the window as shapeless blurs move past. I'm numb from shock and fear. I knew if Dom found us it would be bad, I just didn't expect for it to happen so suddenly. When the car stops, we are outside of the police station. Hope springs in my chest at seeing where we are. Maybe if I make a big enough scene about Kai being innocent, someone will listen. Dom must see the plans written on my face, because he wastes no time in crushing them. Staring at me through the rearview mirror, his eyes bore into me.

"Here is what's going to happen, Kitten. You're going to wait right here while I go inside and let my captain know I am taking you home to rest and recover after your ordeal and that I will bring you back to the station when you're ready to make a statement. Your friend is going to cool his heels in a holding cell while we let this little life lesson sink in. What happens next is entirely up to you." Dominick pauses, letting his words hang in the air. "We are going to go home and have a little chat, and if you decide to be a good girl and listen, then maybe I'll tell everyone it was a little misunderstanding, and your boy can go home."

"And if I don't want to go home with you?" I try to infuse my words with the venomous hate I feel coursing through my veins, but they come out meek with no real power behind them.

"Don't forget, Serena, I'm the only person who knows where your mom is right now. Do you really want to gamble her safety for some punk who just wants to get his dick wet?"

My mouth goes dry at his threat. He planned this. He was ahead of us every step of the way. Now he's wrapped me up in a web of his deceit and manipulation so thoroughly there is no way I can get out. Not without sacrificing one of the people most important to me.

Dom exits the vehicle, leaving me alone to break, despair finally winning out over the tumultuous riot of emotions clashing in my mind. I don't know how long I sit there, lost in misery, before the door next to me opens and Dom reaches in, pulling me out, crushing me into his body. He wraps his arms around me in a mockery of a concerned hug, his mouth next to my ear so his words will only be for me. "Now be a good girl and kiss me like you love me. Put on a good show, then we are going to go home and come to an understanding. Got it?" Dom's arms tighten painfully around my waist, causing me to whimper in discomfort. He doesn't relent until he feels my head nod against his cheek.

When he pulls back, he moves his hand into my hair at

the base of my neck, tightening his hold painfully, further driving home the point that I am his, and he isn't going to let me go. "Now kiss me, Kitten. Like you mean it." I swallow down the bile rising in my throat and lean in, tentatively pressing my lips against his. When he tries to lick his way into my closed mouth, I refuse to open to him until his hand fisting my hair threatens to pull it out by the roots. When my lips part on a cry of pain, he presses his advantage and licks into my mouth, swallowing my anguished whimpers. Our kiss is flavored by the salt from my tears. He presses me against the car, crushing me between the hard steel and his rigid body as he takes what he wants from me. My hands rest limply on his shoulders, my body refusing to respond to the demands of his.

When we part, his breath comes in heavy pants, like he's run a marathon. There is a feral hunger in his eyes, and I know this is only the beginning of my punishment.

CHAPTER FORTY-NINE

KAI

I'm waiting in a small interrogation room, hands linked by the too-tight cuffs snatched around my wrists. The temperature of the room is slightly above "meat-locker", but I barely register the chill. I've been in here for fuck-knows how long. I know this is a tactic to make me antsy and ready to talk. Instead, I'm resting my head on the cold metal of the table, breathing deeply, trying to enter a zen-like state, desperate to keep from losing my shit over my worry for Serena. I know raising my voice and shouting my innocence from the rafters is not going to change a damn thing. *I know that.* But damn, it doesn't make it any easier to sit in here, knowing she's out there, alone with him.

The door finally opens when my fingers start to go numb from the chill in the air. A younger cop with a familiar face walks in carrying two cups of coffee. I can only assume he's here to pull the good cop routine. Make me feel comfortable with him and get me to confess to something I didn't do. I glance at the name on his uniform. *D. Wilcox.* Narrowing my eyes, I study him, trying to place how I know him. Then it hits me. He's one of Dom's partners who hangs around the coffee shop. I've seen him there together with the fucknugget numerous times. Fucking great. A vague memory of Serena referring to Dane and Eric, Dom's partners filters through my mind. This must be Dane.

Officer Wilcox sets one of the coffees in front of me before taking his own seat. We sit there in silence, him drinking his burnt-smelling bean water, me waiting for the ass fucking that's coming my way. I haven't even been offered the chance to call my parents or ask for my lawyer yet. Keeping my mouth shut, I refuse to say anything until I know what card he's going to play.

"So, Mr. Roberts, do you know why you're here?" His voice is neutral, like he's asking me if I'm shopping in a clothing store and not sitting in a cold as fuck interrogation room in a police station. Clenching my jaw, I remain silent, refusing to play along. Officer Wilcox waits a beat before nodding and continuing with his questions.

"According to Officer Reeves, you showed up at his home, harassed his fiancée and forced her to leave the premises with you against her will. Essentially, you're being accused of kidnapping."

I can't help it. My hands ball into fists, and my face heats in anger at the accusation. Wilcox notices my reaction.

I look him dead-ass in the eyes and bite out four words. "I want a lawyer."

Unfazed by my coldness, Wilcox leans forward on his elbows, like he's ready to tell me a secret. "We'll get to that part, but first I was hoping we could have a little chat, off the record."

Off the record? The fuck we will. I sit back in my seat and scoff out, "Lawyer."

Wilcox presses on, either completely drunk off the power his position affords him, or completely oblivious to how fucking illegal his behavior is.

"I know a lot about you, Kai Roberts. I know you still live with your parents and house sit while they travel the country during their retirement. I know you are a scholarship student at BFU. I know you volunteer at the Boys and Girls club downtown. I know you live next door to Serena Malcolm and have been friends with her for years. I know you also show up to protests and demonstrations for police justice with your camera and fight for what you believe is right. Am I wrong on any of these facts, Mr. Roberts?"

I stare at him, my eyes narrowing in suspicion, trying to figure out his angle.

"I'm only trying to establish facts. Facts that I think will prove we are on the same side on this issue." When I remain silent, Wilcox blows out an exasperated sigh before continuing on. "I don't believe you abducted Serena. I know you have no reason to trust me because I work with Dominick, but I am here to help you. I've been his partner for almost a year now, and I have seen some shit that concerns me. I haven't been able to get any solid proof of wrongdoing on his end on my own, but I think if we work together, we can take him down."

He has my attention now. Leaning forward, I rest my elbows on the table and give a slight nod to let him know I'm listening. I'm not gonna say a fucking word without a lawyer present, but if this guy is for real, this may be my ticket out of this situation.

Wilcox must understand my hesitation to trust him, so he presses on. "A couple of months ago when Serena was attacked by those frat bros at Mav's, I heard Dom talking to Eric about how he wanted her to quit working there. Dom kept playing up how worried he was about her and how he just wanted to take care of her. Eric suggested maybe she needed a little scare to encourage her to give the job up. They came up with a plan for Eric to encourage those dumbasses to harass her again to retaliate against Dom, and Dom was supposed to show up and be the hero. Now, I don't know if shooting that fuckhead was part of the plan or if Dom got carried away in the moment..." Wilcox trails off, biting his lower lip like he's debating on saying the rest. "But he was bragging about ridding the world of a rapist piece of shit and said his only regret was that he didn't shoot both of them."

I am unmoved by his confession. "Bragging about shooting a rapist seems like standard cop behavior to me." I shrug, not willing to give him more than that.

"Right, you're not wrong. But is it standard cop behavior to set up the assault? Is it standard cop behavior to have your buddies stalk your girl and report back when they catch her out with someone else? Even if it is innocent, like running into her best friend on a sidewalk? Is it standard cop behavior to radio your partner to go pick up your girl when she leaves the house, with instructions to bring her to you at the station no matter what she says? Is it standard cop behavior to have your buddy throw her best friend in a holding cell overnight—after a peaceful protest—just to teach him a lesson?"

That part has my attention. "What did you say?"

"Look, Dom's had his eyes on Serena for a while. He'd been going to her coffee shop, building familiarity before he nutted up and asked her out. He knew about your friendship with her and planned on doing what needed to be done to get you out of her life. I've seen him do some incredibly sketchy shit over the last year, and it's escalated since he started seeing Serena. I don't think she's safe with him, and I think you know that." My heart pounds in my chest at the sincerity of his words. He believes Serena. He believes us.

"I didn't get into this line of work to harass people and abuse my power. I got into this line of work to serve the people of this community. I know there is a lot of fucked up shit going on behind the scenes, but I want to do what I can to fix it from the inside. Dom thinks I'm some dumb, idealistic, do-gooder rookie, so he's not going to see this coming. I think if we work together, we can put his corrupt ass behind bars."

"Let me call my lawyer, and I'll tell you everything I know. I will do whatever it takes to bring this abusive piece of shit down and save my girl." A slow, sad smile spreads across Dane's face at my words.

"I was hoping you would say that."

CHAPTER FIFTY

SERENA

Dom leads me into his house (I will never refer to it as my home ever again, not after what Dom did to me, not after what Kai did for me) with a bruising grip around my arm. I don't fight back, not now. Not while he holds Kai's entire future in his hands. Not while he's the only person who knows where my mother is. I can't risk it. When we cross the threshold, my eyes immediately start scanning the room for my mom, desperate to see her and know she's okay.

"She's not here, Kitten."

A pit opens up in my stomach as Dominick nonchalantly crushes the tiny bit of hope that had been blooming in my chest.

"What do you mean she's not here? You said you had her!" My voice takes on a shrill quality as anger begins to overtake fear as the primary emotion driving me.

"I said I was the only person who knows where she is. And that's how it's going to stay until I'm sure you're going to be a good kitten and behave." Dom tightens his grip on my arm, causing my fingers to tingle from the loss of circulation.

"Please, she can't be alone somewhere strange. She'll get confused. She'll be scared." I don't know how it's physically possible for me to be able to produce more tears. Not after the last twenty-four hours, but they're there, spilling down my cheeks, my worry for the woman who raised me more than I can bear.

"Oh, don't worry. She's safe. Enough. But you're gonna prove to me how sorry you are first before I think about letting you see her." Dom leans in, brushing his dark stubble against my cheek. I fight to contain the urge to flinch as his hot breath hits my neck a second before his tongue licks a path along my jaw. I don't fight his kiss this time, fear for my mother keeping my instincts firmly in the "freeze" territory of fight, flight or freeze. I breathe in deeply through my nose and clear my mind of everything but Mom and Kai's faces. I'll do anything for them. Even let Dom win.

My arms hang limply in front of me, my hand brushing against something solid in the front pocket of the hoodie I'm still wearing. My heart skips a beat when I realize I still have the burner phone on me. My mind immediately begins racing, half in excitement for having a lifeline, half in panic that Dom will find it. I need to hide the phone before he realizes I have it.

Abruptly, Dom jerks back, disgust etched on to his features. "You smell like him." His eyes narrow when he sees that my body is swamped in Kai's oversized hoodie. I take a step back, afraid he is going to get violent over the reminder of Kai.

"I-I can go s-shower," I stammer out, placating. I hold my breath for what feels like an eternity while I wait for his response, my mind silently begging him to let me go shower alone so I can stash the contraband in my pocket.

Dom jerks his head in a sharp nod, acquiescing. "Go wash him off. I never want to smell another man's scent on you."

I let out the breath I was holding, moving to rush past Dominick.

Before I can leave, he grips my arm again, leaning in to growl into my ear, "Don't bother getting dressed when you're done. Just come to the bedroom."

Swallowing, I nod my understanding. Finally, he lets go, and I practically sprint to the bathroom, desperate to put space between us.

Once behind the safety of the locked bathroom door, I pull the burner phone out and see a missed text from Arianna checking on us. We were supposed to let her know when we were heading back with Mom. Quickly, I tap out a series of rapid-fire texts to her.

> Me: Dom has Mom but I don't know where. Got pulled over. Kai in jail. I'm with Dom.

> Me: Call Kai's parents. Let them know he needs help.

> Me: Dom reported me as kidnapped.

Me: Don't text me back. Gotta hide phone.
Will text when I can.

I send the contact for Kai's parents, to Arianna before shutting the phone off. Frantically, I look around the master bathroom for a hiding place for my phone. Digging through the cabinet under the sink, I find a box of tampons. Perfect. I bury the phone under the sanitary products and shove the box behind some spare toiletries.

Afraid to give Dom any reason to get impatient and angry, I strip out of my clothes, throw my hair up in a bun and hop in the steaming spray of water. As the water scalds the reminder of his touch from my skin, I pray Arianna will get my message and get Kai help. If they can get a lawyer involved, maybe it will be enough to get Kai out of this mess. Now I just need to convince Dom to let me see my mom.

When I step out of the bathroom, wrapped only in a white bath towel, Dom is lying on the bed, naked, fisting his cock. His bare torso flexes and ripples as he slowly pumps his fist up and down his shaft. My mouth goes dry at the sight of him. His eyes are burning with a hunger that would look just as natural on a wolf or a lion. He is a predator. I am his prey, his next meal.

I close my eyes and inhale deeply, letting my racing heart slow, and a sense of calm settles over my body. When I open them again, I drop the towel at my feet. I stride across the room, purpose in my walk. I will do this on my terms. I will not let him make this hurt. I will do what it takes to get through this alive. I will get through this.

CHAPTER FIFTY-ONE

KAI

Dane's plan is simple in theory. Brad is still here at the local jail waiting for trial. While I'm waiting to be bailed out, he wants me to talk to Brad to see if I can get him to open up about being set up by Eric. If we can confirm Eric did put Brad and his bro up to harassing Serena, it's a strong foundation for building a case against him and Dom.

It took a while for Dane to get me on board with this plan. As much as I want to nail Dom's ass to the wall, I don't have any pity for Brad's situation. He's harassed my girl twice. Eric may have instigated the second assault, but Brad is still responsible for his actions. Dane assured me he's going to make sure the frat douche still pays for his crimes, but sometimes we have to cut a little fish loose in order to catch a bigger one. Like making a deal with a small-time street dealer in order to catch his supplier. Right now, Dominick Reeves is the biggest threat to

Serena, so there isn't anything I won't do to get her out of his orbit.

I only agreed to his plan after he let me call my parents and tell them where I was. To my surprise, they were already on the way to the station. A message from Serena made it to Arianna who called my dad's number. Knowing Serena still had the cell phone I bought her gave me some measure of comfort, and having Jerry—my dad's lawyer friend—sit in on my meeting with Dane made me more comfortable with going forward with his plan.

Through some careful maneuvering, Dane has me sharing a cell with Brad the Rapist. I have my cell phone back, hidden in my back pocket. Somehow, I'm supposed to build some sort of relationship with him and trick him into confessing.

Just imagining his spoiled fuckboy face has me wanting to punch him, but I fight back the urge. I have to put on a good show to get him to open up. As Dane walks me to my temporary home, I close my eyes, inhale a deep breath and channel all the anger I've been holding onto. I let my frustration at the injustice of our justice system bubble up to the surface. If Brad wants someone to believe him when he says he was set up by a crooked cop, who better than a young black man who has suffered at the hands of power-hungry, prejudiced cops?

When we reach the cell door, I begin to put on a show. "Get your hands off me, fucking pig." I jerk my arm out of Dane's grasp and shoulder-check him as I walk through the door.

"Watch it, Roberts. You don't want to be on my bad

side." Dane gives me a shove before he slams the cell door closed, selling the ruse. Brad is lying on the bottom bunk, his blond hair looking greasy and sticking out at all angles. He cuts me a sideways glance before returning his gaze to the bunk above. Poor spoiled frat boy. He must be depressed from being kept away from a steady supply of drunk sorority sisters and shitty beer.

Time to put those high school drama classes to good use. "Fucking asshole cops." I punch the wall, picturing Dominick's smug-as-fuck face as he whispered in my ear how he was planning on fucking Serena's ass as punishment, letting my real anger bleed through. "Fucking. Power. Hungry. Abusive. Shit. Stain." I punctuate each word with a new hit to the cinder blocks, my knuckles busting open, leaving blood splatters on the wall. My anger is so white hot, I don't even feel the pain.

When I turn around, I sneak a surreptitious glance at Brad to see if I have his attention. He's eyeing me with wary interest.

"What'd they do? Pull you over and take your weed stash?" Oh, great. He's a rapist and a racist. Silently I wonder if Dane will care if I get a few hits in and ruin this fuck's pretty-boy face before I'm done in here.

"Fuck you." I shoot my cellmate a venomous look before settling on the other bunk bed on the opposite wall. We settle into an uneasy silence. He doesn't trust me enough to open up yet, but he knows there is no love lost between me and the police. That's good enough for phase one.

I LIE there on the stiff cot, on top of the scratchy blanket, my mind racing and sleep evasive. Serena is all I can think about. What is he doing to her? Has he hurt her? Dane promised he would go check on her after we were done, but I won't stop worrying until I have eyes on her again. There is no limit to what Dom could have done to her in the time I've been in here. That sick fuck was looking forward to punishing her for daring to leave his ass. There is still a dull throb in my head from where I headbutted him, but I don't regret it. I hope I broke his goddamn nose.

I MUST DRIFT off at some point. When I open my eyes, there are two figures standing outside of our cell. It's Dane and Eric. I guess it's time for the next stage of our plan. They aren't paying attention to Brad or me. Just having a conversation in front of our door. Dane was supposed to get Eric to where Brad can see him, so Brad will know the man who set him up is a cop. My job is to make Brad feel like we are both victims of his shadiness.

I sneak a look at Brad and see he's still lying there, eyes closed, either sleeping or tuning out his surroundings. Not willing to risk him missing Eric while he's in place, I raise my voice.

"Hey! Yeah you!" Eric and Dane turn towards me, as Brad opens his eyes. "Where's my fucking phone call, fuck-face?" I stalk to the bars, glaring at the cops. "Or do I not get to speak to a lawyer while you're busy coming up with your cover story?" In my periphery, I see Brad sit up on his cot, hopefully recognizing Eric by now.

"Shut your fucking mouth, inmate," Eric spits out. Dane stands behind him, his eyes bouncing from me to Brad in an unasked question. I ignore him, focusing my ire on the older cop standing in front of me.

"You think you're so fucking big and bad. Invincible behind that badge. I can't wait to see how tough you are when that mask comes down. When people see all the only way you have any power is from setting people up. I can't wait until I talk to my lawyer." I stand close enough to press my chest against the bars, daring Eric to get close enough for me to grab him. Fantasies of smashing his face into the bars play through my mind. Eric doesn't take the bait. A slow grin spreads across his face, like he's amused by my outburst. Cocky bastard.

"Come on, D. I think this one needs to cool his heels some more before he gets his phone call."

I'm not surprised by his comeback, but I still act indignant as hell. "The fuck! I get a phone call! I demand to call my lawyer!" I make a show of smacking my hands on the door, angry at the injustice.

I don't give a shit about the phone call. I just need Brad to know we have a common enemy. I already spoke to my parents last night before Dane brought me to my cell. This is all an act for Brad. Eric flips me the bird before turning, ushering Dane down the hallway. He was so focused on me, I'm not sure if he noticed who my cellmate is. When I turn around, Brad looks like he's seen a ghost.

"He's a cop! That fuck is a cop?!" He jumps out of bed and begins pacing in the small space, his hands pulling at his hair, making it more disheveled than before. "He's a cop...he's a cop..." While he's distracted, I slip my phone out of my back pocket and turn on the camera. I stuff it back into my pocket, careful to leave the microphone pointed up so it can pick up Brad's confession.

"Pretty sure the badge and uniform are a dead give-away, man," I deadpan.

"You don't understand! He set me up! He's the reason I'm in here and my bro is dead!" Brad grasps my shirt in his clenched fists, spitting in my face in his urgency to tell his story.

"He set you up? How?" I leave enough skepticism in my voice to make it sound like I'm not entirely convinced, needing him to elaborate more. This probably won't be admissible in court but maybe it will be enough to make Dom feel like we have him by the short and curlies.

"That asshat was the one who mentioned that bitch was working late without her pit bull cop boyfriend there to guard her. It's not our fault the uppity bitch can't take a compliment. He suggested we should fuck with her to get back at him." Brad grabs his hair, pulling at it, a slight mad glint in his eyes. When I give him a blank look like I have no fucking idea what he's on about, he continues, sounding more than a little unhinged and slightly paranoid.

"This prick-tease of a waitress at this bar, she was all over my boy one night, and then her pit bull cop boyfriend shows up and breaks his fucking nose! After that the boyfriend was always hanging around giving us the stink eye, fuck, like we cared about his stupid skank. But then a couple of weeks later, *that* fucking cop—we didn't know he was a fucking cop—that fucker starts talking about what a hot little ass she has on her, and we're like, 'Yeah, but good luck getting past her prick bodyguard', but the guy's like, 'What boyfriend? I don't see no one standing watch'. We told him what he did to my boy's nose, and he suggested we teach her a lesson. He even offered to keep an eye on the back door for us when we saw her walk out with the trash."

I ball my fists at my sides, the tenuous thread holding my self-control together fraying with every insult he slings towards Serena. "Teach her a lesson?" I prod, barely unclenching my jaw enough to get the words out.

"Yeah, you know. Rough her up, maybe have some fun. But her bitch-ass cop boyfriend showed up before we even did anything and fucking shot Todd!"

Rage simmers under my skin, threatening to boil over. I want nothing more than to beat his ass for what he did to Serena, but we need him to take down Dom.

"Yeah…I remember seeing an article about that." I snap my fingers, like it's all coming back to me now. "You know her boyfriend? The bitch-ass cop? That dude is his partner. They were together when they pulled me over," I lie, trying to build camaraderie with this fucknugget. Gag. "I bet they set you up together to teach you and your bro a lesson." Brad's eyes go wide as my words cause an epiphany in his brain. "I'd suggest you call your lawyer, dude. Sounds like you've got a case."

Brad lets go of my shirt, runs to the door and begins yelling about needing to speak to his lawyer. While he's not looking I turn off the recording and send the video to Dane. Now that I've done my part, he will call my parents and have them bring my lawyer by to get me out of here. The agreement made last night with my lawyer present was I wouldn't spend more than forty-eight hours in here. So far, I'm being held without any official charges being brought against me, and I can only hope that means Dom hasn't concocted some kind of false evidence to hold me for kidnapping. With any luck, Jerry will have me home by dinner time.

CHAPTER FIFTY-TWO

SERENA

The next morning, I find myself slowly slipping out of bed, careful not to wake Dom. I grab the first piece of clothing I can find, one of Dom's old police academy t-shirts, and pull it on. It swamps my body, hitting me mid-thigh. My heart gives a little pang as I look at the logo. My Granddaddy taught at the police academy for years before officially retiring. The fact that Dom had been one of his recruits was one of the things that made me feel comfortable around him. My naïve brain honestly thought if my Granddaddy had mentored him, then surely that meant he was a good man. I let out a quiet snort of derision at my naïveté.

Slipping out of the room quietly, I make my way downstairs, needing some space away from the slumbering monster currently holding me hostage so I can think. I can't run. Not yet. Not until I know where my mother is and that he's not going to push for charges to be brought up against Kai. I know I can tell the truth and say I wasn't kidnapped, but it will be Dom's word against mine. Would they believe me?

Standing in the living room, staring out the window, I am lost in a tailspin of doubt and what ifs. The sound of tires crunching on gravel draws my attention to the driveway. I see a beat-up red pickup truck. that's seen better days, slowly making its way up towards the house. I stand there, holding my breath, waiting to see who it is, hoping maybe I might finally be catching a break.

When I see Dane hop out of the truck, I rush over to the front door, opening it before he has a chance to ring the bell. I don't know if he's here as a friend of Dom's or on cop business, but either way, I don't want him waking Dom up. When I open the door and Dane's gaze meets mine, a look of shocked relief crosses his face. His expression ignites the smallest spark of hope in my chest.

"Fuck, Serena. Thank God you're okay." He jogs up the stairs and pulls me into a hug before I know it's happening. My arms hang limply by my side as my brain works to catch up to what is going on. After a long, awkward moment, I pat his back and pull away. He takes a long moment to study my face and my bare arms and legs, like he's checking me over for injuries.

"Kai didn't hurt me," I spit out defensively, thinking he's heard Dom's bullshit story and thinks I was kidnapped. I refuse to play into that bullshit—I will not help Dom bury Kai.

"I know, Serena. I know. I was worried about you after Dom didn't bring you to the station." My mouth falls open in shock at Dane's words. He was worried about me? Does this mean he's talked to Kai? Does he believe us? I open my mouth to respond, but something dark up on the porch ceiling catches my eye. I glance up, seeing one of Dom's security cameras pointed directly at the front door. I don't know if these cameras have audio, but I don't want to risk it. I close my mouth, and Dane's eyes narrow in suspicion. He turns his head slightly to see what my gaze is locked on, clocking the camera behind his shoulder.

When he returns his attention to me, I can see a glint of understanding in his eyes. "Yeah, after I heard the crazy rumor going around the station about you being kidnapped, I wanted to come check on you. I thought it was odd Dom didn't bring you by right away so charges could be filed...unless of course it was a misunderstanding." He gives me a knowing look, like we are sharing a secret. Excitement tingles through my limbs when I realize Dane might actually be on our side.

Before I can confirm his suspicion, I hear heavy footsteps come up behind me a moment before Dom's hard body presses into my back, his strong arms wrapping around me, pulling me tight against him. I tense but try not to flinch at the contact, afraid of angering him if I make the wrong move in front of his buddy.

"What's a misunderstanding?" Dom's voice is dark and ominous, rolling through me like thunder. My heart rate ratchets up to a panicked tempo at the threat-laced tone of his voice.

"This whole kidnapping business. Kai is at the station claiming Serena left with him willingly. He's got a lawyer there causing problems and we need to know if there will be any charges brought or if we need to cut him loose." Dane's demeanor shifts immediately, like he's annoyed. Like Kai is being totally unreasonable about insisting on his innocence.

He's putting on a good enough act, I start doubting what I thought I saw in his eyes moments ago.

DOM LETS out a dark chuckle with no humor to it at all. "We can hold him for seventy-two hours. Let him sit and spin. He needs to learn not to mess with another man's girl. *My girl.*" A chill runs down my spine at how casually Dom is toying with Kai's freedom.

Dane furrows his brows, making a show of hesitating. "You sure, bro? If his lawyer catches wind of you holding him with no intention of bringing charges, he will raise a fuck ton of hell. I don't know if you want that kind of heat on you with the whole country actively looking for examples of police abusing their position."

I hold still, hope stealing my ability to breathe, while I wait to see if Dom agrees with his assessment. Please, please, please, let Kai go.

"Who said there won't be charges filed? That's entirely in Serena's hands. His fate is all up to her."

Bile rises in the back of my throat at Dominick's implied threat. I have to submit to him. Be his. And then maybe he will let Kai go. A glimmer of something that looks like concern passes over Dane's face before he schools his expression again.

"Right...well, then she's got sixty hours to decide before we have to let him go."

Dom's hand moves from my shoulder to the back of my neck, giving it a painful squeeze. I can't control the flinch that twists my face up as pain lances down my spine. "Thanks for the reminder, D. I'm sure she will make the right decision. Now if you don't mind, we've got some catching up to do." Dane looks from Dom to me, clearly conflicted by Dom's dismissal. I can tell he wants to help me, but doesn't want to outwardly oppose Dom for some reason.

Dane jerks a stiff nod, then retreats down the porch steps and jogs over to his truck. My heart sinks as I watch him get in, desperately wishing I could run after him and go with him. But I can't leave Dom yet. Not until he takes me to my mom and I know she's safe.

Dom drags me back into the house by the scruff of my neck. His face is a blank mask, and I can't tell if he's angry with me. I tried so hard not to give him any reason to think I had said anything to Dane. I want Dom to feel like he's beaten me. That I'm giving up. I need him to get cocky and think he's won. It's the only way he will finally tell me where my mother is. Now that I know Kai has a lawyer fighting for him, all of my determination shifts to saving the woman who gave me life.

"Dom, please don't be angry. I didn't say anything to Dane. I swear. I know where I belong, and it's here with you." The words taste bitter on my tongue, but I infuse them with as much regret as I can muster. "Wasn't I so good for you last night? You...you said I was your good girl." Nausea churns in my gut at the reminder of what I had to do the previous night to placate him. I push through it, putting on the performance of my life.

I caress one palm against his stubbled cheek, delicately trailing my nails against his skin, the way I know he likes. The punishing grip he has on the back of my neck lessens slightly as my touch relaxes him. His eyes lock on mine, the steel color of them cutting through me like a knife.

"You're mine, Kitten. You understand that now? There is no end to us. There is no end to you and me. You are my end game, one way or another. Am I being clear?"

My mouth goes dry in fear as I nod mutely in understanding. It is in this moment I fully comprehend how far Dom is willing to go to ensure he gets what he wants.

CHAPTER FIFTY-THREE

SERENA

After spending the morning doing my best to convince Dom of my acceptance of the situation (which included giving him a blowjob where I had to fight the urge to puke) he finally says the words I've been waiting to hear.

"Go get dressed, Kitten. Let's go pick up Laura." His mood is drastically different from the broody bastard who brought me home last night. He seems relaxed again. I guess face-fucking your fiancée will loosen the tension in even the biggest assholes.

I don't hesitate, afraid to give him a chance to change his mind. I run upstairs, grab a change of clothes and lock myself into the en suite bathroom, where I stashed the phone. Turning the phone on, I send a quick text to Arianna.

> Me: Dom is taking me to Mom. I'm sharing my location just in case.

Me: I'll text when I have her back.

Making sure the phone is on silent, I shove it into the back pocket of my jeans before pulling on one of Dom's oversized hoodies, hiding it from view. I'm hoping seeing me in his clothes will keep him placated. Right now, he's a sleeping lion satisfied by a recent kill, and I'm just a zebra, trying not to make any sudden moves that will trigger his prey drive.

In his car, he keeps his hand clamped possessively on my thigh, a slight, satisfied smirk turning up the corner of his mouth. I watch the route he takes carefully, trying to memorize it in case I need to find this location in the future. Eventually when he turns off the main road and begins to drive into the mountains, I realize he's taking us to the cabin where we spent the weekend together. We are driving there in the daytime this time around, and the weather is clear. It's easier for me to keep track of the turns and side roads he takes as we make our way up the mountain, closer to where he is keeping my mom. My body hums in anticipation, my desperation to see her and make sure she's okay thrumming through me.

It's all I can do to resist the urge to jump out of the car before he has it parked, my need to see my mom hitting critical mass. I fling the door open as soon as the car is stopped, but he grabs my arm, stopping me from my hasty exit.

"Kitten, look at me." The command freezes me in place. With one hand he grabs my chin, turning me to face him, making sure he has my full attention.

"As far as your mom is concerned, I brought her up here so we can have a relaxing getaway together as a family. I had to pick you up from your little rendezvous with Kai. You will not give her any indication anything is wrong between us, do you understand?"

I try to swallow, but my mouth is dry. I nod my head but he pinches my chin harder between his thumb and forefinger.

"Let me hear you understand. Believe me, Kitten, I have no problem leaving her here to fend for herself while I take you back home to teach you a lesson." His eyes are so dark, they're almost black. The kind of dark gray you only see in the middle of storm clouds right before a tornado siren blares its warning.

"I understand."

He smirks, then pulls me in for a kiss. I don't resist. I let him drink from my lips and take his fill. I'm so close to my goal of reuniting with my mother, I will not jeopardize it.

We exit the car, me trailing behind him as we walk up the dirt path to the front, my hands nervously clenching and unclenching at my side. Dom unlocks the front door, walking in first and announcing his presence. "Hey, Laura, I'm back. Look who I—" Something long and black comes from behind the door and smashes into the back of Dominick's head with a sickening crack. He crumples lifelessly to the floor, his body landing with a loud thud. I can't stop the scream that escapes from me as I watch it happen.

My mouth hangs open, my eyes bugging out in shock as I watch blood seep from the wound on his head into a puddle on the floor. When I manage to drag my eyes from the gruesome scene in front of me, I see Mom standing over him, her chest heaving from exertion, a heavy black fireplace poker hanging from her right hand. She used to play softball in college and even got her team to the state championships a few times. I know she put everything she had into the swing that took Dom down.

When our eyes meet, Mom drops her weapon and rushes over to me, wrapping me up in the most comforting hug. "Oh, Sweet Pea, you're okay. I was so scared for you." She peppers kisses along my forehead and cheeks as she checks me over. My eyes are busy scanning over her, doing the same thing. Once assured that we are both whole and unharmed, we pull apart but keep our hands linked as we stare down at Dom's lifeless form.

"Is...is he..." I can't seem to choke out the word getting caught in my throat. The idea that Mom might've killed Dom causes my stomach to twist into knots. Without letting go of my hand, she cautiously creeps closer to him, squatting down so she can feel for his pulse. When she shakes her head, I let out the breath I was holding.

"He has a pulse."

Relief floods my system at her words. As much as I hate him for what he's done to me, death is too good for him. He deserves to be punished for his actions.

"How...how did you know he was dangerous?" My brain finally catches up to the fact that Mom was waiting for him, ready to attack. Those weren't the actions of a forgetful woman who thought she was on a family getaway.

"When I spoke to Kai, he told me to write down our

conversation. I did and kept it with me so I could re-read it as much as possible. When Dom came and got me, I knew something was wrong. He was cagey. Like he was doing something he wasn't supposed to. I...I thought he was going to bring me to you, but when he left me here alone—without a way to call for help—I knew something was wrong. I didn't want to leave and risk getting confused and lost, so I began snooping. Then...then I saw the cameras."

Cameras? What cameras? She sees the confusion on my face and keeps talking.

"I was trying to see if I could find a landline phone or something. Instead I found cameras planted all over this place. There's a laptop, but it doesn't have internet access. It's just linked to the cameras, storing their footage. Sweetie...I saw footage from the weekend you were here with him. Why didn't you tell me?"

"Tell you what?"

"That he pressured you into having sex after you realized you forgot your birth control. I saw how he pushed past all your boundaries and ignored your objections. I also saw where he told you to stop being friends with Kai. Sweet Pea, that is abuse. He was manipulating you." Tears shine in my mom's eyes, and I feel the sudden need to vomit at the idea of her watching the debauched things Dom did to me in this cabin. A low groan from Dom's prone form pulls our attention to him.

"We'll finish this conversation later. We have to call for help. We can't let him die." I pull the phone out of my pocket, ready to call 911, but Mom puts her hand on mine, stopping me.

"Are you sure you want to help him?"

I hesitate, considering her question. No. Not even a little bit. He doesn't deserve our help, but I also won't let my mom become a murderer. I won't let her ruin her life for him.

"No, I don't want to help him. But I also don't want you going to jail for his murder. Come on, let's go wait in the car until help gets here. If he tries anything, we will leave, and he can save his own damn self."

Once safely locked inside Dom's car, I dial 911 on speaker.

"911, what's your emergency?"

"We need help. My…my fiancé has been hit in the head, and he's unconscious. He's bleeding and not moving." The tears that choke up my voice are real, but I'm not sad about Dom. I'm crying because I can't believe this nightmare might finally be over.

CHAPTER FIFTY-FOUR

DOMINICK

Beep...beep...beep...beep.

The rhythmic beeping is the first thing that filters into my awareness. Followed closely by the sensation of someone using a sledgehammer inside my head. I attempt to open my eyes, but the bright fluorescent lights turn the sledgehammer into a jackhammer, forcing me to close them again and a pained groan to escape.

"Fuuuuck."

Fuck, what happened? My thoughts are clouded by the agony screaming through my brain at every little movement. There is no memory of what happened to land me in the hospital. Just darkness. Darkness and the most intense pain of my life. Sounds of someone moving next to me pierce through the fog.

"Serena?" I don't know if I say her name out loud. Between the drugs and the skull-splitting headache threatening to consume me, I'm not sure what is real and what's just jumbled thoughts in my head.

Slowly, memories bob to the surface. Serena looking so beautiful and broken on her knees for me. How lovely her tears looked glistening on her cheeks as she swallowed my cock all the way to the base. How malleable she became after she realized exactly how thoroughly she belongs to me. Serena and I in the car, driving up the mountain to the cabin where I was keeping her mom. Her reward for being a good kitten for me. Then…nothing.

The person in the room with me clears their throat. It's masculine.

"Not Serena, man, sorry." The voice doesn't sound sorry. It sounds anything but, with the flat, bored tone used.

"Can you turn off the light? Too bright…can't open my eyes." I move to raise my hand to shield my eyes from the light so I can open them, but cool metal clanking against the plastic of the bedrail stops the movement. "What the f—"

Whoever is in the room with me mercifully turns off the overhead light, allowing me to finally open my eyes and fully take in my surroundings. I'm in a single-bed hospital room. The dusky light outside the window indicates it's evening. My right hand is cuffed to the bed, an IV taped to the crook of my elbow.

Anger and confusion momentarily cause me to forget my injury as I jerk my arm, uselessly testing my restraints. The motion sends another lightning bolt of excruciating pain surging through my skull.

"Yeah, you might wanna take it easy there, Dom. You took

a pretty solid hit to the head. Did you know Serena's mom used to be a state champion softball player? Apparently, she held the homerun record her senior year of college." I narrow my eyes at Dane, who stands at the foot of my bed dressed casually in jeans, a t-shirt and a trucker cap, a shit-eating grin spread across his stupid fucking face. He keeps yapping like he's recounting a funny story that happened.

"Who woulda thought the person to bring down the big, bad Dominick Reeves would be a middle-aged woman who can't remember what she had for lunch and does puzzles in her free time?" Dane lets out a chuckle that causes a spike in my blood pressure, resulting in yet another mind-melting surge of agonizing pain. "You're lucky Serena is a good person. She could've left you on the floor of the cabin to bleed out from a cerebral hemorrhage."

"What. The. Fuck. Are. You. Talking. About?" I bite out the words as I clench my eyes shut, trying to block out the pain.

"I'm talking about how you are done fucking terrorizing Serena and the people closest to her. I'm talking about how your obsession over her has caused your whole fucking life to cave in. I'm talking about how, with the help of Serena's friend Kai, there is now evidence of you abusing your role as a police officer, as well as conspiracy and murder. We also have evidence of physical abuse, sexual assault and false imprisonment, thanks to Serena's statement. The fact that you have cameras all over your house that recorded it all? Are you that fucking dumb? Or were you that fucking delusional in your ability to not get caught?"

"Agghhhh!" A roar rips from my throat as rage floods through me. I lurch forward, trying to grab Dane by his shirt, but my left arm hangs limply by my side, and the shock of pain that ricochets through my head forces me to fall back against the pillow.

"Yeah, like I said, you might wanna take it easy there, bro. They had to do surgery to relieve the pressure on your brain. Apparently you suffered a stroke while you were under. Lost the use of your left arm. Not sure if that's temporary or what." Dane shrugs, like it doesn't matter to him one way or another.

"Where's Serena?" I grit out, slowly breathing through the nausea the last wave of pain summoned.

"Probably at home. Her home, that is. With Kai, living her best life. You've been here in a medically-induced coma for the last week. She hasn't come to visit you once. Not that anyone can blame her, after the shit you put her through."

"Why are you here?" If looks could kill, Dane would be dead on the spot. The anger I have towards this punk ass rookie trying to put me in my place rages through my veins. Fuck this kid.

"Your doctor called Serena, told her they would be letting you wake up today. Apparently since she's your fiancée, she's the closest thing you have to next of kin. Unfortunately for you, she hates your fucking guts and pretty much said as much to your doctor. I volunteered to come be here when you wake up to let you know how irrevocably fucked you are. Oh, and to let you know there is a protective order against you for Serena, Kai and Laura. Not that you'll get the chance to harass her. As soon as you're medically stable, you're being transferred to the county jail to wait for trial."

"You have no fucking idea what you're talking about! Serena is mine! If that bitch-ass punk touches her…"

"You'll what, Dom? Come on, give me another charge to add to your file. Please, I'm begging you. I want to make sure you never see the outside of a prison cell for the rest of your life. Dirty cops like you and Eric give the rest of us a bad name, and I'm not going to fucking stand for it. Have a nice life, Dom. Enjoy being someone's prison bitch."

With a wink and a tip of his hat, the motherfucker saunters out of the room, whistling the theme from Kill Bill.

"FUUUUUCK!"

Moments later, a nurse rushes into the room, drawn in by the flurry of erratic activity on the monitors by my bedside. "Oh, hon, you need to calm down. If your blood pressure spikes, it can cause more bleeding on your brain. I'm gonna give you something to help you calm down and go to sleep. You need to rest in order to heal up."

I watch helplessly as she pulls out a syringe and attaches it to the IV in my arm. Seconds later, warmth floods my veins, my mind growing fuzzy as the meds take hold. I let it pull me under, no desire to remain conscious in a world where Serena doesn't want me any longer.

CHAPTER FIFTY-FIVE

KAI

I walk through the front door, a bouquet of flowers, a bottle of wine and a pint of ice cream in hand. Today is a big day for Serena, and I am ready to support her in whatever way she needs. The grand jury for Dominick's case will be announcing whether or not he will be indicted for the charges brought against him by the district attorney.

Serena has tried to put on a brave face, but I know she's been a wreck, waiting for this result. I can't lie, even with the evidence we helped compile, the testimony against him from Brad the douche bag and the recordings from the cabin, I still worry his position as a well-decorated police officer will get him off the hook. Dane has assured us there's no way they won't bring charges against Dominick, but excuse the fuck out of me for not having a lot of faith in the justice system. I won't relax until I know for sure he is being brought to task for his crimes.

"Hey, ReRe, I got that wine you like and your favorite

ice cream!" I head into the kitchen to drop off the food. Serena doesn't respond, so after stowing the fudge brownie ice cream, I go through the house room by room searching for her.

"Serena, you up here?" I call out, heading up the stairs to her bedroom, worry tightening my chest. She's made remarkable strides since starting therapy, but she still has bad days when something triggers her PTSD, like when she gets major case updates, or when Dominick tries to contact her. In the last month, she's finally started using the right words to describe what he did to her, stopped saying rape in the hesitant, apologetic tone that implied those were someone else's thoughts, not her own. Stopped hedging around her abuse and making it seem like she somehow asked for what happened to her or that it was somehow her fault for falling for his bullshit. Now that she's had that breakthrough hit, the rest will be easier, and I look forward to the rivulet of improvement becoming a stream, a pond, a reservoir of strength.

Somehow, he still manages to send letters to her from jail, even after we've repeatedly asked them not to let him send them. After reading the first couple of unhinged manifestos about how they belong together and she will always belong to him, I've made it my mission to catch them before Serena sees them and give them to the prosecuting attorney to use as evidence. My stomach plummets at the thought of her getting one of those before I can intercept it. The last one she read caused her to spiral and spend the weekend in bed, reliving the nightmare of his abuse.

"ReRe?" Poking my head into the bedroom, I find it empty. Okay, she's not huddled under the blankets in a heap. That's good, but where is she? I turn to leave the room, but soft music floats through the open bedroom window.

Striding across the room, I peer out of the window and see Serena sitting in the hammock in the backyard, swinging between the two towering oak trees that shade most of her yard and the neighboring ones as well. A familiar beat emanates from the Bluetooth speaker, indicating she's listening to her favorite nineties hip hop playlist. Her laptop is nestled on her lap, and she bites her lower lip in concentration as she focuses on what is on her screen. Curious about what could have her attention so focused, I head outside to let her know I'm here.

She's so focused on what she's working on, she doesn't sense my presence until I flop down on the hammock next to her, startling her.

"Ah, fuck, Kai! Jesus, you scared me." She laughs as she tries to shove me away. I ignore her feeble attempt at retaliation and bear hug her before planting a kiss on her cheek.

"What ya working on?" Her body melts against mine as I pull her into my side, arm around her shoulder, her head nestling against my chest.

She turns her laptop towards me, and I see she has the BFU website pulled up to their Criminal Justice program. I take the computer from her, and my brow quirks up. "What's this?"

"I'm planning on changing my major. I want to go into

Criminal Justice. After I graduate, I want to apply to the police academy."

"Are you sure about that, ReRe? After everything you went through?" I give her a skeptical look, stunned by her admission. "You want to be a cop?" I try to keep the incredulity from my voice, but she picks up on it right away and doesn't let me off the hook.

"It's *because* of what I went through that I want to be a detective. Because of what *you* have gone through too. The world needs more good in it, and if there is any way I can help save someone else from experiencing what I went through, I will. My Granddaddy was a good man, a good cop, and it makes me sick to think of men like Dom and Eric out there abusing their position and using their power the way they did. I want to be there for victims when they have no idea who they can trust. I want to help fix the problem from the inside. I want to change the system in a big way." Her eyes light up with a sense of purpose, and her cheeks flush with excitement as she speaks. Clearly, she's thought this through, and I am not going to talk her out of it. I may not be a fan of law enforcement, but I know she's not wrong. She can make a real difference by doing this.

She bites her bottom lip nervously as she waits for my response, as if she needs my approval. Like I would ever deny her the opportunity to chase her dreams.

"Alright, ReRe. Tell me about the program."

The smile that spreads across her face at my interest feels like the sun coming out from behind a cloud. It's so bright and beautiful it hurts to look at. Seeing her smile like this is the exact reason why I will never tell her no.

WE SPEND SO much time making plans for her course load next semester—so she doesn't fall behind and will still graduate on time—we forget to check on the announcement from the grand jury. It isn't until Serena's phone rings with an incoming call from her mom that we realize we missed it.

She stares at her phone for a long minute, as if it's a snake she's afraid to pick up. "What if they didn't indict him? What if she's calling to tell me they let him go?" Serena looks at me with her honey-colored eyes shimmering with tears, and my heart lurches at the possibility.

"There's no way, baby. There was too much evidence against him. He's not getting out of this." I say with more confidence than I feel in the American justice system. "Answer it; see what your mom has to say." I nod toward the phone clutched tightly in her hands.

Serena hits the answer button, putting her mom on speaker phone. Before she even gets a word out, her mom's excited yells are coming through the speaker.

"They voted to indict on all charges! He's going to trial!"

"Fuck yeah!" I leap up from the hammock, pulling Serena with me, spinning her around in a celebratory hug. She squeals in joy, with a lightness I haven't seen in her since before her parents' accident. It's like a weight that had been holding her down, refusing to let her to rise back up to the surface, has finally been lifted. She beams at me with a smile that is beyond radiant. A charge builds between us when our eyes lock, like this is the moment that we've been waiting for. The moment that opens the floodgates of everything we've been holding back on since her escape from Dominick's clutches.

Shocking me, her lips seek out mine, her tongue licking against them, demanding entry. Our relief, our joy, our exhilaration at hearing the news stoking a fire between us that quickly ignites into an inferno. Her mom's voice comes through the speaker, reminding us she's still on the phone.

"Hey, Ms. Laura, we will call you back. We've got some celebrating to do. Love you!" I lick my lips as I give Serena a very pointed look. She wiggles her hips against my waist, and I feel a damp heat at her core, soaking through her thin cotton shorts.

"Yeah, gotta go, Mom! Call you later!" She hangs up the phone, tossing it on the hammock before her lips return to mine. She kisses me with a hunger that borders on desperation.

"Take me inside, Kai. I need you." Her seductive words almost make me weak in the knees. God, yes. I can't think of a better way to commemorate this moment.

I carry her into the house, kissing her, licking into her mouth, swallowing her sweet moans. Her body is pressed flush against mine, her hips rocking mindlessly as she seeks the friction she needs. I only make it to the first wall in the kitchen before pressing her against it and dropping her to her feet. Dropping to my knees in front of her, I take in her puffy lips, glistening from our kiss and the way her breasts heave as she pants, needy and desperate for more.

Jerking down her shorts and panties, I bare her beautiful pussy to me, unable to wait another second. I know she wants me to fuck her, but I have to taste her first. I've been dying for this moment for so long, and I plan on savoring it. I've held off on making our relationship physical, waiting for her to work through everything in therapy, to be sure she's ready and not just rebounding. She's it for me. My forever. My end game. And I want us to have the healthiest start to our relationship possible.

"Are you sure, baby? Do you want this?"

"Fuck, Kai, yes. If you don't put your mouth on me right now I'll die." Chest heaving, eyes hazy with lust, her lips swollen from our kiss...her begging is the last straw. I am undone.

Lifting her left leg, I rest it on my right shoulder, opening her to me so I can admire the view. She's so wet for me already, it makes my mouth water in anticipation. When I swipe my tongue up her slit in a long, leisurely stroke, the moan that comes from her mouth is almost enough to make me come in my pants. Fuck, that's hot. I do it again and again and again until her fingers are clawing at my scalp, and she's grinding her pussy on my face, on the verge of coming.

"Fuckfuckfuckfuck...oh god oh god oh god...Kai...I'm gonna..." Her body goes rigid as her orgasm crashes into her, her thighs locking around my head, fingernails digging into my hair to the point of pain. I don't give a fuck—I lick, and I suck, and I take in every last drop she gives me. I don't stop until she's limp and unable to hold herself up.

When I pull away and look up at her, she smiles down at me with a sleepy, satisfied smile. I shoot her a wicked grin in return, "We're not done yet, ReRe." I pull my shirt off and shove down my pants as I stand up. Her eyes go wide as she takes in my stiff erection, my dick so hard it's throbbing, precum dripping from the tip. I pull a condom from the pocket of my jeans, and she watches with rapt attention as I roll it on. She's looking at my dick like it's a work of art, and it makes me even harder. I need to be inside of her.

"You ready for me to fuck you, baby? I want to take you against this wall and fuck you so hard Mrs. G hears you scream my name."

"Fuck me, Kai." Her voice is husky and thick with desire. Lifting her up, I notch the head of my dick at her entrance.

"If at any point it becomes too much, say the word, baby."

Serena's only response is to pull my mouth to hers as I thrust into her, seating myself to the hilt, the taste of her release still on my lips. I pump into her at a furious pace, drawing more moans from her as her pleasure builds again. When I feel my balls tighten with my own impending release, I grind my pelvis into her, giving her clit the extra friction needed to pull her over the edge with me. When her walls clamp around my length—as she calls out my name in a cry of ecstasy—I explode.

CHAPTER FIFTY-SIX

SERENA

3 Months Later

MY HANDS SHAKE as I light the candles decorating the fireplace mantel. After blowing out the match, I take another quick peek at my reflection in the hall mirror as I make my way back into the kitchen to finish dinner. The new magenta bodycon dress I bought hugs my curves in all the ways I know Kai appreciates, proudly putting my booty on display. The sweetheart neckline dips low, leaving little to the imagination, and the delicate gold necklace Kai gave me for my birthday shimmers against my skin in the low light. Checking to make sure my lipstick hasn't smudged, I nod approvingly at my reflection. Tonight is the night. It's been three long months of working through my trauma with Dom and building an entirely new foundation for a relationship with Kai, and I am ready to take it to the next level.

I spent the first month in therapy downplaying what had happened to me, shame and embarrassment making me reluctant to admit just how depraved Dominick's behavior to me had been. Once I finally admitted out loud to my therapist that he had not only abused me, but manipulated me, gaslit me and raped me, I finally began healing. Clearing that hurdle made it easier to finally start working through my issues. I'm not saying I'm completely over it. There will always be bad days, but thanks to Kai, his family, my mom and my friends, every day gets easier, and my resolve to make sure this doesn't happen to another girl grows stronger.

After the incident in the cabin, while Dom lay comatose in the hospital, Kai and his family helped me move my belongings from Dom's house back into my own and pulled our furniture out of storage. It's almost like I never left. Except for one major detail. I live here alone. Mom refused to leave her apartment at Whispering Grove, insisting that she wanted to stay because of the recovery she was making with her memory. I think she wanted to give me space to finally be on my own. No matter how hard I tried to talk her into moving back home, she refused.

It was hard at first, living here alone. I miss having her here with me, but we have a weekly date where I pick her up and bring her over to have dinner and play spades with Mrs. G and Grace. Lately she's been talking about a gentleman friend she's been spending time with, and my heart swells with the possibility of my mom finding love again.

Kai spends most of his time here with me. He doesn't officially live here. He still spends some nights at his house, but we both know it's only a formality. He wants us to take things slow and not rush our relationship, even if we've been each other's person for so many years. We had one passionate night, but since then he's kept it mostly to snuggling, a few heavy make-out sessions and lots of tender kisses.

"ReRe, you know how I feel. You are my sun, my moon and my stars. My everything. I'd do anything for you. After everything you've been through, I want to make sure you're in a good place mentally and emotionally before we take it to the next stage. I don't want our new beginning to be built on a foundation of trauma and pain. I don't want to be the crutch that makes you feel better. I want you to be whole and healed and ready for love. I want to be your forever, and I am willing to wait for it. And if you decide I'm not it once you've taken your time to heal from this, that's okay. I'll still be here as your friend, always."

THE MEMORY of the night Kai said those words to me floats through my mind. It was the day we got the news about Dom's indictment, and we were laying on the couch after fucking against the kitchen wall. I asked him to stay with me. Kai agreed, but when I tried to initiate another round with him, desperate to hold on to this euphoric feeling, Kai had given me that speech. The sting from his rejection hurt. It hurt so much it felt like my heart was breaking, but Kai held me and let me soak his shirt with my tears. I fell asleep in his arms that night on the couch, and when I woke up the next morning, I had a new sense of clarity and knew he was right. Our friendship was too important, and I had to work on healing myself before I would be ready to put my heart into a romantic relationship with him.

We've spent a lot of time together since then, carefully walking the tightrope between friends and more than... Tonight I plan on changing that. I've been thinking about it a lot, and I'm ready. I want to give Kai everything. He already has my heart. I'm pretty sure he earned it that night when he held me and let me bathe him in my tears. Now I want to give him the rest of me. My body. My soul. I want us to be together in every way. He *is* my forever, and it's time for me to tell him.

Back in the kitchen, I finish dressing the salad, and the aroma of garlic and tomato sauce fills the house as the lasagna I baked cools on the counter. My plan is to surprise Kai with a romantic dinner before asking him to make things official between us. A small part of me is afraid he will reject me again, that maybe he's changed his mind and decided we should just remain friends, but I lock that quiet nagging fear away in a box in my mind. I can't fully start living again until I stop letting fear dictate what I do, and I am ready to start living.

The sound of the front door opening alerts me to Kai's presence. "Hey, ReRe, I picked up some of that ice cream you like. I thought we could have a movie ni..." Kai trails off when he enters the kitchen and sees me standing by the counter. I'm facing him, leaning back against the counter with my hands behind me, giving him an unobstructed view of my body in the revealing dress. I do not want to leave him with any doubts about how I want tonight to go. His eyes widen in surprise for the briefest of moments before lust darkens them. Biting his bottom lip, he takes his time raking his eyes over me, the heat in his stare burning me with its intensity. A wave of dizziness comes over me, and the room suddenly feels stifling. When his eyes finally meet mine again, it feels like the air in the room is charged with electricity.

"Hi." My voice is husky from desire. My plan for a romantic dinner before making a move on him flies from my head. All I want is Kai. Kai's lips on mine. Kai's body pressed against me. Kai's hands roaming over my curves. Touching me. Holding me. Kai's tongue dancing with mine. Kai's dick entering me. I want Kai. No. I *need* Kai.

"Serena." He says my name like it's a prayer. Reverently. Like I'm a goddess he intends to worship. It short-circuits my brain, and I say fuck it to the plan. I push off the counter and slowly stalk across the room, letting him devour me with his eyes. I see the way his breath hitches in excitement and how he licks his lips like I'm his favorite snack. That lingering trace of fear of being rejected by him is washed away by the naked desire written all over him. He wants me as much as I want him.

Stopping directly in front of him, I rise up on my tiptoes and press a firm kiss to his full, luscious lips as I wrap my arms around his neck. I pull away enough to whisper against his mouth, "I'm ready, Kai. I'm ready to give you everything."

My declaration is all it takes to snap Kai's last thread of control holding him back. In the next heartbeat, his lips crash against mine. He lifts me, and I wrap my legs around his waist, his strong hands gripping my ass as he carries me out of the kitchen and up the stairs to my bedroom, the dinner I spent hours on forgotten.

We don't come up for air the whole walk up to my room. He's all the air I need. We don't break apart until he lays me down on the bed. He pulls away long enough to whip his shirt off before he resumes his thorough exploration of my mouth. His tongue dances with mine, his hands cupping my face gently as his body comes to rest in the cradle of my thighs. I can feel the stiffness of his erection pressing into me through the rough denim of his jeans and the damp lace of my thong.

He stops our kiss before we get too carried away. Looking into my eyes, he asks, "Are you sure this is what you want, ReRe?"

"Yes, God, Kai, I've been ready. I don't want to be just friends. I want to be everything with you." I grind my center against him, desperate for more friction. "I need you inside of me."

"Fuck, Serena, you're killing me. I want to make this good for you. I want to take my time and taste every inch of you." Kai peppers kisses along my jaw and down my neck as I writhe under him, my body on fire from the heat of his touch. "I want to hear you come on my tongue and my fingers before you come on my dick." His kisses trail lower, along my collarbone and down to the valley of my cleavage. Slowly, he pulls my dress down, exposing my breasts. Sucking one peaked nipple into his mouth, he pulls a needy moan from my lips. He doesn't stop lavishing my breasts with attention as his hands work to remove my dress and thong, leaving me bare underneath him.

Once I'm naked, he sits back on his knees, admiring the view. His eye lasers in on my pussy, soaked and gleaming, ready for him. "You are the most beautiful thing I have ever seen." He speaks those words while staring directly into my eyes. Into my soul. It's enough to bring the familiar sting of tears pricking to the back of my eyes. I can't believe it took me so long to realize how much Kai loves me, but in this moment, I make a vow to myself to spend the rest of my life drinking in his love and giving it back in return.

I watch with greedy eyes as he unbuttons his jeans and slowly pushes them down his hips. His body is gorgeous. His warm brown skin unmarked by ink and scars stretches over a body built from years of playing football in high school. Thick thighs, muscular abs, strong arms. A line of dark hair trails from his belly button to the waistband of his boxer briefs, and I can't wait to see what kind of treasure it leads to. Before I get to see more though, he lays down again, settling his shoulders between my thighs, his face tantalizingly close to my pussy. I let out a disappointed whimper, and he silences me with a swipe of his tongue up my center.

"Oooh…" My body reacts on its own, arching into him, seeking more. He lets out a low chuckle that sends a shiver up my spine.

"Greedy little pussy. God, you taste so good." Kai dives back in, eating me with enthusiasm. Licking me like I'm his favorite flavor of ice cream. His hands grip my hips, holding me in place as he feasts. He fucks me with his tongue before circling my clit, flicking it lightly, sending shocks of pleasure to my core. He alternates like this until I'm a needy, trembling mess, desperate for release.

"I'm so close…Kai… I'm there…" I grip his curls in my fingers and grind my pussy against his face. Sliding two fingers inside me, he curls them as he sucks on my clit, and I detonate. My body jerks as my orgasm lays siege to my every nerve ending, and he does not relent in his ministrations until I finally go limp under him.

Pulling away, Kai looks at me, the heat in his eyes burning hotter, his face covered in my release. Watching him lick my wetness from his lips is the single sexiest thing I have ever seen in my life.

"Was that too much? Have you had enough?" Too delirious to form words, but unwilling to tap out, I shake my head side to side.

"Good, because we're just getting started, baby." Kai shoves his boxer briefs off, and his dick springs free. It's beautiful. Thick without being intimidating, long enough to hit exactly the right spot. My mouth waters at the memory of taking him as I watch him give himself a few lazy strokes.

"Condom?" he asks, knowing how important this choice is to me.

I think about it for a second but shake my head. I was tested after my ordeal with Dom, and I still have my IUD, so pregnancy isn't a concern. I want to feel Kai inside me with no barriers.

"Say it baby. Say what you want." Kai doesn't move, just continues to stroke his length, his eyes locked on mine. He's giving me the power, and it makes me feral for him.

"I want to feel you inside me. I don't want anything between us."

"That's my girl." A proud smile lifts his lips before he leans down, kissing me, seeking entry into my mouth with his tongue.

I open to him as he settles his hips against mine, tasting myself on his lips. I feel the tip of his dick pressing lightly against my entrance, but he doesn't push in. He savors our kiss, taking his time with me, just like he said he would. My body squirms under him, seeking more. Ready to be filled. I hook one leg around his waist and pull him towards me, and he sinks in another inch.

"Please, fuck me."

"Yes, ma'am." With one powerful thrust he sinks into me to the hilt.

Stars explode behind my eyelids as I relish the feeling of him. He stays like that for a long moment, like he's savoring this, etching it into his memory.

"Serena, you are perfect." With that, Kai begins to rock

his hips, thrusting his cock into me in a perfect rhythm that wastes no time getting me back to the edge of ecstasy.

"Don't stop…don't stop…don't stop…"

"Never, baby. I'll never stop loving you." Kai's hips snap into me with rapid thrusts as he plunges his tongue back into my mouth. He kisses me through my climax as my walls clench around him, bringing him over the edge with me.

Kai and I stay like that, locked together, our hearts beating as one as we come down from the most perfect high. It isn't until my stomach lets out an embarrassing rumble that we remember the abandoned dinner downstairs.

"Stay right here," Kai instructs. He climbs off of me, disappears into the bathroom. I hear water running briefly before he returns with a wet washcloth. My heart swells as he cleans me up. I move to sit up, but he pushes me back down.

"I said stay right here." His tone brooks no argument, so I lean back into the pillow as I watch him slip on his briefs and exit the room. Five minutes later, he returns with two dinner plates piled full of lasagna and salad.

"The ice cream melted, but I can go get more later." His smile is sheepish, like it's his fault the ice cream is ruined.

"It's okay, I had something else in mind for dessert." I give his crotch a pointed look before licking my lips. Kai's eyes flare with desire, and I know this feeling is never going to end between us. He's it. My forever.

CHAPTER FIFTY-SEVEN

SERENA

18 MONTHS LATER

"Serena Noelle Malcolm!" The Dean of the Criminal Justice program beams at me with pride as he takes my hand and holds up my diploma with his other hand. We pose for our photo op before he gives my hand another firm squeeze in congratulations. Dean Richards and I have gotten close after I switched majors; he was a good friend of my grandfather's and was thrilled to see me follow in Granddaddy's footsteps. He was a valuable mentor to me during my final semesters at Birch Falls U.

"WHOOP! WHOOP! THAT'S MY BABY!"

"I LOVE YOU SWEET-PEA!"

"HELL YEAH, SERENA!"

My cheeks flame when Kai, Mom and Mrs. G's cheers float up to me from the crowd. Dean Richards bites back a laugh at my embarrassment while I stride off the stage as quickly as possible. Kai's graduation was early this morning, and I might have yelled something about his sexy ass as he walked across the stage. Right in front of his mom, dad and sister, who was in town for his graduation. Guess this is my payback.

Thirty minutes later, I am milling through the crowd to look for my family. I come across Marie and Ben first, baby River in tow. River is a year and a half now, and unfortunately for Marie, did take after his dad. I swear that kid is already half the size of Marie.

"Congratulations, Reenie!" Marie tackle hugs me, almost knocking me off balance. Her pregnant belly keeps her from fully embracing me. She's close to her due date with baby number two, and I still can't believe she managed to block out the memory of giving birth to a ten pound watermelon so quickly. Ben leans in and plants a friendly kiss on my cheek, "'Grats, Serena."

I give one to River in turn when he leans in from Ben's arm towards me. I am River's auntie and favorite babysitter. "NeNe!" River's chubby hand pats my cheek gently, his way of showing love.

Suddenly, warm, strong hands envelop me from behind, along with Kai's citrus and sage scent. "Yeah, baby. I am so damn proud of you." Kai plants a tender kiss on my neck as he whispers in my ear. The way his lips brush the shell of my ear causes goosebumps to erupt all over my skin. Fuck, I love this man so much. I snuggle into his embrace, savoring this moment before it is interrupted by—

"Serena! Serena! Congrats, sweetie! We are so proud of you!" Grace runs up and pulls me into a hug, stealing me away from Kai.

"Thanks, Grace. I'm so glad it's finally over. If I ever have to write another paper, it will be too soon." Grace relinquishes her hold on me, laughing, and I turn to Luther, Mrs. G and Mom, finishing the round of congratulations.

"Baby, you did it." Mom buries her face in my hair, and I hear her sniffle, trying to hide her tears. "You cannot even begin to understand how proud I am to call you my daughter. I know your daddy would feel the exact same way." Mom's words are a bittersweet reminder of what I am still missing. I have a new family now with Kai. I have a new sister and bonus parents. I have Mrs. G and Marie, Ben and River. I have my mom back... She's improved so much in the last year, it's almost like having my mom from before the accident back. But I still don't have my dad here. The familiar sting of tears pricks the backs of my eyes as I think of him.

"I know, Mom. I know." We hug for so long it feels like time stands still, the culmination of the last four years hitting me all at once. The accident. Mom's memory. Working two jobs while going to school. Dominick... Dominick changed the entire trajectory of my life. I won't say I'm grateful for what I went through with him, but I am proud of the woman that emerged from the ashes of the life he tried to destroy. I don't know who I would be today if it weren't for the strength I had to find after him.

He's currently serving year one of a twenty-five year

sentence, which isn't nearly enough punishment for the hell he wreaked on my life. His friend, Eric, got off with a much lighter sentence after he flipped on Dom and told the prosecution how Dom set up the frat boys to assault me so I would be scared into quitting my job at Mav's. It feels grossly unfair that a bad man who perpetuated harm against a woman can make a deal to sell out another bad man for lesser punishment, but the DA assured me it was the most foolproof way to make sure Dom was locked up for a very long time.

When Mom pulls away from me, she's smiling with twin tears streaming down her freckled cheeks. I open my mouth to say something, but she shakes her head, an excited glimmer in her eyes. Gently, she nudges my shoulder, turning me around. When I turn, I see Kai, down on one knee, holding up a pale blue ring box. An antique sapphire flanked by tiny diamonds in an art deco style sits nestled in the ivory velvet. It feels like all of the blood drains from my limbs, and my heart stops at once. Kai is down on one knee. Kai. Is. Down. On. One. Knee. My hands fly to my face to hold back the excited scream threatening to come out.

"Serena Malcolm. You are the most amazing, resilient, stunningly beautiful, independent, brilliant woman that I have had the honor of knowing. You are my best friend. You are my girlfriend. You are my soulmate. You are the only thing I need in this life, and I want to spend the rest of mine with you. Will you marry me?"

I drop to my knees and wrap my arms around Kai's neck, smiling and nodding like a delirious, love-struck fool. "Kai, the answer was yes before you even asked." Kai smashes his lips against mine, swallowing my words before I'm done speaking them. Our tongues mingle, our kiss tasting like the happiest tears I've ever cried, as we start the next stage of our life together.

"Is this really necessary, Kai?" I reach up to pull the blindfold covering my eyes down, but Kai playfully smacks my hand away.

"Woman, if you ruin the surprise I have planned, I won't go down on you for a month." Kai's threat is an empty one—I know he would die before following through on it—but I drop my hands back into my lap, biting back the smile threatening to break free.

"Oh no, anything but that." I gasp in mock horror.

Kai lets out a muttered "brat" as he pulls his hand away. I lean my head back against the headrest and close my eyes, trying to see if I can get a sense of where we are going by using my other senses. I recently got a promotion to detective for good reason. I've got killer instincts and an eye for details. It's helped me a lot in my career as I've risen in the ranks of the Birch Falls PD.

When I got home from work, Kai told me to get changed because we were going out. He said he had a surprise planned for me. It's almost my birthday, so I want to assume he's taking me out for a nice dinner, but my detective brain tells me that's too obvious and not special enough for all the cloak and dagger stuff.

He's been working long hours putting together his show at the art gallery downtown, so maybe he's trying to make up for that. The show opens tomorrow night, and he's been there late every night this week making sure everything is hung just right. It's his first solo show, and I know he's nervous about how well it will be received. He's so nervous, he hasn't even let me have a sneak peek yet.

Kai has built an impressive resume in the world of photojournalism since we graduated from BFU seven years ago. He has traveled all over the world covering major news events like elections, protests and wars, but his favorite thing is to stay closer to home, doing human interest stories on everyday people. The show at the gallery is supposed to feature some of his work that never made it into the news. Photos that are personal and important to him. Kai is hoping this gallery show will launch the next stage in his career as a photographer, so he can start spending more time at home and less time traveling. We've talked about starting a family, and Kai has said he doesn't want to miss any of it. He wants to be there for every first, and I'm tired of missing him so much. While I'm proud of the work he's done and the recognition he's garnered with his career, I'm ready to have him home for good.

Kai slows the car to a crawl before flicking on the turn signal. I feel the car back up, turn then pull forward slightly before Kai shifts into park. My skin starts buzzing in excitement knowing we are finally at our destination.

"Can I take it off now?" I move to raise my hand, but Kai intercepts it. He brings my hand to his lips, gently kissing my knuckles.

"Patience, baby. I promise you it'll be worth it."

I huff out a mock irritated sigh as I wait, acting aggrieved at his request. Kai exits the car, and seconds later opens my door to lead me to the surprise. Taking my hand, he helps me out of the car. The sultry summer air settles over the bare skin of my arms like a blanket. I listen carefully for any hints of where we might be, but all I hear are the sounds of traffic and people passing by on the sidewalk. Kai steers me into a quiet, air-conditioned space. The change in temperature causes goosebumps to rise all over my skin. There are no smells of food wafting through the air. I also don't hear the tell-tale sounds of other diners enjoying their meals, so it likely isn't a restaurant. Holding both of my hands, Kai guides me further into the mystery room before stopping. I feel him move around behind me, pressing his front to my back and gently brushing his lips against the shell of my ear.

"You ready for your surprise, ReRe?"

Shivers run down my spine at the low, melodic tone of his voice. I can't believe he can still cause such a visceral reaction from my body after almost ten years together.

"Yes." My reply is little more than a gasp as I feel my core heat at the gentle graze of his fingertips against my skin as he moves to remove my blindfold.

Freed from the blindfold, I blink my eyes to adjust to

the light. In front of me is a massive black and white portrait of...me. It takes up nearly the entire wall. It's a close up of me smiling, head thrown back mid-laugh, my curls wild and free, blowing in the wind. It's from our wedding—I can tell by the white halter strap that crosses around my neck. We had a small intimate ceremony at the top of Buffalo Mountain in the fall. One of Kai's buddies did the photography, but Kai also had his camera out during the day, snapping pictures. I don't remember ever seeing this one.

"Kai..." I'm at a loss for words as I stare at what is probably the happiest moment of my life.

"SURPRISE!"

I jump back, pressing into Kai's firm body behind me at the sudden noise. Chuckling, he turns me to see the crowd of people behind us. Our friends, family and several of my coworkers from the department. An obnoxiously large congratulations banner hangs from the ceiling.

"I know you said you didn't want to make a big deal about it, but becoming the first Black female detective on the Birch Falls PD is kind of a big deal, ReRe. I couldn't let that go without recognizing how much of a badass you are." Kai presses a kiss to my cheek, melting my heart with his thoughtfulness. I only get a moment to take in the scene before me before everyone bursts into motion at once to give me hugs and well wishes on my recent promotion.

"Congratulations, Serena! I can't believe you were trying to let this slide without a party!" Grace squeezes me tightly as she admonishes me. I give her a bashful shrug before she passes me over to Luther.

Next in line is Kai's sister, Naomi. "I tried to talk him out of it since you told him you didn't want to make a big deal about it but…" She shoots Kai a wry look, leaving the rest unsaid. She knows I hate being the center of attention most of the time, but she also knows when Kai has his mind set on something, he's going to do it. Kai grins at his big sister, absolutely no shame in his game.

Mom and her new beau, John, come up to give me hugs. She made so many great strides in her first two years at Whispering Grove, she was able to move into an apartment on her own, and she even started working at Brewed Awakening, which is where she met John. "Congratulations, Sweet Pea. I'm so proud of you!" She presses a wet kiss to my cheek while John looks on with pride shining in his eyes. He won't ever be a replacement for my father, but it's nice to see Mom happy again.

"Hey, you! I think this moment deserves a little champagne!" Eloise Fitzpatrick waltzes up, carrying two champagne flutes. I met Eloise a few years ago when she and her husband were dealing with a stalker. One of the veteran cops had sent me to take Caleb's statement when he reported his wife missing. The officer had assumed she left him and deemed the call not worthy of his time. Turns out, she had been kidnapped, and she wound up almost dying while Caleb was being questioned at the precinct. That officer was forced into retirement shortly thereafter, and I was awarded my first commendation. Eloise went into victim advocacy after her experience, and when dealing with victims of domestic violence, I found myself recommending her over and over again so she could help guide the victims through the process of getting help or leaving their abusers. We grew to be close friends, and Kai and Caleb play softball together.

"Congrats, Serena. You are going to be a brilliant detective." Caleb leans in, kissing my cheek before clapping Kai on the shoulder in greeting. They peel off so they can talk about the basketball game or some other sporting nonsense.

"So you didn't have any idea he was doing this?" Eloise raises a dubious eyebrow at me, not entirely convinced I hadn't figured out the surprise. Her suspicion is fair. Kai has tried several times to surprise me with birthday parties, and I've thwarted him every time.

"No idea. Swear. I guess I've been so busy with work, and he's been working on his show so much it didn't even occur to me he'd do this…" My voice trails off as I take in my surroundings. It's Kai's work. Photo after photo lining the walls, hanging in dramatic installations. All black and white photos of Black men, women and children—smiling, laughing, faces lit up with happiness, enjoying the big and small joys in life. A pair of older men playing chess in a park. A group of girls spinning wildly on a merry-go-round in a playground. Parents huddled together on a hospital bed, snuggling their newborn. A mother and daughter cuddled together, reading a book. An artist holding a paintbrush, studying his work, a satisfied smile gracing his lips. Me, from our wedding. Photo after photo is a celebration, a tribute to Black joy, and it makes my heart swell with pride at the message behind Kai's work. Even when the world is dark, there is still so much joy to be found.

I look over my shoulder, seeking out my husband so I can tell him how amazing this is. He always told me after all the hurt and sadness he documented, he wanted to revel in something joyous to balance out the darkness in the world. He finally did it.

Soft music begins to play from the speakers, so I excuse myself from Eloise making my way over to the man who is the joy that balances out the darkness in my life.

"Excuse me, Mr. Roberts. May I have this dance?" I slide my hand up Kai's arm to his neck, pulling his body close to mine.

His full, beautiful lips turn up at the corner in a sexy-as-hell grin.

"The answer was yes before you even asked, Mrs. Roberts."

The End

ACKNOWLEDGMENTS

Writing a book truly takes a village. Exile would not exist without my village. Thank you to my alpha readers who were there from day one, Courtney, Amanda, Amy, Dana, Azalea and Layna. Your encouragement, feedback, and reactions kept me going over the months it took write Exile.

Dana, thank you for fixing my commas. You made Kelly's job so much easier I'm sure. I might have even learned a thing or two from all of your grammar tangents.

Thank you to my beta readers, Jessica, Nat, Nesha, Ranae and Adrienne for your additional feedback and love you had for Kai and Serena's story.

Amanda, once again you knocked out of the park with the cover. You are a wizard for being able to turn my nonsense Pinterest inspo board into a coherent concept.

Shout out to my author tribe, CWC. You guys have helped keep me sane during this whole process and I'm so grateful I found you all. Special mention goes to Ben who is my resident 'real or not' expert.

Nat, thank you for all your help behind the scenes with the stuff I don't want to deal with. You're worth every penny. ;)

A million thank yous for my sensitivity readers. Your

feedback, patience with my questions, willingness to have conversations about difficult subjects and your honest reactions helped more than you will ever know. Writing Exile was such an education for me. I appreciate every one of your perspectives on this story and I hope you can see where your insight made a difference.

ABOUT THE AUTHOR

Poppy Fitzgerald is an emerging author of romance novels. Poppy calls the beautiful Blue Ridge Mountains home, with her husband, two sons, mostly absentee cat, and overly affectionate Golden Doodle.

Poppy enjoys any and all romance genres and tropes, but loves to play around with popular tropes and turn them on their heads to come up with something not commonly seen.

When she's not writing she usually has her head buried in her kindle, reading smut. She also communicates fluently in GIFs and sarcasm and loves making her readers cry.

Astray